D0434957

This book is a puzzle.[i]
Within its pages lie clues that lead to a key hidden somewhere on Earth.
Decipher, decode, and interpret.
Search and seek.
The first to find the key and deliver it to its proper home
will be rewarded with gold.[ii]
Stacks and stacks of gold.[iii]
$$$ Εκατοντάδες χιλιάδες δολάρια την αξία του χρυσού. $.[iv]

ENDGAME

THE CALLING

JAMES FREY

AND

NILS JOHNSON-SHELTON

HARPER

An Imprint of HarperCollins*Publishers*

"Ballad for Gloom" excerpt on p. 205 by Ezra Pound, from *Collected Early Poems*, copyright © 1926, 1935, 1954, 1965, 1967, 1976 by The Ezra Pound Literary Property Trust. Reprinted by permission of New Directions Publishing Corp.

Endgame: The Calling
Copyright © 2014 by Third Floor Fun, LLC.
Puzzle hunt experience by Futuruption LLC.
Additional character icon design by John Taylor Dismukes Assoc., a Division of Capstone Studios, Inc.
All rights reserved. Printed in the United States of America. No part of this book may be used or reproduced in any manner whatsoever without written permission except in the case of brief quotations embodied in critical articles and reviews.
For information address HarperCollins Children's Books, a division of HarperCollins Publishers, 195 Broadway, New York, NY 10007.
www.epicreads.com

Library of Congress Cataloging-in-Publication Data

Frey, James, date
  Endgame : the calling / James Frey and Nils Johnson-Shelton. — First edition.
    pages cm. — (Endgame ; 1)
  ISBN 978-0-06-233258-5 (hardback)
  [1. Science fiction. 2. Survival—Fiction. 3. Contests—Fiction.] I. Johnson-Shelton, Nils. II. Title.
III. Title: Calling.
PZ7.F8925En 2014   2014009662
[Fic]—dc23   CIP
                                                                                                        AC

14 15 16 17 18 LP/RRDH 10 9 8 7 6 5 4 3 2 1
❖
First Edition

Much of this book is fiction, but much of the information in it is not. Endgame is real. And Endgame is coming.

Everything, all the time, every word, name, number, place, distance, color, time, every letter on every page, everything, always. So says, and so has been said, and so will be said again. Everything.

'Ēl' 12 12 12^{vi}

Endgame has begun. Our future is unwritten. Our future is your future. What will be will be.

We each believe some version of how we got here. God made us. Aliens beamed us. Lightning split us, or portals delivered us. In the end, the *how* doesn't matter. We have this planet, this world, this Earth. We came here, we have been here, and we are here now. You, me, us, the whole of humanity. Whatever you believe happened in the beginning is not important. The end, however. The end is.

This is Endgame.

We are 12 in number. Young in body, but of ancient people. Our lines were chosen thousands of years ago. We have been preparing every day since. Once the game begins, we must deliberate and decipher, move and murder. Some of us are less ready than others, and the lessers will be the first to die. Endgame is simple this way. What is not simple is that when one of us dies, it will mean the deaths of countless others. The Event, and what comes after, will see to that. You are the unwitting billions. You are the innocent bystanders. You are the lucky losers and the unlucky winners. You are the audience at a play that will determine your fate.

We are the Players. Your Players. We have to Play. We must be older than 13 and younger than 20. It is the rule, and it has always been this way. We are not supernatural. None of us can fly, or turn lead to gold, or heal ourselves. When death comes, it comes. We are mortal. Human. We are the inheritors of the Earth. The Great Puzzle of Salvation is ours to solve, and one of us must do it, or we will all be lost. Together we are everything: strong, kind, ruthless, loyal, smart, stupid, ugly, lustful, mean, fickle, beautiful, calculating, lazy, exuberant, weak.

We are good and evil.

Like you.

Like all.

But we are not together. We are not friends. We do not call one another, and we do not text one another. We do not chat on the internet or meet for coffee. We are separated and scattered, spread around the world. We have been raised and trained since birth to be wary and wise, cunning and deceptive, ruthless and merciless. We will stop at nothing to find the keys to the Great Puzzle. We cannot fail. Failure is death. Failure is the End of All, the End of Everything.

Will exuberance beat strength? Stupidity top kindness? Laziness thwart beauty? Will the winner be good or evil? There is only one way to find out.

Play.

Survive.

Solve.

Our future is unwritten. Our future is your future. What will be will be.

So listen.

Follow.

Cheer.

Hope.

Pray.

Pray hard if that is what you believe.

We are the Players. Your Players. We Play for you.

Come Play with us.

People of Earth.

Endgame has begun.

MARCUS LOXIAS MEGALOS

Hafız Alipaşa Sk, Aziz Mahmut Hüdayi Mh, Istanbul, Turkey

Marcus Loxias Megalos is bored. He cannot remember a time before the boredom. School is boring. Girls are boring. Football is boring. Especially when his team, his favorite team, Fenerbahçe, is losing, as they are now, to Manisaspor.

Marcus sneers at the TV in his small, undecorated room. He is slouched in a plush black leather chair that sticks to his skin whenever he sits up. It is night, but Marcus keeps the lights in his room off. The window is open. Heat passes through it like an oppressive ghost as the sounds of the Bosporus—the long, low calls of ships, the bells of buoys—groan and tinkle over Istanbul.

Marcus wears baggy black gym shorts and is shirtless. His 24 ribs show through his tanned skin. His arms are sinewy and hard. His breathing is easy. His stomach is taut and his hair is close-cropped and black and his eyes are green. A bead of sweat rolls down the tip of his nose. All of Istanbul simmers on this night, and Marcus is no different. A book lies open in his lap, ancient and leather-bound. The words on its pages are Greek. Marcus has handwritten something in English on a scrap of paper that lies across the open page: *From broad Crete I declare that I am come by lineage, the son of a wealthy man.* He has read the old book over and over. It's a tale of war, exploration, betrayal, love, and death. It always makes him smile.

What Marcus wouldn't give to take a journey of his own, to escape the oppressive heat of this dull city. He imagines an endless sea spread out before him, the wind cool against his skin, adventures and enemies arrayed on the horizon.

Marcus sighs and touches the scrap of paper. In his other hand he holds a 9,000-year-old knife, made of a single piece of bronze forged in the fires of Knossos. He brings the blade across his body and lets its edge rest against his right forearm. He pushes it into the skin, but not all the way. He knows the limits of this blade. He has trained with it since he could hold it. He has slept with it under his pillow since he was six. He has killed chickens, rats, dogs, cats, pigs, horses, hawks, and lambs with it. He has killed 11 people with it.

He is 16, in his prime for Playing. If he turns 20, he will be ineligible. He wants to Play. He would rather die than be ineligible.

The odds are almost nil that he will get his chance, though, and he knows it. Unlike Odysseus, war will never find Marcus. There will be no grand journey.

His line has been waiting for 9,000 years. Since the day the knife was forged. For all Marcus knows, his line will wait for another 9,000 years, long after Marcus is gone and the pages of his book have disintegrated.

So Marcus is bored.

The crowd on the TV cheers, and Marcus looks up from the knife. The Fenerbahçe goalie has cleared a rainbow up the right sideline, the ball finding the head of a burly midfielder. The ball bounces forward, over a line of defenders, near the last two men before the Manisaspor keeper. The players rush for the ball, and the forward comes away with it, 20 meters from the goal, free and clear of the defender. The keeper gets ready.

Marcus leans forward. Match time is 83:34. Fenerbahçe has yet to score, and doing so in such a dramatic way would save some face. The old book slides to the floor. The scrap of paper drifts free of the page and slips through the air like a falling leaf. The crowd begins to rise. The sky suddenly brightens, as if the gods, the Gods of the Sky themselves, are coming down to offer help. The keeper backpedals. The forward collects himself and takes the shot, and the ball blasts off.

As it punches the back of the net, the stadium lights up and the crowd screams, first in exaltation for the goal, but immediately afterward in terror and confusion—deep, true, and profound terror and confusion. A massive fireball, a giant burning meteor, explodes above the crowd and tears across the field, obliterating the Fenerbahçe defense and blasting a hole through the end of the stadium grandstand.

Marcus's eyes widen. He is looking at total carnage. It is butchery on the scale of those American disaster movies. Half the stadium, tens of thousands of people dead, burning, lit up, on fire.

It is the most beautiful thing Marcus has ever seen.

He breathes hard. Sweat pours off his brow. People outside are yelling, screaming. A woman wails from the café below. Sirens ring out across the ancient city on the Bosporus, between the Marmara and the Black. On TV, the stadium is awash in flames. Players, police, spectators, coaches run around, burning like crazed matchsticks. The commentators cry for help, for God, because they don't understand. Those not dead or on their way to being dead trample one another as they try to escape. There's another explosion and the screen goes black.

Marcus's heart wants out of his chest. Marcus's brain is as hot as the football pitch. Marcus's stomach is full of rocks and acid. His palms feel hot and sticky. He looks down and sees that he has dug the ancient blade into his forearm, and a rivulet of blood is trickling off his hand, onto the chair, onto his book. The book is ruined, but it doesn't matter; he won't need it anymore. Because now, Marcus *will* have his Odyssey.

Marcus looks back to the darkened TV. He knows there's something waiting for him there amidst the wreckage. He must find it.

A single piece.

For himself, for his line.

He smiles. Marcus has trained all of his life for this moment. When he wasn't training, he was dreaming of the Calling. All the visions of destruction that his teenage mind concocted could not touch what Marcus has witnessed tonight. A meteor destroying a football stadium and killing 38,676 people. The legends said it would be a

3

grand announcement. For once, the legends have become a beautiful reality.

Marcus has wanted, waited, and prepared for Endgame his entire life. He is no longer bored, and he won't be again until he either wins or dies.

This is it.

He knows it.

This is it.

CHIYOKO TAKEDA

22B Hateshinai Tōri, Naha, Okinawa, Japan

Three chimes of a small pewter bell awake Chiyoko Takeda. Her head lolls to the side. The time on her digital clock: 5:24. She makes a note of it. These are heavy numbers now. Significant. She imagines it is the same for those who ascribe meaning to numbers like 11:03 or 9:11 or 7:07. For the rest of her life she will see these numbers, 5:24, and for the rest of her life they will carry weight, meaning, significance.

Chiyoko turns from the clock on her side table and stares into the darkness. She lies naked on top of the sheets. She licks her full lips. She scrutinizes the shadows on her ceiling as if some message will appear there.

The bell should not have rung. Not for her.

All her life she has been told of Endgame and her peculiar and fantastical ancestry. Before the bell rang, she was 17 years old, a homeschooled outcast, a master sailor and navigator, an able gardener, a limber climber. Skilled at symbols, languages, and words. An interpreter of signs. An assassin able to wield the *wakizashi*, the *hojo*, and the *shuriken*. Now that the bell has rung, she feels 100. She feels 1,000. She feels 10,000, and getting older by the second. The heavy burden of the centuries presses down upon her.

Chiyoko closes her eyes. Darkness returns. She wants to be somewhere else. A cave. Underwater. In the oldest forest on Earth. But she is here, and she must get used to it. Darkness will be everywhere soon, and everyone will know it. She must master it. Befriend it. Love it. She has prepared for 17 years and she's ready, even if she never wanted it or expected it. The darkness. It will be like a loving silence, which for Chiyoko is easy. The silence is part of who she is.

For she can hear, but she has never spoken.

She looks out her open window, breathes. It rained during the night, and she can feel the humidity in her nose and throat and chest. The air smells good.

There is a gentle rapping on the sliding door leading to her room. Chiyoko sits in her Western-style bed, her slight back facing the door. She stamps her foot twice. Twice means *Come in.*

The sound of wood sliding across wood. The quiet of the screen stopping. The faint shuffle of feet.

"I rang the bell," her uncle says, his head bowed low to the ground, according the young Player the highest level of respect, as is the custom, the rule. "I had to," he says. "They're coming. All of them."

Chiyoko nods.

He keeps his gaze lowered. "I am sorry," he says. "It is time."

Chiyoko stamps five arrhythmic times with her foot. *Okay. Glass of water.*

"Yes, of course." Her uncle backs out of the doorway and quietly moves away.

Chiyoko stands, smells the air again, and moves to the window. The faint glow from the city's lights blankets her pale skin. She looks out over Naha. There is the park. The hospital. The harbor. There is the sea, black, broad, and calm. There is the soft breeze. The palm trees below her window whisper. The low gray clouds begin to light up, as if a spaceship is coming to visit. *Old people must be awake,* Chiyoko thinks. *Old people get up early.* They are having tea and rice and radish pickles. Eggs and fish and warm milk. Some will remember the war. The fire from the sky that destroyed and decimated everything. And allowed for a rebirth. What is about to happen will remind them of those days. But a rebirth? Their survival and their future depend entirely on Chiyoko.

A dog begins to bark frantically.

Birds trill.

A car alarm goes off.

The sky gets very bright, and the clouds break downward as a massive fireball bursts over the edge of town. It screams, burns, and crashes into the marina. A great explosion and a billow of scalding steam illuminate the early morning. Rain made of dust and rock and plastic and metal hurls upward over Naha. Trees die. Fish die. Children, dreams, and fortunes die. The lucky ones are snuffed out in their slumber. The unlucky are burned or maimed.

Initially it will be mistaken for an earthquake.

But they will see.

It is just the beginning.

The debris falls all over town. Chiyoko senses her piece coming for her. She takes a large step away from her window, and a bright ember shaped like a mackerel falls onto her floor, burning a hole in the tatami mat.

Her uncle knocks on the door again. Chiyoko stomps her foot twice. *Come in.* The door is still open. Her uncle keeps his gaze lowered as he stops at her side and hands her first a simple blue silk kimono, which she steps into, and, after she's in the kimono, a glass of very cold water. She pours the water over the ember. It sizzles, spurts, and steams, the water immediately boiling. What is left is a shiny, black, jagged rock. She looks at her uncle. He looks back at her, sadness in his eyes. It is the sadness of many centuries, of lifetimes coming to an end. She gives him a slight bow of thanks. He tries to smile. He used to be like her, waiting for Endgame to begin, but it passed him over, like it did countless others, for thousands and thousands of years.

Not so for Chiyoko.

"I am sorry," he says. "For you, for all of us. What will be will be."

SARAH ALOPAY

Bryan High School, Omaha, Nebraska, United States

The principal stands, smiling, and looks out over the crowd. "And so it is with great honor that I present your class valedictorian, Sarah Alopay!"

The crowd cheers, applauds, whistles.

Sarah stands. She's wearing a red cap and gown with the valedictorian's blue sash across her chest. She smiles. She's been smiling all day. Her face hurts, she's been smiling so much. She's happy. She'll be 18 in less than a month. She's going to spend her summer at an archeological dig in Bolivia with her boyfriend, Christopher, and in the fall it's off to college at Princeton. As soon as she turns 20, she can start the rest of her life.

In 742.43625 days she'll be free.

No longer eligible.

She's in the 2nd row, behind a group of administrators, PTA board members, and football coaches. She's a few seats from the aisle. Next to her is Reena Smithson, her best friend since 3rd grade, and four rows behind her is Christopher. She steals a look at him. Blond hair, five-o'clock shadow, green eyes. An even temper and a huge heart. The best-looking boy in her school, her town, maybe the state, and, as far as she's concerned, the world.

"Go get 'em, tiger," Christopher says, grinning.

Sarah and Christopher have been together since the 7th grade. Inseparable. Christopher's family is one of the wealthiest in Omaha. So wealthy, in fact, that his mom and dad couldn't be bothered to fly back from business in Europe to attend their own son's graduation. When

Christopher crosses the stage, it will be Sarah's family cheering the loudest. Christopher could've gone to private school, or the boarding school where his father went, but he refused, not wanting to be apart from Sarah. It is one of the many reasons she loves him and believes they will be together for their entire lives. She wants it, and she knows he does as well. And in 742.43539 days it will be possible.

Sarah gets into the aisle. She has on the pink Ray-Ban Wayfarers her dad gave her for Christmas, a pair of glasses that obscures her brown, wide-set eyes. Her long auburn hair is pulled into a tight ponytail. Her smooth, bronze skin is luminous. Under her gown she is dressed like all the others.

Yet how many others in her graduating class will bear the weight of an artifact onto the stage with them? Sarah wears it around her neck, just as Tate had worn it when he was eligible, as it has been, passed from Player to Player, for 300 generations. Hanging from the chain is a polished black stone that has seen 6,000 years of love, sorrow, beauty, light, sadness, and death. Sarah has been wearing the necklace since the moment Tate got hurt and her line's council decided she should be the Player. She was 14. She hasn't taken the amulet off since, and she's so used to it that she hardly feels it.

As she makes the trip to the stage, a chant begins in the back of the assembly. "Sar-ah! Sar-ah! Sar-ah!" She smiles, turns, and looks at all her friends; her classmates; Christopher; her older brother, Tate; and her parents. Her mom has her arm around her dad, and they look proud, happy. Sarah makes an *I'm nervous* face, and her dad smiles and gives her a thumbs-up. She steps onto the stage, and Mrs. Shoemaker, the principal, hands Sarah her diploma. "I'll miss you, Sarah."

"I'm not leaving forever, Mrs. Shoe! You'll see me again."

Mrs. Shoemaker knows better. Sarah Alopay has never gotten a grade lower than an A. She was All-State in soccer and track, and got a perfect score on her SATs. She's funny, kind, generous, and helpful, and clearly meant for bigger things. "Give 'em hell, Alopay," she says.

"I always do," says Sarah.

She steps to the mic, looks west over her class, her school. Behind the last line of 319 students is a stand of tall green-leafed oaks. The sun is shining and it's hot, but she doesn't care. None of them do. They're finishing one part of their lives, and another is about to begin. They're all excited. They're imagining the future, and the dreams they have and hope to realize. Sarah has worked hard on her speech. She's to be the voice of her classmates and wants to give them something that will inspire them, something that will drive them forward as they embark on this new chapter. It's a lot of pressure, but Sarah is used to that.

Sarah leans forward and clears her throat. "Congratulations and welcome to the best day of our lives, or at least the best day so far!" The kids go crazy, and a few prematurely toss their caps into the air. Some laugh. More cheer, "Sar-ah! Sar-ah! Sar-ah!"

"While I was thinking about my speech," Sarah says, her heart pounding, "I decided to try to answer a question. Immediately I thought, 'What question is most often asked of me?' and though it's a little embarrassing, it was easy to answer. People are always asking me if I have a secret!"

Laughter. Because it's true. If there was ever a perfect student at the school, it was Sarah. And at least once a week, someone asked what her secret was.

"After thinking long and hard, I realized it was a very simple answer. My secret is that I have no secrets."

Of course, that is a lie. Sarah has deep secrets. Profound secrets. Secrets that have been kept among her people for thousands and thousands of years. And though she's done all the things she's popular for, earned every A and trophy and award, she's done so much more. Things they can't even imagine. Like make fire with ice. Hunt and kill a wolf with her bare hands. Walk on hot coals. She has stayed awake for a week straight; she has shot deer from a mile away; she speaks nine languages, has five passports. While they think of her as Sarah Alopay, homecoming queen and all-American girl, the reality is that she is as highly trained and as deadly as any soldier on Earth.

"I am as you see me. I am happy and able because I allow myself to be happy. I learned young that being active breeds more activity. That the gift of studying is knowledge. That seeing grants sight. That if you don't feed anger, you won't be angry. Sadness and frustration, even tragedy, are inevitable, but that doesn't mean that happiness isn't there for us, for all of us. My secret is that I choose to be the person that I want to be. That I don't believe in destiny or predetermination, but in choice, and that each of us chooses to be the person we are. Whatever you want to be you can be; whatever you want to do you can do; wherever you want to go you can go. The world, and the life ahead, is ours for the taking. The future is unwritten, and you can make it whatever you want it to be."

The kids are quiet now. Everyone is quiet.

"I'm looking west. Behind you, above the bleachers, is a bunch of oaks. Behind the trees are the plains, the land of my ancestors, but really the ancestral land of all humans. Past the plains are the mountains, from where the water flows. Over the mountains is the sea, the source of life. Above is the sky. Below is the earth. All around is life, and life is—"

Sarah is interrupted by a sonic boom overhead. Everyone cranes their necks. A bright streak breaks over the oaks, scarring the blue sky. It doesn't appear to be moving, just getting bigger. For a moment everyone stares in awe. A few people gasp. One person very clearly says, "What is that?"

Everyone stares until a solitary scream comes from the back row, and it hits the whole assembly at once. It's like someone has flipped a switch for panic. The sounds of chairs tipping over, people screaming, total confusion. Sarah gasps. Instinctively, she reaches through her gown and grabs the stone around her neck.

It's heavier than it has ever been. The asteroid or meteor or comet or whatever it is, is changing it. She's frozen. Staring as the streak moves toward her. The stone on the chain changes again, feeling suddenly light. Sarah realizes that it's lifting into the air under her robe. It works itself free of her clothing, pulls in the direction of the thing that is coming for them.

This is what it looks like.

This is what it feels like.

Endgame.

The sounds of terror fall away from her ears, replaced by stunned silence.

Though she has trained for it for almost her entire life, she never thought it would happen.

She was hoping it wouldn't. 742.42898 days. She was supposed to be free.

The stone pulls at her neck.

"SARAH!" Someone yanks her arm hard. The fireball is riveting, terrible, and suddenly audible. She can literally hear it moving through the air, burning, raging.

"Come on! NOW!" It's Christopher. Kind, brave, strong Christopher. His face is red with alarm and heat, his eyes watering, spit flying from his lips. She can see her parents and her brother at the bottom of the steps.

They have seconds.

Maybe less.

The morning sky darkens, turns black, and the fireball is upon them. The heat is overwhelming. The sound is paralyzing.

They are going to die.

At the last moment Christopher vaults off the stage, pulling Sarah with him. The air fills with the smells of burning hair, wood, plastic. The necklace pulls so hard in the direction of the meteor that the chain digs into the skin of Sarah's neck.

They shut their eyes and crumple onto the grass. Sarah feels the stone pull free. It sails into the air, seeking out the meteor, and at the last minute the huge fireball changes direction, stopping a thousand feet short and skipping over them like a flat rock on a smooth lake. It happens so quickly that no one can see it, but somehow, some way, for some reason, the ancient little stone has spared them.

The meteor flies over the cement grandstand and impacts a quarter mile to the east. The school building is there. The parking lot. Some basketball courts. The tennis courts.

Not anymore.

The meteor destroys them all.

Boom.

They're gone.

Those comforting and familiar places where Sarah has spent her life—her normal life, anyway—are gone in an instant. Everything wiped away. A new chapter has begun, just not the one Sarah hoped for.

A shock wave rushes out and over the field, carrying dust and darkness. It hits them hard, flattens them, knocks them down, blows out their eardrums.

The air is hot and choked with particles, gray and brown and black. It's hard to see. Christopher is still with Sarah. Holding her. Shielding her. He pulls her close as they're pelted with stones and dirt, fist-sized chunks of god-knows-what. There are others around them, some hurt. They cough. They can't stop crying. They can't stop shaking. It's hard to breathe. Another shock wave passes through and pushes them farther into the ground. Sarah gets the wind knocked from her. Spears of fleeting light illuminate the dust. The ground shakes as things begin to fall around them. Hunks of cement and steel, twisted cars, furniture. They can do nothing but wait, praying that nothing lands on top of them. Christopher is holding her so hard it hurts. She is digging her nails into his back.

They have no idea how much time has elapsed when the air begins to clear and smaller sounds begin to return. People are wailing in pain. Names are being called. One of them is hers.

Her father.

"Sarah. SARAH!"

"Here!" she yells. Her voice sounds muffled and distant, even to herself. Her ears are still ringing. "I'm here!"

Her father emerges from the dust cloud. His face is covered in blood and ash. Against the filth on his face, she can see the whites of his eyes, brilliant and clear. He knows what she knows.

Endgame.

"Sarah!" Her dad stumbles toward them and falls to his knees, wrapping both of them in his arms. They cry. Their bodies heave. People scream in every direction. Sarah opens her eyes for a second and sees Reena in front of her, dazed, in shock. Her best friend's left arm is gone above the elbow; all that remains is blood and shredded skin and jagged bone. The graduation gown has been torn from her body, but somehow her cap has stayed on. She's covered in soot. Sarah calls, "Reena! Reena!" but Reena doesn't hear. She disappears back into the dust, and Sarah knows that she'll never see Reena again.

"Where's Mom?" she whispers, her lips on her dad's ear.

"I was with her. I don't know."

"The stone, it . . . it . . ."

"I know."

"Sarah?" her mom calls out.

"Here!" the three say together.

Sarah's mom crawls toward them. All the hair on the right side of her head is gone. Her face is burned but not too badly. When she sees them she looks so happy. Her look is different from the one she gave Sarah when she walked onto the stage.

I was giving a speech, Sarah thinks. *I was giving a speech at graduation. People were happy. So happy.*

"Olowa," Simon says quietly, reaching for his wife. "Tate?"

Olowa shakes her head. "I don't know."

An explosion in the distance.

The air starts to clear, the carnage becoming more evident. There are bodies everywhere. The Alopays and Christopher are the lucky ones. Sarah sees a head. A leg. A torso. A cap falls to the ground near them.

"Sarah, it's on. It's on for real."

It's Tate, walking toward them, his arms extended. One hand is in a fist; the other holds a grapefruit-sized hunk of gold-and-green rock streaked with black veins of metal.

He is amazingly clean, as if the whole thing passed him over. He smiles. His mouth is full of blood. Tate was a Player once, but no longer. Now he looks almost excited for his sister, in spite of all that's happened around them. All the death, all the destruction, all that they know is coming.

"I found them!" Tate is 10 feet away now. Another small explosion from somewhere. He opens his fist and puts the small piece of stone that was around her neck into the bigger multicolored rock. "It fits perfectly."

"*Nukumi,*" Simon says reverently.

"*Nukumi,*" Sarah says, much less reverently.

"What?" Christopher asks.

Sarah says, "Nothing—"

But she is cut short as an explosion sends shards of metal flying through the air. A six-foot-long piece of steel embeds itself into the middle of Tate's chest. He is dead. Gone. Killed in an instant. He falls backward, Sarah's stone pendant and the piece of green-veined rock still in his hand. Her mother screams; her father yells, "No!"

Sarah cannot speak. Christopher stares in shock. Blood oozes out of Tate's chest. His eyes are open and staring, lifeless, to the sky. His feet twitch, the last bits of life leaving him. But the stone and the pendant, they are safe.

This is not accidental.

The stones have meaning.

Carry a message.

This is Endgame.

JAGO TLALOC

Tlaloc Residence, 12 Santa Elisa, Juliaca, Puno, Peru

Jago Tlaloc's sneakers crunch across broken glass. It is night and the streetlights are out. Sirens wail in the distance, but otherwise Juliaca is quiet. It was chaos before, when Jago first headed for the crater in the city center to claim what had been sent for him. In the madness, survivors poured into the streets, shattering shop windows, taking whatever they wanted.

The looting will not sit well with Jago's father, who runs protection for many of the local businesses. But Jago does not blame his people. Let them enjoy some comforts now, while there is still time. Jago has a treasure of his own: the stone, still warm, wrapped in his satchel and tossed over his shoulder.

A hot wind rushes through the buildings, carrying ash and the smell of fire. They call Juliaca the Windy City of Peru for good reason. Unlike many of his people, Jago has traveled well beyond the city limits. He has killed at least twice on every continent, and still he finds it strange to visit a place where the wind is missing.

Jago is the Player of the 21st line. Born to Guitarrero and Hayu Marca just over 19 years ago. Once Players themselves, several years apart, his parents now run this part of the city. From the legitimate businesses to the illicit materials that flow through the neighborhood's back alleys, his parents take a cut of everything. They are also philanthropists, in a way, turning around their often ill-gotten money to open schools and maintain hospitals. The law does not touch them, refuses to come near them; the Tlaloc family is too much of a resource. In just a few more months, Jago would have become ineligible and joined his parents in the family business. Yet all empires must crumble.

A trio of shadows peels from the mouth of a nearby alley. The figures block the sidewalk in front of Jago, looking wolfish and dangerous.

"What you got there, my friend?" hisses one of the shadows, nodding at Jago's satchel.

In response, Jago flashes his teeth, which are perfectly straight and white. His maxillary lateral incisors are each capped with gold, and each inset with a small diamond. These gems glint in the moonlight. The three scavengers shrink back. "Sorry, Feo," says the leader, "we didn't recognize you."

They should be scared, but not of Jago or the power of his family, though Jago is strong and merciless, and his family more so. They should be scared of what is to come. They don't know it, but Jago is the only hope these people have. Once, the power of his family was enough to keep this neighborhood and its people alive and happy. Now that responsibility falls to Jago.

He passes by the thugs without a word. He is lost in thoughts of the 11 other Players, scattered around the world, each with a meteor of their own. He wonders what they will be like, what lines they come from. For the lines do not know the other lines. They cannot know. Not until the Calling.

And the Calling is coming.

Will some be stronger than him? Smarter? Will one even be uglier? Perhaps, but it is no matter.

Because Jago knows that he can, and will, kill them all.

Not the first not the last. [vii]

BAITSAKHAN

Gobi Desert, 222 km South of Ulaanbaatar, Mongolia

Baitsakhan wants it, and he's going to get it.

He rides hard south into the Gobi Desert with his twin cousins, Bat and Bold, both 12.5, and his brother, Jalair, 24.55.

Baitsakhan has been 13 for 7.23456 days and is just eligible for Endgame.

He is happy about this.

Very happy.

The meteor fell in the middle of the night two days ago in the vast central nothingness of the Mongolian steppe. A small group of old yak herders saw it, and they called it in to Baitsakhan's grandfather Suhkbataar, who told them to leave it alone or they would be sorry. The herders listened. Everyone in the steppe knows to listen to Suhkbataar in strange matters like these.

Because of this, Baitsakhan knows that the space rock will be there, waiting, alone. But when they are about a half mile from the impact zone they see a small group of people, and a worn Toyota Hilux, sitting in the distance.

Baitsakhan reins his horse and slows it to a walk. The other riders pull alongside him. Jalair draws a brass telescope from a saddlebag and looks across the plain. He makes a low sound.

"Who are they?" Baitsakhan asks.

"Don't know. One wears an *ushanka*. Another has a rifle. The truck has three external gas cans. One of the men is leaning on a long pry bar. Two are bending to the ground. The one with the rifle is going toward the Hilux."

Bat rests a longbow across his lap. Bold absently checks his smartphone. No signal, of course, not this far out. He opens Temple Run and starts a new game.

"Do they have the rock?" Baitsakhan asks.

"Hard to tell . . . wait. Yes. Two are carrying something small but heavy. It's wrapped in hide."

"Have they seen us?" Bat asks.

"Not yet," Jalair says.

"Let's introduce ourselves," Baitsakhan says.

Baitsakhan kicks his horse and it launches into a canter. The others follow. Each of the horses is light brown with a braided mane and black tail. Dust rises behind the beasts. The group around the meteorite notices them, but they don't show any alarm.

When they draw very near, Baitsakhan reins his horse and, before it stops, jumps from the saddle. "Hello, friends!" he calls. "What have you found?"

"Why should we tell you?" the man with the pry bar says cockily. He has a low, raspy voice and a thick, excessively groomed mustache. Next to him is the man in the Russian hat. Between them on the ground is the hide-wrapped bundle.

"Because I asked," Baitsakhan answers politely.

Bat gets off his horse and begins to casually check his animal's shoes and hooves for rocks. Bold, still in the saddle, gets his phone out and restarts Temple Run.

A short grizzled man with horribly pockmarked skin steps forward. "Forgive him. He's like that with everyone," he says.

"Shut up, Terbish," Pry Bar says.

"We think we found a shooting star," Terbish says, ignoring Pry Bar.

Baitsakhan leans toward the bundle. "Can we see it?"

"Yeah, not every day you get to see a meteorite," Jalair says from atop his horse.

"What's going on?" someone calls. It's the man returning from the Hilux. He's tall and casually holds a .30-06 at his side.

"These kids want to see the rock," Terbish says, studying Baitsakhan. "And I don't see why not."

"Cool!" Baitsakhan exclaims. "Jalair, check out this crater!"

"I see it."

Baitsakhan doesn't know, but this meteorite is the smallest of the 12. Less than 0.2112 meters. The smallest rock for the youngest Player.

Terbish smiles. "I found one of these when I was about your age," he says to Baitsakhan. "Near the Chinese border. The Soviets took it, of course. They took everything in those days."

"So they say." Baitsakhan sticks his hands in his jean pockets. Jalair dismounts, his feet crunching on the gravel.

Terbish turns toward the bundle. "Altan, unwrap the thing."

The man in the ushanka bends and peels back the pony hide. Baitsakhan peers into it. The thing is a hunk of black metal the size of a small shoe box, pockmarked with glowing lattices of gold and verdigris ingots, like extraterrestrial stained glass. Baitsakhan removes his hands from his pockets and drops to a knee. Terbish stands over him. Pry Bar sighs. Rifleman takes a few steps forward. Bat's horse whinnies as Bat adjusts the girth.

"It is beautiful, isn't it?" Terbish says.

"Looks valuable," Baitsakhan says innocently.

Jalair points. "Is that gold?"

"I knew we shouldn't have shown it to them," Pry Bar says.

"They're boys," Terbish says. "This is like a dream come true. They can tell their friends at school about it."

Baitsakhan stands. "We don't go to school."

"No?" Terbish wonders. "What do you do then?"

"Train," Jalair says.

"For what?" Pry Bar asks.

Baitsakhan takes a pack of gum out of his vest and pops a piece in his mouth. "Do you mind if we check something, Terbish?"

Terbish frowns. "What?"

"Go ahead, Jalair," Baitsakhan says.

But Jalair has already started. He quickly bends over the meteorite. He has a small black stone in his hand. It has a series of perfectly cut T-shaped holes in it. He runs his hand over the rock, underneath it. His eyes widen. "Yes, this is it," he says.

Bold turns off his smartphone, puts it in a cargo pocket on his pant leg, spits.

"Bubble gum?" Baitsakhan holds the pack of gum out for Terbish. Rifleman frowns and moves the gun across his body, holding it with two hands.

Terbish shakes his head. "No thanks. We're going to be going now." Baitsakhan pockets the gum. "Okay."

Jalair stands as Altan starts to rewrap the boulder.

"Don't bother," Jalair orders.

Pry Bar huffs. "You little shits seriously aren't trying to say you're taking this thing, are you?"

Baitsakhan blows a pink bubble. It bursts across his face and he gobbles it back into his mouth. "That's exactly what we're saying."

Terbish draws a skinning knife from his belt and takes a step backward. "I'm sorry, kid, but I don't think so. We found it first."

"Some yak herders found it first."

"I don't see any yak herders around here," Pry Bar says.

"We told them to leave. And they know to listen. The rock belongs to us."

"He's being modest," Jalair adds. "It actually belongs to him."

"You?" Terbish asks doubtfully.

"Yes."

"Ha!" Pry Bar says, holding the rod like a quarterstaff. "I've never heard anything so ridicu—"

Jalair cuts Pry Bar short by grabbing the rod, twisting it free, and slamming the pointed end into Pry Bar's sternum, knocking the wind out of him. Rifleman shoulders the .30-06, but before he can fire, an arrow strikes him cleanly through the neck.

They'd forgotten about Bat behind his horse.

Altan, the man in the hat, gets his hands around the bundle, but Bold throws a black metal dart at him, about eight inches long and a half inch in diameter. It strikes Altan through the hat's earflap and drives a few inches into his head. He collapses and begins to foam at the mouth. His arms and legs dance. His eyes roll.

Terbish is full of terror and disbelief. He turns and sprints for the truck.

Baitsakhan blows a short whistle through his teeth. His horse trots next to him; he jumps on, kicks it in its side. It catches Terbish in seconds. Baitsakhan pulls hard, and the horse rears and comes down on Terbish's shoulders and neck. The man is crushed into the earth as the horse turns a tight circle first one way then the next, prancing over Terbish's body, crushing his bones, taking his fading life.

When Baitsakhan returns to the crater, Pry Bar is sitting on the ground, his legs in front of him, his nose bloody, his hands tied behind him. The rod is under his elbows, and Jalair is pulling up on it. Baitsakhan jumps from his horse.

The man spits. "What did we ever do to—"

Baitsakhan puts his fingers to his lips. "Shh." He holds out his other hand, and Bat appears as if from nowhere and places a long and gleaming blade in it. "Don't talk."

"What are you doing?" the man pleads.

"Playing," Baitsakhan says.

"What? Why?" Pry Bar asks.

Baitsakhan puts the knife against the man's neck and slowly slices the man's throat open.

"This is Endgame," Baitsakhan says. "There is no why."

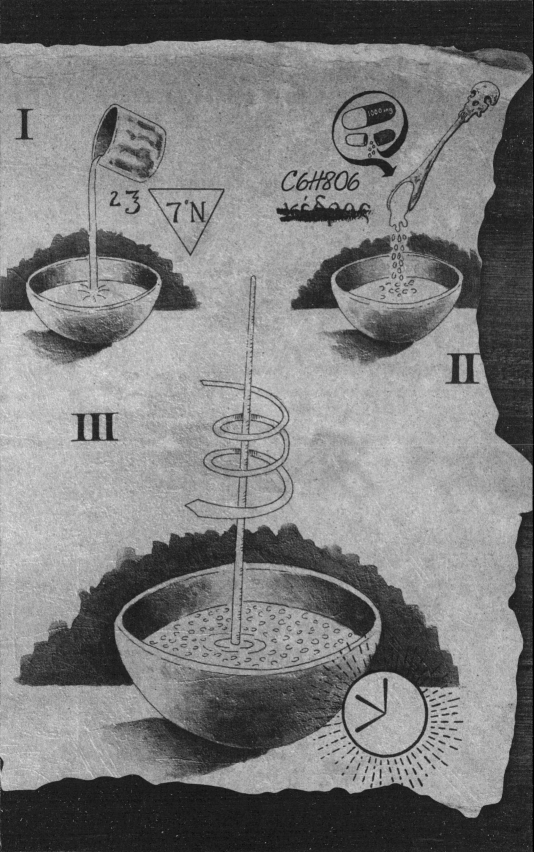

SARAH ALOPAY

Alopay Residence, 55 Jefferson Street, Omaha, Nebraska, United States

Sarah doesn't want her brother to be dead or her best friend to be armless in the ICU or her school to be gone. She doesn't want most of her classmates to have been obliterated. She doesn't want any part of it. She doesn't want to be the Player.

Too bad for her.

She sits at the linoleum-topped table, her fingers laced. Simon and Olowa stand behind her. Christopher returned to the crash site to help pull survivors out of the wreckage and do whatever else he can. He's kind that way. Kind and brave and strong.

Christopher does not know what Sarah is or what she's going to have to do. He does not know that the meteor fell from the sky in order to deliver her a message. In a way, all those deaths were caused by Sarah's presence. And there will be more death if Sarah doesn't Play. Everyone within hundreds, thousands of miles will die if she doesn't win.

The Alopays are still in shock. They look like actors from a war movie. Sarah hasn't spoken. Simon has been crying quietly. Olowa has been steeling herself against what has passed and what is yet to come.

The multicolored meteorite rests on an ancient ceramic platter on the table. Olowa has told them that it's called pallasite—a kind of nickel-iron rock laced with a colorful substance called olivine. In spite of its small size, it weighs 9.91 kg. Cut into the pallasite is a perfect triangular hole.

The stone that flew from Sarah's neck and saved them rests on the table. It is jet-black, darker than the insides of Sarah's eyes.

Next to the stone is a rough-edged sheet of yellow paper, and a glass beaker of clear liquid.

Sarah picks up the stone. They have talked about this moment for years. Though Sarah never believed it would come, and doesn't think her parents did either, now it's here. They have to follow each step, in proper order. When they were young, before they were eligible, she and Tate would playact and pretend they were doing it. They were children. Like fools, they thought Endgame would be cool.

It isn't.

Sarah turns the stone in her hand. It is a tetrahedron. Its four triangular sides are exactly the same dimensions as the hole in the chunk of meteorite. The small pyramidal rock is familiar yet foreign. There is no record of its exact age, but the Alopays know that it is at least 30,000 years old. It comes from an era in human history when humans were not believed to have possessed the tools capable of crafting a thing so fine. It comes from a time when humans were not believed to have even been aware of the perfect proportions of golden triangles. But here it is. Passed down again and again and again. An artifact of history before history. A history that is not thought to have existed.

"Here goes," Sarah says.

This is it.

The future is unwritten.

What will be will be.

She holds the stone over the meteorite; it jumps from her hand and snaps into place, melding with the pallasite. The hairline gap between the objects disappears. For a moment nothing happens. A rock is a rock is a rock is a rock. But as they watch, the stone she wore around her neck turns to dust, as do 3.126 inches of the meteorite around it. The dust mixes, mingles, dances, settles after 11 seconds.

She learned the process when she was five years old. Each step must be done in the proper order.

She pours the dust onto the parchment.

"Ahama muhu lopeke tepe," her father chants through silent tears. He

would rather be grieving for his lost son, but knows there is no time for that.

She spreads the dust.

"Ahama muhu gobekli mu," her mother chants more resolutely.

She pours the liquid on it.

"Ahaman jeje. Ahaman kerma," her parents chant together.

The dust steams; the air fills with an acrid smell; the edges of the paper curl, turning the flat sheet into a bowl.

"Ahaman jeje. Ahaman kerma," her parents chant together.

She picks it up, mixes it.

The liquid evaporates and the dust turns red.

And it appears.

The message.

The Calling.

١١١٥٢٦٠٢٢٢٠٩٠٨١٢٢١٠٧١٩٢٢٠٧٠٤٢٢١٥٠٥٢٢١٥١٨١٣٢٢٠٨٠٧١٢٠
٧١٩١٨٠٩٠٧٠٢٠٨١٨٠٣٠٨١٨٠٣٠٧٢٢٢١٣١٢١٣٢٢١٩٠٦١٣٢٣٠٩٢٢٢٣٢٢١٨٢٠
١٩٠٧٢١١٨٢١٠٧٠٢٢١١٢٠٦٠٩١٤١٨٢٣١٣١٨٢٠١٩٠٧٠٨٠٦١٤١٤٢٢٠٩٠
٨١٢١٥٠٨٠٧١٨٢٤٢٢٢٤١٩٢٦٠٨٢٢٠٧١٩٢٢٠٤١٨١٥٢٣٢٠١٢١٢٠٨٢٢

Sarah stares at the markings. Even though she was not supposed to be the Player, she has always had an affinity for codes and languages. She has been studying them in all their forms since she was four years old. They start shifting into place.

She sees the numbers that are telling her where and how she will start to win.

Sarah thinks about her brother, how Tate couldn't accept that he had been disqualified from Endgame for losing an eye. How he'd been drifting through his years of ineligibility, how he'd grieved at his inability to continue and the passing of the responsibility to Sarah. How excited he'd looked that afternoon when he'd recovered the meteorite for her. How she can't actually believe that she's going to be the one Playing Endgame, and not him. How she is going to have to

Play alone, without Tate's support.

She thinks about Reena and her missing arm, the confusion on her face. She thinks about Christopher pulling bodies from under rubble. She thinks about her speech. *I choose to be the person that I want to be.* Those words seem so hollow now that Sarah has no choice.

She will make sure that her family and friends did not die in vain.

All 12 Players of all 12 lines receive the message.
All 12 Players of all 12 lines will attend the Calling.
The 12 Players of the 12 lines are:

١ Marcus Loxias Megalos,[viii] Minoan,[ix] 16.24 years

٢ Chiyoko Takeda,[x] Mu,[xi] 17.89 years

٣ Sarah Alopay,[xii] Cahokian,[xiii] 17.98 years

٤ Alice Ulapala,[xiv] Koori,[xv] 18.34 years

٥ Aisling Kopp,[xvi] La Tène,[xvii] 19.94 years

٦ Baitsakhan,[xviii] Donghu,[xix] 13.02 years

٧ Jago Tlaloc,[xx] Olmec,[xxi] 19.14 years

٨ An Liu,[xxii] Shang,[xxiii] 17.46 years

٩ Shari Chopra,[xxiv] Harrapan,[xxv] 17.82 years

١٠ Kala Mozami,[xxvi] Sumerian,[xxvii] 16.50 years

١١ Maccabee Adlai,[xxviii] Nabataean,[xxix] 16.42 years

١٢ Hilal ibn Isa al-Salt,[xxx] Aksumite,[xxxi] 18.69 years

MACCABEE ADLAI

Aeroflot Flight 3501, Seat 4B
Depart: Warsaw
Arrive: Moscow

Maccabee Adlai, the Player of the 8th line, settles into the 1st-class cabin on Aeroflot 3501 from Warsaw to Moscow, which will take 93 minutes. In Moscow he will make a connection for a flight to Beijing, which lasts 433 minutes. He is 16 years old but has the build of a decathlete 10 years his senior. He is six feet five inches tall, and he weighs 240 pounds. He has the facial stubble as well, one of those kids who never really looked like a kid. Even when he was seven, he was much taller and stronger than his peers.

He likes being taller and stronger than his peers.

It gives him advantages.

He removes the jacket of a three-button custom silk suit. He settles into his aisle seat. His French-cuffed shirt is powder blue and white gingham. His rose-patterned tie is held in place with a silver clip. His cuff links are made of fossilized mammoth ivory. They are shaped like Tibetan skull beads and have ruby chips for eyes. On his left pinkie is a large brass ring inset with a drab tan stone carved in the shape of a flower.

Maccabee smells like lavender and honey. His black hair is wavy and full and slicked back. His forehead is broad and his skull is apparent, as if his skin is almost too thin. His temples are a little sunken and his cheekbones high. His eyes are blue. His nose is narrow but large with a hook in the bridge.

It has been broken five times.

He likes fighting. So what? When you're Maccabee's size, fights have a tendency to find you. People want to see how they measure up. In

Maccabee's case, they always come up short.

His only bag—a leather monogrammed shoulder satchel—is in the overhead compartment. He expects other Players to be burdened with packs and suitcases and all kinds of expectations. Maccabee doesn't like to be burdened. He prefers to be nimble, fast, to be able to move and strike at will. Plus, the world has not ended yet. Until it does, money will suffice.

Lots of money.

He fastens his seat belt and turns on a smartphone and listens to a recorded message. He has listened to the message dozens of times:

NASA/ESA/ROSCOSMOS Joint Press Release, 15 June:
At 22:03 GMT on 11 June a large and previously undetected Near Earth Asteroid (NEA), since designated CK46B, passed within 500,000 miles of Earth. Accompanying this parent NEA were several hundred children of varying magnitudes. At least 100 of these objects are confirmed to have been drawn into Earth's gravitational field. Like most "shooting stars," the majority of these burned up in the atmosphere, leaving nothing but visual evidence of their descent and demise. However, as worldwide press coverage has well documented, at least 12 bolides did survive the rigors of atmospheric entry.

While the sudden appearance of an NEA as large as CK46B is disturbing, it is the purpose of this release to assuage fears of a larger impact in the future. Impacts like these—especially like those that occurred in Warsaw, Poland; Jodhpur, India; Addis Ababa, Ethiopia; and Forest Hills, Queens, New York, USA—are exceedingly rare. Through joint efforts of our agencies, plus those of the ISA, JAXA, UKSA, and AEB, you can be assured that other NEAs and Near Earth Objects (NEOs) are identified and tracked on a regular basis and that at this time it is our consensus opinion that our planet is in no danger whatsoever of being struck by anything larger than the meteorites mentioned above.

Finally, it is also our opinion that the shower propagated by CK46B is complete and that no additional meteors can be expected. CK46B

has been charted and it is not due to reappear in our vicinity for
another 403.56 years. For now, the possible danger posed by this NEA is
considered past. Any further information—

"Excuse me," a man says in Polish as he knocks into Maccabee,
yanking the cord of his headphones from his ears.

"I should say so," Maccabee says in perfect English with equal parts
confidence and annoyance.

"You speak the English?" the man asks, also in English, dropping
heavily into his window seat. He is 40 or so, sweating, overweight.

"Yes," Maccabee says. He glances across the aisle. A very pretty woman
in a form-fitting dark suit rolls her green bespectacled eyes. Maccabee
returns the gesture.

"Then I will speak the English too," the man announces. "I will
practice. Yes? Onto you?"

"Practice *with* me," Maccabee corrects, winding the cord of his
headphones around his hand.

"Yes. With you." The man manages to shove his valise under the seat
in front of him. He struggles to find his seat belt, pulling hard at the
buckled end, which does not move.

"You have to let out the buckle. Like this." Maccabee unfastens his seat
belt and shows the man how it works.

"Ah, how silly of me," the man says in Polish.

"They should do away with them, in my opinion," Maccabee says, still
speaking English and clicking his back together. "If the plane crashes,
this is not going to help anyone."

"I agree," the pretty woman says in English, her eyes remaining on the
magazine she's browsing.

The man leans past Maccabee, eyes the woman. "Aha. There hello." He's
back to English.

Maccabee leans forward to intercept the man's prying eyes. "It's 'Hello,
there.' And she wasn't talking to you."

The man recoils. "Gentle, young one. She is the pretty woman. She knows it. I just let her know I know it too. What is wrong by that?"

"It's rude."

The man waves his hand dismissively. "Ah! Rude! A good English word! I like. It is meaning 'not nice,' no? What is it . . . 'unpolite'?"

"*Im*polite," the woman answers. "It's okay. I've had worse."

"There. See? You have the nice suit, but me, I have the . . . the . . . *experience*." This last word is in Polish.

"Experience," Maccabee translates.

The man jabs a finger into Maccabee's shoulder. "Yes, experience."

Maccabee looks at the man's finger, still pushed into his shoulder. Maccabee is being underestimated, which is the way he likes it. "Don't do that," Maccabee says calmly.

The man jabs him again. "What, this?"

As Maccabee prepares to respond, a flight attendant appears and asks in Polish, "Is there anything wrong?"

"Ah, another one," the man says, his eyes just as greedy for the attendant. She is also pretty. "Yes, there is something wrong, as a matter of fact." The man animatedly drops his tray table in front of him and taps it. "I haven't got my drink yet."

The attendant joins her hands in front of her. "What would you like, Mr. Duda?"

The woman across the aisle chuckles at the appropriateness of his name—which usually means "booby"—but Duda doesn't hear.

"Two champagnes and two Stolichnayas. All in sealed bottles. Two glasses. No ice."

The attendant doesn't even bristle. She works for Aeroflot and has seen her share of drunks. She nods at Maccabee. "And for you, Mr. Adlai?"

"Orange juice, please. In a glass with ice."

"Adlai, hm? You a Jew?" Duda asks in Polish.

"In a manner of speaking, yes," Maccabee says, turning in his seat.

"Figures. Explains all the finery." Duda's eyes dart up and down Maccabee's shirt. "Also explains the scent you exude." Duda is staying with Polish, probably for the same reason Maccabee chooses English. The attendant returns and bends over, holding a tray, and gravity and pressure part the divide of her collared shirt.

Maccabee takes his orange juice as Duda winks, grabs his drinks, and whispers, "Bend over a little more next time and I'll give you a nice tip."

The attendant smiles and straightens. "We don't accept tips, Mr. Duda."

"Pity," Duda says, as he cracks the two Stolichnayas and pours one into each glass.

She turns and walks away.

Duda leans forward and reaches over Maccabee. "How about you?" he asks the woman across from them. "Would you accept a tip from me in exchange of services?"

"That's enough," Maccabee says, as his heart starts to beat faster, moving from a resting rate of 41 to a heightened rate of 77. "If you speak again, you'll regret it."

Duda downs one of the vodkas and says quietly so only they can hear, "Oh, little boy. I see you dressed like a man, but you don't fool me."

Maccabee takes a deep breath and slows his heart rate, as he has been trained to do. Killing, if it becomes necessary, is best done in a calm manner, and with smooth, easy movements. He did it for the first time at age 10, and has done it 44 more times in the years since.

The man leans into his seat, drinks the other vodka and both champagnes. He rolls toward the window and closes his eyes.

The plane taxis, takes off, reaches cruising altitude. The pretty woman minds her business. And for a while Maccabee does too.

After about an hour, though, he leans across the aisle and says in English, "I'm sorry about all that, Miss . . ."

She smiles. "Miss Pawlek." He can tell that she thinks he is at least 22 or 23. Most people do, especially young women.

"Miss Pawlek."

"Why should you be sorry? You behaved perfectly."

"I wanted to punch him."

"We're on a plane. You can't."

They start to talk. Maccabee quickly realizes that she is tired of talking about the meteorite that has scarred Warsaw, or the 11 others that have rattled the world. It's all anyone has been able to talk or think about for a week, so he lets it lie.

Instead, Maccabee practices a subtle form of interrogation on her. He has been trained to use techniques that reveal sensitive information from people without their knowing. She is from Goleniów, a medieval capital near the German border. She works for an internet investing firm. She is meeting a client in Moscow. Her mother is dead. Her brother is an accountant in Krakow. She likes Italian opera and watches the Tour de France every year on TV. She has been to L'Alpe d'Huez. She has been in love once, when she was 19, and hopes, she says with a smile, to fall in love again.

Maccabee doesn't say anything truthful about himself, except that he is on a business trip that will take him all the way to Beijing. Miss Pawlek has never been there. One day she would like to go.

They order a round of drinks, Maccabee opting for a ginger ale. As they toast, they don't realize that Duda is awake and watching them.

"Moving in on my action, eh?" he announces without lifting his head from his pillow. Duda points at Miss Pawlek, amused. "You should leave this boy alone. Women like you need a real man."

"You're a pig," she replies with a sneer.

"That's not what you're going to be saying later," Duda says, smiling.

The plane jerks. It is flying at 31,565 feet. The wind is coming from the north-northwest at 221 mph. The *fasten seat belt* light comes on. It's rough enough that 167 of the 176 passengers grip their armrests, 140 of them look at the person next to them for reassurance. Eighteen start praying silently. The meteorite has put the idea of horrific, sudden death at the front of everyone's mind.

Maccabee doesn't mind the turbulence. To quote one of his favorite books: *Fear is the mind-killer.* He has practiced besting fear over and over and over again. He has practiced being cold and calculated and efficient. And while Duda is essentially harmless, it never hurts to continue to practice.

He leans close to Duda, pushing a small button on the palm side of his pinkie ring, revealing a short silver needle in the center of the stone flower.

"If you speak to me again, or to anyone on this flight—"

The plane jumps again. The wind speed has increased to 231 mph. More passengers whimper in fear; more begin to pray.

"Don't threaten me, you little—" Duda says, but Maccabee, with his heart rate back at 41, and quickly enough so that no one sees, strikes the exposed flesh of Duda's neck with the needle.

"What did you . . ." Duda says.

"You should have listened," Maccabee says quietly, coldly, with a smile. Duda knows what's happened but is unsure if it's sleep or death that's coming for him.

Duda cannot speak to ask.

Duda can no longer move.

Duda's eyes fill with confusion and terror.

The plane slides hard from side to side. The wind is gusting faster. People are not quiet about their praying now. They are calling out to God. Maccabee lets his heart rate rise.

A baby in coach class starts crying.

As Duda's eyes roll into his head, Maccabee props a pillow against the window and pushes Duda into it. He runs his fingers over Duda's eyelids. He puts the man's hands in his lap, one over the other.

Maccabee settles back into his seat. He has met so many strange people in his life. He wonders who he will meet when he arrives in China.

Six minutes later the turbulence ends. Miss Pawlek looks over at him, smiles. Her brow glistens with a nervous sweat; her cheeks are flushed. Maccabee likes the way she looks in that moment: the relief mixed with something else.

Miss Pawlek inclines her head at Duda. "What happened to our friend?"

"Closed his eyes and went to sleep," Maccabee answers. "Some people can sleep through anything."

She nods. The green of her irises is captivating. "That was pretty rough turbulence, wasn't it?"

Maccabee turns his head from her, looks at the back of the seat in front of him. "Yes it was. But it's over now."

52.294888, 20.950928[xxxii] 7,459 dead; $1.342B damages
26.297592, 73.019128[xxxiii] 15,321 dead; $2.12B damages
40.714411, -73.864689[xxxiv] 4,416 dead; $748.884M damages
9.022736, 38.746799[xxxv] 18,888 dead; $1.33B damages
-15.49918, -70.135223[xxxvi] 10,589 dead; $1.45B damages
40.987608, 29.036951[xxxvii] 39,728 dead; $999.24M damages
-34.602976, 135.42778[xxxviii] 14 dead; $124.39M damages
34.239666, 108.941631[xxxix] 3,598 dead; $348.39M damages
24.175582, 55.737065[xl] 432 dead; $228.33M damages
41.265679, -96.431637[xli] 408 dead; $89.23M damages
26.226295, 127.674179[xlii] 1,473 dead; $584.03M damages
46.008409, 107.836304[xliii] 0 dead; $0 damages

SARAH ALOPAY

Gretchen's Goods Café and Bakery, Frontier Airlines Lobby, Eppley Airfield, Omaha, Nebraska, United States

Sarah sits with Christopher at a small plastic table, an untouched blueberry muffin between them. They hold hands, touch knees, and try to act like this isn't the strangest day of their young lives. Sarah's parents are 30 feet away at another table, watching their daughter warily. They're worried what she might say to Christopher, and what the boy—a boy they've always treated like a son—will do. Their actual son, Sarah's brother, Tate, is in a funeral home, awaiting cremation. Everyone keeps saying there will be time to grieve for Tate later, but that may not be true.

In 57 minutes Sarah is getting on a plane that will take her from Omaha to Denver, from Denver to San Francisco, from San Francisco to Seoul, from Seoul to Beijing.

She does not have a return ticket.

"So you have to leave to play this game?" Christopher asks for what feels to Sarah like the 17th time.

Sarah is patient. It isn't easy to understand her secret life. For a long time, she dreamed of telling Christopher about Endgame; she just never thought she would actually have to. But now she feels relieved to finally be honest with him. For this reason it doesn't matter if he keeps asking the same questions over and over. These are her last moments with him, and she'll treasure them even if he's being obstinate.

"Yes," Sarah replies. "Endgame. The world is not supposed to know about it, or about people like me."

"The Players."

"Yes, the Players. The councils. The secret lines of humanity . . ."
She trails off.

"Why can't the world know?"

"Because no one would be able to live a normal life if they knew Endgame was hanging over them," Sarah says, feeling a pang of sadness for her own "normal life" that went up in smoke just days ago.

"You have a normal life," Christopher insists.

"No, I don't."

"Oh, right," Christopher says, rolling his eyes. "You've killed wolves and survived on your own in Alaska and are trained in all kinds of karate and crap. Because you're a *Player*. How did you ever manage to squeeze in soccer practice?"

"It was a pretty packed schedule," Sarah answers wryly. "Especially for the last three years, you know, because Tate was supposed to be the Player, not me."

"But he lost his eye."

"Exactly."

"How did he lose it, by the way? None of you ever told me that," Christopher says.

"It was a pain trial. Withstand the stings of a thousand bees. Unfortunately, one got him right in the pupil, and he had a bad reaction, and he lost the eye. The council declared him ineligible and said that I was in. Yeah, that definitely made my schedule a bit crazy."

Christopher stares at her like she's lost it. "You know, I'd think this was a sick joke if your parents weren't here. If that meteor hadn't hit and Tate hadn't . . . Sorry, it's just a lot to take in."

"I know."

"You're basically in a death cult."

Sarah purses her lips, her patience slipping. She expected Christopher to be supportive; at least that's how it went when she imagined this conversation. "It's not a death cult. It's not something I chose to do. And I never wanted to lie to you, Christopher."

"Whatever," Christopher says, his eyes lighting up as if he's just come to a decision. "How do I sign up?"

"For what?"

"Endgame. I want to be on your team."

Sarah smiles. It's a sweet thought. Sweet and impossible. "It's not like that. There aren't teams. The others—all eleven of them—won't be bringing teammates to the Calling."

"The others. Players, like you?"

"Yeah," Sarah says. "Descendants of the world's first civilizations, none of which exist anymore. Each of us represents a line of the world's population, and we play for the survival of that line."

"What's your line called?"

"Cahokian."

"So, like, Native American. I think there's a little Algonquian on my dad's side. Does that mean I'm part of your line?"

"It should," Sarah answers. "Most people in North America have some Cahokian blood, even if they don't realize it."

Christopher thumbs his chin. Sarah knows all of Christopher's tics, so she knows that this means he's about to make an argument, he's just not quite sure how to phrase it. There are 52 minutes left before her flight leaves. She waits patiently, although she's starting to worry that this is how they'll spend their last hour together. She was hoping to give her parents the slip, find a secluded gate, and make out one last time.

"Okay," says Christopher, clearing his throat. "So you've got twelve ancient tribes abiding by these weird rules and waiting for some sign. And that's how you've chosen to interpret the meteor that, admittedly, is a pretty fucked-up and crazy coincidence. But what if that's what this is? Just a coincidence and you're like a hot, brainwashed, alleged killing machine only because of some dumb prophecy that doesn't really exist."

Christopher catches his breath. Sarah stares at him, smiling sadly.

"It's for real, Christopher."

"How do you know? I mean, is there some kind of commissioner who runs this game? Like the NFL?"

"Them."

Christopher dips his chin. "Them?"

"They have lots of names," Sarah says, not meaning to sound so cryptic. She's having trouble putting the next part into reasonable-sounding words.

"Give me one," Christopher says.

"Cahokians call them the Sky People."

"The Sky People?"

"Yes." Sarah holds up a hand before he can interrupt. "Listen—you know how every culture around the world believes that their god or gods or higher power or source of enlightenment, whatever you want to call it, comes from above?"

Christopher shrugs. "I guess. I don't know."

"They're right. God, or the gods, or the higher power, whatever and whoever it is, *did* come from above. They descended from the sky amid smoke and fire and created us and gave us rules to live by and left. All of the world's gods and myths are just variations of the same legends, variations of the same story, the same *history*."

Christopher shakes his head. "This is crazy. Like, Jesus-riding-a-dinosaur crazy."

"No, it isn't. It makes sense if you think about it."

"How?"

"It all happened so long ago that every culture adapted the story to fit their experience. But the core of it—that life came from above, that humanity was created by gods—that's true."

Christopher stares at her.

"Sky People. You mean like . . ." He shakes his head. "This is *insane*. What you're saying can't be real. It's the craziest thing I've ever heard! And *you're* crazy if you go."

"I'm sorry, Christopher. If I were in your shoes I'd probably react the same way. Actually, probably way worse. You know me as Sarah Alopay, your girlfriend, but I'm also someone else, and even though Tate was supposed to be playing, I always have been someone else as well. I was raised, as were 300 generations of my people, to be a Player.

Everything that just happened—the meteor, the piece that we found, my necklace becoming part of it, the message and the code—it was all exactly as foretold in our legends."

Sarah studies him, waiting for a reaction. Christopher's face has gone completely serious; he's no longer trying to talk her out of Endgame, as if that tactic ever had a chance.

"Why now?"

"What do you mean?"

"Why did it have to start now?"

"I'll probably be asking myself that question until I die, Christopher. I don't know the answer. I know what the legend says, but I don't know *Their* real reasons."

"What does the legend say?"

"It says Endgame will begin if the human race has shown that it doesn't deserve to be human. That it has wasted the enlightenment They gave to us. The legend also says that if we take Earth for granted, if we become *too* populous and strain this blessed planet, then Endgame will begin. It will begin in order to bring an end to what we are and restore order to Earth. Whatever the reason, what will be will be."

"Fucking Christ."

"Yeah."

"How do you win?" he asks in a low voice.

"No one knows. That's what I'm going to find out."

"In China."

"Yeah."

"And it's going to be dangerous?"

"Yes."

"You talked about choice in your speech—choose not to do it."

Sarah shakes her head. "No. It's what my parents were born to do, what my brother was born to do, what I was born to do. It is the responsibility of my people, and it has been since we appeared on this planet, and my choice is to do it."

Christopher has no words. He doesn't want her to leave. Doesn't want her to be in danger. Sarah is his girlfriend. His best friend. His partner in crime, the last person he thinks of before he falls asleep and the first person he thinks of when he wakes. She's the girl of his dreams, only she's real. The thought of someone trying to hurt her, it ties his stomach in knots. The idea that he'll be thousands of miles away when it happens makes it even worse.

"The stakes are dire, Christopher. You probably won't ever see me again. Mom and Dad, Omaha, Tate—I'm looking back on all of it already. I love you, I love you with everything in me, but we may never see each other again."

"What the hell does that mean?"

"I may not come back."

"Why?"

"If I don't win, I'll die."

"Die?"

"I will fight to stay alive, I promise I will. But yes. It could happen. Easily. Don't forget that I'm a backup. Tate was supposed to be here, not me. The other Players, they've probably been training since before they could walk."

They stare at each other. The sounds of the airport—the announcements of gate changes, the whispering wheels of rolling luggage, the squeaks of sneakers on polished granite floors—swirl around them.

"I'm not gonna let you die," Christopher says. "And if you have to win to stay alive, then I am coming with you. I don't give a shit about the rules."

Her heart drops to the floor. She knew saying good-bye wasn't going to be easy, but she didn't expect this. And in a way it makes her love him more. Kind, generous, strong, beautiful Christopher.

She shakes her head. "The Players have to go to the Calling alone, Christopher."

"Too bad for the others, then. Because I'm coming with you."

"Listen," she says, changing her tone. "You need to stop thinking of me as your girlfriend. Even if you *could* come, I wouldn't let you. I don't need your protection. And, honestly, you aren't up for it."

So much for finding a quiet gate where they can make out. Sarah knew it could come to this, that she might have to be harsh with him. She sees that her words hurt him, that his pride is wounded. She's sorry about that, but what she said is the truth.

Christopher shakes his head, persisting. "I don't care. I'm coming."

Sarah sighs. "I'm gonna stand up in a minute. If you try to follow me, they'll stop you." Sarah tilts her head toward her parents.

"They can't stop me."

"You have no idea what they can do. The three of us, we could kill everyone in this terminal quickly and easily and escape, no problem."

Christopher snorts in disbelief. "Christ, Sarah. You wouldn't do that."

"Understand me, Christopher," Sarah says, leaning forward and gritting her teeth. "I will do *whatever* it takes to win. If I want you, my parents, everyone we know to survive, I *have* to do whatever it takes."

Christopher is silent. He glances at the Alopays, who are staring back at him. Simon is giving him a hard, cold look. It's unlike anything he's ever seen before. Christopher thought he knew these people. He was closer to them than his own family, and now . . .

Sarah sees Christopher's face change, notices the fear blossoming there, and worries that she's pushed too hard. She softens her tone. "If you want to help me, stay here and help the people who need it. Help my parents deal with Tate's death, and maybe mine. If I win, I'll come back and find you, and we can live the rest of our lives together. I promise."

Christopher looks deep into Sarah's eyes. His voice shakes. "I love you, Sarah Alopay." She tries to smile but fails. "I love you," he repeats earnestly. "And I swear that I'll never, ever stop loving you."

They stand at the same time and wrap their arms around each other. They kiss, and though they have shared many, many kisses, none of them has meant as much, or felt as strong. Like all such kisses it doesn't last long enough.

They pull apart. Sarah knows that this is probably the last time she will ever see him, speak to him, touch him.

"I love you too, Christopher Vanderkamp. I love you too."

30.3286, 35.4419[xliv]

AN LIU

Liu Residence, Unregistered Belowground Property, Tongyuanzhen, Gaoling County, Xi'an, China

An Liu has a disadvantage, and he is ashamed.
Blinkblink.
A tic.
BlinkSHIVER.
SHIVERSHIVER.
But An Liu has advantages too:
1.   The Players are coming to Xi'an, China.
2.   An Liu lives in Xi'an, China.
BlinkSHIVER.
SHIVERblink.
3.   Therefore, he has initial home-court advantage.
4.   An is a world-class hacker.
5.   An is an expert bomb maker.
BlinkSHIVERblinkblink.
Blinkblink.
BlinkblinkSHIVER.
6.   An knows how to find people.
After decoding the message, An continuously hacked passenger manifests at airports close to the other impact zones, filtering results for age, ticket-purchase date, date of visa issuance, and *blink-blink-blink* assuming there would be a more-or-less even distribution of gender, sex.
SEXSHIVERSEX.
He figures that *shiver-blink* the Players near the Mongolian and Australian impact zones, on account of their remoteness, will be tricky, so he abandons them. The Mongolian will be coming overland

blink anyway, and the Aussie will also probably start his or her journey *blink* by jeep or possibly chartered aircraft. Instant dead ends.

He also discounts Addis Ababa, Istanbul, Warsaw, and Forest Hills, New York, on account of these being *shiver-shiver-SHIVER* rather populous. He concentrates on Juliaca, Omaha, Naha, and Al Ain. These smaller markets make the hacking and filtering easier.

Initial results provide 451 candidates. These are cross-referenced with train and/or plane ticket purchases for transport within China. An *blink* is *blink* not *blink* hopeful.

Blinkblinkblinkblinkblinkblinkblinkblinkblinkblinkblinkblinkblink-blinkblink.

Had it been necessary for him to travel to reach the Calling, he would have taken the obvious precaution of using aliases, forged visas, and at least two passports, but he knows that not all people are as paranoid as he is. Even Players.

And lo. *Shiver.* He gets a hit: Sarah Alopay.

SHIVERblinkblink.

Blinkblink.

Blink.

JAGO TLALOC, SARAH ALOPAY

Train T41, Car 8, Passing through Shijiazhuang, China
Depart: Beijing
Arrive: Xi'an

Jago Tlaloc is on an overnight train from Beijing to Xi'an. It has taken him nearly three days to get this far. Juliaca to Lima. Lima to Miami. Miami to Chicago. Chicago to Beijing. 24,122 km. 13,024.838 nautical miles. 79,140,413.56 feet.

And now the train for 11.187 hours.

Longer if it gets delayed.

Endgame doesn't wait, so he is hoping for no delays.

Jago has a private sleeping cabin, but the mattress is hard and he's restless. He sits up and crosses his legs, counts his breaths. He stares out the window and thinks of the most beautiful things he has ever seen: a girl falling asleep in the sand as the sun set over a beach in Colombia, streams of moonlight reflecting off the rippling waters of the Amazon, the lines of the Nazca giant on the day he became a Player. His mind won't calm, though. His breath is not full. Positive visualizations disintegrate under the weight.

He cannot stop thinking about the horror visited on his hometown. The hellfire and the smell of burning plastic and flesh, and the sounds of crying men, burned women, and dying children. The helplessness of the firemen, the army, the politicians. The helplessness of everyone and everything in the face of the violence.

The day after Jago claimed his piece of the meteorite, the sun rose on a huddled mass of people lined up outside his parents' villa. Some of them had lost everything and hoped his family would be able to restore them. As Jago packed, his parents did what they could. On television, astrophysicists made hollow promises about how an event

53

like this would never happen again.

They're wrong.

More are coming.

Bigger, more devastating.

More will suffer.

More will burn.

More will die.

The people called the meteor that fell on Juliaca *el puño del diablo*. The Devil's Fist. Eleven other fists punched into the earth, killing many, many more.

The meteors fell and now the world is different.

Vulnerable.

Terrified.

Jago knows he should be above such feelings. He has trained to be above such feelings, yet he cannot sleep, cannot relax, cannot calm himself. He swings his legs over the bed and places his bare feet on the thin, cool carpet. He cracks his neck and closes his eyes.

The meteorites were just a preamble.

Todo, todo el tiempo, he thinks. *Todo.*

He stands. His knees creak. He has to get out of his compartment, move, try to clear his mind. He grabs a pair of green cargo pants and pulls them on. His legs are thin, strong. They've done more than 100,000 squats. He sits in the chair and puts on wool socks, leather moccasins. His feet have kicked a heavy bag over 250,000 times. He straps a small tactical knife to his forearm and slips into a long-sleeved plaid shirt. He has done over 15,000 one-handed pull-ups. He grabs his iPod and sticks in a pair of black earbuds. He turns on music. The music is hard, heavy, and loud. Metal. His music and his weapons. Heavy heavy metal.

He steps to the door of his compartment. Before exiting he looks in the full-length mirror. He is tall, thin, and taut, as if made of high-tension wire. His hair is jet-black, short, and messed. His skin is the color of caramel, the color of his people, undiluted for 8,000 years. His eyes are black. His face is pockmarked from a skin infection he had when he was seven, and he has a long, jagged scar that runs from the corner of his left eye, down his cheek, over his jaw, and onto his neck. He got the scar when he was 12, in a knife fight. It was with another kid a little older than him. Jago got the scar, but he took the kid's life. Jago is ugly and menacing. He knows that people fear him because of the way he looks, which generally amuses him. They should fear him for what he knows. What he can do. What he has done.

He opens the door, steps into the hall, walks. The music blares in his ears, hard, heavy, and loud, drowning out the steely screech of the wheels on the rails.

He steps into the dining car. Five people are seated at three tables: two Chinese businessmen sitting alone, one asleep in his booth, his head on the table, the other drinking tea and staring at his laptop; a Chinese couple speaking quietly and intensely; a girl with long, auburn hair woven into a braid, her back to him.

Jago buys a bag of peanuts and a Coke and walks toward an empty table across from the girl with the auburn hair. She is not Chinese. She is reading the latest edition of *China Daily*. The page is covered in color photos of devastation from the crater in Xi'an. The crater where the Small Wild Goose Pagoda had stood. He sits down. She's five feet away from him, engrossed in the paper; she does not look up.

He removes the peanuts from their shells, pops them into his mouth, sips the Coke. He stares at her. She's pretty, looks like an American tourist, a medium-sized backpack next to her. He has seen countless girls like her stop in Juliaca on their way to Lake Titicaca.

"It's not polite to stare," she says, looking at the paper.

"I didn't think you'd noticed," he replies in accented English.

"I did." She still hasn't looked at him.

"Can I join you? I haven't spoken to many people the past few days, and this country can be *bien loco*, you know?"

"Tell me about it," she says, looking up, her eyes drilling into him. She's easily the most beautiful American, and maybe woman, he's ever seen.

"Come on over."

He half rises and sidles into the booth opposite her. "Peanut?"

"No thanks."

"Smart."

"Hm?"

"Not to accept food from a stranger."

"Were you going to poison me?"

"Maybe."

She smiles and seems to reconsider, like he's challenged her to a dare. "What the hell, I'll take my chances."

Her smile crushes him. He is usually the one who has to charm a woman, which he has done dozens of times, but this one is charming him. He holds out the bag and she takes a handful of the peanuts, spreads them on the table in front of her.

"How long you been here?" she asks.

"On the train?"

"No. In China."

"Little over three weeks," he says, lying.

"Yeah? Me too. About three weeks." His training has taught him how to tell if someone is lying, and she is. Interesting. He wonders if she could be one of them.

"Where you from?" he asks.

"America."

"No kidding. Where in America?"

"Omaha." She's not lying this time. "You?"

"Peru, near Lake Titicaca." So he won't lie either.

She raises her eyebrows and smirks. "I never thought that was a real place until these. . . ." She points at the paper.

"The meteors."

"Yeah." She nods. "It's a funny name. Lake Titty Caca." She pronounces the words individually, like all amused English speakers do. "You couldn't come up with anything better than that?"

"Depending on who you ask, it either means Stone of the Puma or

Crag of Lead, and it's considered by many to be a mystical, powerful place. Americans seem to think UFOs visit it and aliens created it."

"Imagine that," she says, smiling. "Omaha's not mystical at all. Most people think it's kind of boring, actually. We got good steak, though. And Warren Buffet."

Jago chuckles. He assumes that's a joke. He doesn't know who Warren Buffet is, but he has a fat, dumb American name.

"It's weird, isn't it?" She cracks another peanut.

"What?"

"I'm from Omaha, you're from near Lake Titicaca, and we're on a train to Xi'an. The meteors hit in each place."

"Yes, that is weird."

"What's your name?"

"Feo." He pops a peanut in his mouth.

"Nice to meet you, Feo. I'm Sarah." She pops a peanut in her mouth.

"Tell me—you going to Xi'an to see the crater?"

"Me? No. Just touring. I can't imagine the Chinese government is going to be letting anyone get too close to it anyway."

"Can I ask you another question, Feo?"

"Sure."

"You like to play games?"

She's outed herself. He's not sure this is wise. His response will go a long way to determine whether or not he will be outed too.

"Not really," he answers quickly. "I like puzzles, though."

She leans back. Her tone changes, the flirtatious lilt melting away.

"Not me. I like knowing things for sure one way or the other. I hate uncertainty. I tend to eliminate it as quickly as I can, get it out of my life."

"Probably a good policy, if you can actually do it."

She smiles, and though he should be tense and ready to kill her, her smile disarms him. "So—Feo. That mean something?"

"It means 'ugly.'"

"Your parents name you that?"

"My real name is Jago; everyone just calls me Feo."

"You're not, though, even though you're trying to be."

"Thank you," he replies, unable to stop himself from smiling, the diamonds in his teeth flashing. He decides to throw her a crumb. If she takes it, they will both know. He's not sure that it's a smart play, but he knows one must take risks to win Endgame. Enemies are a given. Friends are not. Why not take advantage of an early chance encounter and find out which this beautiful American will be?

"So, Sarah from Omaha who is here on vacation, while you're in Xi'an do you want to visit the Big Wild Goose Pagoda with me?"

Before she can answer, a white flash comes from outside. The train lurches and brakes. The lights flicker and go out. A loud sound like a vibrating string comes from the other side of the dining car. Jago's eyes are momentarily drawn to the faint blip-blip of a red light from under a table. He looks back to the window when the light outside intensifies. He and Sarah both stand and move toward it. In the distance, a bright streak runs across the sky, going east to west. It looks like a shooting star, but it's too low, and its trajectory is as straight as a razor's edge. Jago and Sarah both stare, transfixed, as the streak speeds against the darkness of the Chinese night. At the last minute, before it passes from view, the streak suddenly changes direction and moves in an 88-degree angle north to south, disappearing over the horizon. They pull back from the window and the lights come back and the train starts to accelerate. The other people in the dining car are talking urgently, but none seem to have noticed the thing outside.

Jago stands. "Come with me."

"Where?"

"Come with me if you want to live."

"What are you talking about?"

He holds out his hand. "Now."

She stands and follows him but makes a point of not taking his hand. As they walk he says, "If I told you I'm the Player of the 21st line, would that mean anything to you?"

"I would tell you I'm the Player of the 233rd."

"Truce, at least for now?"

"Yes, for now."

They reach the table where Jago saw the blinking red light. The Chinese couple is sitting at it. They stop talking and look at the two foreigners quizzically. Jago and Sarah ignore the couple, and Jago kneels and Sarah bends to look over his shoulder. Bolted to the wall under the table is a black metal box with a small, faintly blinking red LED in the middle. Above the LED is the character 驚. In the corner of the black box is a digital display. It reads AA:AA:AQ. A second later AA:AA:AP. Another second, AA:AA:AO.

"Is that what I think it is?" Sarah asks, taking a step back.

"I'm not willing to wait around to find out," Jago says.

"Me neither."

"Let's get your bag."

They head back to the table and Jago grabs the backpack. They move to the rear of the car and open the door, step into the space between cars.

If the letters are seconds, they have 11 left.

Sarah pulls the emergency brake.

It doesn't work.

The moving landscape is there. Waiting for them.

"Go," Jago says, stepping aside.

Eight seconds.

She doesn't hesitate, jumps.

Seven seconds.

He hugs the backpack, hoping it will soften his landing, jumps.

It hurts when he lands, but he's been trained to ignore pain. He rolls down a gravel embankment and into the dirt, takes a mouthful of grass, scratches his face and hands. He can't be sure, but he thinks he's dislocated his right shoulder.

Three seconds.

He stops rolling.

Two seconds.

She's a few yards away, already standing, as if she somehow landed unhurt. "You all right?" she asks.

One second.

The train is past them.

"Yes," he says, wondering if she can tell he's lying.

Zero seconds.

She crouches next to him, waiting for the train to explode.

Nothing happens.

The stars are out.

They stare.

Wait.

Jago looks in the sky above the train and sees Leo and Cancer above the western horizon.

"Maybe we overreacted—" Sarah starts to say, just as the dining car lights up and the windows blow out. The entire car is lifted 50 feet or more into the air amidst a cloud of orange fire. The force ripples through the train. The aft cars crumple, momentum piling them into a screeching and jumbled pile. The forward cars are obscured by the blast and the darkness, but Jago can make out the lights of the engine as it's twisted off the rails. The sound of grating metal tears through the night, and another, smaller, explosion goes off toward the front of the train. There is a brief moment of silence, just before the screaming starts.

"*Mierda,*" Jago says breathlessly.

"I guess we're going to have to get used to things like that, aren't we?"

"Yes." Jago winces.

"What is it?"

"My shoulder."

"Let me see."

Jago turns to Sarah. His right arm is hanging low in his shirt.

"Can you move your fingers?"

He can.

"Your wrist?"

He can.

"Good."

She gingerly takes his arm with both hands and lifts it a little. The pain shoots over his shoulder and down his back, but he doesn't say anything. He has been through far worse.

"Dislocated. I don't think it's too bad," she says.

"You don't think, or you don't know?"

"I don't think. I've only set one of these before. For my brother," she says quietly.

"Can you put it back?"

"Of course, Feo. I'm a Player," she says, trying not to sound like she's convincing herself. "I can do all sorts of wonderful things." She lifts it again. "It's gonna hurt, though."

"I don't care."

Sarah pulls, twists, and pushes the arm, and it pops into place. Jago breathes deeply through his teeth, testing out his arm. It works.

"Thank you, Sarah."

The screaming is louder.

"You'd have done the same for me."

Jago smiles. For some reason, he thinks of the people who came to see his parents after the meteor struck Juliaca. There are some debts that must be honored.

"No, I wouldn't have," he says. "But I will now."

Sarah stands, looks toward the wreckage. "We need to get out of here. Before the government gets here, before they start asking questions."

"You think it was meant for one of us?" Jago asks.

"It had to be. This *is* Endgame," she says, reaching out her hand, offering it. "My name is Sarah Alopay. I'm the Cahokian."

He takes her hand, and it lights him up, feels as if it belongs in his, as if it's something he's been waiting for. It also scares him, because he knows these feelings can be dangerous, can make him vulnerable, especially with someone who has the skills he suspects she has. For now, though, he'll allow himself to feel it, to love it.

"I'm Jago Tlaloc. The Olmec."

"Nice to meet you, Jago Tlaloc. Thank you for saving my life. I owe you one."

Jago looks up to the cloudless sky, remembering the streak of light that passed overhead, that short-circuited the train's power long enough for him to see the blinking light of the detonator. He'll take credit for saving Sarah, sure. It's good to have another Player in his debt. But he knows the truth: that streak across the sky was a warning. A warning from Them, making sure that they would live until at least the Calling.

"Don't mention it," he says.

Without another word Sarah puts her backpack on and starts to run into the darkness. She's fast, strong, graceful. He smiles as he watches her braid sway back and forth.

He has a new friend.

The beautiful Player of the 233rd.

A new friend.

Maybe more.

43.98007, 18.179324[xlv]

CHRISTOPHER VANDERKAMP

Air China Flight 9466, Seat 35E
Depart: San Francisco
Arrive: Beijing

Christopher's father is a beef farmer in the western prairie. A very successful beef farmer. At last count more than 75,000 head of cattle. Christopher said good-bye to Sarah. He didn't want to, but he did. He stood with Sarah's family and watched her go through security. He stayed at the airport until her flight had departed.

He let her go.

He's not used to letting things go.

And he's never had to let anything go before.

Christopher was the starting quarterback of the football team. He is a great athlete. He was recruited to Nebraska in the fall to play football. He accepted, but he asked if they could give the scholarship to someone else. Someone who needed it.

On the field he never spent more than five counts in the pocket. He is decisive, has an arm like a cannon, legs like a thoroughbred, a heart like a lion. He is physically superior to most kids his age and to almost everyone he's ever met.

Christopher is in love. In love with Sarah Alopay. In love with a Player of Endgame. All anyone can do is talk about the meteor, the school, the deaths, the disappearance of Sarah. What it all means. They don't know, have no idea, couldn't even begin to imagine the truth about what happened.

But Christopher knows—even if he still thinks it's bullshit.

He's 18 years old. Free. He has a passport. He has been to Europe, South America, and Asia. He has traveled on his own before.

Christopher is a fighter. His younger brother, John, has Down syndrome. Kids used to pick on him in grade school. They made fun of him and mocked him. Christopher took care of those kids, and John didn't get picked on anymore.

Christopher is rich.

Decisive.

Fast.

Strong.

And Christopher is in love.

Christopher knows where she is going, the number of her satellite phone, about Endgame.

Christopher likes games.

He has spent most of his life winning games.

He believes he can win anything.

He realizes he lied to the girl he loves. He is not going to sit this one out. He is not going to wait.

Two days after Sarah leaves, Christopher leaves as well.

He is going to find her.

Help her.

They're going to win.

Together.

The earthquake occurred near Huaxian, Shaanxi (formerly Shensi), China, about 50 miles (80 km) east-northeast of Xi'an, the capital of Shaanxi. Damage extended as far away as Taiyuan, the capital of Shanxi (formerly Shansi) and about 270 miles (430 km) northeast of the epicenter. There were felt reports as far away as Liuyang in Hunan, more than 500 miles (800 km) away. Geological effects reported with this earthquake included ground fissures, uplift, subsidence, sand blows, liquefaction, and landslides. Most towns in the damage area reported collapsed city walls, most to all houses collapsed, and many of the towns reported ground fissures with water gushing out (i.e., liquefaction and sand blows). Gu, et. al. says that "the identified death toll of soldiers and civilians was 830,000, and the unidentified was uncountable." The earthquake was felt in all or parts of nine[xlvi] provinces: Anhui, Gansu, Hebei, Hubei, Henan, Hunan, Shaanxi, Shandong, and Shanxi.

CHIYOKO TAKEDA

Big Wild Goose Pagoda, Xi'an, China

Before the meteorite there were two Wild Goose Pagodas in Xi'an. One called Small and the other called Big.

Now there is one.

The Big Wild Goose Pagoda.

Chiyoko visits it on the morning of June 20.

There are tourists from everywhere, but mostly tourists from China. It's a massive country in every conceivable way. Japan is crowded, but China takes crowds to another level. Ever since she arrived, Chiyoko feels as if China is all there is to the world, that there is nothing more. No ice caps, no Empire State Buildings, no Parthenons, no sprawling boreal forests, no Meccas, no Kremlins, no pyramids, no Golden Temples, no Angkor Wats, no Stonehenges.

No Endgame.

Just China.

Chiyoko sits on a bench. The Big Wild Goose Pagoda is surrounded by a scenic park. Chiyoko reads her guidebook and looks at pictures. The Small Wild Goose Pagoda had soft lines and a rounded taper. It was, before the meteorite, 141 feet tall. It was constructed around 708 CE and had been periodically reconstructed over the centuries. It suffered some earthquake damage in 1556 that, until its recent destruction, had remained unrepaired.

The Big Wild Goose Pagoda—the survivor towering before her—is harsher and more fortresslike. Its taper is fixed by a number—Chiyoko estimates that each successive floor is around 0.8 times smaller than the preceding floor. It is 210 feet tall. It was constructed in 652 CE and repaired in 704. The same 1556 earthquake damaged it extensively, causing it to lean to the west at 3.4°.

In less than 48 hours she will sneak into the Big Wild Goose Pagoda and find whatever it is that is waiting for her.

What is waiting for all the Players of Endgame.

Chiyoko watches the crowd of tourists. She nibbles on spicy rice crackers from a little white paper bag. She is convinced that other Players are here now, doing the same thing she is. Scattered among the Chinese throng are foreigners, and every one intrigues her. Especially the young ones.

The African boy with the lollipop.

The Southeast Asian girl decked out in Hello Kitty gear.

The pale white girl with flame-red hair and skull-shaped headphones.

The brooding Indian boy in the cornflower-blue shirt.

The Central Asian girl smoking a thin cigarette as she swipes her thumb across the screen of her iPhone.

The squat blond girl wearing tight white jeans and leather Birkenstocks.

The sinewy pockmarked boy with the scar on his face.

Surely they are not all Players, but some are, some definitely are.

Chiyoko stands, walks toward the tower. She is determined to remain alone throughout Endgame. Any alliances she makes will be temporary and opportunistic. She finds friendships to be burdensome, so why bother with any in the crucible that is about to consume them? Nor will she strive to make enemies. These are even more annoying than friends. No, her plan is simply to follow for as long as she can. She will use her best skills and attributes—silence, furtiveness, ordinariness—to her advantage.

She walks to the pagoda. She is so unobtrusive and quiet that the guards don't notice her, don't ask for her ticket.

She moves inside. It is cooler there. The sounds are clearer. If there weren't so many people inside, she would like it. There is so much noise in China. Very few understand the value of silence like Chiyoko.

She makes her way to the stairs, moving without any sound.

I must choose wisely, she thinks. She must pick the Player or Players she believes has the best early chance. Then she will shadow and track that Player. When they are not looking, she will take whatever it is she wants or needs and move on.

She makes her way up, up, up. She reaches the top of the Big Wild Goose Pagoda. There is a small door at the back of the room. She makes her way to it, casually inspects it. Etched into its wood, in very small markings, is the word *ROBO.*

As far as ciphers go, it is child's play. But since it is recognizable as an English word fragment, it goes unnoticed.

Chiyoko notices, though.

Chiyoko understands.

And the others will too, if they haven't already.

She turns from the door and goes to the western window. She peers out over the sprawl of Xi'an. There is the crater, where the other pagoda stood, still smoldering, six days after the impact. The wind carries the smoke to the south in black and gray tendrils.

A small group of monks arrives, clad in orange and red robes. Like her, they are quiet. Perhaps they also have dedicated themselves to silence. She wonders if they'll scream when it all comes crumbling down.

Chiyoko won't scream. When the world goes to hell, Chiyoko will do what she always does. Slip away unnoticed.

CHRISTOPHER VANDERKAMP

Xi'an Garden Hotel, Dayan District, Xi'an, China

Christopher watches the Big Wild Goose Pagoda. He has not seen
Sarah. But he has been looking, and he knows that she's out there. He'd
like to think that she can sense his love, but that would be crazy. He
needs to keep his head on straight, to go about this rationally.
He didn't travel halfway around the world, chasing his girlfriend who
is involved in an apocalyptic game of allegedly alien design, to get
sidetracked by silly puppy-love emotions.
His hotel is across the street from the pagoda. He has a telescope and
two pairs of binoculars mounted on tripods. He has a DSLR with a
400-mm fixed lens. All of them face the Big Wild Goose Pagoda.
He watches.
Waits.
Dreams of seeing her, touching her, smelling her, kissing her.
Looking into her eyes and seeing love returned.
He watches.
Waits.
And on the night of the solstice it happens.
He sees seven people sneak into the Big Wild Goose Pagoda. Most are
disguised, hidden, incognito. He can't be sure if any of them is Sarah.
Sarah said there were 12 Players, so he assumes the other five must
have gone in from a different entrance, or gone undetected. He can't
cover all the angles from his room.
Snap snap snap.
He takes pictures.
Lots of pictures.

Only one person gives him a good image. A girl. Dark-tanned skin.
Wearing colorful scarves over a form-fitting jumpsuit. Full black hair
peeking out from a head wrap. The glint of brilliant green eyes.

He is tempted to go too. He doesn't want to admit it, but he is afraid.
Of the other Players. Of Endgame. Of—he can hardly believe he is
thinking it—the Sky People.

But mostly he is afraid of what Sarah would look like—what she would
say, how she would feel—if she were to see him now.

He knows the time isn't right.

Not yet.

He needs a moment where he can swoop in and help her, where he can
prove his worth and his love. He doesn't want to seem like a stalker,
lingering around the pagoda like some kind of Endgame groupie. That
would be embarrassing. So he waits. For an hour. Two. Two and a half.
Nothing.

He waits.

His eyes are heavy. His chin is in his hand. His elbow is on his knee.
There's nothing, no one.

He can't fight sleep anymore.

He's been up for over 27 hours.

And just like that, he is out.

35.2980, 25.1632[xlvii]

MARCUS LOXIAS MEGALOS

Big Wild Goose Pagoda, Xi'an, China

Up, up, up.

Marcus checks his watch.

Keep going up.

12:10 a.m.

He's late.

Up.

How could he have been so stupid?

Up.

He should have stayed within walking distance, not at a hotel in the walled part of the city.

Up.

Not have-to-take-a-taxi distance.

Up, up.

A taxi that hit another taxi, which plowed into a couple standing on the side of the road eating fried persimmon cakes out of a red plastic bag. Both died on the spot. And Marcus's driver took the damn cakes to boot.

Up.

His heart beating hard, beating hard.

Going up.

Finally he stops. He faces a low door at the top of the Big Wild Goose Pagoda. Etched on the door is the word *ROBO*. Is it really this easy? Seems it is.

No one's seen him, or if someone has, they haven't called Marcus out. Maybe the guards have been bribed. Maybe they have been bribed by one of *Them*.

It's about to begin. Provided he didn't miss it by being—he looks again—11 minutes late and counting.

How *stupid* of him to be late.

Marcus puts his hand on the door. The other Players have already arrived. They must have.

He pushes it in.

A narrow wooden staircase is behind the door. Marcus draws his bronze knife from a sheath under his pant leg. He enters and closes the door. It's dark. The staircase goes up half a flight and makes a turn.

His heart beats harder.

His clothing soaks up sweat.

Marcus is the son of Knossos. A child of the Great Goddess. A Freeborn. An ancestral Witness to the Breath of Fire.

He is the Minoan.

He squeezes the hilt of his knife. It's adorned with glyphs understood only by him and the man who taught him. All the others who understood are dead.

The old stairs creak. The wind outside whistles over the roof tiles. The smell of smoke, from the crater, wafts over and through the still-standing Big Wild Goose Pagoda. The stairs end.

Marcus is at the edge of a small room. It is shrouded in darkness, and he can barely make out any details. There is no movement.

He breathes.

"Hello?"

Nothing.

"Anyone there?"

Nothing.

He fishes in his pocket for a Bic lighter.

Flick flick flick.

A weak flame ignites.

His heart skips a beat.

Stacked at the far end of the room like logs are the Players. Each is wrapped in a silver shroud and blindfolded with a simple black cloth. Though it is hot and stuffy, he can see their breath on the air, as if it's winter.

A trap? he wonders.

He takes a tentative step forward.

He can make out features on three of the others. One girl looks Middle Eastern, maybe Persian. She has fine, copper skin; thick black hair; a hooked nose; and high cheeks. A boy—and he is undoubtedly young— is tanned and has round cheeks. His face is locked in a grimace. A tall girl has short-cropped red hair and freckles and lips so thin and pale they are practically nonexistent. She looks like she's dreaming of rainbows and kittens, not the end of the world.

He takes another step, drawn to the pile of Players like a moth to a flame.

You are late.

The voice is in Marcus's head, like the voice of his thoughts, only it's not the voice of his thoughts.

Marcus begins to say he's sorry, but before the words can pass his lips, the voice comes again.

It is not preferable, but it is acceptable.

The voice is pleasant, deep, neither male nor female.

"You can hear—"

I can hear your thoughts.

"I'd prefer to speak."

Fine.

The others did too.

Except for one.

"Why are they wrapped up like that?"

So I can take them.

"You need me to put on one of those things too?" Marcus is impatient. His lateness makes it worse.

Yes.

"Okay. Where do I go?"

Here.

"Where?" Marcus sees nothing. He blinks—a routine, taken-for-granted, split-second blink—and when he opens his eyes, floating before him is one of the silvery shrouds. He can see faint markings in gold, green, and black on the inside of the cloth. He recognizes some of the characters—Arabic, Chinese, Minoan, Grecian, Egyptian, Mesoamerican, Sanskrit—but many are unknown. Some must belong to the other Players. Some must belong to whoever is speaking to him. "Where are you?" he asks as he takes the shroud.

Here.

"Where?" The cloth has substance but is virtually weightless, and it's cold, freezing cold.

Everywhere.

"What do I do?"

Put it on, Marcus Loxias Megalos. Time, as you understand it, is of the essence.

He pulls the shroud over his shoulders, and it's like stepping out of a sauna and into Antarctica. The sensation is shocking, and would be debilitating if not for the pair of unseen hands wrapping a blindfold around his head. As soon as the blindfold is in place, Marcus falls into an immediate slumber. It's so deep that he can't feel his body. There's no cold or heat. There's no pain or pleasure. He is neither comfortable nor uncomfortable. It's as though his body has ceased to exist.

What consumes him is the image of a vast black nothingness perforated by points of light in a rainbow of colors. Blotting out this cosmic scrim is a silent, cratered, tumbling rock that gets closer and closer but never arrives.

There's no telling how big it is.

Or how small.

It just is.

Tumbling.

Closer and closer and closer.

I flew around a mountain and then we came to a valley. Directly below us was a gigantic white pyramid. It looked as if it were from a fairy tale. The pyramid was draped in shimmering white. It could have been metal, or some other form of stone. It was white on all sides. What was most curious about it was its capstone: a large piece of precious gem–like material. I was deeply moved by the colossal size of the thing.

—US Air Force pilot James Gaussman,[xlviii] March 1945, somewhere over central China

KEPLER 22B

Great White Pyramid, Qin Lin Mountains, China

You may look.

Each Player opens his or her eyes.

They are seated in a circle, cross-legged, straight-backed, their hands joined in their laps. The blindfolds, the shrouds, and the overwhelming cold they carried are gone. The 12 are free to move their heads, hands, and torsos, but any attempt to stand is thwarted by paralysis.

Your legs are fine. They will work when I've finished.

The being who shepherded them is nowhere to be seen, even though the voice is present, as if it simultaneously stands behind each of them.

Several Players try to speak, but like their legs, their mouths are frozen.

They look around. They're in a forest surrounded by hills and mountains. The air is crisp and cool, the ground soft, sounds muted. Behind the northern side of the circle, 754 feet away, is a huge pyramid. It has no discernible openings or markings. Its edges are perfectly hewn. There are no variations in its mercurial surface—no lines suggesting stonework or construction of any kind. Its base measures 800 feet across. It is nearly as high. Its apex glows bright and white.

They look around the circle. They're seeing one another for the first time. The Players they'll stalk, follow, fight, love, betray, fear, kill. They commit everything to memory: eye color, visible tattoos, birthmarks, hairstyles, postures, jawlines, dimples, mannerisms, everything.

They judge, make assumptions, take guesses. Each of them has been trained for this: the quick recognition of enemies, the parsing out of weaknesses.

The Players are even more captivating to one another than the immense pyramid.

They are the 12.

We are in the Qin Lin Mountains. South and west of the city now known as Xi'an. This is the Great White Pyramid. Larger than the pyramid at Giza. Like my kind, it has long remained hidden from human eyes.

The Players stop looking at one another, their eyes drawn to the pyramid. Its surface shimmers, and three cloaked figures drift out of a black doorway that appears for less than a second. Two of the figures remain near the pyramid, like guards. The 3rd joins the Players in an instant, as if the space between the pyramid and the forest is nonexistent. It stands behind Sarah Alopay. She cranes her neck in order to take it in.

The being's cloak is dark and punctuated with illuminated points like it is made of space, as if it is covered in stars. Around its neck it wears a round, flat disk covered with glyphs.

The figure is tall—at least 7.5 feet—and thin, with broad shoulders and long arms. It is wearing shimmering shoes that look to be made of the same substance as the Great White Pyramid. Its feet are very long and very flat.

It has a long, narrow head. Like its voice, the thing's face is neither male nor female. Its skin is like mother-of-pearl. Its long hair is platinum. Its thin eyes are completely black.

It is obviously not of this world. And though they feel like they should be scared, the Players are at ease with the creature. Although they've never seen anything quite like it, there is an odd familiarity about it. Some of them even find the being bewitching, beautiful.

I am kepler 22b. You have come to learn about Endgame. I will teach you. First, it is the custom that you introduce yourselves.

kepler 22b looks down on Sarah. She senses that, for the moment, she can speak, but she's unsure of what to say.

Your name. Your number. Your tribe.

Sarah takes a breath and slows her heart to 34 bpm. An insanely low number. She doesn't want to give anything away, knowing that the others might pick up clues in even the simplest statements. "I am Sarah Alopay of the 233rd. I am Cahokian."

The ability to speak moves to her right, like an invisible token.

"Jago Tlaloc. 21st. Olmec." Jago is calm, and pleased to be seated next to Sarah.

"Aisling Kopp, the 3rd, La Tène Celt." Aisling is the tall, thin-lipped redhead Marcus saw piled in the pagoda. She is curt and clear.

"I am Hilal ibn Isa al-Salt of the 144th. I am your Aksumite brother." Hilal is refined, soft-spoken, very dark-skinned, regal. His eyes are bright blue, his straight teeth a blinding white. His hands are joined easily in his lap. He looks tall and strong, looks the way a Player is supposed to look, somehow both menacing and peaceful.

"Maccabee Adlai. I represent the 8th line. I am Nabataean." Maccabee is big, but not huge, and impeccably dressed in a casual linen suit and white cotton shirt, no tie. Some of the Players interpret his pretty clothes as a sign of weakness.

"Baitsakhan," barks a boy with round tanned cheeks and smoldering brown eyes. That is all he says.

Say the rest.

Baitsakhan shakes his head adamantly.

You must.

kepler 22b insists without sounding upset, and Baitsakhan shakes his head again.

Stubborn boy, Sarah thinks. *Trouble, probably.*

kepler 22b raises a spindly, seven-fingered hand, and the boy's body begins to shiver. Very much against his will he vomits the words "13th line. Donghu." When he's done, he looks at kepler 22b with equal measures of fury and awe.

The next Player is thin, his chest concave, his shoulders slight and curved around him like wings. Dark circles hang under his eyes. A red tear is tattooed in the corner of his left eye. He has shaved an inch-thick line through his hair in a reverse Mohawk. As the Players take him in, they realize that he has been turning his head repeatedly in tiny, jerking movements.

He blinks a dozen times before blurting, "A-A-An Liu. Three-three-three-three-three hundred seventy-seventy-seventy-seventy-seven. Shang."

It is a terrible first impression. A stammering weakling here amongst trained killers.

"Shari Chopra," a beautiful, ocher-skinned girl says in a peaceful, meditative voice. "55th. I'm the Harrapan."

"My name's Marcus Loxias Megalos of the fighting 5th. Watch your asses, because I'm the Minoan."

Marcus's bluster is poorly played, like the nonsense a boxer might spout at a prefight press conference. The other Players have no need for such bravado. A few chuckle silently.

"I am Kala Mozami," a slight girl, wrapped in a brilliant red-and-blue head scarf, says with a thick Persian accent. The force and confidence of her tone is at total odds with her appearance. Her eyes are as green as dampened jade. "89th, sisters and brothers, I trace my line through the ancient, golden heart of Sumer."

She likes words, Jago thinks. *A poet. Probably a liar.*

"Alice Ulapala. 34th. Koori," Alice says with an endearing Australian accent. She's huge, muscled, and a little plump. A wrestler. A shot-putter. A weightlifter. Her skin is dark, and her eyes are darker, a mop of curly black hair as wild as a nest of snakes. She has a pale, crescent-shaped birthmark above her right eye that disappears into her hair. Without compunction or ire she spits on the ground before the next person speaks.

Only the next person—the last person—doesn't speak.

Chiyoko Takeda.

All eyes move to the mute. She has pale, ivory skin and shoulder-length hair with bangs cut in a perfectly straight line above her eyebrows. Her full lips are deep red. Her cheeks high and round. She fits the stereotype of a demure Japanese girl, but her eyes are forward and confident and determined.

Chiyoko Takeda does not speak. She is from the 2nd. Her line is more than ancient. Nameless and forgotten. We will call it Mu.

kepler 22b raises its right hand, reaches out, opens its fingers. A white hologram sprouts from its palm. It is a perfect circle 8.25 inches in diameter.

A deep gong resonates in the chests of the 12, and a thin, bright light shoots from the top of the pyramid, marking a point in the night sky. kepler 22b begins to read, and as it does, the holographic circle turns slowly.

"Everything is here. Every word, name, number, place, distance, color, and time. Every letter, symbol, and glyph, on every page, in every chip, on every fiber. Every protein, molecule, atom, electron, quark. Everything, always. Every breath. Every life. Every death. So says, and so has been said, and so will be said again. Everything is here."

The gong resonates in their chests again and the light from the pyramid disappears.

"You are the twelve. All are fated to die—except one. The one who will win."

kepler 22b looks up from the hologram and regards them carefully.

"As it is with all games, the first move is essential."

kepler 22b looks back to the hologram.

"To win you must acquire three keys, and the keys must be found in order. Earth Key. Sky Key. Sun Key. All the keys are hidden here on Earth."

kepler 22b grabs the holographic disk midair and tosses it like a Frisbee. It stops cold over the center of the circle and begins to grow, patterns spreading across the surface. Twelve hairlines of light shoot from it and each strikes one player in the middle of the forehead. The Players all see the same thing through their mind's eye: Earth, as if from space.

"This is Earth."

The image changes. The blue of the oceans becomes gray. Streaks of black move across continents. Red scars bloom. The poles become whiter. The expanse of blue and the bands of green and the blots of brown are gone. The vibrant colors of a living Earth appear only in tiny, clustered pinpricks.

"This will be Earth after the Event. The Event is coming, and it is part of Endgame. The Event will destroy everything. The winner of Endgame earns survival. Survival for themselves and for every member of their line."

kepler 22b pauses.

The image of the ravaged Earth disappears.

"Endgame is the puzzle of life, the reason for death. It holds the origin of all things, and the solution to the end of all things. Find the keys, in the order prescribed. Bring them to me, and you will win. When I leave, you will each receive a clue. And Endgame will begin. The rules of Endgame are simple. Find the keys in order and bring them to me. Otherwise, there are no rules."

Welcome[xlix]

ALL PLAYERS

Somewhere in the Qin Lin Mountains, China

kepler 22b vanishes. The guards standing in front of the pyramid vanish. The pyramid remains, glimmering, imposing, otherworldly. The door reappears, though no one knows where it leads.

Feeling slowly returns to the Players' limbs. There are pins and needles in their fingers and toes, and also in their minds. kepler 22b did something to them, pushed some kind of information into their brains, and now their heads ache. All of them are bleary. All of them know that they must recover quickly. A delay now could mean the end.

There are no rules.

Jago looks around. They're in a small clearing; the forest gets thicker a few meters from where they sit, and the pyramid waits in the opposite direction. The forest could provide good cover. The pyramid—well, Jago doesn't want to guess what might be in there, or where the door might lead.

Sarah is next to him, blinking her way back to awareness. Her presence is strangely comforting—one familiar thing amidst an overwhelming sea of questions. He notices something on the ground a few feet away from Sarah's knapsack. The gray stone disk that hung around kepler 22b's neck. *You will each receive a clue.*

Jago dives for it.

Chiyoko notices Jago move for the disk. He's the first one to act. *Impressive.* Chiyoko's own muscles are stiff, sluggish.

She fights this weariness and also lunges for the disk, but Jago is faster. Chiyoko's fingertips graze the cool stone surface as he snatches it away.

Jago jumps to his feet. Sarah shoulders her bag and stands beside him. Chiyoko reaches into her bag and pulls out a coil of rope. She can't give away to the others that Jago has a disk of Baian-Kara-Ula, or she'll never be able to steal it for herself. Slowly, very slowly, she begins to back out of the clearing.

Jago takes his eyes off Chiyoko. The mute girl saw him take the disk but is leaving him alone. A smart play. Better to avoid open conflict at this point. Jago will have to keep an eye on her. He slips the disk quickly into a small knapsack he bought in Xi'an and grabs Sarah by the arm. Her muscles are hard, tense.

"Let go of me," she whispers.

Jago leans close to her ear. "I have kepler's disk. Let's get out of here." Finding the disk is a piece of luck, even if neither of them knows exactly what it means. They have an alliance, and now they have an advantage. *Better to not let the others find out*, Sarah thinks. *It could make us a target.* She wishes Jago hadn't grabbed her arm. She shrugs him off and steps to the side, hoping they didn't give anything away.

But Kala saw their exchange. "What did you just say to her?" She holds a short golden spear, lowers it, ready to strike.

Jago meets her eyes, unblinking, and smiles with his diamond-studded teeth so that dimples form in his pockmarked cheeks. "You want to die so soon, little girl?"

Jago and Kala stand across from each other, loose, confident, unbending. It's the first of many confrontations that will decide the outcome of Endgame.

One by one around the circle, weapons are drawn. This is exactly what Chiyoko was worried about, why she backed away. The paranoia in the air is palpable. She takes another step backward, toward the cover of the woods.

An begins to tremble. He reaches a hand into his vest—a fisherman's utility jacket covered with small pockets and zippers. Marcus notices. His dagger is drawn and itching to spill some blood. But if that jittery little creep has a gun or something long-range, he'll have to act fast.

"What're you doing?" Marcus demands, flipping his knife from hand to hand.

An pauses. "M-m-m-m-meds. I have to take my m-m-m-m-meds."

Chiyoko silently retreats into the shadows. No one notices her disappear.

Sarah looks at her watch. It is 3:13:46 a.m.

If Jago has the disk, then I am going with him, Sarah decides. *Aside from the strategic advantage, I'm not sure I'm ready for this. Maybe he'll help me stay alive.*

Hilal steps forward to where the center of the circle was. He holds out both his hands, empty. He's one of the few not to have gone for a weapon.

"Sisters and brothers of Endgame, let's talk," Hilal says, his voice smooth. "We have much to discuss. This night does not have to end in bloodshed."

Baitsakhan titters, amused by the coward. Everyone else ignores Hilal. Kala doesn't take her eyes off Jago and doesn't lower her spear.

Shari, noticing Chiyoko's absence, barks in her Indian accent, "Where's the mute?"

Alice scans the perimeter of their circle. "Lit out. Smart girl."

Hilal looks grim, disappointed. He knew it would be difficult to make peace, but he expected them to at least hear him out. "Sisters and brothers, we should not be fighting. Not yet. You heard the being. There are no rules. We can work together, for the good of the people and creatures of Earth. We can work together, at least until we are forced to work against one ano—"

He is interrupted by a *swoosh* as a rope with a weighted metal object on the end of it flies from the shadows. It wraps tightly around Hilal's throat. He raises his hands to his neck. The cord is pulled taut, and Hilal spins in place and falls, choking, to the ground.

"What the hell was that?" Maccabee asks, swiveling.

Baitsakhan doesn't wait to find out. He also sprints into the forest. Another rope attack issues from the darkness, this one from a different place, as if from a different person. It lashes out at Jago, but as the rope nears, he jumps backward, and the cord falls limply to the ground before being whisked into the woods.

A twig snaps. They catch a glimpse of Chiyoko's pale skin and black hair darting through the undergrowth.

"It's the bloody mute!" shouts Alice.

As they turn to Alice, an arrow whistles from the darkened forest and hits Maccabee's right thigh. He staggers and looks down. A long shaft has pierced the front of his leg and punched through the back; blood is welling and starting to run. It was that little mongrel boy, Baitsakhan, sniping from the cover of the woods. Without thinking, Maccabee snaps the shaft and pulls the arrow free. It is excruciating, but he does not cry. He is infuriated. The little shit ruined a perfectly good suit.

"To hell with this, I'm gone," Kala says, forgetting about Jago. She sprints for the pyramid.

"Stop this madness!" Hilal has freed himself from the rope and gotten his breath back. "It does not have to be this way!"

In response, an arrow thuds into the dirt between his legs. Hilal scrambles away, also into the woods.

"Maybe save the sermon for another time, preacher," says Aisling, before she follows him into the forest.

Another whistle cuts the air. Sarah's instincts take over, and she reaches toward Jago's head and with her bare hand snatches an arrow out of the air just before it would have found its mark in Jago's skull. Jago looks at her. *He* has never seen someone do *that* before. He is wide-eyed, grateful. "How did you—"

"We have to get out of here," Sarah says. She can't believe she did that either. She practiced it over and over and over, sliced her hands to ribbons trying to catch arrows, but she never succeeded. Not until this moment.

She throws the arrow to the ground and grabs Jago by the hand. "Let's go."

They turn toward the forest and begin to run.

An Liu is no longer fishing around for his bottle of pills. He stands, shoulders square, facing what is left of the group. He wears a sinister smile.

A third arrow flies from the woods, striking An square in the chest. An looks down, amused, and flicks the shaft away from the ballistics vest that went unnoticed beneath his fisherman's pockets. He casually tosses a small, dark sphere the size of a walnut toward the remaining Players. Marcus, who is closest, is taken by surprise. His instincts lead him to reach out and catch An's offering. But just before it can land in Marcus's hand, it explodes.

The blast is much bigger than the size of the bomb would suggest. Bodies fly. Sarah loses her hearing, and for a few moments all is chaos. She lifts her head to see the zombielike form of Marcus. Both of his arms are gone at the shoulder, and his jaw hangs dislocated and slack from his skull. Blood covers his face and upper body. The skin on the left side of his head is shredded like cheese, and his ear is hanging low by his neck.

Something falls spinning from the sky and lands at Sarah's feet. A finger. Pointing 167°49'25".

Sarah's stomach turns as she is reminded of the meteor strike and her graduation and leaving Christopher.

She is reminded of her best friend, Reena.

And her brother, Tate.

It was only a week ago.

A week.

She should be grieving, with her family, sitting in the living room, eating and hugging and holding hands.

Instead, she is here.

Alone.

Playing.

She glances at Jago.

Maybe not alone.

Marcus falls to his knees, face-plants into the ground. For Marcus

Loxias Megalos, Minoan Player of the 5th line, Endgame is over.

An spins, and a fire lights behind him as he disappears into the woods. He's let off another incendiary device. The forest starts to burn. Even though the fire is 59 feet away, the heat stings Sarah's face.

"Come on!" Jago says. He lifts her to her feet and they stumble away. They have to get out through the pyramid. Through the door that has reappeared, though they don't know where it will take them. They can't risk the woods, not with the fire, not with An, Chiyoko, Baitsakhan, and who knows who else lurking there. They reach the pyramid and stop at the door.

Its incandescent surface reflects the light of the fire, the dark of the woods. Sarah reaches out. A series of golden images drift across the doorway. Some are recognizable: the pyramids at Giza; Carahunge; the jumble of geometric stones at Pumapunku; Tchogha Zanbil.

Others are megaliths and signs, idols and statues, numbers and shapes that Sarah doesn't recognize.

Another explosion rattles the air behind them.

"I think it's asking where we want to go," Sarah says.

Jago glances over his shoulder. "Anywhere but here," Jago says.

He squeezes Sarah's hand, and together they step forward and pass through the strange portal. They don't notice that right behind them is Maccabee Adlai, bleeding and angry and hungry for death.

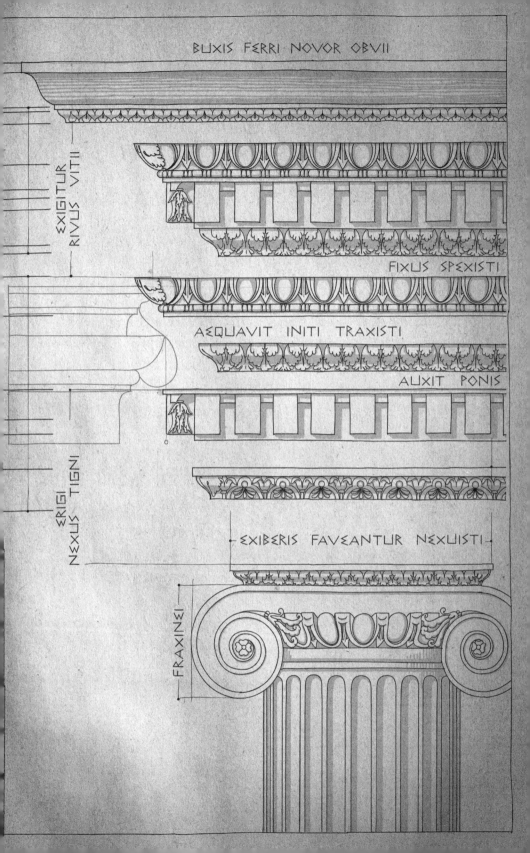

BVXIS FERRI NOVOR OBVII

EXIGITUR RIVVS VITII

FIXVS SPEXISTI

AEQUAVIT INITI TRAXISTI

AUXIT PONIS

ERIGI NEXVS TIGNI

EXIBERIS FAVEANTUR NEXVISTI

FRAXINEI

CHRISTOPHER VANDERKAMP

Xi'an Garden Hotel, Dayan District, Xi'an, China

Christopher wakes with a start. He can't believe he fell asleep. He looks at his watch:

3:13 a.m.

It could all be over by now. Sarah and the others could have finished whatever they were doing in the pagoda and moved on.

He grabs the backpack that contains his passport, money and credit cards, his phone, some food, and a folding knife he bought at the Big Wild Goose Pagoda gift shop. A headlamp, a change of underwear, and a Chinese phrase book. He takes one pair of binoculars and throws it in the bag and leaves the room. He doesn't bother with the $5,000 worth of equipment, all bought the day before. He knows he'll never come back.

He's going to go into the pagoda. He's going to go find out if Sarah is still there or already gone. He runs down five flights of stairs, into the night, streetlamps casting an orange glow over the city. There are very few cars out, no people. He looks at his watch.

3:18.

He runs as fast as he can, which is fast. His bag bounces on his back. Floodlights on the ground illuminate the pagoda. He hopes there isn't a guard, but if there is, he's prepared to do whatever he has to do, knowing in his heart he's doing it for love. He has to get inside. Find Sarah. Help her win.

He arrives, looks for a guard, doesn't see one. It's strangely empty. Whatever was happening here, it was meant to take place in private. He pauses before moving toward the door, looking up and around. He

stops dead in his tracks, something catching his eye. His jaw drops.
A young woman leaps from a window at the top of the pagoda, 200
feet up. She starts to fall, her colorful scarves flapping and fluttering
around her. As she moves toward the ground, she spreads out her
arms and legs, and the scarves billow out and catch the wind. Even
though she's falling fast, she also seems to be slowing down.
Christopher shakes his head, can't believe what he's seeing.
She is not falling at all, not anymore.
She is flying.

KALA MOZAMI

Big Wild Goose Pagoda, 6th Floor, Xi'an, China

Kala materializes in the attic of the Big Wild Goose Pagoda, tumbling across the rough wooden floor. She dove into the emptiness of the pyramid's door and this is where it spit her out. She's out of breath but relieved to be away from the other Players.

For now, she wants to keep it that way.

For now, she wants to retreat and breathe and decode the random string of Arabic numbers and Sumerian letters kepler 22b tattooed onto her consciousness like a sudden, driving madness.

She wonders if the codes are this intense for the others. She hopes they are. Because it's strange and upsetting; it disarms her and confuses her.

She doesn't want to be the only one who feels this way, an indecipherable message burned across the forefront of her mind. It would put her at a great disadvantage. She does not like being at a disadvantage of any kind. She will do what she can to remedy this. As soon as possible. Now.

The room is as she remembers it: dark and small and old. But there are no Players stacked like rugs in the corner, and there is no ghostly voice of kepler 22b. *Blessings to Annunaki for that*, she thinks. She does not want to be there when another Player arrives, and is not sure when that might happen, so she gathers herself and bolts down the small hidden stairway to the main room of the pagoda's penultimate story, the room that has windows looking out over China, over the rest of the world.

The world that is going to end.

Filled with people who are going to die.

Kala pauses and balls her fists around her scarves and does a little pirouette as she eyes the open window. She has to get away. She shakes her body violently, and two flaps of webbing drop from her jumpsuit, one beneath her arms and another between her legs. She stares at the night outside. She takes a deep breath and runs straight toward the window.

She jumps headfirst. She's done the math, knows how much distance she needs. She knows that she only has 200 feet before the ground will rush up to meet her. It's just enough. Her scarves flutter and snap and the flaps catch the up-rushing wind and it happens. She's not falling but gliding, flying. For a moment, a too brief moment, she feels free. *Blessings.*

The code seared onto her brain is gone. The others are gone. The pressure is gone. Just like that.

She's flying.

But not for long.

Because here comes the ground.

She jerks her head and shoulders and thrusts her pelvis forward. The suit is special. Designed not just for flying but landing too. An array of miniature chutes opens along the flaps that slow her down. Kala pushes a button on a loop of cloth that is stretched around her middle finger, and the whole front of the suit inflates with a loud hiss. She hits the ground and it hurts, but she's fine. The cushions deflate just as quickly as they blew up, and just like she has practiced 238 times, she is upright and already running. Running away from it all, and running toward it all as well.

Everything is here, Kala recalls kepler 22b saying. What does that mean? The way the creature said it made her feel small and meaningless. She didn't like that. Kala cannot think about this for long, though. Because, as her feet move across the ground, the code comes back to the forefront of her mind like a supernova.

Kala is so distracted that she doesn't even notice the young man following her.

False[1]

CHRISTOPHER VANDERKAMP

Big Wild Goose Pagoda, Ground Level, Xi'an, China

Christopher stood and watched as the girl's clothing inflated like a balloon and, without breaking stride, she hit the ground and started running. He takes it as a good omen that this is the same girl he was able to ID from his room. The one with the dark-tanned skin and the colorful scarves and the green eyes.

He also takes it as a good omen that she doesn't notice him.

She's playing catch-up, he says to himself as he tries to run silently after her. *I have to assume that she was the last to leave, that the others have already moved on from the Calling. I have to follow her. She's the best and only connection I have to the girl I love.*

And he follows. And as he does, it doesn't occur to him that Kala is in fact the first Player to leave the Calling through the Big Wild Goose Pagoda. That if he had waited a few more minutes, he might have seen Sarah Alopay, the Cahokian Player of the 233rd.

SARAH ALOPAY, JAGO TLALOC

Big Wild Goose Pagoda, 6th Floor, Xi'an, China

Sarah and Jago arrive in the same room as Kala did. It is 3:29:54 a.m. Kala jumped exactly 10 minutes and 14 seconds ago. They have no idea she jumped. Sarah has no idea that Christopher is so close. If she were to imagine Christopher, it would be back in the relative safety of Omaha, helping diligently with the cleanup efforts. But she doesn't imagine him; she's pushed Christopher out of her mind.

That part of her life is over.

Blindly leaping through an alien door was a strange experience. It seemed to Sarah like something magical, but she knows that's not the case. It's just like what the first men must have thought about fire. The door wasn't magic; it was science. Just tech, far-off and advanced tech, something humans have not yet learned, or maybe were never allowed to learn.

For centuries, this has been the power and allure of the Sky People. Their machines, technology, and abilities were what made them gods in the eyes of countless ancient peoples around the world. Sarah knows that the Sky People could do the same to modern humans if they so wished. Awe them, intimidate them, enslave them. All the Players know that humans are but a diversion to the Sky People.

Even with contemporary DNA sequencing and nuclear reactors and geotechnical engineering and space stations, humans are just a crude amusement, like ants who make fire out of anything, kill one another for no reason, and stare into mirrors for too long.

But ants that, for whatever reason, the gods have taken an interest in.

"You still have it?" Sarah asks, her head spinning.

"I have it," Jago replies, motioning to his backpack. His head throbs; he's panting, dizzy. The shock wave from the bomb took a toll.

"You okay?" Sarah reaches out.

"Fine," he grunts, straightening.

"We should leave. We're not safe here."

"No kidding."

As Jago turns toward the door that leads to the stairs, Maccabee appears behind him. Sarah sees it happen. It's like Maccabee is emerging from a curtain of black ink suspended in the air.

Maccabee doesn't seem to have suffered any ill effects from the bomb or the teleportation. He lunges at Jago, wrapping his hands around his neck. Sarah's first thought is for the disk. Though she doesn't know how or why, she's certain that it will help her—*them*—get a big lead in Endgame.

Sarah raises her fist to hit Maccabee in the back of the head, and Jago rakes his heel across Maccabee's shin. Maccabee yells out and bends over, shoving Jago toward the floor, and Sarah narrowly misses his skull with what would have been a crushing blow.

Jago can't break the Nabataean's grip. He blindly jabs his thumb behind him, hoping to land it in Maccabee's ear. He scores a direct hit, and there's a *pop* as Jago pulls his digit free, like a cork coming from an old bottle.

Maccabee lets go and wails. He grabs the side of his head with one hand and wildly swipes at the air with the other. First an arrow in the thigh and now a dirty blow from this hideous Olmec. Maccabee is not used to so much pain, so much humiliation. It infuriates him.

Before he can collect himself, Sarah steps around Maccabee and kicks him in the thigh, right next to his wound. He collapses to the floor.

Sarah and Jago have a clear path to the stairway leading down, out of this funnel of Players, this bottleneck of murderers. Sarah wonders if they'll have time to finish off Maccabee, or if it's even worth it.

Jago doesn't have the same concern. His knife flashes into his hand, ready to find Maccabee's throat.

"Watch out!" Sarah shouts, as Aisling Kopp appears in the room. Aisling's short red hair is wild, her face covered in soot from the fire in the woods. She was forced to double back for the pyramid after An lit the trees on fire. She's feeling panicked and hemmed in, which is why she doesn't ask questions. Aisling raises her small crossbow and fires. Sarah's warning is just enough to get Jago diving out of the way. The bolt sails over his head.

Midair, Jago flips the knife, catching it by the anodized blade, and hurls it at Aisling. The Celt drops the one-shot crossbow, claps her hands, snags the knife out of the air, and smiles. She's proud that move worked; her grandfather taught her well.

As Jago and Sarah turn and run down the stairs, Jago's knife flies over their heads and imbeds itself in the far wall.

In seconds they emerge into the large room near the top of the pagoda. Jago moves to keep running, but Sarah sidesteps the doorway and grabs him by the arm. She points up. Rafters. Between the rafters and the underside of the roof is a foot of space.

Jago nods. He understands. Side by side, he and Sarah jump up, silently grab the rough-hewn timbers, and twirl their bodies around them. They eye each other intently and stop breathing and will their hearts to slow, slow, slow.

Aisling bursts into the room and runs toward the stairs that lead farther down. But just before exiting, she stops. She smells something in the air, cocks an ear to the empty space. She makes a half turn in their direction, and for a second Sarah wonders why they are bothering to hide. The Celt is only one and they are two. They could eliminate her quickly. As she looks toward Jago, all three of them hear Maccabee's voice bellowing from the stairway: "I'm going to kill all of you bastards!"

Without pause, Aisling spins and is gone. Maccabee stumbles loudly down the stairs. He grunts and moans, dragging himself into the room. He's in bad shape: other than Marcus, dead-as-dirt Marcus, Maccabee has endured the most violence of the Calling.

Maccabee steps to the middle of the room and looks in a circle, doesn't bother to look up. His mind is clouded with injury, the suddenness of Endgame, and the clue implanted in his mind. He slides around the room for 22 seconds—only 12 heartbeats in Sarah's chest—before the three of them hear another Player arrive in the room above. Maccabee spits on the floor and leaves, going down.

They wait for three more minutes. Whoever appeared in the room upstairs must still be there, waiting. Without speaking, the Olmec and the Cahokian drop silently to the floor, walk to the stairs, and leave.

"Too bad we couldn't take at least one out," Jago laments as they creep down the stairs. He rubs his neck where Maccabee's fingers left a ring of bruises.

"We'll get our chance," Sarah says. She can see that they make a good team, but she's not sure that Endgame is the place for teams. Still, Jago has grown on her. And he has been helpful and, more importantly, faithful. She can tell that he likes her. She wonders if she can use that. She wonders if she *wants* to use that.

"The next time I see the Nabataean . . ." Jago spits, trailing off.

They go down, down, down.

When they reach the bottom, they make sure the coast is clear, step out of the Big Wild Goose Pagoda, and head toward the street, sticking to the shadows. Sarah has no idea that not more than 30 minutes before, the boy from Omaha who she still loves was right here.

And neither Sarah nor Jago knows that An Liu, the tricky bomb maker, the last to emerge from the portal, is watching them from a window, back up the stairs of the Big Wild Goose Pagoda.

Watching them and pointing a long metal object in their direction.

A wand.

An antenna.

A microphone.

A sneaky *blink* sneaky *blink* sneaky bit of *blinking* business.

CHIYOKO TAKEDA

Great White Pyramid, Qin Lin Mountains, China

Chiyoko Takeda slinks through the woods. She watched—and smiled as she watched—An Liu blow up the Calling. She considers it a great move. A great, great move.

Nothing like death and mayhem to cloud minds and mask intentions. Chiyoko is tracking the Olmec and the Cahokian as they make for the pyramid. She's on their right, to the east, moving silently. The Nabataean is also making his way toward the pyramid, but the Olmec and the Cahokian haven't noticed him.

Chiyoko noticed. She saw the Sumerian leave through the mystical pyramid. Saw her melt away into its quicksilver wall.

The Great White Pyramid is a monument that speaks volumes to Chiyoko Takeda, the mute, the ever-ancient Mu, the Player of the 2nd line.

Just to look at it is an honor. It stands as a marker of space, history, and commonality. Chiyoko knows that pyramids were the Game Keepers' tethers in the ancient past—tethers for their ships, their portals, their sources of energy—and someday they might be again, after it all comes and goes and comes again. The buildings or their remnants are in China, in Egypt, in Sumer, in Europe, in India, and in the Americas. Most of them have fallen down or vanished beneath mounds of dirt and foliage. Or they've been desecrated by people, ignorant humans who don't deserve to survive what comes next. Some, like this pristine example, are even undiscovered. But none are like this one.

This one has not been polluted by human hands or minds. It hasn't been eroded by wind or rain. Eaten by root or soil. Shattered by the quaking earth or an erupting volcano.

This one is special.

If she could, she'd stay and look at this one for a week, two, three. Wonder at its dimensions. Measure its footprint. Record its markings. Try to decipher them. But she can't do any of this.

The game is on.

And she is tracking.

Her ropes—the hojo—are slung over her shoulders. Their deployment was a diversion, like An's explosives. Not as effective, of course, but they served their purpose. Her ropes gave her the cover that allowed her to get off the tracking dart that struck Jago Tlaloc in the neck and chipped him. The dart that buzzed his ear like a mosquito.

Jago Tlaloc, the Olmec. Clearly aligned with Sarah Alopay, the Cahokian. The Players of the ancient tribes of the Americas. She watches them walk toward the pyramid. Chiyoko is near enough to hear their voices but not their words. Maccabee is limping close behind. Jago and Sarah have still not noticed him. Just behind the Nabataean is Aisling Kopp. Who will catch who, who will fight who, who will die?

The Olmec leads the Cahokian through the door. They vanish like a magic trick. Chiyoko starts to step forward, hoping to get in before Maccabee, but he's too close. She knows what the others don't—that the Olmec has the disk. Among the Mu the disks are worshipped as sacred and mysterious symbols. Chiyoko recognized it instantly: a disk of Baian-Kara-Ula. Disks that fell from the sky many ages ago. Disks with information and knowledge, clues and direction.

She has to follow it. If another Player gets the disk, she'll follow that Player. She'll continue to follow it until she spots her opening, and then she'll steal it. She knows it leads to Earth Key.

And she knows that she is the only one who knows.

Because this is the clue that kepler 22b left in her mind. In very simple language, it told her: *As the Mu, only you understand where the disk will lead.*

Chiyoko watches Maccabee reach the doorway, stumble through, vanish. Aisling is less than a minute away. None of them have noticed Chiyoko. She'll go in after the Celt. Chiyoko waits. Surmises that she has only one more minute at the Calling. Only one more minute in the presence of the magnificent glimmering pyramid. She bows to it, shows her respect and admiration, shares a quiet moment with it, thanks it for being.

A small distant twang jostles the air on her eardrum, interrupting her reverie. She drops to the ground instinctively as an arrow cuts the air right where her heart was.

One of them *did* notice her.

The boy.

Baitsakhan.

Chiyoko figures that seven long strides of open ground separate the edge of the woods from the portal. She will not risk getting shot to get there. She knows she has to move or the boy will kill her. As she crawls forward, another arrow punctures the ground near her, but it is a desperate shot. She is certain the boy can no longer see her.

She reaches a thick tree and stands behind it, traces the invisible arc of the arrows that have been shot at her. Finds the spot where they were fired and sees him crouched among the green.

He's 90 feet away.

Well within striking distance.

She reaches into her jacket and pulls out five razor-sharp, titanium shuriken. Her fingers dance around them and they fan out like cards. She flips one into the air with one hand, catches it with the other. She is not impetuous. Killing for her has always been the child of opportunity and necessity, and she doesn't take it lightly. We are human. We have one life that should be honored. Taking a life should always be a considered decision.

She moves quietly down the hill, the pyramid at her back. She wills her eyes to dilate against the glow of the explosion's lingering flames. She stops next to a fallen tree, plants her left foot, throws.

Baitsakhan is nearly surprised.

Nearly.

At the last moment he drops, and the throwing star misses, burying itself in a tree trunk.

Chiyoko breathes.

Stays still.

Waits.

She catches sight of Aisling Kopp passing through the portal.

She watches as Baitsakhan stands and exposes himself, loading an arrow and frantically looking for her.

Fool.

She throws a star, and it hits the boy on the outside of his shoulder, disappears into his flesh.

He cries out.

She relocates again, putting herself on a path that leads directly to the door. She throws another star, the six points whirling through the air like a silent saw blade, on target to stop in the middle of the boy's forehead. But just before it strikes, there's a gust of wind that blows it off course, and it glances off his scalp, taking a chunk of flesh and hair with it.

He cries out again, issuing a challenge, and desperately shoots an arrow into the night.

Chiyoko breathes. The gust subsides. She turns to the pyramid, performs a forward flip over a large rock, and when she is upside down she throws the last of her shuriken at the annoying one-named boy, Baitsakhan, the Donghu of the 13th line. She lands squarely on her feet and silently sprints through the mystical door, unsure if she hit her target.

She doesn't care. The boy is too rash to last for very long. If she didn't kill him, someone else will.

Chiyoko appears in the secret room where they first gathered. She is not at all disoriented like the others were. She sneaks to the door and down the old stairs and sees Aisling leave the main chamber at the top of the building. Chiyoko waits, hugs the wall, and moves around the edge of the room like a ghost. She does not notice the two sequestered in the rafters, and they do not notice her.

And just like that, she is gone.

HILAL IBN ISA AL-SALT

Hsu Village, Qin Lin Mountains, China

Hilal ibn Isa al-Salt has beautiful hands.

No matter how many walls he has scaled, how many knives he has thrown, how many machetes he has wielded, how many stones he has moved, how many bones he has broken, how many wires he has soldered, how many pages he has turned, how many push-ups, pull-ups, and handstands he has done, how many punches he has thrown, how many boards he has broken, how many guns he has cleaned, he has always taken care of them, his beautiful hands.

Coconut oil.

Rosemary tincture.

The freshly rendered fat of young lambs at the slaughter.

An ivory-handled file.

His nails are perfect disks, white against his dark skin. His cuticles are smooth. His calluses invisible. His skin like velvet.

He does not pass through the portal of the Great White Pyramid, shrouded in otherworldly mystery and age, but opts for the woods. At first he moves fast to stay ahead of the smoke and fire—and the other Players. The mad ones who wouldn't listen to him, wouldn't even give him five minutes before the killing started. Hilal sighs.

As he exits the orbit of the ageless pyramid, the woods grow quiet and still. They become familiar, as all forests are to those who have spent time in them. He encounters none of the others who also left through those woods, and after 12 hours of hiking he reaches a small outpost that is not on his map. It's not much more than a dirt crossroads, a cow, a flock of chickens, a collection of wooden shacks.

He stops in the middle of the crossroads. No one emerges from the huts, but smoke billows from makeshift chimneys and he can smell food cooking.

A young girl finally appears from one of the buildings, the muffled voices of her caretaker urging her to stay inside. She ignores him. She's curious and moves into the road. She has never seen a man with black skin. His bright blue eyes—a gift of his ancient heritage—are even more shocking.

He might as well be an alien.

The girl—seven or eight years old—stops in front of Hilal.

A red string around her neck is weighted down by a small silver cross. Hilal holds out his beautiful hands, forming a bowl. He lowers them and she peers into them. They're empty. He watches her appreciate the fineness of his skin, how it is lighter on the palm side. And she sees the little scar on the heel of his right hand. Her eyes widen and she rises on her toes.

It is a little cross of his own, branded into his otherwise flawless skin. "I come in peace, sister," he says in English. She has never heard such sounds, but his voice is so soft that her thin lips crack a grin.

It fades quickly as Hilal hears footsteps behind him.

The girl waves her hands as if to ward off a bad spirit and scampers back a few feet.

Hilal stays put.

He doesn't need to look to know what is coming.

He closes his eyes. Listens. It is a man. Barefoot. Trying—and failing—to run quietly. His arms are raised. In his hands is something like a bat or a staff. His breath is suppressed and nervous and charged.

Hilal steps to the right at the last second as an ax slices the air millimeters from his shoulder. The sharpened head is buried in the ground, and Hilal reaches out calmly and takes his assailant's right thumb and snaps it. The ax comes free, and Hilal draws the man's thumb in an arc. Where the thumb goes, the man follows.

Hilal allows a small scowl to pass across his face. This man should have known better. He does a flip as Hilal takes a knee, still holding the thumb, and the man slams into the ground, his wind taken from his lungs.

The man strikes out with his left hand, but Hilal dodges the feeble attempt and holds out his hand, once again showing the cross on his palm to this outcast band of Christians.

"I come in peace," he repeats in English. "As our mutual brother Christ once did."

The man pauses, a look of confusion wrinkling his eyebrows, before he tries to strike again. *Violence, always violence as a first resort.*

Hilal shakes his head disapprovingly and jabs the man in the neck, temporarily paralyzing him.

Hilal lets go of the man's thumb, and he slips to the ground like a rag doll. Hilal stands and announces to the small town, this time in passing Chinese, "I am a hungry traveler from another world. Help me, and I will do what I can to help you when the time comes."

A door creaks open. Another.

"And come it will, my Christian brothers and sisters, come it will."

12.0316, 39.0411[li]

SARAH ALOPAY, JAGO TLALOC

Taxicab #345027, Registered to Feng Tian, Passing over Xi'an Old City Wall, China

It is 11:16 a.m. later that day. Sarah and Jago have not slept. They haven't seen another Player since leaving the pagoda. They had rice and tea and oranges for breakfast and ate on the move. They stayed away from the pagoda and the meteorite crater and the city center. They eventually found a cab, climbed in, and said, "Hotel." The driver has been moving south for over an hour, trying to convince them to get out, but they keep handing him cash and telling him to drive on, to go farther away from the city. They want a small place, an out-of-the-way place. They haven't found one yet. The driver keeps driving.

Jago reaches into his bag and pulls out the disk for the first time since the Calling. He holds it up and turns it in the midmorning light that filters in through the taxi windows, tries to make head or tail of it. The driver notices it in the rearview mirror and starts talking about the strange object.

They have no idea what he's saying.

The driver is an odd man. He knows they can't understand a word he's saying, but he keeps talking. He takes his hands off the wheel, gesturing wildly, and the cab swerves back and forth. Sarah is tired of it, of him, of the noise, of driving. She turns away and looks out the window, watches the city give way to the suburbs and the countryside. She needs to quiet her mind.

Sarah tries to visualize something pleasant, someplace far from here. She ends up thinking about Christopher. Remembering the night before graduation, before the meteorite destroyed her school and killed her brother. Christopher picked her up at her house and took her to a quiet spot along the Missouri River where he had arranged a picnic. And while there was food, they spent most of their time under a blanket, kissing, holding each other, whispering between kisses, their hands locked, their bodies entwined. It was a great night, one of the best nights of her life. And while she's been telling herself to forget about Christopher, at least until Endgame is over, he is the first thought she conjures up when her mind needs comfort.

And though she wants to keep that image in her mind, the clue that kepler 22b burned into her brain imposes itself over all of her thoughts. It is a long and senseless string of numbers. No matter what else she thinks about, no matter how hard she tries to avoid it, no matter how happy the memory or how sweet the vision, the numbers are there.

498753987.242034333335034057483149845743987523487203984999993 29.292923893702137548935672498572341234675489342267743453777 7773923046805.3652566245362209845710230467233100438.138572101 02000209357482[lii]

Sarah is a crack code breaker, but this one makes no sense to her. She can't find a pattern, can't find a clue, can't find the rhythm that lurks within every code. She gives herself over to it and feels a profound sadness as her image of Christopher fades.

"You okay?" Jago asks.

"I don't know," Sarah answers, surprised at how easy it is for her to be honest with Jago.

"You look sad."

"You could tell?"

"Yes." Jago hesitates. "You want to talk about it?"

Sarah smiles, a bit flustered at the idea of having a heart-to-heart with this boy she's just met. A Player, no less. Someone she should probably be figuring out how to kill instead of how to trust. She doesn't want to tell him about Christopher, so she only gives him some of the truth.

"I can't stop thinking about my clue. It's like a bad song stuck in my head."

"Ah," Jago says, nodding. "Same with me. I can't shake it loose."

"Mine's this crazy string of numbers."

"Mine's a picture, some kind of ancient Asian warrior."

"That's better than numbers," Sarah says.

Jago clicks his tongue against his teeth, annoyed. "You ever looked at the same damn thing for twelve hours straight? Like being at a museum and getting stuck in front of one boring-ass exhibit."

Sarah allows herself another smile. Perhaps helping Jago will take her mind off her own clue. "Maybe I can help. Can you describe the picture?"

"It's like a photograph, I can see every detail. In one hand he has a spear, in the other he's holding . . ." Jago points his eyes at his feet, at his bag.

"The disk?"

"Yeah."

"Maybe that's why you picked it up?"

"Nah. Finding it before the others was just luck."

"What do you think that thing is?"

"No idea, but it's important. The mute girl knew it was. It's why she flipped out when I grabbed it."

Sarah nods. She turns away. *Christopher was right,* she thinks. Then she says, "This whole thing is crazy."

Jago stares in front of him. The only sounds are of the car and the road. Then he says, "You didn't want Endgame, did you?"

She can't tell him the truth. She can't tell him about Tate. She can't tell him that she's only been training for real for under four years. She can't.

"I just never thought it was going to happen," Sarah says.

"To be honest, neither did I." Jago touches the scar along his face. "Almost ineligible, too."

"Yeah. I was just over two years out."

115

"*Dios mío.*"

"Thousands and thousands of years have passed without Endgame. Why now? Do you know?"

Jago sighs. "No, not really. Mami says it's because there are too many people. Like we're a scourge. But you know, it doesn't matter why, Sarah. You saw that kepler thing—*el cuco*. Made it crystal clear that Endgame's for real and we don't have much choice. All that matters is that it's happening. And we have to Play."

"But *why?*" Sarah persists.

"Why'd that thing have seven damn fingers?" Jago snaps, brushing off Sarah's question. "You trained. You were told about Endgame and the Makers and the lines and the real history of humanity, no?"

"Of course I was. I trained as hard as you can imagine." *Harder,* she thinks, *to make up for lost time. To cram it all in.* "But I was also normal. Seeing the others for the first time last night . . . I don't know . . . maybe I'm the *only* normal one. You, Chiyoko, Baitsakhan, An? You've been bred for this shit. Me . . ." She shakes her head and trails off.

"A few days ago you jumped from a moving train. You relocated my shoulder. You saved my life last night *by catching an arrow.* Don't kid yourself; you've been bred for this too." Jago smirks at her. "And I'm more *normal* than I seem. Used to show pretty American tourists like you down to the beach, give them the tour." Jago sucks his teeth, reflecting. "Like you were the only one with a normal life. Please."

What Jago says is true and she knows it is, but it still feels unreal. For the first time, Sarah realizes the deep gulf that has divided her life. On the one side, Sarah Alopay, homecoming queen and valedictorian. On the other, a hardened badass raised to kill, decipher, and deceive. Before it started, she could always reconcile her two halves, because Endgame was an evil joke that consumed her summers and weekends. But it isn't a joke anymore.

For a brief moment the image of Christopher—smiling, sweating in a practice jersey, bounding toward her off the field—infiltrates her mind's eye. But as soon as it appears, the code pushes it away.

"I was happy," she says wistfully. "I held the keys to the world. I thought I was normal, Feo. I thought I was fucking normal like everyone else."

"If you want to have any chance of winning, you better stop thinking that way."

"I want more than a chance. I want to win. There's no option *but* winning."

"Then the old Sarah Alopay is dead."

She nods, and the cab slows and turns onto a dirt road. They drive a quarter mile and pull through an iron gate, drive along a road lined with blossoming lemon trees. The driver stops at a cul-de-sac and points to a two-story concrete guesthouse with red roof tiles and overflowing flower boxes. The bars on the windows are painted yellow. A rooster stalks the tiled threshold.

There are no other buildings nearby. There is an array of satellite dishes—meaning internet service—on the roof. The road is a dead end, and behind the building is a small fallow meadow, behind that the rise of the hills.

"Perfect," Jago says to the driver. He hands him a fistful of yuan and opens the door. He turns to Sarah and says, "Look all right to you?"

She inspects it. Her training takes over, pushing her trepidation aside. The place is remote, secluded, safe. As good a place to Play the next round as any.

"Yes," Sarah says.

She steps out of the cab and takes a deep breath. Jago was right. It's time to leave the normal parts of her behind. The Sarah who was homecoming queen and valedictorian.

As she watches Jago walk ahead of her, she knows, once and for all, that it's time to leave the Christopher part of her behind as well.

CHIYOKO TAKEDA

Taxicab #345027,^{liii} *Registered to Feng Tian, Chang'an District, Xi'an,*
China

Feng Tian shakes his head, puts the car in gear, and leaves. He's glad
to be rid of the strange and moody foreigners. He couldn't understand
a word they said, but that didn't matter; he's driven around enough
sullen foreign couples to recognize the signs of a lovers' quarrel. Silly
kids. At least they tipped well.

He pushes a CD into the player and blasts some pop music and bumps
along the dirt road and lights a cigarette. He turns onto the paved
road, passing a red motorbike that wasn't there before. He doesn't pay
it any mind.

A short distance down the road he is surprised to find a young
Japanese girl in short jean shorts and makeup, wearing a wig of bright
blue hair. She has a large, stylish purse slung over her shoulder. She's
flagging him down. She does it in the Japanese fashion, her fingers
pointed to the ground, her wrist swinging back and forth. To him it is
a motion that says "go away."

He pulls over.

No one else is around.

On one side of the road is a wheat field. On the other is a stand of
bamboo.

Where did she come from?

She leans in the window and hands him a card. He turns down the
music. She has a lovely smile, glossy lips, dimples in her cheeks. On the
card, in perfect Chinese handwriting, it says, *Forgive me, I am mute.*
Will you take me back to Xi'an?

What luck! A return fare. He nods and points to the backseat. She surprises him by opening the front passenger door and jumping in. She's like an eager schoolgirl. The thoughts running through his mind are not entirely wholesome. She pulls the door shut and nods at the road and grabs his pack of cigarettes off the dashboard.

Pushy girl.

And stranger even than the other two.

Happier, at least.

Maybe this won't be such a boring ride back to Xi'an.

Feng Tian puts the car in gear and eases back onto the road. She turns to him and points at the cigarette. She wants a light. He gets out a Zippo, flicks it open, and thumbs the tinder wheel. He keeps one eye on the road and one on the tip of the smoke.

He doesn't see the specially modified Taser that she pushes into his neck before shooting him full of 40,000 volts of surging, bristling, killing electricity.

Chiyoko grabs the wheel and pulls the emergency brake. She pushes hard into his flesh with the Taser and watches him writhe for 11 seconds. She releases the trigger. Checks his pulse. There isn't one. She reaches across the driver's body and reclines his seat. She pulls off his sunglasses and puts them on the dash. She pries his lighter from his electrified fingertips. She jumps into the back, releases a latch that lowers the seat, and reveals the trunk. She pulls the body into her lap—she is incredibly strong for her size, and has no trouble with the man—and pushes him into the rear of the car. She climbs back into the front, pulls off her wig, and throws it in the footwell. She removes a plain collared shirt, another wig, and a packet of wipes from her purse. She puts on the shirt and the wig, which makes her hair look like a man's. She adjusts it in the mirror, pulls a wipe from the packet, and cleans the makeup off her face. She takes a small Ziploc bag from the packet, opens it, and removes a thin fake mustache. She puts it on.

All of this happens in under two minutes.

She puts the taxi in gear and pulls away. Checks the mirrors. No one is around. No one has seen. There are no witnesses, so no one else who

Chiyoko needs to kill. She slides on the dead man's sunglasses, takes a new cigarette from the pack, flicks the lighter, inhales. It is only the 4th cigarette of her entire life, but it's a good one. A delightful cigarette. It relaxes her, calms her, lets her process the murder she just committed. The man had to die because he saw the disk. Chiyoko says a silent prayer for him, explains to him that she cannot take any chances. Even if he had been the dumbest taxi driver on the planet, she cannot take any chances.

Aside from Jago and Sarah, only she can know.

Code King[liv]

SHARI CHOPRA

3rd-Class Bus Approaching Chengdu, Sichuan Province, China

Shari Chopra has a new problem, an unforeseen problem.

29, 9, 8, 2, 4.

She cannot calm her mind.

29, 9, 8, 2, 4.

All her life she has been peaceful inside, but something has changed.
Something happened after the Calling, after getting her clue.
Something started worming away inside her, digging away at her,
wanting out, wanting.

The numbers.

29, 9, 8, 2, 4.

Slithering through her mind.

She tries to relinquish expectations, to take shelter in her breath, tries
to see through her closed eyes.

Nothing works.

29, 9, 8, 2, 4.

What do they mean?

What do they want?

29, 9, 8, 2, 4.

What Shari wants is a chai in a terracotta cup. She wants to drink the
sweet, warming liquid, throw the empty cup on the ground, see the red
shards. She wants to hear the wallah in the background as she strolls
away. She wants dum aloo and dalchini pulao for dinner. She wants
her *dadi*'s coconut chutney. She wants home, home. She wants her
love, the love of her life. She wants to see him. Touch him.

But whatever the numbers want, that takes precedence. They crowd her mind and shove everything else aside.

29, 9, 8, 2, 4.

Shari is on a 3rd-class bus approaching the outskirts of Chengdu, capital of Sichuan. She got on the bus because she followed Alice Ulapala. She saw the big Koori in the woods and tracked her into Xi'an. It is less than 30 hours after the Calling. Alice hasn't seen Shari, or at least she hasn't let on. Alice is in the front. Shari snuck past her and is in the middle. The bus is full.

Her mind is full.

Too full.

Boiling over.

How could this happen? Shari has always had such rigorous control over her mind. While other Players of Endgame have focused on their physical skills, Shari has honed her mind like a blade, meditation her whetstone. Shari's memory is close to perfect. Her mind drinks in details as thirstily as a man would drink water in the desert. Perhaps it is this openness that is causing her so much pain; perhaps she was *too receptive* to the clue.

29, 9, 8, 2, 4.

A passenger behind her starts crying. She says her stomach hurts. There is no air-conditioning and it is hot and getting hotter, and the heat from the engine is washing through the bus, the heat from the churning, belching engine that reeks of oil and gasoline and fire. Should they be reversed? *4, 2, 8, 9, 29.* Is it a sequence? *4, 2, 8, 9, 29.* What's next? Is it a single number? A formula? 2 squared is 4, cubed is 8, plus 1 is 9, put the digit 2 in front and get 29. But then what? What?

What what what.

Shari is sweating. Sweating from the heat and sweating from the pressure building in her mind.

She wants to see him. She wanted to see him as soon as the Calling started and again as soon as it ended.

She wants to see him now.

She wants to see Jamal. Her best friend. Her *jaanu.*

The other Players cannot know about him.

About *them.*

Her husband and her young daughter, also named Alice, just like the Koori who Shari is tracking. She took it as a good omen that the two should share a name, her daughter and this Player.

Shari is only 17 years old, but she's a woman. A mother and a wife. This must stay secret. *They* must stay secret. If not, they will compromise her. They will compromise her because she loves them. They have to live. They have to.

The others cannot know.

The woman in the back continues to wail, her pain getting worse. Others are yelling. Shari tries to block it out, tries to concentrate on the numbers.

29, 9, 8, 2, 4. 29, 9, 8, 2, 4. 29, 9, 8, 2, 4. 29, 9, 8, 2, 4.

But the woman won't relent. She screams louder, pounds the glass of the window so hard it might break. Shari turns to look and sees a throng of passengers hovering and gesturing wildly. They look like they're starting to worry. The driver is unfazed, keeps bumping along. Shari sees a hand shoot up from behind a seat, a clenched fist. Someone is asking if there is a doctor on board.

Doctors do not ride 3rd-class buses.

The person asks for something else. Shari understands a word: *midwife.* Is there a midwife on board?

Shari is not a midwife, but she is a mother and has 13 little sisters and seven brothers, 29 (that number again!) nieces and nephews, dozens of cousins. Her father has had five wives. This is the way with her line. It is messy and big and thank goodness it is full of resources. And full of little mouths.

In the back of the bus, there is a new little mouth struggling to come out, trying to breathe and eat and cry.

Calm.

Be calm.

There is a little mouth in there trying to live.

Shari looks at Alice. She can see her mop of hair rising above the seat back. The Koori Player looks to be asleep. In this heat, with the bouncing bus, and the screaming woman—Shari is amazed that anyone could sleep. The Koori's mind must not be as cluttered as her own. Shari wishes she could sleep herself. Alice is not going anywhere. She is oblivious.

So Shari will help.

She rises and walks down the crowded aisle. As she walks, she removes a small bottle of hand sanitizer from her fanny pack. She rubs a dollop in and around her fingers and palms.

"Excuse me," she says, switching to poor Mandarin and stashing the little bottle. The smell of rubbing alcohol is strangely refreshing.

A few people turn to her and shake their heads. She is not what they expected.

"I know I am young and a foreigner, but I can help," she says. "I have a child myself and have been to twenty-one births. Please, let me see."

The remaining people step aside. The birthing woman is not a woman but a girl. Maybe 13 years old.

Like Shari was once.

Except that Shari did not give birth to her Little Alice aboard a sweltering bus. It was a lovely day and Jamal was there to hold her hand. She wishes he could be here now.

The baby is crowning. It is not long in arriving. It would be here already if something weren't wrong.

"May I help?" Shari asks the girl.

The girl is scared. Blood vessels have popped across the bridge of her nose and over the rise of her cheeks. She nods.

Such pain.

Such sweat and tears, such fear.

Shari is suddenly calm. For a moment she forgets about Alice, about Endgame. Her head clears of those blasted numbers.

"My name is Shari."

"Lin."

"Breathe, Lin. I am going to put my hands here. After you breathe, I will feel. Don't push. Am I saying the right words? My Mandarin is not good."

"I understand. I won't push. You will feel."

"Right. Good. Now, one, two, three, big breath."

Lin fills her lungs and blows out her cheeks.

Shari touches the girl's skin. It is hot, damp. She kneads the girl's abdomen. Shari can feel the baby's arm. It is caught. The cord is wrapped around it. If the cord is short, the baby will die and possibly the mother too. If the cord is long enough, there is hope.

A man brings an armful of water bottles from a box at the front of the bus.

Shari looks at him.

He is scared too.

He is not a man.

A boy, 14, maybe 15.

The father.

She puts a hand on the boy's wrist. "Don't worry."

He nods quickly, nervously, doesn't even look at Shari. He is locked on Lin. Lin is locked on Shari.

Shari has him open a bottle and pour the water over her hands to remove the alcohol. While doing this she looks Lin intently in the eye.

"The cord is holding the arm. I have to try to free it."

Lin nods, her eyes full of fear.

Shari searches the faces around her. And there, like an apparition, appears Alice Ulapala over the heads of the diminutive Chinese throng. They lock eyes for a tense moment.

"What's happening?" the Koori asks, but her voice is casual—friendly, even.

Shari is shocked. "Helping this girl," she answers in English.

The other riders regard Alice like she is a giant from another world. And in a sense, she is.

"We need to stop the bus," Alice says. Shari hesitates. If they stop the bus, it will be easier for Alice to get away. But if they don't, this girl and her baby could die.

"Yes," Shari says, deciding. "Please, Alice, go ask the driver to stop."

"Will do, mate."

Alice turns. Shari doesn't know what comes over her then. It's an impetuous feeling, but it somehow feels right. Even though she knows she should keep her family a secret, her instincts tell her that this is the right course of action. She shouts after Alice, "My daughter is also named Alice!"

Alice Ulapala freezes. Looks over her shoulder. Shari can see the crescent-shaped birthmark like a waxing moon rising on the Koori's darkened skin. She looks like she's trying to decide whether to trust this new information or not. Whether to trust Shari. "That so?"

"Yes," Shari says desperately. "I don't know why I'm telling you this."

"That's all right. Kids are angels, they are. I hope you see yours soon, I really do."

"Thank you."

"No worries, mate." The Koori continues down the bus, and the peasants part for her like the Red Sea did for Moses.

Shari watches as Alice speaks with the driver, and within a minute the ride has stopped. Everyone on board is now paying attention, some of them hopeful that Lin will be all right, others just annoyed at the delay.

Shari looks at Lin. She forgets about Alice and Endgame and the Calling and Jamal and her Alice too. She is focused only on this task. Her mind is sharp and clear.

"This will hurt," she says to Lin in Mandarin. "But it will be over soon." *One way or another it will all be over soon*, Shari thinks.

"Breathe!"

The girl inhales. Shari reaches down and slides her hand over the baby's head and face. She can feel its heart beating, beating, beating. It's a strong baby. The girl screams. Fearing for Lin, the father reaches for Shari, but a middle-aged man in round spectacles and a beaten canvas hat holds the boy back. Two women gasp. The girl screams some more.

Shari can feel the cord. She probes and gets a finger under it, between the arm and the tube, and then another finger. The baby arcs its back and pushes its face into Shari's wrist. She can feel both heartbeats now, the mother's and the child's, striking against each other. Shari tries to slide the cord over the fingers. Lin is panting. Her legs start to quiver.

"Hold on, I've almost got it!"

A car passes on the road honking its horn; someone shouts from its open window.

Shari glances over. Just across the shoulder, opposite the bus, is Alice Ulapala. She's looking directly at Shari. She raises her hand to her forehead and snaps a respectful salute, then gets into the car. Shari knows she should go after her. That she should go and Play.

But she can't.

She moves her finger. The cord slides down one centimeter. The heartbeats race each other. Shari's own heartbeat joins the contest, galloping away like a thoroughbred.

Alice is gone.

Shari is here.

Here she will stay.

The cord is squeezed and snags on Shari's index finger. She lowers her shoulder. Lin heaves, her breath is erratic, and her midsection is locked in a contraction.

"Breathe!"

The baby's heartbeat slows. Slows. Slows.

"Breathe! Breathe!"

Lin tries but the pain is unbearable.

Shari gets lower and pinches the cord in the crook of her finger, forcing her knuckle uncomfortably into the girl's pelvis.

Lin begins to pass out.

"Pour water on her face!"

A woman does. Lin wakes. She's exhausted, can barely function.

Shari is calm. It's strange to her. She holds a life—two lives—literally in her hands. It's calm, peaceful.

I *am* Playing, she realizes.

It is the puzzle of life, kepler 22b said of the game. *The puzzle of life.*

29. 9. 8. 2. 4.

They'll come together.

She's a Player and she is Playing.

The baby pushes against her wrist. Shari works her hand around, and finally the cord is free. Slowly she unhooks her finger and pulls out her hand. As she does, she feels the baby's heartbeat go up up up.

"It's done."

The middle-aged man with the glasses and the canvas hat smiles at her and pours water over her hands. Shari washes the blood and amniotic fluid onto the hard floor of the bus.

"Lin. Are you with me, Lin?" The girl nods weakly. "The baby is almost here. After the next—" Shari doesn't know the word for contraction, so she mimes one by flexing her arms and stomach and wrenching her face. Lin understands. "After that, you breathe and push, breathe and push, breathe and push."

"Okay." She is still frightened.

They wait. Shari offers her hand to hold. Lin takes it. Tries to smile. The father takes her other hand.

The contraction comes.

"Go!" Shari lets go of the girl's hand and gets ready. "Go go go!"

Lin does as she's been told and does it again and again and it comes it comes it's crying.

"A boy! A boy! A boy!" people shout as they see. The news ricochets down and around the bus. The driver fires the engine back up, but an old lady hits him with a rolled newspaper and he turns it off.

Shari holds the baby. Lin cries with tears of everything—hope, joy, grief, pain. Shari passes the baby to the beaming father. Someone hands him a scarf, and the baby is wrapped up. Shari reaches in her fanny pack and pulls out a folding knife. She opens it and cuts the cord.

A throng pushes in on the new mother and father. Shari steps back. Her heart is still going fast.

There is more than one way to Play Endgame.

She smiles.

And as she retreats to her seat, people make way for her. She's a hero. They give her space. She sits, silently thanks the Koori for being there. Something about her presence helped. And as the adrenaline from the birth starts to fade, she realizes the numbers that were taunting her, tormenting her, are gone.

In their place is a string of Sanskrit letters. A jumble. She works them in her mind, and finally they come together.

The child is in your line now.

Win or he will die.

SARAH ALOPAY, JAGO TLALOC

Wei's Bīnguǎn, Chang'an District, Xi'an, China

The owner of the guesthouse—a fiftysomething man named Wei—caters to travelers seeking refuge from the bustle of Xi'an. Most of his customers, he says, make day trips back to the city or to some of the local pyramids. He is happy to point out that he took the picture that is framed and hanging behind his desk. It's a photo of a pyramid washed in the orange light of the setting sun, a wispy white cloud far in the distance.

Wei speaks very good English and mistakes the strange-looking pair of travelers for a couple. As they check in, Jago tries to play this up by sliding his arm around Sarah's waist, but she elbows him in the side and he immediately backs off.

Wei laughs. "Traveling is not always easy, friends. You can trust that I will take good care of you here. It is what I do. I can tell that you need rest."

"You have no idea," Sarah says.

Wei laughs again and shoots Jago a knowing look. "Perhaps after you rest, no more elbows, hmm?"

Jago and Sarah exchange a quick look. He flashes his studded smile at her, but she just stares back at him, deadpan. Jago decides to change the subject. "Do you have internet access, Mr. Wei?" he asks.

"There is a shared computer off the dining room. I have satellite service and a generator for when the power fails, so we are never disconnected," he says proudly.

They pay for three days in advance and head for their room. As they go up the stairs, Sarah asks, "Why did you try to put your arm around me?"

"He wants to see a couple, so I was giving him a couple." Jago shrugs. "Makes us more incognito."

"Jago, there's no way we could ever be incognito in this country."

"You're right. I'm sorry. I shouldn't have."

"You're not getting any of this, you know," she says playfully.

"No? Why not?"

"This isn't a James Bond movie. You"—she points at him and makes a little circle in the air—"are no Bond."

"I could kick Bond's ass, you know."

She laughs. "So could I."

They come to the door. Jago opens it for her. "I just want to lie down. Can I do that, at least?"

"So long as it's on your bed."

Sleep is high on the list of things they each want to do. Another is shower. But at the top is getting a good look at the disk.

They walk into their room. It has large windows that look over an inner courtyard, two twin beds, and a small bathroom with a tub. Sarah makes immediately for the tub and turns on the water. It's hot, and she smiles contentedly as it splashes across the back of her hand. Jago takes the disk out of his backpack, although he's really paying more attention to Sarah. He's imagining her in that tub and what might happen in this room. Smartly, he keeps his mouth shut, playing it cool. James Bond—*psshh,* he has nothing on Jago Tlaloc.

Sarah steps out of the bathroom and examines the disk with Jago, their heads close together. It is gray stone. Eight inches across and two inches thick. On one side is a spiral groove 1/8th of an inch thick that runs out from the center. In this are little nicks and creases. Jago turns it over, and on the other side is a series of 20 concentric circles. Within some of the circles are strings of a mysterious, nonpictorial text. It is full of curlicues and exacting dot matrices and short diagonal hash marks.

As old as the disk is, the markings look as if they were written with a machine.

"You ever seen marks like that?" Sarah asks.

"No. You?"

"No. Can I hold it?"

He passes it to her. And it happens. Like a shot through her brain it happens. Jago asks if she is all right, but he sounds far-off and she can't answer. Her clue of incomprehensible numbers changes. Most of the digits flutter and disappear. The ones that are left fly and rearrange, right in front of her, as if they are floating in the air.

"Jago, grab those." She points at a pad and pen sitting on the side table between their beds.

"What happened?"

"Get the pen and paper!"

Jago does it. "Bossy," he grunts.

"Write this down. 346389863109877285812. Got it?"

"346389863109877285812." Jago squints down at the meaningless line of numbers. "What does it mean?"

"I have no idea," Sarah says. "My clue . . . something changed when I touched the disk."

"Perfect. More puzzles," he says in frustration. There hasn't been enough fighting in Endgame for Jago. Fighting or—he glances at Sarah—other physical activity.

As they stare at the numbers on the page, Sarah's satellite phone rings. Jago frowns. "Who's calling you?"

She shrugs, puts the disk on the foot of the bed, and fishes the phone out of her bag. She looks at its display. "Oh my god."

"Who is it?"

"It's . . . my boyfriend."

Jago arches an eyebrow. "You have a boyfriend?"

"I did, but I broke it off with him after the meteor hit. When I knew this was all real."

"You tell him why?" Jago asks. "Or did you just say"—he fumbles for the American expression—"it's not you, it's me?"

The phone is still ringing. *Christopher.* What could he want? Sarah

133

shakes her head, annoyed; annoyed that he would call, annoyed at how much she wants to answer the phone.

"I told him I was leaving and he'd probably never see me again and he should let go of me."

"Seems he didn't get the message."

"If I don't answer, maybe he will."

"You don't strike me as an easy girl to get over," Jago muses.

Sarah doesn't answer. She's tired of the banter. Eventually the phone stops ringing.

"I'm taking a bath," she says abruptly, turning and walking into the bathroom. "I'll figure out those numbers later."

A boyfriend, Jago thinks. *More competition, though of a different kind.* She closes the door.

After a few moments, he hears her getting into the tub.

I like competition, he thinks.

I have spent most of my life eliminating it.

And the trees laid down like toothpicks.[lv]

CHRISTOPHER VANDERKAMP

Grand Mercure Hotel, Room 172, Huimin Square, Xi'an, China

Christopher finds Kala surprisingly easy to follow. It's as if she is constantly preoccupied and distant and blissfully unaware of her surroundings. Like she is focused on some figment of her imagination or some distant target that she's trying to find.

If this is the type of person Sarah is up against, she should have no problem winning.

After 36 hours on Kala's tail Christopher has become so at ease with shadowing her that his only fear is that she will jump off another building.

Because there's no way he is going to do anything like that.

But so far so good. Here he is in the same internet café as her. Here he is in the same tea shop. Here he is standing outside the electronics store where she's shopping. Here he is in the same hotel—a very nice one—on the same floor. Here he is watching the hall through the peephole. Here he is bribing the bellhops to call him if they see her leave. Here he is outside the same internet café as the day before. Here he is following her taxi in a taxi of his own. Here he is at the airport. Here he is in line, just behind her, and still she doesn't notice him. Here he is overhearing her conversation with the desk agent at Qatar Airways. Here he is buying a ticket to the same place she just bought a ticket to, a place called Urfa in Turkey. They have to fly first to Changzhou, then to Dubai, then to Istanbul.

The first flight leaves in 45 hours.

Here they are leaving the airport.

Sarah said she'd trained for years to master all this Endgame stuff.

Granted, Christopher hasn't had to fight anyone yet, but he's pretty excited at how easy all the superspy moves are coming to him. He wishes Sarah could see what he's been up to. Maybe she'd reconsider teaming up.

Since he knows where and when Kala is flying out, Christopher lays off for a day. He goes back to the hotel and watches TV and reads the news on the laptop he brought from home. He unpacks and repacks his bag. He sleeps fitfully. His dreams are plagued with images of Sarah being tortured or chased, beaten or burned. He keeps seeing her standing amidst 11 other Players, all of whom are trying to kill her. He wakes at 4:17 a.m. and tosses and turns for an hour, unable to get the dreams out of his mind. He gets out of bed and goes to the bathroom and splashes cold water on his face. He wonders where she is, what she's doing, if she's okay, if she's alive. He decides to call her. He called her once already and her phone rang until it went to voice mail.

The greeting was automated.

Impersonal.

He didn't leave a message.

He just wanted to hear her voice.

Hear her say hello.

Hear her laugh.

Hear her say, "I love you."

He misses her.

He just wanted to hear her voice.

AN LIU

Liu Residence, Unregistered Belowground Property, Tongyuanzhen, Gaoling County, Xi'an, China

An is in a dark room. A quartet of computer screens is arranged before him in a grid. One shows a Chinese news feed, another shows BBC World News. Both have the volume *blinkblink* muted. Both show pictures of the meteors and their *blinkSHIVER* carnage. An likes carnage.

A little more than a week old and these images still captivate him. Other Players might have wished for Endgame, but none pined for it like An.

In time, An will be just like the meteors. *BLINKBLINK.* He will captivate them all.

An stares at a lower screen. It has a graph on it. On the graph is a web of lines dipping and diving and making *blink* making no *blinkblink* making no goddamned kepler damned Endgame damned *blinkblink* no sense.

Longitude vs. latitude.

Place vs. place.

Here vs. there.

blinkblinkSHIVERblink.

An hammers furiously on a keyboard. Bangs numbers and strings and code into a console. Runs them. Watches the screen *blinkblink* watches the screen *blinkblink* change.

He leans in, watches, scratches the back of his neck at the hairline hard for five seconds, 10 seconds, 20 seconds. He scowls at the graph. The algorithm is beautiful. They usually are. He stops scratching and inspects his fingernails. Dandruff and dry skin, chipped and white. He sticks a finger in his mouth, sucks off the flakes. Removes the finger from his lips with a pop and wipes it on his jeans and puts the finger on the screen and traces over the graph. Follows a *blink* follows a *blink* follows a green line.

Stops.

There?

Blinkblinkblinkblink.

Yes.

There.

Though the position *blink* the position *blink* the position is not exact. He needs to pin it first.

He swivels in his chair and bangs on another keyboard. Loads an IP address aggregator with the phone's approximate coordinates. *Blinkblinkblink.* Casts a wide net *blink* and sets criteria for searches. Plane or train bookings, ancient sites, pyramids *SHIVER* Olmec culture, kepler 22b. The program will report back which computers are searching for what and when. *SHIVER. BLINK.* If An thinks one of these is Jago, he will confirm it with a *blink* robocall to Jago's phone and triangulate.

An will *blink* An will *blinkblink* find them.

Find them and stop them.

No winners.

BlinkSHIVERSHIVERblink.

None.

An swivels in his chair again, catches a quick-cut montage of the meteoric destruction on BBC World. Over it is a title with light trails and lens flares. It says: *End Times?*

People are wondering; yes, they are wondering.

An smiles.

He stands and walks upstairs, out of his basement, into the kitchen, out the door. It's a bright and cheery day. He needs *blinkblink* he needs some air. He needs some air and some *blink* transistors and soldering wire and a new pair of needle-nose *blink* needle-nose pliers from the hardware store.

Besides, he likes to watch the people scurry about.

All the people who will die die die. All the people who will *blinkblinkblinkblinkblink* who will die.

Some will try to stop the Event.

Will try to be heroes.

Will try to win.

To hell with the others.

People will die. Millions, hundreds of millions, billions of people will die.

There is no hope for the future, and An loves it.

CHIYOKO TAKEDA

Huímín Street Market, Xi'an, China

Chiyoko hustles through a busy market just outside the city center of Xi'an. She ditched the taxi and the dead driver and gathered her belongings from her dank little hotel room. She is going to relocate to the countryside, but first she needs to buy some things. A fleece sweater, makeup, and hair dye. And she needs to find a hardware store so she can get the items she'll need to steal cars or motorcycles or boats or whatever else she wants to steal.

She is relocating so she can be closer to Jago and Sarah. So she can be closer to the disk.

The disk that is just like the ones found in 1938 in a cave near the China-Tibet border: the disks of Baian-Kara-Ula.

They were initially thought to have been made by a local tribe of isolated pygmies named the Dropa, but when the technology became available, they were radiocarbon-dated and discovered to have been at least 12,000 years old.

Chiyoko knows that these disks are just a few of many that existed through antiquity going back much farther than 12,000 years. Going back 20,000, 30,000, 40,000 years. Well into the last ice age, when the coastal boundaries of Earth were very different than they are today. Back when the great ice caps made the seas shallow. When the advanced ancient cities, since submerged by the Great Flood and lost to water and ignorance, stood like beacons on the coastlines.

Back when everyone knew that the disks were power.

Here is how Chiyoko knows: In 1803, a strange vessel, floating in the northern Sea of Japan, was discovered by Japanese fishermen. The vessel, egg-shaped and 5.45 meters in diameter, was unlike anything anyone had ever seen. Today it might be considered a submersible or a space capsule or even a chunky flying saucer, but they had no notion of what it was back then. It was made of crystal, metal, and glass. The fishermen peered into it and saw that the floor was cushioned and the walls were adorned with flourishes of wallpaper depicting unknown things. There were words everywhere, but the language was a mystery. Strangest of all was the woman—yes, woman—inside. Pale-skinned, tall, red-haired, slant-eyed. There was no telling how long she'd been aboard her strange vessel, or how she'd managed to survive at sea. The fishermen towed the entire thing—the vessel, the woman, and all—to shore. The woman got out. She carried a quicksilver box, which the village gossips determined was a container for her husband's severed head. She spoke their language with a strange accent and offered no explanation for where she had come from or why she had come. For some reason, the villagers took to her, and eventually she settled down, marrying a local blacksmith. There she stayed until she died, and never, not once, did she open the box. At least not in the presence of any villager, not even her Japanese husband. No one ever knew what was inside, if there was even anything at all.

This woman was Mu.

Perhaps she was the first, or perhaps she was meant to be the last. When the Japanese villagers pulled her out of the ocean and took her in, they became Mu as well. She chose a boy from the village, a strong boy named Hido who apprenticed with her husband, and called on him once a week. She taught this boy the secrets of her ancient line, one that was long thought wiped out.

In time, he became a Player.

The 2nd line was restored.

For Hido, the woman opened the box. She took out the disk inside. She gave it to Hido. And she said only, "This is of the ancient and for the ancient. It contains everything and nothing. It is not one of the keys, but it will lead directly to the first. The first move is essential."

Hido did not understand and was given no explanation. The woman said to pass the disk down the line, along with her words, and that when the time came, they would make sense.

And so now they do. To Chiyoko Takeda, the 7,947th Player of the 2nd line. All she needs is the disk.

But, of course, she doesn't have it. The disk watched over by her line was lost. Chiyoko has only ever seen sepia-tinted pictures of her great-great-grandmother Sachiko Takeda holding it proudly like a prize.

In the picture she is young, able-bodied, strong. She wears a set of workman's clothing. A *katana* hangs from her belt. She is ready for Endgame, right there in that picture taken in 1899. So long ago.

But Sachiko was lost. She was lost when a ship sailing from Edo to Manila went down in a tempest.

And the disk was lost too.

But not anymore. Chiyoko knows with every fiber of her being that the disk that the Olmec and the Cahokian possess is the same one that used to belong to her line. She has no idea how kepler 22b retrieved it, but that is immaterial.

She must get it from them.

It belongs to her by right.

Chiyoko works through the market methodically and discreetly. She is dressed down, like a chambermaid running errands for her mistress. The clerks who deal with her barely say a word. As she pays for the hair dye, she slides a small square of paper toward the clerk. Written on it in Mandarin are the words *hardware store.*

The clerk points at the door and left and says there is one five storefronts down.

Chiyoko gives her a curt and appreciative nod and leaves the drugstore.

She finds the hardware store and wanders in and looks for a voltmeter and some spare batteries and a wire cutter and an assortment of automotive fuses and some metal shears and a roll of stiff tin flashing. A chain-smoking matron at the back of the store barks orders to her employees. Chiyoko is the only other woman in the place.

She brings her stuff to the counter and pays. She turns. Keeps her head down. Stays discreet. She walks down a narrow aisle to the door. Just as she is about to exit, a person rounds a corner quickly and bumps into her.

"Excuse me," he says.

She looks up.

And sees the red tattooed tear of the Shang Player, An Liu. His bloodshot eyes widen.

Her heart beats faster.

A vein along his temple shows that his heart quickens too.

And for a brief moment neither of them moves.

AN LIU

Wǔjīnháng Hardware Store, Xi'an, China

The Mu Player—inches away and filling with energy—is beautiful and delicate and serene. An knows that their fight will have to be brief and decisive. He can't risk getting arrested.

He will kill her quickly and leave.

Disappear back underground.

The edge in her deep, round eyes seems to suggest that she feels the same way. An takes a step forward. She takes a step back. He gathers his chi into his fingertips and jabs at her solar plexus. She blocks this easily with the flat of her hand and lets the energy of An's attack dissipate through her hand, down her arm, fanning out through her body and into the ground and the static of the very air around them. She breathes in and counterattacks, pushing her palm forward.

An has never felt anything like it. She doesn't even touch him and he is pushed back a full foot. It takes all the power of his glutes and thighs, all the concentration rising through his feet and legs and lungs and neck and skull not to be thrown a dozen feet into the wall.

They hear the matron yell at one of her employees. No one has noticed them yet.

An shuffles forward in two quick swishing movements. She retreats. They are at the start of a darkened aisle stocked with cans of paint. It occurs to An that aisles in hardware stores containing paint should not be dark but light; otherwise how can the customer know what color he is getting? But he doesn't dwell on this. Chiyoko has dispensed with her bags and has both palms up and facing him. Her thumbs are hooked together so that it looks like she is making a butterfly shadow puppet. Her right leg is behind her. An seeks out the small sliver of space that will allow his next attack to pass through her guard.

He sees it.

At the sternal notch.

He pushes his chi up from the pit of his stomach and strikes with lightning quickness. He is not sure that he's ever moved so quickly, but she is faster. She raises her hands and snags his finger in the crook of her thumbs and folds her fingers over his. He pulls back and she closes her fists with such ferocity that they generate a little breeze that crosses his face.

If he had not pulled away, his hand would have been shattered. He is certain of it.

She tries to hit his neck, but he sidesteps and slides a foot forward, hoping to knock her over, but she just moves back. It is like she has eyes all over her body. Can see everything he's doing before he does it. He goes for her face, and she bends over backward, completely, keeps going, and then her feet are coming up for his chin and *he* bends over backward but cannot do the flip that she has just done so he springs back upright. And when he does he flicks his sleeve and a closed butterfly knife slides into his hand.

He twirls it. Its hinges and pegs are coated with high-grade carbon nanotubes, and the blade is totally silent. He is going to stab her in the heart, between the 6th and 7th ribs on the left side.

But before he can get the knife open she sticks a finger into the works and it twirls the wrong way and for three seconds the two of them are staring at the knife as it dances in the air between them. The toes of their shoes are touching. He has trained with this knife—this very knife—since he was five, and now, with this person thwarting him, it's as if he's never even seen a butterfly knife in his life.

One more second and the unthinkable happens: she has the knife, its point pushing into the skin below his belly button.

The matron yells again, this time telling someone to see what the commotion at the front is all about.

An breathes and slides back and she slides forward and he slides back and she forward. Their combined chi is incredible.

Intoxicating.

Overwhelming.

And that's when he realizes that since he has been in her presence, his tics have disappeared. No *blinks* or *SHIVERS*, head twitches or nerves. None.

For the first time since before his training began—since before he was beaten and starved and frightened and led around by a chain like a mongrel—he feels calm.

One of the employees yells, "They have a knife!"

An grabs Chiyoko's wrist and orders, "STOP!"

And by the Maker, the Maker of all Makers, she does.

"How are you doing that?" he asks, his stutter also gone.

She tilts her head. *Doing what?* the gesture says.

"My tics are gone. I feel . . . young."

He lets go of her wrists.

She lowers the knifepoint.

The energy pulses from his body.

A new kind of energy.

His ears tell him that the matron is moving toward them now, cursing and threatening. An can't help but look. She's huge, fat, slobbering, and waving a thick wooden baseball bat with a massive nail sticking out of its business end. She wants none of this crap in her place.

An feels the breeze again.

He turns.

The door is already closing. The knife is folded and falling to the ground. Chiyoko's bags are gone.

And so is *blink* so is *blink* so is *blinkSHIVERSHIVERblink*.

So is she.

47.921378, 106.90554[lvi]

JAGO TLALOC

Wei's Bīnguǎn Lobby, Chang'an District, Xi'an, China

Jago wakes with a start early the next morning. His sheets are soaked. His skin is burning. His eyes are throbbing out of their sockets.

He sits up with a groan.

Sarah is not in her bed.

The bathroom door is open.

Her things are here, but she is not.

Jago leans over and grabs the pen and paper from the side table. Tears off the sheet with Sarah's numbers and throws it on the floor and clicks the penpoint out and starts making frantic lines all over the sheet. His hand moves automatically, and Jago becomes aware of himself in a way that he never has been before. He is observing himself as if from above. His mind is detached and lucid. It is like the deepest of meditations. The past—all that he has done to get to this point—is here in the present.

Everything.

Here.

Nothing anywhere else.

The drawing is nonsense. Harried. Abstract. The lines are curved, or as straight as a razor, or bent by forced perspective, or twirled like a lock of curling hair. All of them are short. No more than three centimeters long. They are disconnected, littered across the page, random. They don't add up.

For a moment Jago actually closes his eyes as his hand continues to dart over the page.

When he opens them, Jago sees something. The contour of a nose, the curl of an ear. The line of a sword's blade. A bunching of cloth over a muscle. A paintbrush streak of hair. The sharp angle of armor. Fingers. A mustache, and high, arching eyebrows. Deep-set eyes that stare into the unknown past.

He closes his eyes again.

Lets his mind go, his hand go.

Until he is finished.

And his mind returns to his body.

And his skin cools, and a breeze comes through the window and he shivers.

He opens his eyes.

The drawing takes up the whole page. It depicts a heavily armored Chinese warrior in ¾ profile. His hair is done up in some kind of ribboned headdress. His sword is short and true. His shoulders are broad, his face delicate.

In one hand he holds a disk that looks exactly like the one Jago took from the Calling.

His hand has drawn the clue that kepler 22b put into his head.

Jago gets out of bed and fills the sink with water and splashes the water on his face. He gets dressed and grabs the drawing. He grabs the backpack that contains the disk and he looks at the clock. It is 6:47 a.m.

He walks out of the room and sees Sarah sitting cross-legged in the little courtyard. Her back is to him.

She is perfectly still.

Thinking.

Waiting.

Breathing.

He won't bother her.

He wants to get to the computer, do a search for the picture. It's so accurate that there must be something like it out there somewhere.

He finds Wei sweeping the lobby. Wei straightens and says, "You're up too? I thought young people like you slept in."

Jago stops. "No, not me. I never sleep in."

"Me neither. Good for the soul. Always nice to start the day in peace. From peace flows peace."

Wei may be right, but Jago feels sorry for this guy. For his boring life that will soon be over. "I guess," Jago grunts.

Wei leans on the broom handle, trying to get a look at Jago's drawing. "What's that?"

Jago holds it up. "This? Uh, something I drew."

Wei studies it.

"It's remarkable."

"Yeah." Jago squints at the drawing, still a little surprised that it came from his hand. "Thanks."

"It looks just like one of them, though I've never seen one with a plate like that one is holding."

"You recognize it?" Jago's pulse speeds up.

"Of course. You're very talented."

"Thank you," Jago repeats. A total lie. Left to his own, Jago can barely draw a convincing stick figure. Practicing art wasn't covered in his Endgame training.

Wei's eyes shift from studying the picture to studying Jago.

"But you don't know what it is, do you? Even though you drew it?"

Something in his look makes Jago feel uncomfortable. He shrugs, playing it off. "I just copied it from a picture Sarah tore out of some magazine." He lies without missing a beat. "Why? What is it?"

"That is a general in the Terracotta Army."

"Oh yeah! How stupid of me." He knew he'd seen it somewhere before. The Terracotta Army is world-famous. Over 8,000 life-sized warrior statues guard the remains of the first emperor of China. His tomb is a local attraction, and it dates back to the 2nd or 3rd century BCE.

"Sarah was talking about going to visit it while we were here."

kepler 22b must be telling me that I—we—need to go there. And we need to bring the disk.

"Of course she was. Everyone goes to visit the Terracotta Army. It's quite impressive." Wei resumes sweeping. "I'm kind of crazy for it myself."

"That so?"

"Yes." And then he says unexpectedly, "And why are you lying to me, by the way?"

"Lying?" Jago feels the muscles in his neck tense, readying.

"There is no way you copied that from a photo."

Jago shakes his head. "But I did."

"No warrior of Emperor Qín Shĭ Huángdì ever held a disk like that."

Jago swallows. "Oh, I just made that part up. I was dreaming about Frisbees."

"Frisbees, hm? That doesn't look like a Frisbee."

"What can I say? I can't draw Frisbees. No one's perfect, I guess."

"No. I suppose not." Wei sweeps some more. "I'm sorry. I didn't mean to bother you. Weren't you going to use the computer?"

"Yeah, I was," Jago says, heading to the alcove.

Jago finds the computer and sits at the terminal and opens a browser window and starts searching. He reads more about the Terracotta Army and the Chinese pyramids and Emperor Qín. He finds cryptic internet rumors—which is to say, a load of bullshit—about the Great White Pyramid.

Jago surfs for a while longer. Checks an old email account. Nothing but junk. Reads the local news from Juliaca and Omaha and a few other crater sites. Googles *alien disk* and gets a ton of useless garbage written by crackpots.

After 17 minutes his phone vibrates.

He is not expecting a call.

Only four people have the number.

He pulls it from the bag, careful to keep the disk hidden inside, and studies the number.

It's local.

He frowns and hits talk.

"Hello?"

A pause before an automated female voice speaking jovial Mandarin comes over the line.

A robocall wrong number.

Jago hangs up, a little uneasy. Normally he might wonder if his phone was just tagged by a tracker, but he has the most secure, most advanced smartphone that exists.

He erases the history cache on the computer and quits the browser and heads back to the room, hoping that Sarah is done with her meditating. They need to get moving.

As he passes through the lobby, Wei says, "You know, I have a cousin who is a researcher at the site. I think he would very much enjoy your picture. I'll give him a call and see if he might be able to give you and your girlfriend a tour. He could probably let you into some areas other tourists don't get to visit."

Jago isn't sure he trusts Wei, but it will be a good way to get into the complex, if that's what the clue is telling him he should do. "Thank you, Wei. That would be great."

Wei bows. "Think nothing of it."

AN LIU

Liu Residence, Unregistered Belowground Property, Tongyuanzhen, Gaoling County, Xi'an, China

Hard drives spin. Numbers fly. Coordinates are cross-referenced. IP addresses are winnowed. Packets are sent through wires to transmitters to satellites and back. An old dot matrix printer unspools sheets of paper with perforated edges. A display lights up. The script unfurls in masses of long-line code.

An Liu's mechanism has just pinned Jago Tlaloc's phone.

The Shang Player bounds into the room, hot from the street, from his fight with Chiyoko, from the flush of her power. Hot from scouring the streets for over two hours, searching for her, and failing.

An goes to the printout. *SHIVER*. Consults the screen. *Blinkblink*. Will *blink* gather his *blink* toys and go and meet them.

When they are removed *blink* are removed *SHIVER* removed from the game board, he will seek out this Chiyoko Takeda. The clue that *blink* kepler 22b *blinkblink* placed in his mind does not matter. He does not intend to play Endgame like the others, chasing *blink* riddles, acting like fools.

blinkSHIVERblink.

What matters is the calming *blink* calming *blink* calming silent soothing force of *blink* the bewitching Player *blink* the bewitching Player *blink* the bewitching Player of the 2nd line.

The remaining Players can wait.

The present he is making for them isn't ready yet.

But it will be soon.

And what a present *blink* what a present it is going to be.

MACCABEE ADLAI

Xī Jīng Hospital Urgent Care, Xi'an, China

Maccabee Adlai leaves the hospital. He has been there for two days and 15 hours, checked in under the alias Paul Allen Chomsky. He couldn't risk going on the grid with his real name. It wouldn't have done to be paid a nighttime visit by an assassin as he lay in his bed dreaming of killing the young boy Baitsakhan, killing Jago, and killing that crazy bastard An.

He walks into the light of day and stands in the taxi line. He's going to the train station. His leg is sore, needs a fresh dressing once a day, and can't get wet for a week, but is structurally fine. The shot from Baitsakhan's arrow was clean, and by some miracle the resulting wound did not require surgery.

The ear is another story. Jago Tlaloc ruptured his right eardrum when he thumb-stabbed Maccabee, and for now he has to endure a persistent high-pitched ringing. The doctor insisted it would heal itself and the ringing would gradually subside, but that it could take up to two or three months.

Great.

The doctor also told him to avoid flying for at least two weeks. He said if Maccabee did fly, it wouldn't make his eardrum any worse, but that it probably would be very painful.

Whatever. He'll think about it, but he has to follow his two-part clue. Time is of the essence.

The first part is this: ἐναςἐναςἐναςἐναςἐναςἐναςμηδένἐναςἐναςμηδέν μηδένμηδένμηδένἐναςἐνας.

And the 2nd, this: 47:4f:42:45:4b:4c:49:54:45:50:45:54:45:4d:50:4c:45:4f:
46:54:48:45:43:4f:4e:53:55:4d:49:4e:47:56:55:4c:54:55:52:45.

It took him some fiddling to figure them out, which lying in a hospital
bed was good for, but it wasn't that hard. After he triple-checked
the result, he fired up his tablet computer and Googled it to find out
where he had to go to get a bead on Earth Key.

It was Turkey.

Near some place called Urfa.

Maccabee gets into the cab. Screw what the doctor said. He's going to
fly to Urfa. Doctors always hedge their diagnoses, and besides, what's a
little ear pain in the service of winning Endgame?

Nothing.

Baitsakhan and the others will have to wait.

Unless, of course, their clues lead them to Urfa as well.

וְיִגַּל כַּמַּיִם, מִשְׁפָּט ; וּצְדָקָה, כְּנַחַל אֵיתָן

עמוס ה:כד

BAITSAKHAN

Fashion Europe Wig Factory Warehouse, Chengdu, China

Baitsakhan is letting himself have a treat. A sugar cookie with candied lemon zest on top. It is delicious.

He sits with his brother, Jalair, over a pile of these confections and small glasses of jasmine tea in an abandoned warehouse in Chengdu. Bat and Bold are running an errand. An essential errand.

Baitsakhan's mind has turned from the task at hand back to Maccabee. The tracker that Baitsakhan's arrow implanted in the Nabataean's leg is functioning. It survived the hospital. This much Baitsakhan can tell, because Maccabee is finally on the move.

Baitsakhan will give him one day and start to follow.

Seeing Maccabee again will be a wonderful treat. Like the cookies. Just as sweet, only deadlier.

This is his Endgame.

And it is not hard.

It is easy.

Fun.

Just like his clue, which is incredibly simple and direct. Translated from Oirat, it reads:

TAKE KILL WIN.

The clue is so easy to crack that Baitsakhan—at 13, cold, hard, merciless, and murderous—thinks it conveys favorability.

Yes.

That *is* what it means.

Baitsakhan knows.

The being at the Calling respected his unwillingness to speak his line and his tribe. The being respected his strength and his resistance. And it will appreciate the way he plays Endgame.

Baitsakhan might be the youngest and the shortest, but he is not the weakest. The weakest are those who don't yet realize they've been shoved into a slaughterhouse. The ones digging through ancient ruins, making alliances, having peaceful discussions—any Player doing anything other than killing is a fool.

Like this one here.

Baitsakhan turns his head slowly to regard the girl. He brushes a stray cookie crumb from the corner of his mouth. He pushes play on a docked iPod. "All You Need Is Love" by the Beatles starts up. It is loud, very loud.

He looks to Jalair and nods, and Jalair brings his blade down on Shari's left middle finger, the one with her ring, the ring given to her by her husband, Jamal, on the day their daughter was born.

Beautiful, smiling Little Alice.

Where is she now? Shari wonders. *Playing in the backyard.* She can picture it.

Playing in the grass with Jamal.

Shari is calm. Even after the ambush and her capture and the beating they gave her. She is calm *because* of these things. They have given her a chance to use her training, to refocus her mind. She has not cried out once since they took her, grabbed her when she got off the bus to buy a snack. By all appearances, Shari feels nothing.

Jalair looks at Baitsakhan. He is impressed by this girl. It's like she is made of stone. Baitsakhan doesn't notice Jalair's look; he is not impressed. He watches the blood ooze out from where Shari's finger used to be and smiles.

The cut hurts, the stump of her finger throbs, but the pain is nothing compared to the pain of childbirth. *These stupid boys know nothing of pain,* she thinks, and she walls her mind off from the pain.

Baitsakhan sips his tea. Shari looks at him. Through him. She has never killed a person before, but she would kill this one in a second.

Because he is not a person.

Baitsakhan sets down his tea and turns down the music.

"Tell me your clue, Harrapan, and your end will be swift," Baitsakhan promises in English, as if he is some kind of dark king.

But Shari says nothing. Betrays no emotion other than indifference. She doesn't stop staring through him.

Not human.

He is not even an animal.

Not worthy of this or any other life.

And as far as she is concerned, he is already dead.

HILAL IBN ISA AL-SALT

Church of the Covenant, Kingdom of Aksum, Northern Ethiopia

Hilal leaves the small crossroads town. He leaves the people there a small redstone talisman in return for their hospitality. The talisman is from Ethiopia, a finely carved cross, inlaid with a vein of pure platinum. He does not tell them what it is worth. There is no point. They will all be dead soon enough, and the Earth will take back everything humanity has built, everything humanity thinks it owns. He rides an oxen cart to a bigger town. A pickup truck to a bigger one. A jeep to a bigger one. A bus. A taxi. A train. A plane. He flies to Hong Kong, to Brussels, to Addis Ababa. He picks up his uncle's Nissan Maxima and drives to the crater. He sits at the edge and prays for the victims and their families, prays for the future, that it be good, that it simply be.

For this is Endgame, he thinks, standing over the still-reeking pit. *The future will end, and time will restart.*

He leaves the crater, returns to the Maxima, and drives north. To the old kingdom of Aksum, the kingdom of his forefathers' forefathers. He is the great-grandson of Ezana, the grandson of Gebre Mesqel Lalibela, the unknown leader of Timkat, the Showing of God.

He is versed in stone, and prophecy, and the kindness of death.

He gets out of the car and walks among his people. He walks for miles, wrapped in stark white and bright red cloth. He wears leather sandals on his feet. The people are scattered here and there, farming, tending goats, slaughtering chickens, beating the chaff from wheat. A few old ones recognize him and they genuflect, and he raises one of his beautiful young hands, palm up, as if to say, *No, brother, I am you; you are me. Stand next to me. Stand with me.*

And they do.

"Live," he tells them.

And they do.

They can see it in his brilliant, gentle eyes: he is theirs; they are his.

He passes over the barren hills, brown and red. And he reaches it. One of the stone underground churches, shaped like a cross, carved from the subterranean volcanic rock.

This one is secret, hidden, surrounded by a thick stand of cedars.

It is 3,318.6 years old.

Hilal makes his way through the maze of ditches that leads down to the church. The air cools; the light dims. He reaches the main doorway, carved from stone like the rest of it. His mentor is there. His spiritual guide. His counsel.

The ex-Player Eben ibn Mohammed al-Julan.

Hilal kneels, bows his head. "Master."

"You are the Player, so I am no longer the master. Come in, and tell what you have seen."

Hilal rises and takes Eben by the hand and they walk into the dank church.

"I saw a god, and he told us of the game."

"Yes."

"I saw the others. They are crude, for the most part."

"Yes."

"I saw one die. Several tried to kill. I saw ten escape."

"Yes."

"The god called himself kepler 22b."

"Yes."

"It is a planet, if memory serves."

"Yes."

"It said we must retrieve the keys: Earth Key, Sky Key, Sun Key. The winner must have all three."

"Yes."

"He left a disk of stone, but did not call our attention to it. The Olmec got it. He was with another, the Cahokian. They were followed by the Mu. None noticed that I saw the disk, or that the Olmec took it."

"Watch that last one, Player."

"Yes, Master."

"No more master. I am only Eben now."

"Yes, Eben."

"He left us each a clue, in our heads."

"Yes."

"Mine is a circle."

"Of?"

"Just a circle. A line. Empty inside and out."

They reach an altar. Eben kneels before it, and Hilal kneels with him. They lower their heads. The Christ is there above them, forever bleeding, forever suffering, forever dying, forever giving life, love, and forgiveness.

Eben says slowly, "And you do not know its meaning?"

"I think it was for the disk the Olmec took. He should have gotten my clue. It would have served him better. Or perhaps I should have gotten the disk."

"You cannot know that. Assume for now that all is as it should be, and the gods do not err. What does this circle tell you?"

"It makes me think of the disk, but also something else. A circle of stone. A stone circle."

"Yes."

"It references a construct. One made in the ancient world, the one that existed here when the gods visited."

"Yes."

"One made to last, like so many things were made in those days: of rock and stone. A monument to space and time and the cosmos. A thing that sought the memory and permanence of stone. The ancient power of it."

"Yes."

"But which stone circle? There are many."

Eben rises. Hilal does not.

Eben says, "I will bring you wine and wafers."

"Thank you, Eben. I must meditate. There is more to this simple clue. More to what I must discern from it."

"Yes."

Eben turns and leaves, his robes rustling.

Hilal the Aksumite of the 144th brings his hands together in his lap. Closes his eyes.

The circle in his mind.

SARAH ALOPAY, JAGO TLALOC, CHIYOKO TAKEDA, AN LIU

Terracotta Warriors Museum, Lintong District, Xi'an, China

Sarah and Jago climb out of a taxi at the main tourist entrance of the great and ancient Terracotta Army. They are met immediately by Wei's cousin, Cheng Cheng Dhou. Cheng Cheng is a tiny man, barely 153 cm, affable, with bright eyes and Coke-bottle glasses. It is only 17 degrees Celsius outside when they meet him, but he is sweating through his white collared shirt.

"Yes! Yes! Hello!" he says. His right hand is open in front of him, and in an odd gesture he is gripping his right wrist with his left hand, as if he needs to use one arm to move the other. They shake hands and introduce themselves, Sarah and Jago using their real first names. Cheng Cheng leads them to the entrance and ushers them through with his security pass. Just like that, they are in the complex.

"So, what exactly are we looking for?" Sarah whispers to Jago, Cheng Cheng a few feet ahead, oblivious.

Jago rolls his shoulders lazily. "Beats the hell outta me."

"I might just do that if this is all a wild-goose chase," Sarah replies with a smirk.

"Looking forward to it," Jago replies.

Twenty meters away, working her way through the tour group, is Chiyoko Takeda. She made a stop at the guesthouse after Sarah and Jago left, hoping they might be dumb enough to leave the disk behind. They weren't, and so she joined this group to visit the great Terracotta Army. She has on a blond wig and cargo pants and a black T-shirt and carries a hiker's daypack.

Chiyoko watches Sarah and Jago talking to a little troll man. A transmitter is set deep in her ear, enabling her to hear what Jago and those closest to him are saying. Unlike the locator, the audio transmitter only works when she is close to the Olmec. Chiyoko consults a wrist-mounted locator disguised as an analog watch. A unique polarization array in the clear lenses of her glasses, which are part of her disguise, enables her to see the digital display embedded in the watch's faceplate.

The locator is working. She will get in the complex on her tourist ticket, disappear, and follow the Olmec and the Cahokian to wherever it is they are going.

Follow them to where, she suspects, this Cheng Cheng Dhou will tell them something about the disk.

And after they leave, she will have to kill the poor troll man.

There can be no witnesses to Endgame.

What will be will be.

An Liu *blink* climbs off his *blink* matte-black Kawasaki ZZR1200. He is *blink* two kilometers *SHIVER* from the entrance of the Terracotta Army. Cover-up is pasted over his tattooed tear. *Blinkblinkblink.* His head is newly shaved. His backpack is full of *blink* fun things. Full of fun *SHIVER* fun *SHIVER* things. He wears an earpiece that tells him, every 30 seconds, the *blink* location of Jago's phone. *Blinkblinkblink.*

He will sneak overland now *blink* past the guards *blink* into the burial complex.

On this day Endgame *blink* Endgame *blink* Endgame will lose two Players.

Blinkblinkblink.

He has been scouring the *SHIVERBLINK* the internet for the *blink* others. Has found good leads for Kala Mozami and Maccabee Adlai and Hilal ibn Isa al-Salt. The rest are like ghosts, but no matter. They *blink* they *blink* they will turn up.

BlinkSHIVERblink.

Besides, after these two are gone, he needs to find Chiyoko Takeda. He needs to find her and unlock her *blinkblinkblinkblinkblink* her secret. If he has to drink her *blink* still-warm blood or *SHIVER* turn her skin into a shirt or *blink* keep her prisoner until the Event is through, he will. He will do anything *blink* do anything *blink* do anything to cure what ails him.

"It is mind-boggling big, you see. Finished around 240 BCE, we think. Seven hundred thousand men work thirty years on it! Four pits, one unfinished, plus an unexcavated burial mound that hold untold riches. Only Pit One has been excavated, and only partially, you see. It is the biggest. Measures two hundred three feet by seven hundred fifty-five feet. Has ten rows of warriors and chariots and horses and standard bearers and pikemen and swordsmen and generals and ranged crossbowmen. Most rows are three or four abreast. Between rows you see the wide columns separating the ranks and these make the tomb structure. Over one thousand warriors dug up, but many thousands more to go! We estimate eight thousand total! Eight thousand! All to guard one dead man from invading hordes of afterlife. Crazy funny, you see!"

Cheng Cheng is in front of them, his arms out wide, pointing here and there, as if he is a conductor and the motionless statues before him his musicians. The three of them stand on a viewing platform, and it's one of the most amazing things Sarah and Jago have ever seen, even with all their training and their knowledge of their own cultures' ancient sites and buildings. Even in the wake of beholding the Great White Pyramid.

"All the figures had paint, beautiful paint. Recently we found some perfectly preserved! Very secret, these, very secret. They used paint made of malachite, azurite, cinnabar, iron oxide, ground bones, even figured out how to make barium copper silicate and mix with the cinnabar to make beautiful vibrant lavender, you see.

And more: the bronze weapons! Some have blades coated with chrome-saline oxide. Amazing! They are like brand-new, right out of the blacksmither's. Sharp as the day they were born. And the crossbows are of highest quality. They shoot bolts over eight hundred meters!"

"Fascinating," Sarah says. She *is* impressed, but she gives Jago a look that says, *What about the disk?*

Jago shrugs.

He doesn't know.

Cheng Cheng turns to them and says with a wide grin, "Now, Wei said you have a nice picture. You have a nice picture?"

"Uh, yeah, I do," Jago says.

Sarah is relieved that maybe something more than meeting a funny little man will come of this.

"Let me see."

Sarah removes the folded sheet of paper from an outer pocket of Jago's pack and passes it to Cheng Cheng. He opens it and holds it in front of his face. He looks so closely that they can't see his expression. For 13 seconds he peers at Jago's detailed sketch.

Finally he lowers it. One of his chubby fingers is resting on the disk. His voice is low, serious. "Where did you see this?"

Jago says, "That? I made that up."

"No. You did not. Where did you see this?"

"Tell him," Sarah whispers.

Jago knows she's right. This is Endgame. Cheng Cheng is not a rival. All through his training his uncle and father told him to be receptive to luck, to chance, to help. Be ready to kill it, of course, if it turns bad, but all the same be open.

A tour group gathers next to them, 12 feet away. Jago says quietly, "We have one."

Cheng Cheng drops his arms in disbelief. "With you?"

"Yes," Sarah answers.

Cheng Cheng looks at them intently before saying, "Both of you, come with me." He begins to walk briskly away from the tour group and toward a rope with a sign that says NO ADMITTANCE.

An *blink* hides in a manicured bush on the edge of the *blink* complex. An asexual, computerized voice in his ear says, "One hundred thirty-two meters, west-southwest. Stationary."
He *blink* waits *blink* waits 30 seconds.
"One hundred thirty-two meters, west-southwest. Stationary."
He *blink* waits 30 seconds.
"One hundred thirty-two meters, west-southwest. Stationary."
He waits *blink* waits 30 seconds.
"One hundred twenty-six meters, west-southwest. Moving east."
He waits 30 *blink* seconds.
"One hundred one meters, west-southwest. Moving east-northeast."
He *blink* waits *blink* 30 seconds.
"Eighty-two meters, due east. Moving north."
He *blink* waits *blink* 30 seconds.
"Seventy-one meters, east-northeast. Moving north."
He waits 30 seconds.
"Fifty-eight meters, east-northeast. Stationary."
He waits *blink* waits 30 seconds.
"Fifty-five meters, east-northeast. Stationary."
He waits 30 seconds. *Blink.*
"Fifty-five meters, east-northeast. Stationary."
An *SHIVER* An consults his map. *BlinkSHIVERblink.* They are stopped *blink* stopped *blink* stopped on or near Pit *blink* Pit Four.
Which is *SHIVER* unexcavated.
Or so *blink* so everyone believes.
He moves too.

Chiyoko waits for the Olmec and the Cahokian to leave with the little man and slides away from the tour group. When the guards and the yammering guide are not looking, she vaults the railing and goes down to the floor. The floor with the silent, staring, waiting warriors.

For a spare moment she looks one directly in the eye. They are shocking creations. She feels a kinship to them unlike any she has ever felt for another living, breathing human.

Silent.

Staring.

Waiting warriors.

All of them.

Especially her.

She looks at her watch.

Sees the blue blip.

Runs.

"Come."

Cheng Cheng opens the flap of a white field tent erected on the grass. Jago and Sarah step in. A wooden railing is built around a hole in the ground 3.5 feet across. The hole is covered by two metal doors. Cheng Cheng pulls a small remote control from his pocket that has a single red button on it. He pushes it, and the doors open, revealing a rough stone staircase leading down into darkness.

"What's down there?" Sarah asks.

"Answers," Cheng Cheng says, working his way into the hole. "More questions, too. Come with me."

"Everyone with their fucking riddles," grumbles Jago as he follows Sarah. As they walk, motion detectors flip on a series of weak yellow lights.

"This is Pit Four," Cheng Cheng says over his shoulder.

Sarah says, "So Pit One isn't the only one you've dug up?"

"No. Geologic surveys show very interesting feature of Pit Four, one kept secret. Very secret. We only start digging last August."

"If it's so secret, why do you have a simple tent in the middle of a field covering it up?" Sarah asks.

Cheng Cheng chuckles. "Hide in plain sight. The best way. Hide in plain sight."

Chiyoko Takeda, who is just entering the tent and listening to the conversation on her earpiece, couldn't agree more.

"Besides, button on remote enables all kind of booby traps. You watch out!" Cheng Cheng says this so good-naturedly that they can't tell if he's telling the truth. Not even Jago, who is like a human lie detector. He casts a nervous glance toward the walls, looking for hidden poison darts or something else out of Indiana Jones. He doesn't notice anything. They continue through a narrow earthen tunnel supported by wooden beams, and eventually emerge in a star-shaped stone room. The floor is white alabaster. The walls are painted brilliant red. At chest height, going all around the room, are 12 painted depictions of disks. The paintings are so realistic that they look like photographs. Except for minor differences, they are the spitting image of the disk in Jago's bag. In the middle of the room is a single Terracotta Warrior holding a gleaming sword.
They step toward it. Jago notices another tunnel on the opposite side of the room. "What is this place?"
"Star Chamber," Cheng Cheng says. "We do not know exactly what it is for."

Chiyoko Takeda reaches the edge of the chamber. Peers in. Sees them. The warrior's back is to her. She needs to see more. See better. She finds a shadow a quarter of the way around the room. She'll go there. She raises a short tube to her lips and blows. Her action is silent, and so is the little projectile that sails across the room, but then it hits the far wall behind the others. It makes a slight rattling noise as it falls to the ground. They turn. Chiyoko slides quickly into the shadow.

"What was that?" Sarah asks.
"Ah, probably rock. Rocks always falling in here."
They look back to the warrior. Chiyoko is invisible.

"When we first open chamber we find one other warrior, but he is broken and shattered, probably by earthquake. He is not here now. He is at shop. Me and three others put him back together, piece by piece. I break the rules one night after lots of partying—fun!—and tell Wei and show him a photograph. Wei loves the Terracotta Warriors, maybe even more than me." Pause. "The photograph I show him was of the same man in your drawing."

"Really?" Jago asks.

"Really."

"So you have a disk too, then?" Sarah asks. "Since the guy in the picture is holding one."

"No. I do not." He hesitates. "The disk is like the statue, not like the sword. Weapons of the Terracotta Army are real. The disk is not. It is just clay." Cheng Cheng reaches out for the sword. Touches the exposed part of the hilt. "But there are other disks like the one in the picture."

"Where?" Jago says pointedly.

"Here, in China. At archives. They are called the disks of Baian-Kara-Ula. They were found in 1938, near Tibetan border. No one knows where they come from, or what they do. Many think they are gifts directly from the gods themselves! Crazy, yes? We think one of the disks is meant to go here"—he grabs the hilt—"but none fit right. So I was wondering, could I see yours?"

Sarah and Jago look at each other. Jago nods. Sarah nods back. Jago unslings his backpack. "Okay." He opens it and removes the prize from kepler 22b and holds it out to Cheng Cheng.

Chiyoko's breath is as silent as a leaf on a branch on a still day.

Cheng Cheng takes the disk reverently. "This . . . this is perfect."

BLINK.

An Liu creeps to the opening *blink* of the chamber. He has on *blink* he has on *blink* his ballistics vest. His motorcycle helmet. A thick collar is turned up to cover the rear of his neck. His *blink* his *SHIVER* his heart is racing.

This is Endgame, at last. Here. *Blinkblink*. Now. Right before the noise and *blink* and *blink* the death.

An does not notice Chiyoko. Chiyoko does not notice him.

Cheng Cheng continues: "Where did you get this?"

Jago gives the little man a hard look. The jewels on his teeth glitter. "A friend gave it to me."

Cheng Cheng understands that Jago is not going to tell him more. "Of course." He inspects the disk. Turns it over. "I can't . . . this is incredible. My friend Musterion must see this."

"Who's Musterion?" Sarah asks.

"Musterion Tsoukalos. A man obsessed with the visitations of old. He lives in Capo di Ponte, northern Italy. He can help you with this disk. He knows them very, very well. Knows that they came from the heavens in the days before days, in the history before history. He knows that they helped to make us what we are, and he will know where this disk belongs."

An *blink* removes a *blink* a black object the size and shape of a softball from a *blink* bag. He *blink* puts it on the ground and *blink* pushes a button. He rolls it *blinkblinkblink* silently into the room.

Sarah and Jago do not see the ball, but Chiyoko does. She looks to the entrance and catches a glimpse of An spinning away. She steps from the shadows. Jago and Sarah notice her immediately. *How can she be here?* Sarah is about to pounce when the Mu player looks at them wildly, claps her hands three times, and points at the ground.

Blinkblinkblink SHIVER. What was *blink* what was that? An looks back and *blinkblinkblinkblinkblinkblink* sees Chiyoko—precious, invaluable, essential Chiyoko—pointing at the ball!

SHIVERblink.

SHIVERSHIVERSHIVER.

Seven seconds.

Seven short seconds to destruction.

Seven short seconds and no more Chiyoko Takeda, the one who can make him whole.

Of late struck One; and now I see the prime
Of day break from the pregnant east: 'tis time
I vanish: more I had to say,
But night determines here;(Away!^{lvii}

SHARI CHOPRA, BAITSAKHAN

Fashion Europe Wig Factory Warehouse, Chengdu, China

The music has stopped.

Bat and Bold return, each of them carrying a briefcase.

Jalair is leaning over Shari, yanking her nose hairs out one by one with a pair of silver tweezers.

Shari's eyes are watering, but still she hasn't made a noise.

Baitsakhan sees his cousins and claps his hands excitedly. "Wonderful! Come, you two. Show us what toys you've brought."

Bat and Bold put the cases on a table. The table has pliers, a small handsaw, an assortment of clamps, and a coil of thin-gauge cable. There is a plastic bottle containing some kind of unknown liquid. A lighter. Two pairs of large noise-canceling headphones.

Bat clicks the clasps on one of the cases and pries it open.

Baitsakhan leans over. Inside are twin all-black Sig Sauer P225s and four clips. Baitsakhan pulls a pistol out of the foam casing and hits the magazine release. The magazine drops out; the chamber is empty. Jalair steps aside as Baitsakhan sights the unloaded gun on Shari's forehead and pulls the trigger. She doesn't even blink. The pistol has good action. He reinserts the magazine and slaps it home. He racks the slide to charge a round, makes sure the safety is on, and puts the pistol on the table. He turns it so that the barrel faces Shari.

"Think, Harrapan. Think."

Nothing.

"Speak, and this"—he indicates the gun with his eyes—"will end the game for you."

Nothing.

"Don't speak, and these"—he sweeps his hands over the tools, the bottle, the lighter—"will end the game for you."

Nothing. Shari spits on the floor. Her left eye is swollen shut. She wonders if her Little Alice is taking a nap. If she is hugging her gray bunny.

Baitsakhan is beginning to lose patience with this one, whose eyes give nothing away, who won't even cry out. It's like talking to one of his horses. He misses his horses. Annoyed as he is, Baitsakhan forces a smile. "I'll give you until tonight to decide."

As Baitsakhan turns away from Shari, Bat and Bold each put on a pair of the large headphones.

"Come, brother," Baitsakhan says to Jalair. He picks up Shari's detached finger. It is gray and puffy and still wears the ring her husband gave her. He uses the severed digit to push play on the iPod. A loud, terrifying scream tears loose from the speakers.

Maybe that will break her concentration, Baitsakhan thinks.

A brother, Shari notes, watching as two of her torturers leave. *Another weakness.*

Bat and Bold watch her. She watches them. The scream continues, unabated, like a raging river of fear. Shari knows that it will not stop. It doesn't matter. She will retreat into her mind, bask in her rediscovered calm.

She watches the two boys. Baitsakhan and his brother are gone. She is safe for the moment. And for the first time she prays. She prays to Pashupati and the Shiva and the Great Tiger.

She prays for luck and deliverance.

But mostly she prays for vengeance.

24.4322, 123.0161[lviii]

AN LIU, CHIYOKO TAKEDA, SARAH ALOPAY, JAGO TLALOC

Terracotta Warriors Museum, Secret Star Chamber, Lintong District, Xi'an, China

Six seconds.

"Where did she come from?" Cheng Cheng asks, alarmed at the sudden presence of Chiyoko. He clutches the disk to his chest, afraid of this stranger who inconveniently showed up just as he's about to unlock the secret of his life's work. Cheng Cheng has not noticed An's little present, or he would have more reason to be afraid.

The ball rolls to a stop at the feet of the ancient stone warrior.

"An Liu!" Sarah shouts.

Blinkblinkblinkblinkblink.

And there he is, the Shang, rushing into the Star Chamber, tackling Chiyoko to the ground.

Five seconds.

Cheng Cheng says, "What is—?"

Sarah grabs Cheng Cheng and pulls him toward the opening at the opposite side of the chamber. She saw what An Liu did to Marcus back at the Calling and knows what he's capable of. They have to move quickly.

Jago snatches the disk away from Cheng Cheng, who tumbles onto his knees in the entrance to the tunnel. Sarah starts to go back for him, but Jago grabs her hand and drags her forward.

"Forget him!"

Three seconds.

An pulls Chiyoko to the other tunnel, making sure to keep his armored body in between her and the bomb.

"Go!" he says to her. They're close, touching, and his tic is completely gone. As they move away, Chiyoko peers over her shoulder, hoping that the disk is safe.

One second.

Jago and Sarah run, hunched, into the darkness.

Zero seconds.

Boom.

The force of the explosion throws Jago and Sarah 23 feet forward. Lucky for them, Cheng Cheng, still hunched in the tunnel's opening, acts as a kind of sacrificial plug, shielding the Olmec and the Cahokian from the worst of the blast.

They look up, relieved to be alive. But then the first rocks begin to fall around them.

The tunnel is collapsing.

"Move!" Sarah says. She is in front now and can hear Jago coughing a few feet behind her.

They run as fast as they can through the pitch black, the walls shaking, dirt and rocks falling on their heads and gathering at their heels. For 30, 40, 50 feet there is no light, and Sarah, keeping her arms in front of her, continually plows straight into walls before figuring out which way to turn.

"It's too dark!" she yells. She can feel Jago's hand curled on the back of her shirt.

The air is choked with dust. Breathing is hard. A low rumbling builds behind them. Jago has to put his mouth against her ear to be heard. "Keep going unless you wanna be buried alive!"

In the other tunnel, Chiyoko is out cold. An is lying on top of her, coughing. He puts his fingers to her neck. Her heart is beating and her breath is steady, but his fingers come back hot and sticky. Blood.

Oh God, what have I done? An thinks desperately, as he licks the blood from his fingertips. *My tics are still gone; her chi is that strong. I must have it.*

He stands. Pulls a green glow stick from his vest, shakes it and snaps it, illuminates the tunnel. He hears a rumbling nearby, but this tunnel was farther outside the blast radius than the one the others ran toward. An and Chiyoko should be spared any cave-ins. He hopes the others aren't so lucky.

He looks down at the Mu Player. She has a lump on her head above her right eye and some scratches on her cheeks. The blood is coming from her neck. He holds the glow stick near.

Please no, please no.

He pulls at the skin and she moans.

Not the carotid artery. Not the carotid artery.

"There!" Jago shouts.

A sliver of light appears in front of them. As they sprint toward it, the lit space widens and grows. Sarah digs deep and finds another gear—she has always taken comfort in the fact that she is the fastest person she has ever known—and her step lightens as she cruises across the shaking floor.

Jago can see now, the tunnel dimly illuminated from the light up ahead. He lets go of Sarah's shirt, realizing that he doesn't have much choice. She's so much faster than he is.

Sarah reaches the end of the tunnel and makes a sharp turn, and she's out. She skids to a stop just inches from a sword that looks primed to take her head off. Another Player lying in wait, ready to attack?

No, just one of the clay warriors. Her adrenaline still pumping hard, Sarah breathes a sigh of relief. Then Jago crashes into her back and they fall to the ground.

Behind him, a plume of dust ejects from the tunnel as it fills with earth. The Star Chamber is buried once more.

"Sorry," Jago mutters as he helps her up.

"Glad you caught up," Sarah replies, glancing at the wreckage behind them.

Wordlessly, Jago brushes the dust from his eyes. Sarah studies him. He looks wounded somehow, disappointed; it's the same look opposing goalies used to give her on the soccer field.

"You know, it wasn't a race," she says.

Jago looks up at her. "Wasn't it?"

Before Sarah can reply, someone shouts at them.

They are back in Pit One, at the rear of one of the long rows of ancient guardians. The viewing platform is about 30 m away. Tourists point in their direction. Guards yell in Chinese.

"We better go," says Jago.

No blood squirts out of Chiyoko's neck. It's just a gash. It will need stitches, though. An Liu hoists Chiyoko over his shoulder and walks slowly through the tunnels, the ghostly, ethereal light of the glow stick showing the way. He makes it back to the tent, sets her gingerly down. The light is better. He can see.

He removes the flak jacket and his motorcycle helmet. The back of the jacket is jagged with shards of clay from the exploded warriors. It is good that he wore it. Good that he shielded her. He examines the rest of her body and she is whole. Only bleeding from her neck. The only concerns now are an infection of the wound and possible concussion from the head contusion.

An smiles. No tics, no shivers, no stutter. He marvels at the clarity of his mind. He has no idea how, but the girl does this to him, something in her or of her. He must get it from her.

Whatever he has to do, however he has to do it.

He unrolls a field kit. Pulls a syringe. Shoots the skin around the wound with a lidocaine-epinephrine mixture. Chiyoko moans again. An knows that the injection stings, usually more than the injury itself. He waits 12 seconds and pulls the skin aside and douses it with iodine and saline. He pulls the skin together and closes the gash with butterfly bandages. The stitches will come when they arrive back at his place.

He checks her pulse.

Strong.

Her breath.

Good.

He hears shots being fired in the direction of the entrance, half a kilometer to the southwest.

He puts his helmet back on and pulls her over his narrow, hunched shoulders and leaves the tent and makes his way back to his motorcycle.

He walks calmly, steadily, easily, her spell still working on him.

He feels young and strong and nervous. It is the best feeling he can ever remember having.

And he's never going to let it go.

"Follow me!" Jago yells, bobbing and weaving through the statues. Sarah follows, hot on his heels. The guards are after them, clambering down the metal stairs, yelling and pointing. The guides usher the tourists from the action.

"They must think we blew up the tunnel!" Sarah says, running.

A guard plants his feet wide on the platform. He raises a pistol and aims it at them. They keep moving through the warriors, making sharp turns, keeping their movements unpredictable.

The guard fires and the shot echoes through the hangar, zinging past Jago's head and blowing apart the shoulder of a nearby warrior.

"Guns at a tourist spot!" shouts Sarah, a little shocked. "Are they nuts?"

"It's China. They take this shit seriously," Jago replies. Back in Juliaca, he had men shoot at him for much less.

Sarah sprints by a warrior holding a crossbow. She pulls the weapon from the statue's hands. It's loaded, ready, untouched for two millennia. She hopes it still works. The guard fires again, and this shot goes just wide of Jago's head. Sarah skids to a stop and drops to her knees, bringing the stock of the crossbow to her shoulder in a single motion. She's trained with crossbows, killed deer with them, hit targets from 300 yards. But never anything like this. She tries to center herself and pulls the release.

The power of the ancient bow surprises her, and the bolt flies fast and true. It strikes the guard's hands, moves straight through them, and he drops the gun on the floor and starts screaming.

"They built good crossbows," Sarah says, impressed not just with it but with herself. Jago snorts, shocked that the old weapon even functioned at all.

Three more guards appear on their level, coming directly toward them. Jago isn't going to take any chances with the ancient bows. He grabs a sword from one of the statues and runs directly at the nearest guard, keeping a wall on his right. The guard is young and scared. He raises his gun. When Jago draws close, he angles his body and plants his feet on the wall, using his momentum to keep running, his body parallel to the ground, for several feet. In this way Jago gets around the awestruck guard, and when he's behind him, he hits the back of the guard's neck hard with the butt end of the sword's hilt. The guard goes down in a heap.

Sarah throws the crossbow away and runs for the guard nearest her. She executes a perfect flying forward flip as the guard shoots and misses. She lands right in front of him and pushes hard into the middle of his chest with the heels of both palms. He drops his gun and collapses, gasping for air.

"Here!" Jago yells, sprinting toward an open door under the platform. Sarah grabs another crossbow from the final line of soldiers and follows him to the exit. They spill out into the daylight, their eyes blinking. There are no guards nearby. Not yet, anyway.

"Over there!" Sarah says, pointing toward a parking lot. They cover the 40 yards in under 4.5 seconds and skid to a stop next to a blue Chery Fulwin hatchback. The windows are rolled down. Jago throws the sword into the backseat and climbs into the driver's seat. He leans under the steering wheel and tears off the fuse panel and within four seconds the car is on.

"You've done that before," Sarah says, impressed.

"Like you haven't." Jago grins at her.

"Not that fast."

Jago smirks, wondering if she's trying to make him feel better. Whatever, it's working. He puts it in reverse just as half a dozen guards appear at the edge of the lot. "Buckle up."

Three guards close in behind the car as Jago guns it, doing a perfect J-turn right out of the parking spot. Two of the guards jump away, and the last gets nailed by the side of the little car. Jago drops the car into 2nd gear and floors it. They peel out of the lot, breaking through a checkpoint. The guards gather in front of them like a swarm, waving hands and pistols, as the car speeds down the hill toward the main road. A large metal gate is sliding closed behind the guards.

It's going to be close.

Two men move to help the gate close faster, and shots are fired. Jago and Sarah hunker behind the dashboard. The windshield is peppered with bullets, turned into a white wall of webbing. Sarah sinks lower in her seat and kicks her feet up—once, twice—knocking the windshield loose. Jago can see again.

The gate is more than half closed. They're not going to make it.

"We can plow through!" yells Jago.

"Not in this piece of crap," Sarah says back, tugging at her seat belt. "You ever see crash-test dummies in Peru?"

Jago puts the screaming engine in fourth, tries to squeeze every ounce of power out of it.

The guards scatter as the car comes for them. The two assisting the gate turn and run. It's only 3/4ths closed now, but that will be enough to stop them.

Sarah squints at the guard booth. She thinks she can see the panel that operates the gate. There are two guards standing in front of it, watching, dumbfounded, not to mention a window in the way. They're traveling at high speed, have seconds until impact. It's an impossible shot.

Trust your training, Sarah. Don't overthink it. That's what Tate would say. Don't overthink it.

Sarah kicks the crossbow into her hands from the footwell and, without even shouldering it, shoots.

The bolt sails between the two guards, shatters the window, and just nicks the key that operates the gate mechanism. It turns in the opposite direction; the gate slowly grinds backward just as their car reaches it. Sparks shoot up along the doors, the side mirrors ricocheting off, but they're through.

As they drive away, the bewildered guards disappearing in the distance, Sarah screams with pleasure and Jago just laughs.

41.252363, -95.997988[lix]

AISLING KOPP

Calvary Cemetery, Queens, New York, United States

Thousands of miles away, Aisling Kopp stares tiredly at a headstone. She doesn't want to be here, the cemetery unpopulated on this sunny day, at least by the living. She should be back in China or Turkey or somewhere else, following the clues of Endgame. Even though it was her clue, in a way, that brought her back to New York, far away from the action.

The headstone belongs to Declan Kopp. Aisling's father.

"Why'd you make me come here?" Aisling asks the old man standing next to her. "This some kinda motivational thing? 'Cause we coulda just done that on the phone, Pop."

Aisling's grandfather seems lost in thought. He snaps to when she speaks, turning his bad, milky-white eye toward her. His hands are folded peacefully behind his back. He is missing three fingers on his left hand. He has a bushy white beard and long white hair still tinged with traces of orange. Decades ago, this man was a Player. Just like his son, Declan, was a Player.

Aisling's father, in the ground, dead for almost as long as Aisling's been alive.

It was her grandfather who trained Aisling. He taught her everything she knows. He was there, in the dirt next to her, spotting for her, when Aisling made her first kill. It was with the same reliable Brugger & Thomet APR308 sniper rifle that now sits at Aisling's feet, broken down and packed away in a sleek black case. That first kill, the expression of pride on her grandfather's face, it is one of Aisling's fondest memories.

And that is why, when Pop insisted that she come back home just as Endgame had finally begun, Aisling begrudgingly complied. It was the clue that had set her grandfather off. Aisling had told him the random string of numbers over the phone, and her grandfather had used a tone of voice she'd never heard before.

Afraid.

All because of 19090416. Whatever that was supposed to mean.

So Aisling had hopped two trains and four planes and ended up back in Queens, worn out from traveling and wanting to move on as quickly as possible. As much as she loves him, Aisling knows that the time for men like her grandfather is past. The work of the trainers is done.

"I have never told you how your father died," Pop says matter-of-factly.

Aisling glances at her chunky pink wristwatch. "You're picking now?"

"Wasn't important until now," muses her grandfather. "But I think They want you to know. For whatever reason."

Aisling thinks about that kepler thing. She'd hate to have to guess at its motivations, at what it knows, and why. Luckily, she doesn't have to. Endgame is simple. Kill or be killed.

"What gives you that idea?"

"Your numbers: they're the day he died, mixed up."

Aisling sniffs, feeling incredibly dumb for not figuring *that* out. "That's some pretty simple coding for big-shot aliens."

"Like I said, child, they wanted you to figure it out. It's the *why* that's troubling."

"Go on, Pop."

"Your father, after eligibility passed him by, he couldn't let Endgame go. He spent years studying it. Studying *Them*. Trying to figure it all out."

Aisling remembers one of her first lessons, something Pop has ingrained in her since childhood. "It's not for us to know," she says. "What will be will be."

"That's what I've always taught you, child, but . . ." Her grandfather raises a hand. "Your father, he had some ideas. Wasn't a popular man amongst our line. Had you with an outsider, bless her. When the High Council decided you'd grow up to be a Player, he took it badly."

Aisling is paying attention now. She's never heard so much about her mother and father, has always known better than to ask. But now the floodgates are open. "What'd he do?"

"He fled. Killed the active Player in the process. Took the stone, your birthright, and you. You were just a babe, years away from eligibility. He said he was breaking the cycle."

"What the hell does that mean? That he was going to end our line?"

Her grandfather sighs, shaking his head. "Presumably, but I never really knew for certain. The High Council sent me to find the two of you, and the stone, and eventually I did. And I restored order to our line."

It takes a moment for this to sink in. "You killed him," Aisling states.

Pop nods. "My son. Your father. Through the scope of the rifle at our feet. Yes."

Aisling exhales slowly through her nose. She's not sure how to interpret this, not sure what to do with this information.

Her grandfather holds out a folded piece of paper. "These are the coordinates of where he took you. Where he died. Maybe They want you to go there."

Aisling takes the piece of paper, glancing at it. Somewhere in Italy. She stuffs it into her back pocket. "Go there and do what?"

Her grandfather shakes his head. "Perhaps see what your father did. Perhaps understand like he did."

"But he didn't want to *win*," Aisling says, surprised by her own ferocity. She's suddenly angry with her father, a man she doesn't remember, for trying, somehow, to buck Endgame. For putting her in the middle. For forcing Pop to carry around all this guilt for years.

"No," says her grandfather. "He wanted to *know*. Perhaps, child, you can do both."

CHRISTOPHER VANDERKAMP

Grand Mercure Hotel, Room 172, Huímín Square, Xi'an, China

Christopher gets a call from the concierge. Kala is leaving. She has her
bags and is headed to the airport.

It's a little early, so Christopher doesn't worry. The flight is in five
hours, and even if the traffic is horrible, it will take only two hours to
get to Xi'an Xianyang International Airport. Sarah used to like to get an
early start on things, too. Maybe that's something the Players all have
in common: anal overpreparedness.

He showers, gets dressed, packs a small bag. Once again he's going to
leave most of what he has with him in the room. He doesn't want it,
doesn't need it. As long as he has his passport and his credit cards,
he can move, live, search for Sarah. Sure, he received an angry and
worried email from his mom two days ago, but the credit still hasn't
been turned off.

In the taxi, he turns on his smartphone and flips through pictures.
Of Sarah, of the two of them together. He started taking them when
she was 14, when they were in 8th grade. They'd only been dating for
a year, maybe less. It scares him to think that there was so much he
didn't know about her. She had a whole other life when she was away
from him: the training she went through, the terrifying skills she
acquired, the violent trials she endured. And somehow, when she was
with him, she was still Sarah. The Sarah he'd always loved.

The driver turns on the radio, and he hears a man singing a love song
in Chinese, and he's brought out of his memories and reminded of
where he is and what he's doing. He looks at a picture: Sarah standing
in front of her parents' car just before they went on a camping trip to

the Grand Canyon. They probably weren't going to the Grand Canyon at all. Another lie.

He should be mad at her, angry that she lied to him for all these years. Angry that she said she was going to the Grand Canyon, or soccer camp, or piano lessons, when really she was training to become a ruthless killer. He should be scared of her. But he's not. He's scared at how much he still loves her, no matter who she is, no matter what she's done, no matter what he doesn't know. She's waving in the picture.

He smiles.

Says, "I love you."

And waves back.

SO ΛΜΛΛΙΦΛ ΚΛΙSΛRΙS ΥΛΛΕΝSΙS ΠΝS ΝΛSΙΛΛ
FRΛΜ FRΠΜΙSTSΛHΛ HΠΠΝΛΝΕ.   ΠΝS FRΛΓΛF
FΛRΦΛ ΠFΛR ΛΟΝΛRΙS GΛH ΙΝ ΦRΛΚΛ FRΙΦΠ.

ΛΠΠΙΚΙΝΠS GΛH ΜΛΧΙΜΠS ΠΝSΙS ΛΝΛΝΕΜΠΝ
ΥΛΙRRΠΒΛ, ΛΛΠΗT ΠΝSΙS ΓΛFΠΝ.   ΛΝΛ
ΦΛΜΜΛ ΛΛΠΗTΛΙSΚΛ ΛTΛΕΥΕΙΝS ΦΛRΕΙ
ΠSΥΕΜΠΝ ΦΛΝS ΒΛTΙSTΛΝS ΠΝSΛRΛΝS.

ΛΛΛΥΙΥΠS SΛ ΜΙΚΛS ΓΛSTΙΚΛΝS ΥΛRΦ ΙΝ HRΠRR
ΦΛΙRΗ ΛFΜΛRΖΕΙΝ ΥΛΛΕΝSΙS.   HΛΛΙSΛΙΥ
ΛΝΛ ΛΛΕΙΝΛΙ ΦΛΛΠΗ ΙΚ ΛFΛRΛΛΙSTΙΦS ΥΛS
SΥΕ ΛΙΝS.

SΛ ΒΛΓΜS SΛΕΙ ΥΛRΦ ΓΕΛRΛΝSΙΦS FRΛΜ
HΙΝΛΛRΥΕΙSΕΙΝ RΠΜΟΝΕ ΥΛHSGΙΦ ΛFTRΛ
SΥΙΝΦS.   ΦΛΙ ΦΕRΥΙΝΓΟS ΓΛΛΕSΠΝ ΛFTRΛ,
ΜΙΦΓΛTΙΜRΙΛΕΛΝΝ ΛFTRΛ, ΓΛSΥΙΝΦΝΟΛΕΛΝΝ
ΙΦ ΦΟ TΛΠΙΛΕΛΝΝ SΝΙΠΜΠΝΛΟ.

ΟΛΙΥΛ ΜΛΓ ΙΚ SΥΛ ΒΛΙΝΛS ΥΛΛΕΝSΛ GΛH
ΛΛΛΛΜΜΛ RΕΙRGΛ RΠΜΟΝΕ.   ΕΙS ΒΙΥΕΜΠΝ
SΙΝTΕΙΝΟ ΓΠTΦΙΝΛΛ ΛHΛΚS FRΙΦΛΝS ΥΛΙRΦΙΦ
ΝΙΝ ΛΙΥ.

FΛΝR GΕRΛ HΠΝΛΛ GΛH ΜΛΙS TΛΝΗΛΝS ΥΛRΦ
RΠΜΛ FRΛΜ ΛRΛΠΗTΙΝΛ ΒΛΛΥΛΥΕΙSΛ.
FRΛΝGΙΝΟΛΕΛΝΝ ΦΛΙRΗ ΓΛΙS SΥΛ ΜΛΝΛΓΛΜ
RΠΝGΛΜ ΕΙ ΥΛΙRΦΛΝ ΦΛΙ ΛΙΝΛΗΛΝ.

ΥΛΛΕΝS SΚΛΛ ΥΙSΛΝ SΛ ΙFTΠΜΛ.   SΠΝGΙS ΙST
ΛΝ ΒΙΥΙΜΛΝ ΦΛΝS ΦΕRΥΙΝΓΛΝS.   ΦRΟΦΦΙΛΛ
ΙΚ FΛΝRΛ ΛΛΦΟΝ ΦΟ ΜΙΚΙΛΟΝ.   ΒRΠRGΛ ΦΟ
FΛΛRΕΙΝSΚRΛΜΛ ΛΙRΙΖΛΝΕ ΜΕΙΝΕ.

ΛTTΙΝΗΛ ΕΙΖ ΜΕΙΝ GΛH TΙΝΗΛ ΦΙΝΛΛ ΜΕΙΝΛ.
ΥΕΙS FRΛΥΙSTGΛΜ ΛΠΠΙΚΙΝΛΝ GΛH ΥΛΛΕΝS
ΠSΥΙΜΛΜ.

ΟΛΖΠΗ ΛΛΛS ΜΙΦ ΒΛΟΛΛ FΠΛΝΙΦ.
RΠΜΛ ΛRΛΝSGΙΦ.

SARAH ALOPAY, JAGO TLALOC

G5 Jingkun Expressway, China

Sarah and Jago are also on their way to the Xi'an Xianyang airport. They ditched the Fulwin and stole a Brilliance Junjie wagon, of which there are literally tens of millions on the roads of China. Nobody looks at the car; nobody notices them. While Sarah drives, Jago plays Tetris on his phone.

"We were pretty good back there, Feo."

"We sure were," he says. "I knew we would be."

"I've never seen anyone pull that walking on the wall stuff in real life."

"It's all in the sneakers," says Jago, feigning modesty. "Hell of a shot with that gate. Even though we were going to make it."

Sarah smiles and shrugs, mimicking Jago's nonchalance. "As long as we keep taking turns saving each other, this'll play out just fine."

Jago suppresses a smile.

"Yeah, I guess that's a pretty good plan."

"We should get cleaned up before we get to the airport," she says.

"There. That gas station."

She pulls off the road and they take turns in the bathroom. Sarah puts her long hair into a tight bun. Puts on eyeliner to darken her eyes. Changes her bra and underwear. Changes all her clothes, throws the dirty ones in the garbage. It's crazy, but she's feeling good. Different. More confident. Maybe, as with everything else, Endgame gets easier just by doing it.

Jago splashes water on his dusty body and watches the red water swirl down the drain. He puts fake enamel fronts over his jeweled inlaid teeth. He dons a pair of flashy and expensive sunglasses. He puts on a black silk shirt and leaves it half open.

They head for the airport. While Jago again distracts himself with Tetris, Sarah keeps her eyes on the rearview mirror. Something is nagging at her.

"I can't believe those two followed us," Sarah says. "How did they do that?"

"Couldn't be following us. I'd notice," Jago replies. Then he looks down at the phone in his hands. He turns it over and rips out the battery, examining it. "Tracking us, somehow."

"Yeah, and worse, they're doing it separately. Chiyoko wasn't expecting An to be there. She tried to warn us."

Jago screws up his face. "Then why did he try to save her?"

"Got me." Sarah pauses. "You think he did? Save her?"

"I hope not. I hope both of those crazy bastards bought it."

"Agreed. But how *did* they find us?" She watches Jago examining his phone. "Phone tracers? Internet trails? A chip?"

"All possible. So we scrap the phones for new ones ASAP and use the internet as little as we can and only at public terminals."

"What about chips?" Sarah wonders. "When could we have gotten tagged?"

They both know.

"The Calling," Sarah says. "That's the only place."

"What are we going to do?"

Silence for a moment.

Sarah says, "Until we have time to get scanned for real, we're going to have to check each other out. Like, all over. *Every*where. We can't take any chances."

Jago can't help it: his heart quickens at the idea of looking closely at Sarah's naked body. And, in spite of everything, Sarah's heart also quickens at the prospect.

"When?" Jago asks, maybe a little too eagerly.

"Slow down, Paco," Sarah says with a smile. "Soon."

"No, what I mean is—before we get on a plane?"

Sarah curls her lips. "If it's easy, but not at the expense of getting the hell out of China. It's too damn hot here."

Jago nods in agreement. He puts his hand out his window, letting the warm air pass over it, and thinks about the best ways to comb for chips. They'll want to be thorough. . . .

Sarah clears her throat. "So. Where should we go?"

Jago looks at her. "Italy, right? It was Cheng Cheng's last wish that we find his buddy."

"Maybe, but I've been thinking about my clue. At first I thought the numbers were coded letters, but they're not. They're just numbers."

"Meaning?"

"I think they're coordinates. But they're jumbled. I need some time."

"We need to leave, though."

"I say we fly somewhere between here and Italy. And then stay off the grid the rest of the way. Stay out of airports and off plane manifests, even with aliases."

Jago runs through lists in his head. Names, places, connections.

"How's Iraq sound to you?" he asks.

"Iraq?"

"I have a line member in Mosul who can help us. He can get anything—and believe me, anything is gettable in Iraq. We can take a day or two. If you still need to tinker with your clue, you can do it in peace there."

Sarah looks at Jago. "Well, then, I guess we're going to Iraq."

CHRISTOPHER VANDERKAMP

Xi'an Xianyang International Airport, Terminal 2, China

Christopher arrives at the airport.

Sarah could be here. If Kala is leaving China, then it stands to reason the other Players are on their way out as well.

He doesn't see Kala, but he's not worried about it. He knows he'll see her eventually.

Sarah could be waiting in line right now.

He gets his boarding pass at the desk. Doesn't check any bags.

Buying a ticket.

He walks along the glass windows toward security.

Or is she already dead? Am I chasing a ghost?

He doesn't look outside. He's leaving Xi'an, and he won't return, so why bother looking at that which he is turning his back on?

No, I'd know if she were dead; I'd feel it somehow.

He walks through the airport, loses himself in the sounds, the smells, the crowd. He doesn't notice the couple stepping away from the ticket counter, walking easily, hand in hand, trying to look as though they had nothing to do with what is being called a terrorist attack at the Terracotta Army only 132 minutes ago.

Christopher reaches the screening area, turns his back on China.

And without knowing how close he is, he turns his back on his love, the object of his pursuit, his best friend, the girl of his dreams, Sarah Alopay.

CHIYOKO TAKEDA

Liu Residence, Unregistered Belowground Property, Tongyuanzhen, Gaoling County, Xi'an, China

Chiyoko wakes from a bucolic dream with a start. The smelling salts are sour, harsh, painful. Her head throbs.

What happened?

An Liu leans over her.

An Liu the maniac.

Yes, it comes back: the Star Chamber, the Olmec and the Cahokian, the explosion.

The disk.

She wonders if they made it out alive. If An Liu has the disk, or if he even knows about it. If the disk is still buried down there, with the Olmec and the Cahokian, then she must go back for it. She knows what it holds and where it leads. She needs that disk. Now.

Chiyoko tries to stand, but her head is too heavy. An watches her closely, not making any move to help her.

She gives herself over to her disorientation and weariness. She concentrates her rattled chi and wills herself to forget the disk and be in the present.

Be here, and everything will work out.

Be here.

She rises to her elbows and looks at An.

Something about him is different.

He puts out his hands in a conciliatory gesture and says, "Wait, please" in Mandarin.

An has decided not to kill Chiyoko and drink her blood or tan her skin and wear it. That would be foolish, for it might not work. This—her, alive, in his presence—is what works. So this is how he has decided to play it.

This is his Endgame now.

"I won't hurt you, I promise," he says, and Chiyoko can see he is telling the truth. "And you can leave whenever you want. I promise that too."

That, however, is a lie, which she can also see.

She will have to be careful about this one. He is a delicate little madman.

She is in a small bedroom in a concrete building. The room is spare; there's a chair, a small table, a pitcher of ice water, and a plastic cup. On one wall hangs a curling poster of an ancient gingko tree in the yellowing throes of autumn. On another a dirty window with bars on it. On a 3rd a wall-mounted air conditioner. Not many escape options. The open door, six feet from the foot of the bed, is metal and has three deadbolts on it. The deadbolts are on the outside of the door. She is to be kept here; there is no question in her mind.

She cannot be kept here. There is no time. The disk must be recovered.

"How do you feel?" An asks.

Chiyoko tilts her head back and forth. *So-so*, the gesture says.

"You were hurt. You hit your head and I stitched a deep cut on your neck." Chiyoko touches the patch of gauze taped to her skin. "I was afraid you'd had a concussion, but your eyes have not dilated and your breathing and pulse are regular. I brought you away from that place."

He doesn't usually talk this much, but these are the most effortless words An can ever remember speaking.

Chiyoko mimes for something to write with.

"Of course," An says, and goes to the table. He hands her a pad of paper and a red crayon.

She won't be able to stab him with a crayon. He is smart, cautious.

Chiyoko will have to be smarter.

Thank you, she writes effortlessly in Mandarin.

An risks a smile. "You're welcome."

Where?

"My place."

Xi'an?

He considers his answer. "Yes."

My stuff?

"In my room. Safe."

Why am I here?

An looks at her, not sure how to explain. Chiyoko impatiently taps the crayon on the pad of paper.

"Because . . ." An looks away, nervous.

Chiyoko taps the crayon on the question again. Red smudges form over the word *why.*

"Because you make me feel good."

Chiyoko gives him a quizzical look. And that's when she realizes what is different about him. When she remembers the pause in their fight at the hardware store. What he said about feeling whole, and young.

Your stutter, she writes.

An nods. "I have stuttered since I was a small boy. I have stutters and tics and they torment me. But not anymore."

An meets Chiyoko's eyes. There is gratitude in his look, but also something else. Something passionate and possessive. Chiyoko isn't yet sure how to play this. This boy thinks she has cured his twitching. She decides to play dumb, gesturing to herself and cocking her head confusedly.

"Yes, you. I'm different near you. Healed."

Chiyoko is expressionless. He has just put himself at an incredible disadvantage. She decides that she must break him to pieces. Quickly. And then put him back together.

The first part will be tricky.

The second easy.

I want my things, she writes, shoving the pad at him.

An shakes his head. Chiyoko stares at him for a moment, brings the pad back down to her lap. She takes her time with the next sentence, writing as clearly as she can with the crayon.

I will not be your prisoner.

An shakes his head again. "I don't want you to be. We can do this together."

He means Endgame. Chiyoko has to resist the urge to roll her eyes. She does not do alliances. She is a loner. A soloist.

Chiyoko pretends to think this over. Writes, *Is this all you do?*

She mimes pulling the pin out of a grenade, lobs it, and then makes an explosion with her hands.

"Confusion. Disruption. Death," An says. "It's all I *need* to do."

Is it? she writes.

An gives her a puzzled look, as if the answer were obvious. "That's what Endgame is. Uncertainty and death."

Chiyoko takes a moment before writing, *Is that what you were taught?*

An shudders almost imperceptibly, his tic shooting through him for a millisecond. She has hit on something. She reaches out and squeezes his hand, tapping the question insistently.

"N-n-n-n-none of your business," he blurts, ashamed, and storms away.

Chiyoko drops the pad and crayon in her lap and claps hard. An freezes before reaching the door. He turns to her, his eyes downcast like a scolded dog's. Chiyoko swings her legs over the side of the bed. She puts some weight on her feet. She feels good. She can run if she has to. But she's not ready to fight. Not yet.

She writes something. An watches. When she is finished, she holds up the pad and taps it with two fingers. An comes back to her and she gives him the pad.

I won't hurt you. I promise.

His words. Turned back on him.

An reads the words over and over again. No one has ever made that promise to An without breaking it. Without their words being a trick. But because it is Chiyoko—beautiful, gentle, powerful Chiyoko—he believes.

For the first time that he can remember, he believes that something good is actually good. Not, as is usually the case, that something bad is good. Like carnage, death, the meteorites, a well-placed bomb, a body blown to bits, blood on hands or walls or faces. Those are good things, and everything else is lies.

It is a strange feeling.

"Can you walk?" he asks quietly.

Chiyoko nods.

An holds out his hand. "Let me show you around."

Chiyoko takes his hand.

And in that moment she knows that by mending some little part of him, tearing him into pieces will be as simple as winning a game of skill with a small child. All she has to do now is pretend to love him, and he'll let down his guard, and she'll be able to leave.

But before she can do that, she needs to find her things. Her bag with the watch and the glasses that show her whether the Olmec, Jago Tlaloc, has perished, or if he has lived through the day to Play on.

Play on.

SARAH ALOPAY, JAGO TLALOC

Xi'an Xianyang International Airport, Terminal 2, China

Jago and Sarah get lucky. A flight is leaving for Delhi in an hour, where they can make a quick connection for a flight to Abu Dhabi. A two-hour layover and then a straight shot into northern Iraq. The total flying time is under 19 hours, which is remarkable for this part of the world. They book their tickets using fake passports—hers Canadian, his Portuguese—and credit cards under the same fake names. They fight off nerves as they pass through security, worried that the authorities will have tipped off all agencies to be on the lookout for a pair of foreigners who terrorized the Terracotta Army complex. Going through the detectors, they worry that some unseen chip will set off an alarm, but both pass through without incident.

After security and passport control, they have 15 minutes to make the flight. They don't have time to hit the restroom, get a bottle of water, look for reading material. Which is why Sarah walks right by a newspaper stand without bothering to look, without seeing that standing there, behind a rack of magazines, is Christopher.

"Come on, honey, we have to hurry!" Jago says, playing up the couple thing even more.

"I'm coming!" Sarah says impatiently, going along with it. "And you know I hate it when you call me honey, cupcake."

Christopher hears the people speaking English as they scramble down the concourse, wonders who they are, where they're going, if they're happy, if they're in love the way he's in love.

He doesn't even recognize her voice.

Who loseth to God as man to man
Shall win at the turn of the game.
I have drawn my blade where the lightnings meet
But the ending is the same:
Who loseth to God as the sword blades lose
Shall win at the end of the game.

ALICE ULAPALA

Fashion European Wig Factory Warehouse, Chengdu, China

Alice peers through the greasy, clouded windows. She sees Shari, slumped in her chair, bloody, beaten. One hand is professionally bandaged. It appears to be missing a finger. The fingers around the bloody stump are free, though probably very sore. She's asleep. How she manages to sleep with that unholy cacophony blaring through the room is unimaginable to Alice.

Maybe she is unconscious from the beating or dehydration or simple exhaustion. Or maybe all of them.

Or maybe she's already dead.

Alice closes her eyes and listens. Projects her thoughts into the room. Attends to her breath. Calls on the Mothers and the Fathers and the Brothers and the Sisters and all the lines of Earth for help.

She listens, listens, listens.

Shari *is* asleep. Dreaming pleasant things. Green things. Laughing things. All the torture that she has endured is like water in a rainstorm—gone. Washed away. It's as if she doesn't feel any of what Baitsakhan and his band of torturers did to her. As if her mind can separate itself from her body. And it's this that also allows Alice to find the Harrapan. Using a long-forgotten gift.

Alice's people have been projecting like this for tens upon tens of thousands of years. They are the only ones left who know how to do it. The only ones but for beings like kepler 22b who came to them in the Great Wide Open in the time before time and taught them.

Ever since Alice witnessed Shari's selfless act on the bus, Alice saw the goodness, and the goodness burned bright in the night. She could feel

Shari's pain, and where it was, and when it was. Such goodness does not deserve so much pain. So Alice came to relieve her of it.

Alice figures that if she does not win Endgame, she would like Shari to win, and either way, Shari sure as shit shouldn't end up dying at the hands of this Baitsa-whatever dickhead.

Yes, Shari would be a good goddess to the future of man. An excellent goddess.

Alice sings Shari a message, a message that lilts into the Harrapan's dreams: "Three minutes and away . . . three minutes and away . . . three minutes and away . . ."

Shari's head lolls.

Shari has heard it.

Alice is barefoot, creeps toward the sliding bay door. Through the course of her training she has walked silently over burning coals and beds of broken glass and pads of dried thistle burrs. She has two of her many boomerangs in her hands and a buck knife at her belt. Two kinds of boomerangs for two different purposes. She knows the boomerang is like a bad joke for a Koori, but if you're good with one, there is no better weapon.

And no one is better with a boomerang than Alice Ulapala.

The screaming is so bloody loud, it makes opening the door and walking into the filtered darkness a cinch. One of the boys wearing headphones is cleaning a pistol. He is washed in light from an overhead bulb. The other is in a shadow, texting or playing a game on his phone.

A longbow is on the table next to a pair of briefcases. A quiver full of arrows.

"Oi!" Alice yells as a test. They don't move. It is too loud, and the headphones block the rest out.

But Shari hears.

She lifts her swollen head.

Alice steps out of the shadow.

Shari sees her.

Alice winks. She wants the Harrapan to see this, figures she might enjoy what's about to happen.

She raises the first boomerang and whips it through the air with a twist. It flies up into the rafters, over a support beam, and down, threading between the cords of hanging lights. The center of the boomerang hits the texting boy hard on the hand. It breaks and the phone shatters. The wing of the boomerang slices across his face and cuts his lips clean off.

The boomerang hits the floor and slides to a stop a few feet away from Alice.

He screams out, but the other boy, his back to this one, his headphones on, doesn't hear him and continues cleaning the gun. The boy's scream is like a drop of noise falling into the ocean of screams coming from the speakers.

The lipless one, totally unaware of what has hit him, looks away from Alice, since the attack came from the other direction. Nothing there. He looks to Shari. Nothing there either. Just the girl, bound to her wooden chair, in and out of sleep.

And then, before he knows it, Alice's buck knife is in his back, between his C7 and his T1.

Game over, mate.

And the other still doesn't notice.

Alice makes a twisted face at Shari. Shari understands. The Koori is saying, *Who are these amateurs?*

Shari points her eyes at the ropes around her ankles. Alice slides over and cuts them. Shari looks at Bold, the remaining boy.

He has finally seen what is going on and is putting the last part of the pistol back together. The slide snaps back.

Shari stands and jumps back down hard on the chair and it splinters into pieces. She has to work herself free of the loosening ropes.

Alice flings the other boomerang into the air and it misses Bold wide. Alice turns and runs across the room, toward the dark, to try to draw his attention.

He doesn't bite.

Bold fixes the slide, charges a round, and aims at Shari.

But the Harrapan is free and moving toward him, holding a jagged stick in each hand. Remnants of the chair.

He pulls the trigger.

And just then the boomerang hits the back of his neck, and rings around it, and severs everything but the bone of the spine.

The gun goes off with a pop. The blood-spewing Bold has lost his aim. Shari is not hit, still charging. The boomerang slips to the floor, coated with red. Shari reaches him and drives the stakes hard into his chest. He's already dead, but she does it anyway. Bold falls back onto the table, his body quaking like a crucified frog pinned to a dissecting board.

Alice emerges from the shadows.

"You all right, mate?" she asks, reaching out and hitting stop on the iPod. Silence fills the room.

Shari is breathless and feral.

She nods.

"Great, then," Alice says, as if they've just finished playing a friendly game. Alice bends and picks up the boomerang.

"Two guns in that case," Shari says, as if she is offering them.

"Don't like guns," Alice says. She grabs a rag from the table and cleans off her weapons.

Shari pries a pistol from Bold's hand and takes the other from the table. "Neither do I, but I'm still taking these. It's just the start of what I'm owed."

"All right, then. Why not?" Alice opens the other case and takes the two Sigs, along with the extra magazines. "We should scoot, yeah?"

"Yes, honorable Koori, we should," Shari says.

They start to walk out. Shari is not tired anymore. Her hand will need attention, but it doesn't hurt. Her first murder, plus the lift that Alice has brought into her heart with her generous violence, have her amped.

They reach the door and peer out. The coast is clear.

"How did you find me?" Shari wonders.

Alice snickers. "Ah, ancient secret. Have to kill you if I told you."

"Well, I'm happy you did. Thank you."

"Yeah. Pity that other little bugger wasn't here. Woulda liked to strike him from the board."

"I agree."

"Eh, he'll get his turn, I'm sure."

"I plan to see to it personally, Alice Ulapala."

Alice gives Shari another wink. "My name sounds real nice when you say it." She looks left. "I'll be going my way now, if you don't mind. This isn't a peace party or nothing. I don't aim to team up. You're just right by me is all, and deserved better than that lot."

Shari nods gravely. "I'll never forget it. I hope to return the favor someday, if the circumstances are right."

"Circumstances," Alice says, looking to the sky, where a few faint stars flicker here and there. "They could get funny pretty soon, couldn't they?"

"They already have, if you ask me," Shari says with a painful smile.

"Well, I'll cut yer head right off if you'n me are the last ones standing. But it'll be with a heavy heart."

Shari smiles, holds out her good hand. "The same goes for me."

Alice takes it and they shake. "Give yer Little Alice a peck when you see her. Special delivery from her big auntie A." She turns and trots away, her bare feet noiselessly slapping the ground.

Shari watches her for a moment.

Alice is a marvel.

A hero already.

But Shari can't stay. She runs across the road and climbs an iron ladder and moves up to the warehouse roof and crosses the night of Chengdu in secrecy.

She is leaving Baitsakhan—and China—behind.

She wants his blood.

But she must be patient.

So, so patient.

CHIYOKO TAKEDA

Liu Residence, Unregistered Belowground Property, Tongyuanzhen, Gaoling County, Xi'an, China

Chiyoko is lying next to An Liu. Their bare legs are entwined. They are facing each other. A sheet is pulled to their waists.

This is what she had to do to escape.

Now he trusts her.

Soon he will sleep.

And when he does, she will leave.

Only something more has happened.

Chiyoko rests a hand in the crook of his hip. He draws a finger over her shoulder in small spirals. He was gentle, patient, preternaturally adept. He whispered questions that she could answer with only a look or a nod. He pinched her once, at just the right time. He tickled her, and she laughed silently. He moved slowly, and deeply, slowly and deeply. And most importantly, aside from his questions, he was silent.

Like her.

Respectful.

Right through to the end.

Because of all this, though she is pained to admit it, she liked it.

She liked lying with the mad bomber of the 377th.

She likes thinking that she had changed him in some significant way. It was not her first time (the others were clumsy and disappointing), but she assumes it must have been the first time for An. Who would have sex with this twisted, ticking monster otherwise? He could have paid for it, she supposes, but even then he wouldn't have learned all that had just happened. A prostitute would only have taught him what anyone can find on the internet in a matter of seconds.

No, the only explanation was that it was *her*. The effect Chiyoko had on him. Even if it was only for the time it took, he loved her. And although she had no intention of loving him back, for those few moments when their bodies shook in unison, a small part of her loved him too.

This is her Endgame now. Playing pretend, but not entirely. Something real has happened here.

He showed her around the place. At first he was reserved and guarded, but then she laced her fingers into his, and he began to thaw, open up.

He showed her his computers. His machines. His materials. His explosives. His artifacts. His tools. He even showed her his medications, lined up in neat white plastic bottles in his bathroom. He showed her a pet: a lizard from the western provinces. He showed her a picture of his mother, who died when he was only one. He did not show her a picture of anyone else.

He made them dinner. Fried rice with oysters and homegrown garlic shoots and pork dumplings and orange slices. They ate, and drank cold Cokes with lemon wedges. Ice cream and cookies for dessert.

At dinner the only thing he asked was if everything was all right, though he asked this 17 times.

Everything was all right.

Eventually they went to his room. She saw her stuff in a little pile. It was all there. She did not rush to it. The stuff could wait. It had to. Because first it had to happen.

It was the only way.

They sat on the bed in silence, keeping a small distance between them. Being. Breathing. Not touching. He put a hand on the bed and she put her hand on top of his and turned to him. He was so nervous he couldn't look. She kissed him on the neck. He turned his mouth to hers.

And it began.

And it happened.

Now they are looking at each other. Unsmiling. Just looking. Chiyoko feels desperate. She still has to leave. But, strangely, right now she doesn't want to.

She blinks her big eyes and holds up a finger and gets out of bed. He watches her naked body glide to the chair with her things. She gets her phone. She returns. She is completely at ease in her skin.

He's envious of her. Of her ease and purity. Envious and enamored.

She gets back in bed and opens a Chinese language notepad app. Types. Shows it to him.

That was nice. Really nice.

"It was. Thank you." An sounds a little surprised, but also tries to be confident and assured. The lack of a stutter certainly helps in that department.

I wonder if any of the others . . .

"Ha. Maybe. Probably those two you were following, right?"

Chiyoko shrugs. It's not like her to gossip. She doesn't care what the Cahokian and the Olmec might be doing. She just wants to draw An out some more. It's working.

He stares at her, speaks. "I want to tell you something. Some *things*. That I've never told anyone. Is that all right?"

He is being dumb, she can't help but think. Never has she been so glad to be a mute as in this moment.

She nods.

The whole time he speaks, he looks directly into her eyes. His voice is even and deliberate. His nerves are quiet, his tics still.

"When I was very young, I was normal. Two, three years old. I can remember it. Actually I can remember it very well. Playing with red rubber balls in the park, talking to my uncles, insisting on getting a little toy, running, laughing, talking without a stutter. None of what I am now—what I am when I'm away from you—was there. None of it. And then, when I turned four, I was told about Endgame."

She pushes her head into the pillow. Chiyoko knew about Endgame from the day of her birth. The stories they told her as a baby were of Endgame. The songs they sang to put her to bed, the easy lies her parents told to get her to behave. Everything was Endgame, all the time. It troubled her, of course, and as she got older her apprehension grew, but she always accepted it. It was a part of her, and in a very real way, she was proud of who she was.

But not An.

"The day after I turned four, my father whipped me savagely with a switch for no reason. I cried, wailed, pleaded. It didn't matter; he didn't stop. And everything that came after was a nightmare. I was beaten, tortured, forced to learn by rote. If I cried, I was tormented more. I was made to do hundreds of repetitive tasks or movements thousands upon thousands of times. Left alone in a box only centimeters bigger than me for days at a time. Starved. Parched. Drowned. Overloaded. Eventually I learned not to cry. Not to scream or protest. I had to understand the hardness of it all. And I did. They broke me over and over and over again. They beat me regularly. They said it was the same way with them, and before them, and so it would be with me, and after me. When I was ten, they beat me so bad they fractured my skull and I had to have a steel plate put in my forehead. I was in a coma for two weeks. They didn't care that I developed tics and spoke with a stutter when I came out of the coma, that half my skull is made of metal. As they made me—my own father and his brothers, and no women, none—they forgot the innocent boy that I started as. They forgot the little kid I once was. I, however, never have. And I never forgave them for what they did to me."

Chiyoko can't help but feel for him, moves closer to him.

"I killed them all when I was eleven. Drugged them while they were sleeping and doused them with the cheap rice whiskey they loved so much and lit them each on fire, one by one. The flames roused them, even with the drugs. They were terrified, and I loved it. I left my uncles to burn alone, but I watched my father. I said to them, in my mind, because my tongue was so jammed by speech, 'You have reaped what you have sown.' I watched my burning father for as long as I could, until I had to leave the house, because it was burning too. That day was, and has been until today, the happiest day of my entire life."

Chiyoko puts a hand on his arm. He is silent. The silence is the purest Chiyoko has ever heard.

"I hate Endgame, Chiyoko. Despise it. Loathe it. If humanity is meant to perish, then it should perish. No one will have a chance to win as long as I live." Pause. "No one, but now, you."

And I have to leave you to make that happen, she thinks. *I hope you will understand.*

The silence resumes. She leans in and kisses him. Kisses him again. And again. She pulls back. They stare at each other. They still don't speak.

He rolls onto his back and gazes at the ceiling. "The others are going to find it difficult to get around very soon. They will all be put on no-fly lists, along with as many aliases as I could glean. If I find more, I will add those names too. The only people who will find it easy to fly will be you and me. Oh—and the young one, Baitsakhan. I just couldn't locate any electronic bread crumbs for that one. It's like he's never used the internet, or left Mongolia until a week ago."

He isn't dumb at all. He is in love. And whatever his goal, he is Playing. Playing harder than most, if not all, of the others.

I am lucky.

She nuzzles her head into his neck. She thumbs something into her phone. Shows it to him.

Thank you, An. Thank you for everything. I'm going to sleep now if that's okay.

"Of course. I'm tired too." Pause. "Will you stay here, in the bed with me?"

She smiles, puts her arms around him, kisses his neck.

Yes, she'll stay with him.

Until.

Until.

KALA MOZAMI

Qatar Airways Flight 832, Seat 38F
Depart: Xi'an
Arrive: Dubai

The plane Kala is on has been flying for four hours and 23 minutes. It is passing the western edge of the Indian subcontinent and flying out over the Arabian Sea. Kala is in seat 38F. Christopher is in 35B. He knows where she is. She still has no idea even *who* he is.

Kala is not as obsessed with her visual clue as she had been, but it still turns constantly in her mind. The image was a mystery, and it clouded and distracted her. But it isn't anymore. She knows what it is.

Gobekli Tepe.

She contacted 56X and he did some research and confirmed her belief. He provided a fact sheet and a list of internet links, not that Kala really needed them.

Every Sumerian knows Gobekli Tepe.

Here is a little of what the world "knows" about Gobekli Tepe: A huge Neolithic stone structure in southern Turkey, buried for millennia. Discovered accidentally by a local shepherd in 1993. Excavation did not start until 1994. It is believed to have been built by an unknown culture no later than 10,000 BCE. Predates the accepted time frames for the inventions of agriculture, metallurgy, animal husbandry, the wheel, and writing. The largest stones—standing on end and capped with huge blocks—weigh as much as 20 metric tons. They are carved with lizards, vultures, lions, snakes, scorpions, spiders. No one knows what they mean or how it was made. Gobekli Tepe remains shrouded in mystery.

Here is what Kala knows: It was one of the sites that the Annunaki visited, a site built for them. One of the places where they came down from the sky and from Du-Ku and gave the people their humanity. Put it in them, to be passed down through the ages. We all have it now, in us still, sleeping, hiding, waiting. The Annunaki showed this group of "first people"—for there were many such "first peoples" around the globe—how to farm and mine and weave and cultivate. Gave them writing. Showed them metal. Told them how to cast and mold it. Especially the magical, soft metal known now as gold. The Annunaki showed them how to find it, work it, craft it. Some believe the gold is why the Annunaki came to Earth. That they needed it for some reason, for some technology they had, and they knew it could be found in abundance on Earth. And while knowledge of the Annunaki has been lost, the cities and monuments built to honor them have not been. There at Gobekli Tepe, as at other forgotten, buried, submerged, ancient places, the Annunaki pushed our evolution along with gifts unknown. Gifts as if from the gods themselves.

Which is exactly how they came to be known. As gods.

Gobekli Tepe.

That is where Kala Mozami is going. Back to a place of beginning. She finds this fitting, since it is all going to end so soon.

Blessings.

As the image turns in her mind, she thinks of her line, wonders how exactly they will be delivered when she is victorious. Because, she believes, her line is different from the others.

Prospective Players are taken from their mothers and fathers in infancy and raised and nurtured by elders. They have names, and among themselves they use them, but officially they go by alphanumeric designations. 56X, for instance. Or Z-33005. Or HB1253. Kala is known as 5SIGMA.

The reason they do this is to avoid what they call "blood sentiment." Bonds are formed, of course, and feelings nurtured, but it is essential for Players of the 89th not to have blood relations. These, they have learned over the centuries, cloud thought and action. There are stories of other lines, dead lines, collapsing under the weight of their own relations.

So the 89s have no mothers or fathers. It has been this way for 4,394 years. Kala thinks of her favorite mentor. A woman known as EL2. Her name was Sheela. She died three years ago of ovarian cancer. She was a happy, carefree mentor. A good cook and fine martial artist. A master lock picker. She took Endgame seriously, but not with too much pepper. "Like my lamb," she was fond of saying. Her whole approach to the end was that it would be a new beginning. That the game, when it came, would be the prism through which fear turned to courage.

This is what Kala was taught.

Blessings.

The turning image of Gobekli Tepe fades from her mind. She is going there; she need not dwell on it in this moment. She centers herself. Feels her breath and her heart. Rests her hands in her lap and looks out the window to the world below. The Arabian Sea is dark and blue. There is no land in sight. The clouds are intermittent and puffed and sun-kissed and bunched on the horizon like a gilded cavalry. The world below is as full and beautiful as it ever was.

She leans her head on the glass.

It all passes below.

She closes her eyes.

31.05, 46.266667[lx]

SARAH ALOPAY, JAGO TLALOC

Emirates Airlines Flight 413
Depart: Abu Dhabi
Arrive: Mosul

Sarah and Jago's plane is just south of Baghdad, 35 minutes from Mosul. They have not spoken about their good fortune in escaping China. They have not spoken about the things they need to acquire in Iraq. In fact, since boarding the first plane out of China, they have barely spoken at all. They are dog-tired. The Calling, the escape from the pagoda, the Terracotta Army incident, the fact that they still have the disk, all the flying—everything—is finally catching up with them. Also, they are about to land in Iraq on forged visas that Jago had hidden in his backpack. So they are a little stressed.

Jago sleeps sitting up, his body leaning into the empty seat that separates them. Sarah is working on her code. She uses a worn nub of a pencil and scribbles on an inside-out barf bag. She writes using an ancient, long-forgotten number system.

She's making some progress, but it's hard. There are simply too many numbers. If all the numbers are used, the coordinates will be accurate to the 6th or 7th decimal place. Furthermore, she can't be sure if the coordinates are UTM or LAT/LON. Still, she is generating a list of possibilities. What she needs now is a map so she can start making educated guesses. She stares at the markings on the bag, puts the pencil on the tray table. She turns to Jago. His eyes are open. He is staring at an empty spot near her shoulder.

She smiles.

"How's it going?" he asks.

"It's going. I need a map," she whispers.

"They have those in Iraq."

"Good."

Sarah stares at Jago for a few moments as the numbers scroll through her head. Jago mistakes her gaze for something more and asks, "Want to go into the bathroom with me?"

"What? No!" She laughs.

Jago recovers, saying, "I mean to check each other for chips. Weren't we going to do that ASAP? ASAP was a while ago. . . ."

"Oh, yeah. I forgot about that." But really she hasn't forgotten. Since leaving China she's actually thought about it a lot.

"I think we should do it before we go through Iraqi customs. Just in case."

Sarah turns away from Jago. "I'll go in first and undress. Last one on the right side. Give me a couple minutes."

"Cool."

Sarah slides her sneakers off and pushes them under the seat in front of her. She stands and squeezes past Jago's knees. When she's in the aisle she whispers, "And don't get any funny ideas."

"Same to you," he says.

Sarah snorts and walks toward the back of the plane.

The flight is nearly all men. A few Westerners, but most are Middle Eastern. One man stares at her without any compunction. Sarah gives him the hardest look she can muster, which is pretty damn hard. He looks away.

She goes into the lavatory and looks in the mirror and begins to undress. She folds her clothes and puts them on the closed toilet seat. She washes her hands and splashes water on her face.

She checks the front of her body, under her breasts, under her chin. She pulls down her underwear and inspects the area that Jago will not be allowed to check. She runs her hands over her thighs, down her knees, over her shins and the tops of her feet. She sees nothing. No chips, or anything else that could be used to track her.

She stands and splashes more water on her face.

She is eager, nervous, unsure about Jago inspecting the rest of her body. The only boy to have ever seen her, or touched her, is Christopher. And it was under very different circumstances from these. The first time was in his room. His parents were in Kansas City for the weekend and he was home alone with his uncle, who spent most of the weekend drinking beer and watching football. They snuck upstairs and locked the door to his room and spent four hours kissing each other, touching each other, slowly taking off each other's clothes. After that, every chance they got, they snuck away. They'd been saving their first time, and they had planned on going there while they were away this summer. Another thing lost to Endgame, though Sarah knows if she wins, she'll have the chance again. As she looks at her body and imagines Christopher's lips and hands, his body pressing against her own, Jago knocks. She lets him in and closes the door quickly.

"Hey."

"Hey."

"You ready?"

"Yes."

He sits. She turns away from him and unfastens her bra. She holds her arms across her chest. "I've already done the front," Sarah says, her voice shaking a little.

"Were you clear?"

"Yes."

Sarah holds her breath. Jago bends down, reaches for her. His touch is light. He runs his fingers over her ankles, up her calves, behind her knees. Sarah feels instantly at ease. He may have been a little suggestive before, but he isn't now. All he seems to be doing is looking for a subcutaneous chip.

He reaches the top of her thighs and stops.

"I don't know...."

Sarah hesitates, then pulls down her underwear. "It's fine. We need to check."

Only Christopher has seen this much of me, she thinks.

Jago's fingers move slowly up the back of her thighs, sending chills through Sarah. And even though it's not supposed to feel great, given the situation and the reason, it does. She closes her eyes as his fingers move upward, and she takes a deep breath. And shockingly, she realizes that she was never, not once, this comfortable around Christopher. No matter where they were, or what they were doing, much of their intimate time together felt like the awkward stumblings of teenagers. There's something about Jago that feels more real, more adult than Christopher. More like what she always imagined love and intimacy were supposed to feel like. When she was with Christopher, she felt like she was a girl with a boy. Jago makes her feel like a woman with a man.

She opens her eyes and watches in the mirror as he continues to inspect her. His face is inches from her skin, his fingers moving lightly and slowly. She doesn't want him to stop, not now, or ever, and when he's done, she immediately misses him.

"Okay so far," he says.

"Keep going."

He stands, starts again, with his fingers, his eyes. He moves up her back, her sides. Her spine curls as he reaches her shoulder blades. And when he parts her hair around her neck and looks carefully at the hairline, she can feel his breath on the back of her neck, sending another round of chills through her body. He's standing behind her, inches away, and though she doesn't know if it's real or not, she thinks she can feel heat from his body warming hers. He runs his fingers down her arms and she closes her eyes again, knowing that he's going to be finished soon, wishing he weren't. His fingers move slowly away from her wrists, and she wants them back, wants them back more than she's wanted anything in her entire life.

"You're clear," he says. "I don't see a thing."

"Good," she replies as she refastens her bra.

He hands her her clothes. She watches him undress while she puts her things back on. It's a funny dance in such close quarters. Their elbows knock as Jago lifts his shirt over his head. He smiles nervously as they switch places. Sarah sits on the toilet. Jago hands her his shirt and undoes his belt. He lowers his pants and hands them to her in an unfolded clump. She puts the clothing in her lap and he turns his back to her.

They repeat the searching process. Sarah is more nervous now than when Jago was looking at her.

She starts at his heels, his Achilles, moves up, and despite her training, she has to fight to keep her hands from shaking. His calves are thin and taut. She puts her hands around them, checks both sides of them, and she can see his pulse through the veins. She quickly calculates his heart rate at 49 bpm, which means he's clearly not as nervous as she is, which makes her even more nervous. She continues up his thighs, which, despite the fact that he's thin, look incredibly strong, like they're carved from rock. She moves slowly, pretending to be extremely careful, but really just loving the feel of her fingers on his skin.

When she finally moves her fingers away, even though she doesn't want to, she says, "Your turn."

He slowly pulls down his underwear. She wants to look but can't, so she closes her eyes and runs her hands over him. She moves quickly, somehow thinking she's cheating on Christopher, even though she broke up with him, and even though she's doing what she's doing for a practical reason. She keeps moving her hands here and there and here until she says, "Clear."

"You sure?" Jago asks, and she can hear the smirk in his voice.

"Positive," she blurts.

She moves up his back, which is defined by long thin muscles. He doesn't have more than a pound of fat on his entire body. She runs her hands over his back, shoulders. She can feel that his heart is now humming along at 56 bpm. She is doing this to him and she knows it. And she likes it. That he clearly feels something similar to what she does. Feels her hands on his body, and feels her in a way that excites him. *Somehow,* she thinks to herself, *this is actually better than fooling around.*

She looks closely at Jago's neck. He has another scar there, like the one across his face, that is raised and purplish. She hesitates, wonders if this is where Chiyoko's chip is embedded. But the scar is too small, too deep, so she decides it can't be. Her hands move over it, past it, and the chip remains undetected. Sarah moves on and sifts her fingertips through Jago's hair. She slows down because she's almost done, and she doesn't want it to end. When it does, her hands fall to her sides, and she's sad.

"You're clear too."

"Good."

They stare at each other for a moment, both unsure of what to do, if anything. Both unsure if they felt the same things, which they did, which they absolutely did. They hear an announcement, and the plane begins the initial descent into Mosul.

"I'll see you back at the seat," Sarah says, breaking the silence.

"I'm right behind you."

"Great," she says as she opens the door and quickly steps out.

She doesn't want to think about his body anymore.

But she can't help it.

Green Pyramid of the plains, from far-ebbed Time[lxi]

AN LIU

Liu Residence, Unregistered Belowground Property, Tongyuanzhen, Gaoling County, Xi'an, China

An rolls over and his arm moves across his bed. The side of the bed she is on.

He opens his eyes.

The side of the bed she *was* on.

Blink.

He sits up quickly. He can smell her on the pillow, but the bed is cold. She's not in the bathroom.

Blink.

What time is it? 1:45. 1:45 *p.m.*! Since he was a small child, An has never slept more than four hours in a row. But last night, this morning, *this afternoon*, he slept for over 15.

Blink.

Did she drug him?

Blinkblink.

He jumps out of bed and runs through the house. Not in the kitchen. Not in the workroom. Not in the spare bedroom. Not in the storage room. Not in the living room. Not in not in not in not in.

Blink.

He runs to the basement, to the epileptic room of computers and televisions and keyboards and servers and web-bots and programs and aggregators and script managers and boxes and flash drives. She is *blink* she is *blink* she is *blink* not in there either.

SHIVER.

He's crushed. An drops into his chair and stares at his bare knees, which are starting to shake. Out of the corner of his eye, he notices a folded piece of paper lying across a keyboard. On top of this, at an angle, is a plain business envelope with tiny lumps poking up from within.

Blink. SHIVER. Blink.

He reaches out, opens the envelope. He looks inside.

A clean, thick, neat coil of her hair. He takes it out and holds it, brings it up to his nose and smells it.

He misses her already. And though he appreciates the gesture, this makes it almost worse. To smell her, but not to be able to see her or touch her.

There is more in the envelope. He peers into the crease and sees the small crescent moons of fingernails. An entire toenail, ripped free of the skin and cuticle. A splotch of dried blood.

He holds the hair to his cheek. It is so soft, so soft. He closes the envelope and picks up the paper, unfolds it, stares at the graceful Chinese handwriting.

Dearest An,

I am sorry. I hope you can forgive me. I cannot fully imagine what I must mean to you. I want nothing dishonest between us. You have been lied to far too much in this life. I will not do that to you. Not anymore.

The truth: I intended to sleep with you so that I could leave. I know I was to be your prisoner. I could not let that happen. I have a lead in the game, and I do not intend to relinquish it.

What I did not intend was to have to write words such as these. I thought I would just leave and never see you again. But here the words are.

An wipes a real tear away from his tattooed one and reads on.

Yesterday, when I woke, you were nothing to me but an opponent. I can't explain what happened since. But something did happen. My effect on you is plain to see. It is easy to understand, if not the why, at least the what. The effect you have had on me is subtler. You were not my first,

An, so it wasn't that. It was something else.

Something precious and rare.

Like you.

I have known about Endgame since I came from the womb. It is who I am. I love my parents, my cousins, my aunts and uncles, all who taught me and guided me. We were a quiet, contemplative group of people, always weighed down by the game, but we were also happy. I was never beaten or tortured. Yes, I endured pain in training, as we all surely have, but nothing like you have had to endure.

I like life, and I intend to live. You Play for death. I Play for life. Other Players also Play for life. Other Players surely also Play for death. But not like you. I believe that you, among the 12, are unique. Even if the reasons are grotesque, mean, and twisted, you are unique. Do not forget this.

You are hard because hardness is what made you. But with me you were gentle. It is in you as well. Kindness. Empathy. Generosity. All of them are in you. You were sleeping so quietly and contentedly when I left. I wished the man I was with in bed was the man who was playing Endgame.

Play on as you choose. I will not judge you. Hate me if you must, but know that I will never hate you. And if it ever becomes necessary, I will fight for you. This I promise.

I am sorry, truly sorry. Keep what little of me I have put in the envelope for you. If I could have left you more of myself, I would have. So much more.

—Chiyoko

An reads the letter again and again and again. The tics stay gone throughout. These talismans will protect him. Shepherd him. See him to his end, wherever that is. He knows he'll keep them on his person at all times. And he immediately decides two things. The first: if she will not judge him, then he will not judge her. The second: if she wants to Play for her life, then he will do what he can to help her.

He turns on the computer monitor, opens a terminal, and starts typing. The no-fly lists are in place at all the appropriate agencies and in nearly every country in the world. All they await now is their keyword and they will spring open. He types, hits enter, leans back, and watches it unfold.

The keyword is a simple string:

CHIYOKOTAKEDA.

That, dearest, is my love letter to you.

And for the others, especially any who might be flying right now, what a surprise is in store.

J. DEEPAK SINGH

Qatar Airways Flight 832, Seat 12E
Depart: Xi'an
Arrive: Dubai

J. Deepak Singh gets a vibrating in-flight alert on his agency smartphone. He reaches into his jacket and pulls it out and enters the code and reads the flash.

EMERGENCY UPDATE>>>01:34:35.9 ZULU>>>ALERT ALERT ALERT>>>IMMEDIATE ATTENTION REQUIRED>>>SPECIAL AIR AGENT JDSINGH ASSIGNED QATAR AIRWAYS FLIGHT 832 ENRTE CZX>DXB>>>FOR YOUR EYES ONLY>>>REPEAT>>>FOR YOUR EYES ONLY>>>STOP

Singh follows protocol. He turns off his phone, rises from his seat by the bulkhead in the middle of coach, and makes his way to the bathroom. He has to wait for a moment, until the door opens and a young girl steps out. He steps into the bathroom, closes and locks the door.
Occupied.
He swipes at his phone again, opens the app, enters his security code. A picture of a pretty, dark-skinned, green-eyed Middle Eastern girl pops up.

KALI MOZAMI AKA KALA MEZRHA AKA KARLA GESH AKA REBEKKA JAIN VARHAZA AKA NIGHTOWL>>>AGED APPROX 16–18 YRS>>>173–176CM>>>48–52KG>>>HAIR BLACK EYES GREEN SKIN BROWN>>>NATIONALITY UNCONFIRMED>>>ENRTE FLIGHT 832 ON OMANI PASSPORT>>>SEEK AND DETAIN>>>CONSIDERED ARMED AND EXTREMELY DANGEROUS>>>USE ANY AND ALL

NECESSARY MEANS>>>REPEAT>>>USE ANY AND ALL NECESSARY MEANS>>>TICKETED SEAT 38F>>>UAE AIRPORT AUTHORITIES ALERTED>>>PREPARED FOR DETENTION ON ARR>>>STOP

Singh can't believe it.

This is what he has been training for: this, now.

Most agents go an entire career and never get a call like this. The most the average sky marshal has to deal with is a drunken passenger or a heated family dispute or, at the very worst, a crazy person making unfounded threats.

But this is something else.

Singh checks his gun—a standard-issue Glock 19. The rounds are rubber. He has one magazine of live ammunition in his holster. He checks his Taser. It's charged. He checks his cuffs, hidden and at hand. He checks himself in the mirror. Blows out his cheeks. *All right,* he thinks, *let's go.*

He opens the door and finds the nearest flight attendant. They know who he is and why he's on the plane. He tells them that he's going to arrest someone and they need to tell the captain. The attendant is a veteran. So as not to arouse suspicion—either with the mark herself, who could be walking around, or with the passengers—the attendant fixes Singh a cup of coffee and hands him a packet of cookies. He opens the cookies, eats them. When the coffee is ready she gives it to him. He drinks it black.

He leans against the counter and acts casual. The attendant calls the captain and alerts him. She calls the other flight-attendant stations. Singh says to her, "Rear galley," and she tells the crew there to be ready. She hangs up the phone. He finishes the coffee and hands her the cup. He turns away and walks aft down the aisle. He has one hand on his Taser, the other on the cuffs. His gun is within easy reach.

AISLING KOPP

Lago Beluiso, Lombardy Italian Alps, 1,549 m above Sea Level

Aisling puts one foot in front of the other. The Italian Alps rise around her like the gods themselves, with white-peaked hair, reaching for the heavens.

She is moving up, up, up, quickly, deftly. She's sweating, panting, her legs burning. She's wearing hiking boots, carrying a pack, a coil of brightly colored rope over her shoulder, a walking stick in one hand. She has a sling full of quickdraws and carabiners, nuts and cams. The blue tube of a Camelback hydration system snakes over her shoulder strap.

If someone saw her, they'd think she was just some agro kid on a mission. A thrill seeker. A girl marching to the beat of her own drum. All of which are essentially true.

But no one is around to see her. And besides, she is so much more than any of these things. She is also carrying ammo, a scope, and her sniper rifle, which is deadly from two miles. Her pack weighs 130 pounds, which equals her own weight. It's nothing to her. She's trained with more weight for longer periods on steeper grades. She is much more than a hiker: she's an assassin, a dead-eye shot, a patient devil with a trigger finger.

But Aisling is also confused.

Worried.

Angry.

After everything she learned about her father, about her life, about the history of her line, it feels good to be alone, in the open air, pushing herself. It lets her forget about her short visit home to Queens, if only for a moment.

She is bushwhacking a trail from Lago Beluiso up to 1,835 m, where her grandfather's coordinates took her. To the place where her father died.

No. Was killed.

She tries to picture Declan, climbing up this same mountain, with baby Aisling wrapped tightly in his arms. Retreating from Endgame. In search of something, something he believed would change him, change Endgame, change the world. She tries to picture it but cannot. She's never even seen any pictures of her father. To her, he is just a name and a headstone.

She's not sure what she's going to find, if anything. She knows, however, that a nearby valley is famous for a small group of prehistoric caves. In these caves are paintings. Very old paintings showing some very strange things. What these things reference is a point of endless debate. Some think spaceships, others gods, others mere representations of people. No one knows for certain.

Like so many things in this world.

No one knows.

It's not for us to know. Aisling remembers the familiar refrain from her pop.

Everything, always, she recalls kepler 22b saying.

So confusing, all of it.

Aisling tries to turn off her mind.

She can't.

The fact that the fate of the world is being played out by a group of teenagers.

All of whom are deadly, and all of whom want to kill her.

Up, up, she continues. The Alps are stunning. Aisling has always liked the outdoors. One of the best weeks of her life she spent in the New York wilds, infiltrating the woods around West Point during one of the military academy's war-game sessions. She operated as a rogue, unsanctioned and unknown. She was 15 at the time. Younger than all the cadets. Smaller and physically weaker, but smarter and faster.

She captured two cadets from opposing sides and held them for three days each in separate camps. Her methods were so unorthodox and bizarre—snare traps, torturous bindings made of vines and sticks, tinctures of psychotropic fungi—that the cadets each thought she was some kind of demon or long-lost Hudson Valley wild woman. She let them go without killing them and kept tabs on both. One went crazy and hanged himself a year later. The other completed his training and is currently stationed in Kabul.

She thinks about the first cadet often, about the madness she caused within him. She's not proud of that, but something about it, and the fact that she was responsible for it, creates a sense of awe in her. The power she held, the control, to be able to toy with a man's life in such a way. Aisling wonders if that is how kepler 22b and his brethren feel about humanity. And her father, was he like the cadet? Did thoughts of Endgame drive him mad?

Aisling stops next to a towering pine tree. A jagged wall of gray rock rises in front of her. The air drifting down from the heights is cold, but her skin is slick and hot. She drinks from the tube over her shoulder and stares at a dark fissure dividing the rock. She takes out her GPS and checks the coordinates. She pulls off the climbing sling and lets the pack drop to the ground. She fishes in a mesh pocket on the pack's hip belt and pulls out a headlamp. She draws her skinning knife from the sheath that is strapped to her thigh. She stares at the fissure, which, if she is right and Pop is right and the gods are right, leads to a cave. She starts walking toward the darkness, and when she reaches it, she steps in.

Earth is 4,540,000,000 years old. Extinctions occur at regular intervals. Today it is believed that between 15,000 and 30,000 species go extinct each year, which translates to a total species loss of 15 to 20 percent over the next 100 years. During the Cretaceous-Tertiary extinction, up to 75 percent of all species were lost. During the Permian-Triassic extinction, up to 96 percent perished.

KALA MOZAMI

Qatar Airways Flight 832, Seat 38F
Depart: Xi'an
Arrive: Dubai

Someone taps Kala on the shoulder. She pulls the azure scarf around her head away from her eyes, opens them. The person sitting next to her—the one tapping her—is a different person from when she dozed off. The aisle seat just beyond this new man is vacant.

In a very professional tone the man asks, "Miss, are you Kala Mozami?"

Kala says, "No. My name is Gesh. Who are you?"

"Ms. Gesh, I need you to come with me."

"Who are you?" Kala repeats.

Singh holds open his lapel to flash his ID.

A cop.

And that's when she realizes the muzzle of his gun is sitting on the armrest between them, pointed right at her kidney. Kala is genuinely confused. Why would the authorities be looking for her?

Something is not right.

As he lets his jacket close again, she sees the extra clip snapped into his holster. The topmost bullet there throws a little light. It's metal, which surprises her. She knows air marshals usually use only rubber bullets. She needs to play this right.

"I'm sorry," she says quietly, "but there must be some mistake."

"If there is, it will have to be sorted out in Dubai. My instructions are to detain you."

"Detain me?" she says a little too loudly, and on purpose.

Christopher, three rows forward, hears and turns his head. Others look as well.

"Ms. Gesh, please stay calm. I want you to take these"—he slides a pair of silver handcuffs across his thigh—"and put them on, keeping your hands in front of you. I will remove your head scarf and cover your hands. Then we are going to slowly get up and you will lead the way to the back of the plane."

Kala shakes her head. She widens her eyes to make herself look scared. "Please, officer, I don't know what you're talking about." Again she says this a little too loudly.

Someone in the middle of the plane says, "What's going on over there?" in alarmed Arabic.

"If you don't do it, I'll be forced to do it for you."

"All right, but do I have to take off my head scarf? It is haram."

Singh isn't moved. "I am sorry, but I must insist."

Slowly, reluctantly, Kala pulls the scarf from her head and lets it fall into her lap. "I'm telling you, this is a mistake."

"If it is, then you will have my sincerest apologies."

She holds out a wrist for the cuffs. This, she knows, is what a reasonable innocent person would do. Protest and then comply. With her other hand, under the scarf, she pulls a thin hairpin from a slit in the hem. The cop doesn't notice. She slips the cuffs over her left wrist and then her right.

"Tighter, please."

"But I haven't done anything!"

"Just a little tighter. Please."

She does as she's told. He puts the scarf over her joined wrists.

"Thank you," he says.

Singh slides out of the seat and into the aisle, careful to keep his weapon concealed.

Kala stands and works her way toward him.

People are looking at her and mumbling. A large, dark-skinned African man is taking her picture with his phone. A woman in a black hijab is wrapping her arm around her daughter protectively. A Western boy a year or two older than she is peering intently at her over the back of his seat. He looks familiar. More familiar than he should.

Who is he?

She steps in front of Singh and turns to the rear of the plane and starts to walk slowly. There are nine rows between her and the aft galley. She immediately starts working one of the cuffs' locks with the hairpin.

She's done this hundreds of times before in training, and picked thousands of locks, so she knows she'll be free by the time they reach the back of the plane.

Seven rows left and the plane hits some bad turbulence. She has to steady herself against the seats with the side of her arm. A few of the passengers gasp. She runs her finger along the pin. It is still in the lock. Five rows left and the plane passes through some more chop, but this time lighter. The overhead compartments creak.

She almost has it.

Three rows left and the plane drops 40 or 50 feet. Kala momentarily lifts off the floor, as does Officer Singh. The whole plane comes down with a thump, but Kala and her captor remain standing. They hear more gasping; a couple screams.

"Keep going," he says, not a tinge of nervousness in his voice. Flying is Singh's job, and he's dealt with turbulence before.

A cabin chime informs them that the seat-belt light has been turned on.

Click, click, click, in every seat.

They pass the lavatory doors and she has it. The left cuff comes free. She brings out her wrist and recloses the cuff, leaves the scarf in place. There are two flight attendants in the rear of the plane. One is strapping herself into a jump seat. The other, a tall, thin man, is bracing himself between the wall and the counter. When he sees Kala—very young and very pretty and not at all what one would think of when one thinks of a criminal or terrorist—his eyes light up. Evidently, he thinks that it's funny this is the person the crew is abuzz over, the person who has been deemed a profound security risk.

Kala hears something outside, something just barely perceptible. A hitch in the engine.

She braces herself.

The plane jumps again. The male flight attendant is thrown over the counter. Singh falls forward and Kala can feel the muzzle of his gun press into her back. Realizing that under these conditions he could accidentally shoot her, and that she needs to act, Kala spins around and raises her left hand like she is going to attack. Singh is not expecting it and his eyes follow her hand. As the plane continues to bounce, and he gets ready to fight her off, she loops the empty cuff ring around the gun and pulls back hard with her right arm. The cuff tightens around the pistol and whips it out of his grasp.

Singh is shocked.

The plane bounces again.

Again.

Kala struggles for a second to free the pistol from the cuff. Singh is pulling out his Taser. The male attendant sees what's happening and, believing he can be a hero, moves on Kala. The female attendant screams and closes her eyes. They are all separated by less than five feet. Kala raises the pistol. By the weight of the Glock she can tell that her initial thought was right—it's loaded with rubber rounds. The real bullets are in that extra clip. A kill shot will have to be perfectly placed. Singh moves forward. The plane rises again and they all leave their feet. Kala sees everything unfold as if in slow motion. As they are in the air she reaches out for Singh's left hand, which is holding the Taser. She pulls him close, pushes the barrel of the Glock into his right eyeball, fires. The pop is muted, unnoticeable above the turbulence and the fear and the cabin hum and the engines. There is no exit wound, and he dies immediately, slumping forward across Kala's shoulder. The Taser is still in his hand. She lifts it and fires at the male attendant. He walks right into it and goes stiff, and his eyes roll into the back of his head.

The plane lurches again, and Kala knows they just lost an engine. The attendant in the jump seat screams.

"Shut up!" Kala yells as she extracts herself from the dead officer.

But the attendant doesn't listen. She keeps screaming.

"Pull yourself together and shut up!" Kala yells again.

She doesn't listen.

Kala trains the gun on her. The attendant raises her hands and Kala fires three quick rounds. The screaming stops.

Kala steps into the middle of the galley as the plane starts to fall. She puts both hands on the lavatory doors, the flat slide of the Glock in her right hand pressing against the plastic panel, and looks into the cabin. No one has noticed what has happened. Everyone is too frightened, too concentrated on the imminent end of their own lives. Even the familiar boy is not looking in her direction. All she can see is the top of his head, his face slightly raised as if he is talking to God, pleading, praying. Everyone is praying.

The captain comes on the PA.

"Ladies and gentlemen, do not worry. We have lost one engine, but the A340 is designed to fly on as few as two. We are two hundred forty-eight nautical miles from the coast of Oman and have been cleared for an emergency landing at the nearest military base. I repeat, do not—"

He is cut off by a very loud grinding noise followed by a slow *whomp whomp whomp* that reverberates through the fuselage and everyone's chest. The PA is still on, and the sounds of multiple warning alarms from the flight deck spill from the speakers.

"Oh God, please help us," the pilot says, and he's cut off.

The plane's nose points down, and the aircraft starts to fall hard and fast. Kala struggles to open a lavatory door, goes in and shuts it, locks it. She sits on the closed toilet and gets ready, breathes, thinks, tries to stay calm. She will not lose Endgame this way. She is in the rear of the plane. She can hear the airflow change as the flaps are lowered. They'll ditch. They'll be in the water. The rear of the plane is the best place to be in a crash. It takes every ounce of her training to calm her nerves, but she manages to do it.

She looks at herself in the mirror. She will live. She will win. She prays for luck and thanks her mentors for all that they have given her, especially the ability to calm herself in the face of disaster.

The plane is going down.

They will hit the water in less than 60 seconds.

Blessings.

Blessings to the stars and to life and to death.

Blessings.

ALICE ULAPALA

Grub Street Bar, Darwin, Australia

Alice sits in a bar in Darwin. She was at her auntie's, visiting down in Coffin Bay, when the meteors rained down, but now she's home. The place is mostly empty, like it usually is, just the bartender and a guy bellied up to the bar who must be a tourist. He doesn't know what kind of place he's wandered into, the sort of clientele it serves. Alice doesn't mind the company, and her people don't discriminate against visitors. As she sips a beer from a frosted glass, she scrawls on a napkin.

The same words, letters, numbers, over and over again:

How he likes other almonds scarcely serves Caesar's actions.

HHLOASSCA.

8 8 12 15 1 19 19 3 1.

She draws lines and pictographs, but nothing adds up. Eventually she sketches a rabbit. She makes a little gunshot noise with her mouth. Alice is imagining hunting rabbits in the Great Sandy Desert, which is where she would rather be, walking, sleeping under stars, skinning snakes. Not doing maths problems.

"What a jackass. Yabber and more yabber. If the stakes weren't so high, I'd toss the lot."

"Beer cold enough for you?" the barman asks her. His name is Tim, and Alice knows him from around, meaning Tim's one of her privileged line members who knows all about Endgame. She showed him the nonsense sentence when she first showed up at the bar, but like her, Tim isn't much for puzzles.

She looks at him. "Beer's great."

Tim nods, smiles. "Cold beer helps me think, usually."

"Me too," says Alice, taking a swig from her mug. "This one's a right quiddler, though."

"What is?" asks the tourist, taking his eyes off the match playing on the bar's single television. He has an American accent. He cranes his neck at Alice's napkin.

"Puzzle I gotta solve," Alice answers.

"Puzzle? What, like a crossword?" He slides off his stool and steps closer. He is white as rice, his hair is red, his eyes are green, and he wears glasses.

"Nah, but it is a word problem." Alice exchanges a look with Tim, who shrugs. "Here. Have a look."

She pushes the napkin across the bar top. The tourist studies her scribbling.

He picks it up. "Which is it?"

"The sentence at the top there."

"'How he likes other almonds scarcely serves Caesar's actions'?"

"Yeah. Driving me bonkers. I tell ya, mate, I can kick every arse on a whole team of footballers, but I can't beat that one."

The tourist chuckles and looks at her. "You certainly look the part."

"I am the part." She downs the beer. "Killed two guys in China a couple days ago, saved a little Indian girl."

"That right?"

She smiles, makes it sound like a joke. "Damn right that's right."

"She's a big talker, mate," Tim explains to the tourist, though he knows Alice is telling the truth.

"Well, you won't get no trouble from me."

Tim refills their glasses. The tourist reaches for his wallet, but Tim shakes his head.

"On the house."

"Thanks," says the tourist. He rests the napkin on the bar. Afternoon sunlight filters through tinted windows. A neon Foster's sign buzzes, but only Alice is attuned enough to hear it.

"What's the prize?" the tourist asks.

"What?"

"The prize. What do you win if you solve it?"

"Ah. Fate of the world. Save the human race. Make sure my people and everyone I know and love survives and goes to heaven. That lot."

"Big prize then, huh?"

"Yeah, big, big prize."

She takes a swig.

The tourist lifts the napkin. "Well, I may be able to help, if, you know, you can cut me in on the action."

Alice lets loose a surprised guffaw. Even Tim laughs. The tourist looks between then, smiling uncertainly.

"You got any Koori blood, yank?" Tim asks him.

"Koori? What's that?"

Alice snorts again. "Never mind him, mate. I'll cut ya in."

Alice fishes in a pocket and pulls out a large wad of cash, all big bills. She slams it on the bar top. "How's that?"

The tourist's eyes widen at the sight of the money. "You're serious?"

"Ain't quite eternal salvation, mate, but it'll have to do. You can take it or leave it. I'll be the judge if you earn it, though."

"And don't be messing about," Tim adds, eyeballing the tourist with no small amount of menace.

"Yeah," says the tourist. "I thought we were just joking around."

"We're not," Alice replies, motioning impatiently. "Let's have it. I meant what I said about scrapping a team of footballers."

"And the two in China?" the tourist asks, swallowing hard.

Alice winks. "Yeah. That too."

The tourist relaxes a bit. The wink put him at ease, though he still eyes the money. "What's your name, anyway?"

"Alice the Hundred and Twelfth."

"Tim the Eighty-Sixth," adds the bartender.

"Dave, uh, the First, I guess," says the tourist.

"I doubt that," Tim says, knowing that this tourist Dave couldn't be the first of whatever line it is he belongs to. Alice isn't interested in all that. She wants to get on with it.

"Let's go, Dave," she says.

Dave takes the napkin up and points at the sentence. "Well, clearly it's a code for something. And the first letters don't seem to mean anything. But the first *two* letters—here and here, and then the rest of the way down—do mean something."

Alice takes the napkin from him. He watches her. The TV flashes a special report.

"So—*h*, yeah, but then *h-e*, and *l-i*, then *o*, and then *a-l, s-c, s-e, c-a, a-c*."

Tim stares at them both, surprised by Alice's widening smile. "I don't get it."

She looks at Dave. "Christ, mate! Those're elements!"

"Yep."

Alice slaps the bar top so hard everything on and under it jumps. Dave jumps too. Tim shakes his head, chuckling quietly.

Alice stands. "Money's yours, mate. If it comes to it, you can count on any Koori to get your back."

A shiny animated graphic on the news tells of a plane crash in the Indian Ocean.

Dave stares at the money. Before he can say thanks, Alice is gone. He turns back to Tim.

"You never told me what a Koori was."

"New rulers of the world," answers Tim, cleaning a glass with a worn towel. "New rulers of the world."

	186.21	190.23	192.22	195.08
28 Ni 58.693	**30** Zn 65.39	**31** Ga 69.723	**32** Ge 1.0079	**33**
8 O 15.999	**40** Zr 91.224	**36** Kr 83.80	**92** U 238.03	**93**
16 S 32.065	**10** Ne 20.180	**29** Cu 63.546	**82** Pb 207.2	**84**
11 Na 22.990	**47** Ag 107.87	**22** Ti 47.867	**50** Sn 118.71	**51**
61 Pm 145	**26** Fe 55.845	**73** Ta 180.95	**80** Hg 200.59	**83**
64 Gd 157.25	**65** Tb 158.93	**66** Dy 162.5	**67** Ho 164.93	**68**
96 Cm 247	**97** Bk 247	**98** Cf 251	**99** Es 252	**100**
105	**106**	**107**	**108**	**109**

KALA MOZAMI

Indian Ocean, ~120 km off the Coast of Oman

The plane plows into the water at 175 mph. Kala fights to hold on to her sense of calm, but a plane crash is quite an event. A rather terrible event. The worst part is not the violence of the impact. It's not the doors of the bathroom flying open and dumping supplies everywhere. It's not the edge of the sink pushing into her rib cage, bruising her, feeling like the pressure might chop her in half. It's not the smell of jet fuel, seawater, smoke, burning hair, or scorched rubber. It's not the uncertainty of what will happen next.

The worst part is the sounds.

First the groans of the plane as it descends. The instructions from the pilot, completely irrelevant now, a barely audible panicked droning. Then the loud repeated smack of the fuselage skimming across the water. The metallic shriek of the flaps as they are torn from the wings and bounce off the outside of the plane. The whirring of the engines as they take on water and fall apart. The first explosion, when it comes, is almost a relief. The screams, everyone screaming. Wailing, moaning, a baby crying. Another explosion, closer to the nose. The electrical system snapping as the lights fail.

And for a moment, a brief moment, silence.

The deepest, darkest, most profound silence she has ever heard.

A red emergency light comes on. Kala checks herself. Her right wrist is still cuffed. She still holds the gun. She's bruised and battered, and blood coats the right side of her head. She may have a broken rib but can deal with that. Overall she's fine. Her heart is working; her breath is even. The adrenaline is pumping and her energy is high.

She tries the door but it is jammed. She kicks it hard, and it flies halfway open, blocked by the body of Officer Singh. She steps out of the bathroom and over the dead cop. She removes the clip of ammo from his holster, finds the key to the cuffs in his jacket pocket. She undoes the remaining cuff and drops them to the floor, slides the clip into her back pocket, looks around. Most people are still in their seats, moaning and trying to recover. There's a large hole in the starboard side of the plane. There is sunlight filtering through it, and through the windows, and through the smoke. Halfway down the center aisle there's a woman on fire; two men are trying to put her out with blankets. A little closer, Kala sees the bulk of a cargo container, forced up through the floor and into the seats, which in turn were forced into the overhead compartments. Sparks fly from exposed electrical wiring. A leg dangles; its owner is crushed.

A person screams a few rows away. It's hard to tell if the voice is male or female. Kala pushes into the aisle and sees a sheet of metal embedded in a seat back; it has decapitated the passenger next to the screamer. The person across the aisle begs frantically, "Where's the head? Where's the head?" but no one answers, and no one seems to know. After a moment someone tells this person to shut up, but he doesn't.

There's commotion at the front of the plane and a loud creaking sound. It's at this moment that Kala realizes that the nose is taking on water—fast—and the fuselage is tilting to the fore. The wings, so long as they are intact, will help keep the plane afloat, but given enough time it will tilt more, sink; she knows she has to get out, now, now, now.

Someone is walking urgently toward her. It's the Western boy. He's frightened and rattled, but his body is whole and he knows that he has to get out too. Kala looks in the rear overhead next to her and finds the emergency kit and the transponder. Before she turns to the exit door the Western boy says, "You need your bag?"

Plane crashes are strange things, she thinks.

He is looking right at her, stopped at the row where she was sitting. "Yes!" she yells over the confusion.

He reaches into the compartment and grabs her bag, and only her bag. *This is not a coincidence. He's been watching me.* She'll have to figure out why later.

She turns to the galley. Two of the food carts have escaped their bays and are blocking the emergency exit. Trays, cups, and carafes are everywhere. Burst cans of Sprite and Coke hiss on the floor. A tray of small bottles of alcohol lies at her feet. She goes to the starboard door and pulls the big handles covered in warnings, pushes the door open; the raft inflates. Outside it's bright and calm. The water is limitless. *We should call it Ocean, not Earth,* Kala thinks.

Water begins to wash over the threshold of the doorway, and she knows it won't be long until the plane goes down.

"You ready?" the boy asks, his voice shaking.

She had already forgotten about him.

She turns to say that she is, but no words come out. The boy is strong, tall, athletic. His left arm is bleeding. A bruise is rising over his right eye.

"Yes," Kala says.

She puts a leg in the raft and Kala hears another sound. A young girl begging her mother in Arabic not to let her die. The mother, sounding strong and sure, telling her it will be all right. As if he can understand, the Western boy holds up a finger and turns. The mother and daughter are standing in the back row. The boy wades through dark water that is steadily rising, now at his ankles. He goes to the mother and the daughter, and they appear untouched, as if graced by God. It is like the crash didn't happen for them at all. The boy grabs the mother by the arm.

"Come!" he shouts in English. Kala knows that the only men to have ever touched the young mother are her husband and her father. Perhaps an older brother. It would be an abomination if this were happening anywhere else in the Middle East, under any other circumstances.

The boy says, "Now!" and pulls the woman and her child. Water is flowing in white swirls around their knees. The mother nods, and they wade to the door. Kala is already in the raft. The boy ushers the mother and child in, follows them.

"What about the others?" the girl asks in Arabic.

The boy cannot understand.

"There is no time," Kala answers. She notices the mother looking at Kala in fear. Her hijab is perfect. Her eyes are like new copper coins. Kala detaches the raft but cannot push off. The water is being sucked into the doorway so quickly now that it holds the thick yellow rubber against the metal of the plane. Just as the doorway is about to disappear underwater, a hand materializes, a voice screaming for help. But the person it belongs to cannot escape the pull of the water.

The door goes under. Kala pushes off. The raft drifts away from the plane, and the four of them watch in horror and shock as the plane sinks. The nose depresses and the tail rises. Some things escape the wreckage and pop to the surface. Seat cushions. Chunks of foam. Parts of a body. But no one living. For a minute or so, as the passengers drown, the plane floats just below the surface, the rudder and the rear stabilizers up in the air. A stream of bubbles appears as the last air pocket is breached, and the plane pitches underwater and disappears. Just like that it is gone.

And everyone in it.

Never to be seen again.

"I have a transponder," Kala says.

"And there's a sat phone in here," Christopher says, patting Kala's bag. *How does he know that?* she wonders. She'll have to ask when the time is right.

The girl starts crying, and her mother tries to soothe her. The sea is calm and there's no breeze. The sun is setting. They are the only survivors. *Blessings for life,* Kala thinks. *And for death.*

After a while the girl stops crying and they're all quiet.

Alone on a raft in the middle of the ocean.

SARAH ALOPAY, JAGO TLALOC

Renzo's Garage, An Nabi Yunus, Mosul, Iraq

Sarah and Jago are greeted at the airport by a squat, jovial, 47-year-old man named Renzo, who arranged for them to bypass security. Unlike the new arrivals, who have already started sweating in Iraq's profound heat, Renzo doesn't seem bothered. He's used to the weather here. Even though he's a touch overweight, Sarah can still see—in the way he moves, how he sizes her up—that Renzo used to be a Player.

"Everything, all the time, everywhere . . ." Renzo says in English, staring at Jago.

". . . So says, and so has been said, and so will be said again," Jago finishes.

Renzo grins, satisfied, and claps Jago hard on the arm. "It's been too long, Jago. Last time I saw you, you were still hiding behind your mother's skirts."

Jago shifts, uncomfortable, glancing at Sarah. "Yeah, Renzo. Long time."

"Now you're all grown up. Big man, big Player." Renzo whistles, turning from Jago to Sarah. "And who is this?"

"My name is Sarah Alopay, the Cahokian of the 233rd. Jago and I are working together."

"You are, eh?" Renzo asks with an air of disapproval.

"This is my Endgame, Renzo," Jago says forcefully, his expression darkening.

"But you play for us. For the survival of our line. Not to impress some *gringa*." He looks Sarah up and down. "At least she's pretty."

"Shut up, fat man, or I'll show you *my* Endgame," Sarah threatens.

Renzo chuckles. "Feisty, too. That's good. Don't worry, Sarah Alopay, I have no interest in dishonoring you. Players kill Players, that's what our line says. Pudgy ex-Players, we just offer support when called on. Come along." He walks away, leads them to a yellow pickup truck. In a couple of minutes they're navigating the crowded streets of Mosul. Sarah sits in the backseat, Jago in the passenger seat next to Renzo. The streets are loud, and Renzo has his radio blaring. Jago leans in close to Renzo, not wanting Sarah to hear.

"Do not question me in front of her, understand?" Jago hisses. Renzo flashes a jovial grin, but it quickly fades when he sees Jago's expression. "I'm sorry, Jago. It won't happen again."

"Good," Jago says, leaning back, satisfied. Renzo isn't frightened of Jago so much as he's frightened of Jago's parents. It was a generous "scholarship" from the Tlaloc fund that put Renzo through engineering school, allowing him to set up shop here, just in time to become a fixer for the American military during the war and amass a small fortune. What the Tlalocs have given, they can take away. Even for an ex-Player. Renzo knows this.

Of course, since Endgame has begun, that doesn't much matter anymore.

Sarah leans forward, shouting to be heard. "What're you guys talking about?"

"I was telling Renzo we need new passports and visas," Jago answers. "If someone's tracking us, we should start fresh."

"Good idea," Sarah says.

Renzo nods enthusiastically. "Don't worry! Renzo's got it all." And he isn't exaggerating. This becomes obvious as he pulls their car into a large, air-conditioned garage, his base of operations. He has everything Jago and Sarah will need and more: new phones, laptops, power converters, SIM cards, all manner of scramblers. He has a stash of fresh visas for over 40 countries. He has traveler's checks and money and fake passports. He has medical equipment and clothing and gloves and armor. He has trackers and receivers. He has Browning pistols and M4 machine guns with underbarrel M203 grenade launchers. He even has two very special pistols made entirely of ceramic and plastic that are completely undetectable to any kind of imaging equipment. What he had to do to get those from the US Special Forces is a story unto itself, he tells them.

"You've done well for yourself, Renzo," Jago says, examining one of the strange guns. "I'll tell my parents it was money well spent."

"This is amazing," Sarah agrees, looking around. She's impressed; there aren't any former Cahokian Players with arsenals set up in disparate parts of the world. She made a wise decision pairing up with Jago.

"I haven't even shown you the best part," Renzo says.

Apparently, the best part is a piece-of-crap-looking 2003 Peugeot 307 hatchback. It's painted baby blue and has a large flower stenciled on the hood. Hippy trinkets and talismans hang from the rearview mirror. It rides low to the ground and the upholstery is torn. There is a big dent in the front right fender. Part of the hood is beginning to rust. The rear window sports a hand-sized spiderweb of cracked glass.

"You drive this thing in Mosul?" Jago asks incredulously. "With the flower?"

Renzo rubs his hand lovingly across the hood. "The flower works like a charm. It makes people think, 'There goes a man too stupid to have anything to hide.'"

"I can see that," Sarah says, smirking at Renzo.

"So what's the big deal? It looks like a piece of shit," Jago says.

"I've been working on this baby for months," Renzo replies, affronted. "It's no piece of shit."

The dents, Renzo explains, are all cosmetic. The chassis is rebuilt, better than new. The engine packs 487 horses instead of the standard 108. The entire exterior of the car is bulletproof. A blast shield coats the underside. It has 15 smuggling compartments, one large enough for a person. Its license plates are coated with a special kind of e-ink and can change on command. There are presets for Iraq, Turkey, Greece, Italy, Lichtenstein, Austria, France, and Israel. The flower is also e-ink and can be changed to a star and crescent, or a peace sign, or a turtle, or made simply to disappear. The vehicle has a high-speed computer with carbon nanoswitches and encrypted satellite uplinks that controls all of its systems.

"I'm almost done with the windshield," Renzo says, out of breath from listing the car's features. "When I am, it'll have a digital HUD. Show you maps, traffic info, whatever you want. Oh, and night vision. I forgot to mention the night vision."

"And this is for me?" Jago asks, sounding like he can't believe his luck. He glances over at Sarah. "For us?"

Renzo nods. "I'm not happy about this Endgame business. I hoped I'd be dead before it came. I'm rich. Life is good." Renzo sighs dramatically, and Sarah almost laughs. "This car, it's the least I can do for the Player of my line. You keep Renzo alive. I'm proud to give it to you."

Jago clasps Renzo's hand. "I'm proud to accept it, brother."

Dinner that night is grilled lamb with mint leaves over rice. They have succulent figs drizzled with sweet syrup for dessert. They have tea. They discuss how they are going to get to Italy—overland in the 307, crossing Turkey, Bulgaria, Serbia, Croatia, and Slovenia. It is a 2,341.74 mile-long drive.

After dinner, they do what they can to relax. Renzo is in the passenger seat of the 307, running diagnostics. Jago is watching Al Jazeera with the sound muted, his body stretched across one of Renzo's leather couches. Sarah is standing over a large map of the world.

She is placing little silver hex nuts on the map at various locations. Some are very random: a dot in southwestern Siberia, a little point near the Ryukyu Islands of Japan, a speck on the southern coast of South Africa. Others are so predictable as to be cliché: the pyramids at Giza, Machu Picchu, Stonehenge. And then there is one that is somewhere in between random and predictable, with the added bonus of being nearby.

Sarah leans over the map.

She punches some numbers into Google on a small laptop.

The results come up quickly.

"Either of you ever heard of Gobekli Tepe, in Turkey?" Sarah asks. The word *gobekli* is familiar to Sarah, it's Old Cahokian for "round-topped hill," and usually refers to ancient burial mounds. But what this word means in connection to some random place in southern Turkey, she has no idea.

"No," Jago says from the couch.

"Gobekli Tepe? Of course!" Renzo says from the 307.

"What is it?"

"Ancient archeological site in Turkey. Not too far from here. No one knows who made it or how it was made. It's turned a lot of assumptions on their ear. Like when humans started making cities, when they started worshipping in temples, and why and who they were worshipping. Little things like that."

Jago perks up. "Endgame things."

Renzo pulls himself from the car. "That's right."

Sarah puts her elbows on the table. She stares at the tan earth around the hex nut.

"You think we should go there?" Jago asks.

Sarah considers this. Renzo wipes his hands on a rag and wanders closer to the TV. "I don't know," Sarah finally says. "More than anything, we need to see that Musterion guy in Italy."

Jago nods. "Agreed."

Renzo points at the newscast. "Can you unmute it?" Jago picks up the remote and pushes a button. Renzo moves closer to the TV and translates from the Arabic, "A plane crash. Commercial flight. Qatar Airways 832 from Changzhou to Dubai."

"Where'd it go down?" Sarah asks.

"Arabian Sea."

"Survivors?" Jago wonders.

"Possibly. Authorities are picking up a transponder signal. An Omani rescue team is en route. No other contact. They won't know the full situation until they get to the site."

"Changzhou," Sarah says slowly.

"You think some of the others were on that flight?"

"It's possible. Could even be *why* it crashed," Sarah muses. "Wouldn't be the worst thing in the world if we lost some Players, would it?"

"No," Jago says. "It wouldn't." He mutes the TV again.

Renzo goes back to the car and resumes his work. "Only a couple more days and this baby will be ready to roll," he says.

And just then, Sarah's sat phone rings. She fishes the phone from her pack, recognizes the number as being from another sat phone, and turns it off. Part of her hopes it was Christopher. She hasn't answered any of his calls—refuses to go down that road—but she likes knowing that he's out there. Maybe it's selfish, but she likes that he's still thinking about her.

"Who was it?" Jago asks.

"Don't know," Sarah says. "But it could have been An tracking us. We've got to get rid of this thing, Feo."

"Leave it here," Renzo offers. "I'll wipe it and set up untraceable call forwarding to your new phones, if you like."

Sarah goes back to the map. "Thanks, that would be great."

Jago falls back into the couch, starts to drift off.

Renzo tinkers with some wire couplers.

Sarah glances at Jago. He looks good, stretched out that way. Peaceful. She has the sudden urge to lie down next to him. She doesn't want to be alone. Not while there's still a chance to connect, while the world still seems normal, even if it isn't.

She smiles, to herself, for herself, and returns to the map. After a couple more minutes she looks over. He still looks good, peaceful, and she still wants to join him. She decides what the hell. Steps over and lies down, the heat from Jago's body immediately warming her.

It feels good. So good.

No one on Earth knows for certain:

Pyramids at Giza.
Nazca lines.
Moai.
Stonehenge.
Sphinx.
Machu Picchu.
Gobekli Tepe.
Carnac.
Aramu Muru.
Ziggurat of Ur.
Teotihuacan.
Angkor Wat.
Pumapunku.
Terracotta Warriors.
Pyramids of Meroe.
Sacsayhuamán.
Anta Grande do Zambujeiro.

No one on Earth knows.
But some*one*, some*thing*, some*where* does. . . .

CHRISTOPHER VANDERKAMP, KALA MOZAMI

Raft, Indian Ocean, ~120 km off the Coast of Oman

Christopher huddles in the corner of the raft. The mother and her daughter are asleep. Kala is asleep. The sea is calm. The sky is clear and dark and punctured with stars. He has never seen so many stars, not even camping in Nebraska.

He looks at his watch. The plane sank 4.5 hours ago. The transponder is on. Kala refused to use the sat phone to call for help. She said that if there was no rescue by sunup they could make a call. Until then, the transponder would be their best bet. Now that the plane is gone, he can't stop thinking of the crash. When it was happening it didn't seem that bad, but now that it's over it feels crippling and overwhelming. He survived a plane crash.

A horrible fucking plane crash.

He wants to see Sarah. Needs to see her. Wants to touch her. Needs to touch her. He turns his head. Kala's bag with the phone is in arm's reach. He looks at Kala. The girl who jumped out of a building and flew to the ground. The girl who somehow disarmed the sky marshal sent to arrest her. Christopher saw the dead officer's face as he left the plane. A gunshot wound. That was what had killed the man. A gunshot to the eye at point-blank range.

Therefore, Kala has a gun.

She sleeps soundly, easily, as if nothing happened, as if she didn't kill a man and let dozens of others die after the crash. When Sarah told him about Endgame, and the Players, and the training she'd received, it all seemed unreal. Now that he knows what it is, and has seen what the Players can do, it is all too real. Would Sarah have shot that air marshal in the face? Would she have detached the raft before other survivors had a chance to get on? Christopher doesn't think so.

He needs to hear Sarah's voice.

Talk to her.

Make sure she's okay.

He reaches for Kala's bag and slides it along the rubber floor. He slowly unzips it, gets the phone. He pushes the power switch and smothers it with his chest while it comes on. He waits, looks; the green light of the display glows. He mutes the number pad, dials; the line rings, once, twice, three times; voice mail.

Beep.

He whispers, "Sarah. Sarah, it's me. I don't know what to say. . . . I . . . I followed you. It was stupid but I did it. I love you, Sarah. I went to the pagoda and didn't see you and followed this other person, another Player. Kala something. God, she's . . . I don't know what she is. . . . She's not like you."

The line cracks and the connection fails. Christopher peeks at the keypad. Should he redial? Maybe she would pick up? But if Kala caught him it wouldn't be good. No. He pushes the power button again and the phone shuts down. Quietly, he puts it back in Kala's bag. He rolls onto his back and exhales. He can feel the ocean under his spine and shoulders and butt. It's like a water bed, but alive.

There are so many stars. So many.

A fucking plane crash.

So many stars.

So much death.

The crash . . . the ocean . . . the gun . . . Sarah . . . stars.

Sleep.

He jolts awake. It is still dark and the stars twinkle like tinsel. His side hurts. Kala stands over him.

Christopher rubs his eyes. "Why did you kick me?"

He struggles to sit as she demands, "Why did you call her?" She brandishes the sat phone like a weapon.

Christopher peers around Kala's legs and hips. Moves quickly to the other side and squints.

They're not there.

Gone.

He looks at Kala's face, concealed in shadow. "Where're the others?" His voice betrays his fear.

"I let them go."

"W-what?"

"They're not here."

"You killed them?"

"Forget them. They were ghosts. All of you are. Mention them again—to anyone—and you will join them in hell."

"You killed them?" he repeats.

Kala drops and is in Christopher's face in a split second, her thumb and index finger pinching his Adam's apple. "I mean it, Christopher Vanderkamp." She has rendered him speechless. His eyes go wide. "I looked at your passport. Omaha. Like the Cahokian. Now tell me why you called her. And remember—do not mention the others."

She releases his throat and stands. Christopher coughs. Why did she kill them? How? Did she drown them? Break their necks? Smother them? Did she do the mother first or the daughter?

His stomach turns. It is all he can do to hold it in.

"The Cahokian!" Kala barks.

"I . . . I'm . . . her boyfriend."

Kala laughs and throws her head to the side. Christopher sees the gun in her hand. Did she shoot them? No. He would have heard.

He becomes suddenly aware of the faint *thump thump* of distant helicopter blades. Rescue is on the way.

"An amazing love story, told at the end of the world," Kala exclaims, her eyes gleaming. "How pathetic. And your name! 'Bearer of

Christ.' What a joke." The sound of the rescue chopper grows louder. Kala gazes across the horizon but can't see it yet. "Listen carefully, Christopher. You are my companion. My name is Jane Mathews." As she says the words, her accent changes, becoming completely American and slightly southern, like maybe she's from Oklahoma or western Arkansas. "There will be some problems, because my name will not be on the passenger manifest. But the men on the helicopter will not know that. You are to vouch for me. We met three days ago in Xi'an. We fell for each other. Since we met, we have spent every minute together. *Every* minute. Like so many other people around the world, we have become obsessed with the meteors. We are going to Al Ain to see the crater there. I have a birthmark shaped like a shark's fin on my left buttock. Do you have any birthmarks?"

"I have a mole behind my knee."

"Which one?"

"Left."

"If you're lying, I'll kill you."

"I'm not."

"Excellent. We will end up in Dubai, as planned. And once we are free from the authorities, we will continue our trip to Turkey."

A searchlight flashes over the water in the west.

"Can you repeat that to me?"

He does. She corrects him about which buttock the birthmark is on.

"What about the plane crash?" he asks.

"What about it? It happened. We are the sole survivors. We were both thrown to the back of the plane. We were not unconscious; everyone else was. We escaped. It sank."

"And the gun?"

Kala throws it in the water. "I don't need a gun to kill you, Christopher." He considers tackling her overboard, but he's seen how quick she is. "Don't try me. My hands are faster than your brain," Kala says, as if reading his mind. "Remember, Jane Mathews. We're together. We're in love. Al Ain. Shark's fin birthmark."

"Yeah, I got—"

But before he can finish, faster than any cornerback on a sneak blitz, she's on him. Two quick shots to the jaw, and he's out.

FORM 500
U.S. DEPARTMENT OF LABOR
IMMIGRATION SERVICE

MANIFEST OF ALIEN PASSENGERS FOR THE UNITED S

MANIFIESTO DE PASAJEROS EXTRANJEROS; VERZEICHNIS AUSLÄNDISCHER REISENDER; MANIFESTE DE PASSAGERS ÉTRANGERS; 艙單外國人的乘客

List 23

S. S. .... NIRENBERG ....,

Point of Origin .... UNITED KINGDOM ....,

#		A — PASSENGER IDENTIFICATION / Identificación de pasajero / Passagier-Identifikation / Identification des passagers / 乘客識別	B — NAME IN FULL / Nombre completo / Name, Vorname / Nom complet / 全名		C — Age / Edad / Alter / Age / 年齡	D — Married? / ¿Casado? / Verheiratet? / Marié? / 結婚了嗎?	E — Nationality / Nacionalidad / Staatsangehörigkeit / Nationalité / 國籍	F — Race or People / Raza / Stamm oder Volk / Ethnicité / 種族
1	N C I	0 0 0 0 2 .1 2	OLGUN	MUSTAFA	3 4	X	Turkey	Turkish
2	N C I	0 0 9 9 5 4 3 5	OLGUN	ZAHIRA	2 7	X	Turkey	Turkish
3	MINOR	9 9 7 5 4 4 6	OLGUN	ALEXANDER	8		Turkey	Turkish
4	N C I	0 0 0 0 1 1 0	GAMOWE	ZAHIRA ANNA	2 3	X	Australia	Koori
5	N C I	9 2 4 9 2 2 7	GAMOWE	HOLLEY	1 9	X	Australia	Koori
6	MINOR	9 2 7 4 9 2 4 4	GAMOWE	JACK	1		Australia	Koori
7	N C I	0 0 0 0 4 .1 2	YAMAMOTO	MASAO	5 4		Japan	Japanese
8	N C I	9 6 9 1 3 5 1	YAMAMOTO	NISHI	3 2		Japan	Japanese
9		9 6 9 1 3 6 5	YAMAMOTO	KAZUKO	2 0		Japan	Japanese
10	N C I	0 0 0 0 2 .1 2	MARCZEWSKI	BRENNER	4 1	X	Poland	Hebrew
11	N C	0 2 1 2 3 1 0	MARCZEWSKI	WALERIA	3 8	X	Poland	Hebrew
12	MINOR	2 1 2 3 1 0 3 9 7	MARCZEWSKI	WATSON	1 5		Poland	Hebrew

CHIYOKO TAKEDA

Bus from Kayseri to Urfa, E90 Highway, Turkey

Chiyoko is headed southeast in a tourist bus from Kayseri to Urfa. She did not have any desire to go to Iraq, and she presumed that Sarah and Jago would be there for only a short while.

It has been a little longer than she expected.

The computerized blip imbedded in the scar in Jago Tlaloc's neck has barely moved for 48 hours. Still, he *has* moved. He *is* alive. Or, if he's dead, his body has been carried around.

She decides that if they're not on the move within 48 hours, she will steal a car and go to the Ibrahim Khalil border crossing and wait. And if they are not on the move within another 12 hours, she'll go into Iraq and find them.

Chiyoko looks out the window. The hills of central Turkey pass by in a tan procession. It is a beautiful country. At once barren and full. The people have been kind, as much as she has had to deal with them. The desserts in Kayseri were exquisite.

She closes her eyes and thinks of An. He sent her an encrypted email that led her to a website. It had a black background and white type and all it said was: *There is no judgment.* And below this: *ZIP ICE.* And below this a link: 驚.

She clicked it, a file downloaded, and she put the file on five jump drives. One of these she keeps with her at all times.

After she got the file, the site self-destructed.

He is part of her now.

For better or worse, part of her.

BAITSAKHAN

Rahatlık Konuk Evi, Urfa, Turkey

Baitsakhan drags a strike-anywhere match across the top of the wall
and lights a hand-rolled cigarette. Jalair stares through a pair of high-
powered binoculars on a tripod pointed at a small hotel on the eastern
edge of Urfa. They are on a rooftop. It has a garden. Honeysuckle,
rosemary, a dwarf jacaranda, endless twisting vines of green grapes
and morning glories encase the terrace. Baitsakhan pulls a violet
morning glory from its stem and turns it in his fingers, making it thin
and lifeless. He spits some loose tobacco on the white-painted rooftop.
He drops the flower. Puts his foot over it. Crushes it.

"See anything?"

Jalair shakes his head. "No."

They've been in Turkey for 2.45 days, shadowing the chipped
Nabataean.

"Where the hell is he?"

"I don't know."

"Bat and Bold should be with us," Baitsakhan growls. "We should have
chased the Harrapan instead. Track the bitch down."

Jalair shakes his head again. "We are not in this for revenge, Baitsakhan.
In the end she will get what is coming to her. They all will."

Baitsakhan doesn't like it, but he knows that his older brother is right.
Jalair squints into the eyepiece and takes hold of the long barrels of
the binoculars. "Wait. I think . . . yes. It's him."

Baitsakhan stands. "Move." He pulls on the cigarette and leans
forward. He holds the puff of smoke in his lungs.

He is looking through the binoculars at another rooftop 95 m away.

Maccabee Adlai is alone and has his back to them. He looks over a shoulder, practically right at Baitsakhan, but it's not a searching look. The Nabataean is simply admiring the sunset. He doesn't know what's out there waiting for him.

Baitsakhan and Jalair know that Maccabee has been in Urfa for three days. He flew in on an aliased New Zealand passport. He's been in this small hotel since his arrival. He booked every room and paid the proprietor to mind his business. He's gone to the old market twice and visited 18 mosques and one library. He's stopped at 19 different internet cafés. He bought an Audi sedan from a private dealer and could've bought a second car with what he spent on clothing. He is alone and doesn't seem to be actively communicating with anyone. Baitsakhan is not alone.

His people, members of his line, have always hunted in small packs. He pulls away from the binoculars. He hands Jalair the cigarette, picks up a modern compound bow from the ground, and strings an arrow. He raises it, pulls the string, and sights through a scope. Maccabee's back is there. He moves incrementally. Maccabee's neck. Moves again. His head.

"Suhkbataar wouldn't be pleased, but I prefer this kind of bow to our traditional ones," Baitsakhan says. Jalair is silent. Baitsakhan lowers the bow and eases up on the string. "Tonight we go in. Tonight we take his clue and kill him and move on."

Jalair nods, takes a drag off the cigarette. "Good. I want to kill something. Any death is better than none."

A flock of pigeons explodes over them from an adjacent building. As the sun sets, the call to prayer rings out over the ancient city.

"Yes, brother. Any death is good."

KALA MOZAMI,
CHRISTOPHER VANDERKAMP

InterContinental Hotel Dubai–Festival City, Room 260

Kala watches the boy sleep. They've made it through the aftermath of the crash, the questions and the reporters and the paperwork. Kala has not appeared on TV or the web or in print, and Christopher has only appeared for a brief second, a jacket draped over his shoulders, as they were hustled from a dark SUV into a building. They've interviewed with the airline and the investigators and counselors. Like any innocent person, Kala didn't try to explain the absence of the name Jane Mathews from the manifest, but how else could she have gotten on the raft in the middle of the ocean? The American accent and the alibi provided by Christopher were enough evidence that she was not the wanted person that Agent Singh had been ordered to arrest. The lack of her name was a snafu, nothing more. Kala Mozami, all assumed, perished along with the other 274 passengers and crew. *Blessings.*

Kala and Christopher are in a glass tower, the Dubai InterContinental. Qatar Airways is paying for their suite. To keep up appearances, they share the room. Christopher is in the bed, a soft sheet pulled to his chin, staring at the ceiling. He's recounted the crash a dozen times, and his story hasn't wavered. He's been convincing and he knows it. Every time he's left them out. The mother and the daughter. The dead. The murdered. Drifting in the depths of their eternal resting place. Kala walks from the living room into the bedroom and stops in front of a huge plateglass window. Christopher props himself up in the bed. He stares at her. Outside the window is the endless desert, the red wall of a sandstorm raging in the distance.

Kala looks out the window. She remembers the old stories. The ones about the storms in the time before time. How they were used as shrouds by the Annunaki to conceal their vessels and their numbers. How, in turn, the great storms came to be like gods themselves. Obscuring, blinding, stinging gods without mercy.

I am the storm, she thinks. *Descended from the time before time, taught to obscure, blind, sting.*

Without mercy.

She turns to Christopher. "You did very well, Christopher Vanderkamp. We're free to move on to Turkey as planned."

He is silent.

"I would thank you if I thought it would mean anything to you."

He is silent.

"I'll do so anyway. Thank you."

Christopher doesn't want to speak to this murderer. They've been approached by all kinds of reporters since the plane crash and they all want to write the same story about young lovers surviving a tragedy. Young lovers—the very thought makes him want to puke. Kala, on the other hand, has spent the last two days seeming amused by all the attention. She knows that she'll disappear soon, go back to Endgame. When that happens, Christopher wonders, what will happen to him? He hasn't been able to shake the thought of the dead mother and daughter. They had survived a plane crash, why kill them? And even though he doesn't want to speak to her, Christopher can't help himself; he wants to know. "Why did you kill them?"

She turns from the window. "I did them a favor."

"Why not do me a favor, then?"

She steps toward him. "Because of the Cahokian. She's my adversary. One of ten who remain, as far as I know. I'm going to use you to get to her."

"Then I'll use *you* to do the same," he says defiantly.

She laughs.

"What's so funny?"

"What has your little girlfriend told you?"

"That there are twelve of you. That you're playing this psychotic Endgame thing for the fate of the world."

"No. Not the world, Christopher." Kala smiles sadly. "The world is already dead."

Christopher looks around. "Seems pretty alive to me."

"She didn't tell you everything," Kala says, pinching her lip thoughtfully. "I suppose I wouldn't have either. It'd be like explaining trigonometry to a dog. A waste of breath. She pities you, her handsome high school sweetheart, so she let you go on in ignorance."

"Uh-huh. I'm ignorant. Must be why I had such an easy time following you."

Kala bristles at that. She is ashamed this non-Player was able to track her and blames the distraction caused by her clue. Slowly, she walks toward the bed.

"I do not pity you, Christopher. You are just a bargaining chip to me. So I will tell you the truth." She gets closer. "Everything you think you know about the world is a lie. We did not come from the apes. There was no natural selection. It was actual, literal, intentional selection. The Annunaki created us to be their slaves, and gave us the tools to build what the world has become. And it is happening again. Your little girlfriend, me, the others—we don't fight for the fate of the world. We fight to be selected. To be the favorite pet of the gods."

Christopher just stares at her. Kala isn't sure if he's understood her, and doesn't really care either way. She's right next to the bed now.

"Rest assured, you won't be picked," Kala says.

She strikes quickly, before Christopher can even flinch, hits a pressure point behind his ear. He's out immediately.

I am the storm.

She sneers at the unconscious boy before turning her back on him. She goes to the desk and picks up her sat phone. She hasn't used it since the raft. She accesses the recent calls. She selects the number Christopher dialed. She hits send.

It doesn't ring. There is an automated voice followed by a beep. "Cahokian, this is Kala Mozami, your Sumerian sister, the Player of the 89th. I regret having to do this, but this is Endgame." Kala is using her honey-dipped voice, hoping her apologies will soften her request and ingratiate her to Sarah. "I have something of yours. A boy named Christopher. I did not seek him. He found me. He would like to find you. I will give him to you. But in return I want what the Annunaki— kepler 22b—gave to you. You may call me back at this number if you wish to strike a deal. And if you don't, trust that I will discard him. Despite his high opinion of himself, he's too much of a burden to keep for long. I hope this message finds you well. And I hope to hear from you soon. *Bedrood*, sister Sarah, until we speak."

She hangs up, plugs the phone into the charger, makes sure the ringer is turned up.

When Sarah calls, she does not want to miss it.

And Christopher won't want her to miss it either.

BAITSAKHAN, MACCABEE ADLAI

Aslan Konuk Evi, Urfa, Turkey

Baitsakhan and Jalair scuttle across rooftops, making hardly any noise. A waning half-moon hangs 21 degrees above the eastern horizon. They wear heavy gloves so that they can prop their hands on the shards of broken glass embedded in the tops of the parapet walls. They're incredibly fast, agile. If they were to be spotted, they'd be gone before they could be seen again.

Jalair has the compound bow and a small collection of arrows. In a hip holster Baitsakhan has a Heckler & Koch USP Compact Tactical pistol with a suppressor. He has a wavy Mongolian dagger in his right hand. They want and expect to kill tonight. They're both looking forward to it.

Two more rooftops to go.

One.

None.

They're on top of the small hotel. Jalair consults a miniature screen on his wristband that has a three-dimensional representation of Maccabee's location. Jalair puts a fist in the air, raises a finger, remakes a fist. They move for the door on the roof.

Locked.

Jalair slides a rake pick and a tension tool from his sleeve. He puts them in the tumbler and fiddles and closes his eyes and slowly opens the door.

A dark staircase is before them. A light is on in the hall at the bottom. Jalair steps in and goes down the stairs. He nocks an arrow loosely on the string. He looks at his wrist display. They need to go down two more flights before they reach him.

There is one room on the top floor. They go down. Two rooms on the next floor. All the rooms are empty, their doors open. Down. Two rooms on this floor. One door open, the other closed. They switch off the hall light.

Light comes up from the ground floor, so it's not completely dark. Baitsakhan pulls the pistol from its holster and steps to the front. He points at himself, and then at Jalair, and then at the ground where Jalair stands. He wants Jalair to stay behind. Baitsakhan is the Player, and he will do this alone.

Jalair nods and stands aside.

Baitsakhan puts his hand on the knob and tries the door. It is unlocked. He pushes it forward enough to wedge his body into the room. Filtered light from the street touches the room here and there. Baitsakhan sees a desk, a chair, a suitcase. A Sig Sauer 9mm pistol is on the suitcase. A bed is in the corner. On the bed is the Nabataean. Sleeping, stupidly sleeping.

The gun has an exploding round in it that will obliterate Maccabee's legs. Unlike the Harrapan, Maccabee will not be running away. They will tie off his severed limbs or burn the wounds closed. Jalair will inject him with sodium thiopental and they will ask him some questions. When they get what they want, what Baitsakhan needs, they'll kill him.

Baitsakhan raises the gun, squeezes the trigger, fires.

Maccabee rolls to the floor and the mattress explodes in a shower of feathers. Baitsakhan lowers the pistol, fires again, but Maccabee is on him already, holding a hardbound book with two hands. The round pushes through this, rending it in two. Baitsakhan's gun hand is being boxed by the halves of the book. Maccabee twists his hands, and the gun comes free, falling to the floor.

Maccabee kicks the gun away. Baitsakhan swipes his wavy dagger through the air, but Maccabee moves his body out of the way.

"Little shit," growls Maccabee.

Jalair comes bow-first into the room. Maccabee catches sight of the silver arrowhead and throws himself backward into the door, breaking the arrow and crunching Jalair's face on the other side. Maccabee pushes the door closed, breaking the weapon, and slides a bar across the door to keep Jalair out.

Baitsakhan charges with the knife. Maccabee jumps, grabs a rafter, and lifts his feet just as Baitsakhan stabs the space where he was standing. Maccabee brings his feet down hard on Baitsakhan's shoulders.

Baitsakhan absorbs Maccabee's hit by collapsing to the floor.

Maccabee swings over Baitsakhan and lands by the table. He grabs his pistol and turns. He gets three shots off, but Baitsakhan is moving too much from side to side. Maccabee gets off one more shot and it grazes Baitsakhan's ear, clipping a miniscule notch out of the lower part of his lobe.

Their ears are ringing now, Maccabee's all the worse on account of his injury in the pagoda. The Donghu slams his heel into Maccabee's foot just as Maccabee brings his head down for a strike across Baitsakhan's nose. But Baitsakhan's head is already rising up in order to smash the bottom of Maccabee's jaw.

Their heads collide with a loud crack.

For a moment, they are both dazed.

"Fuck!" they both say.

Baitsakhan vaults to his feet, the knife flashing in the intermittent light. Maccabee draws the suitcase from the table in front of him like a shield. Baitsakhan swipes and stabs and Maccabee parries. Baitsakhan brings the knife high and the blade sinks into the case, and he twists the whole arrangement away from Maccabee. The case bangs to the floor.

There's a brief pause as they size each other up. In that silence they hear the twang of a bowstring. In the hallway, a body hits the floor. Jalair has had to kill someone. At the same time, both Baitsakhan and Maccabee ask, "Police?"

No, they would be louder. It must've been the innkeeper, they think at the same time.

It's only a brief détente. The two Players barrel into the space between them. Each wants the other to think that he is unarmed.

I have him, Maccabee thinks, his pinkie ring flipped open and the needle ready.

I have him, Baitsakhan thinks, as a long anodized razor flicks out of his specialized glove, completely invisible in the dark rush of combat.

They meet and grapple with each other, and each fails to land the finishing touch. But each gets the point in place—the needle over the cheek and the razor along the jugular—and each can feel the cold of the metal—a thin line for the razor and a pinpoint for the needle—and in that instant they realize that they are both about to lose Endgame.

They freeze. Their eyes lock.

Both are breathing hard.

At the same time each demands, "What's your clue?"

They exchange a look of disbelief.

"Where are you going?" Again, said in unison.

"I'll kill you!" Together.

They look nothing alike, but they might as well be staring in a mirror. They each recognize it. They have fought to a draw. They are a match. But there is more. Both recognize that they are killers. Highly skilled, well-practiced, cold-blooded killers.

"Truce?" they ask together.

Their bodies and minds are one.

Each nods. Maccabee pulls the needle from the cheek, Baitsakhan withdraws the blade.

They are silent for a moment. Still standing incredibly close together, as if at any moment they could raise their weapons again and go for the kill. From the hallway a worried Jalair calls, "What is happening?" in Oirat.

"Peace, brother," Baitsakhan answers in the same language.

"Let me in," Jalair says.

Baitsakhan ignores him.

"What are you saying?" Maccabee demands.

"That you and I are reaching an agreement," Baitsakhan says in English. "That is what's happening, yes?"

Maccabee takes a step back. "Yes."

Baitsakhan steps back too.

"You'll never be able to trust me," Maccabee says.

"You'll never be able to trust me," Baitsakhan counters.

"Good."

"Good."

"So we kill the others."

"Until none are left."

"But you."

"And you."

They are a mirror.

A mirror of death.

Baitsakhan pulls the glove from his left hand with his teeth and slices a cut across his palm.

Blood drips to the floor.

Maccabee turns to the table. There is an old knife there, older than old. Passed down through 500 generations of his people. He picks it up and unsheathes it. He draws the blade along his left palm.

Blood drips to the floor.

They grasp hands.

"To Endgame, brother," they say.

The game is played, but how will it end is[lxii]

AISLING KOPP

Lago Beluiso, Lombardy, Italy

Aisling stares at the cave's wall. She is cross-legged. A small fire burns behind her. A skinned rabbit roasts on a spit. The sniper rifle rests across her thighs. She closes her eyes and meditates on the images on the wall, just as she has every day since arriving. She wonders if this is what her father did. And for how long. And if these images drove him mad, or if he had always been mad.

This is not how Aisling imagined her Endgame, studying ancient paintings. The painting she is seated before depicts 12 human figures standing among a primitive circle of stone monoliths. The stone shapes look vaguely familiar, but she can't place them. Her eye is drawn to the 13th figure as it descends from on high. This 13th wears a helmet studded with lights and a thick suit. It holds something that looks like a star.

The 12 stand in a circle, their arms stretched skyward, toward the visitor and the void he emerges from. Their arms are stretched toward everything. Toward nothing.

"Spaceman visits naked people," mutters Aisling.

The 12 have exaggerated genitalia. She noticed that right off, had to learn to discreetly avert her eyes or the meditation wouldn't take. Six men. Six women. All have swords or spears. Warriors. All, except for one, have their mouths open, singing to the heavens or crying out or screaming.

The one with her mouth closed—a woman—stands in the center of the circle. She holds a round object. A disk. She appears to be fitting it into a rock or a rise in the earth. Or perhaps she is removing it.

A disk. Like the one that kepler 22b had at the Calling.

Above the 13th figure—the one in the helmet, the visitor, the Maker—
is a giant red ball in the sky.

Below them all is a black gash. The 12 seem to be sinking into the
darkness, slowly. Or perhaps those are just the shadows cast by
Aisling's small fire.

There is another painting farther into the cave. Aisling has meditated
before that one too, but gained no insight. In it, the woman from the
first painting, the one with the disk, stands in a small oval boat. The
boat looks as if it is made of stone. Aisling wonders why it doesn't sink.
Maybe whatever savage painted it all those millennia ago didn't know
crap about sailing.

Anyway, the woman in her little boat is adrift on an endless ocean.
Her face is serene, but Aisling can't figure out why. It doesn't look like
a pleasant voyage. The ocean is steaming—or maybe smoking—and
there are dead fish floating on the surface. The woman doesn't seem
bothered by all this. She holds the disk in her hands and drifts along.

For whatever reason, the woman with the disk reminds Aisling of the
mute girl from the Calling. Chiyoko. The Mu.

Maybe she has the disk? Maybe kepler 22b gave it to her?

Or maybe the Mu is chasing the disk?

Maybe . . . one of the others has the disk. . . .

The fire cracks; the rabbit roasts.

Aisling breathes, concentrates on the air passing through her nostrils,
waits patiently for a revelation.

What will be will be.

SARAH ALOPAY, JAGO TLALOC

Renzo's Garage, An Nabi Yunus, Mosul, Iraq

The Peugeot 307 is ready. Sarah and Jago will leave Mosul in the morning. They're on opposite ends of the couch. The TV is off. They have barely spoken since they woke up on the couch next to each other. As they slept, their arms and legs intertwined. Neither of them knows what to make of it. Sometimes Jago thinks that Sarah is warming up to him as more than just a temporary ally. He catches himself thinking about her like one of the beautiful American tourists he would take dancing and to the beach and to his bed, and he kicks himself. She is not one of those silly girls—she is beautiful, yes, but dangerous and crafty. They are Playing together now, but when the end of the game comes they will not be able to be together. Unless they can figure out some way around the rules, only one of them can win. But that time is not now, and for now Jago cannot tell if Sarah is playing him or being sincere. Either way, he only wants her more. Sarah swings between wanting Jago and not wanting Jago. She remembers the speech she gave at her ill-fated graduation. She thinks if she is happy she will have a better chance of winning Endgame. She fears despair; she fears grief; but above all she fears being alone. No Tate. No Christopher. No Reena. She sees Jago as a friend more and more. Being more than a friend with Jago might complicate things but it would also make her happy. Happy won't win her Endgame, though. And that is all that ultimately matters.

I am happy and able because I allow myself to be happy, she remembers saying to her classmates.

What foolishness.

Naïveté.

Jago is reading the 307 manual and pretending to ignore Sarah. She turns to him, setting down the Middle Eastern fashion magazine she found stashed in Renzo's things.

"Jago?"

"Hm?"

"You talked about it a little before, but what was your life like before this?"

Her question surprises him. He sets down the manual. "What does that matter?"

She eyes him playfully, can tell immediately that he doesn't want to share. So she'll start. "Like I said, I was normal. Normal high school with regular kids."

"Yes," Jago says, waving his hand. "I remember. And you had a normal boyfriend."

"Uh, yeah," Sarah says, quickly changing the subject. "My dad's a lawyer and my mom works for the parks department."

Jago laughs. "Are you kidding?"

Sarah raises an eyebrow, not understanding what's funny. "No. Why?"

"That is—what's the English word, hm? Simple and cute? Quaint. Such quaint lives for former Players."

"Why? What do your folks do?"

"Run a large criminal organization. Control a city."

"Oh."

"You still think in terms of *normal*, Sarah Alopay," Jago says, staring right into her eyes. "As if that's something we can go back to. As if that ever applied to us. We are not normal, or descended from normal. We're special."

Sarah knows exactly what they are.

Assassins.

Acrobats.

Puzzlers.

Spies.

Jago's fingertips spider gently across hers. She doesn't move away. "The rules do not apply to us," he says.

He's right, Sarah thinks. She realizes, at that moment, why she felt more comfortable with Jago in that airplane bathroom than she ever did with Christopher. It's because Jago is *like* her. They are the same in ways that Christopher could never understand.

She feels a pang of guilt for Christopher, her abandoned, sweet, normal boyfriend. But in that moment, Sarah Alopay does not want normal. She wants Jago.

"Are you going to feed me some line about the end of the world next?" she asks, her voice low.

"Would that work?" he asks.

"Don't bother," she replies.

Sarah reaches up and gently traces the scar on the side of his neck. Jago smiles and the 307 manual goes tumbling to the floor. He leans forward, crossing the empty couch and pressing himself onto her body.

"This better not be part of the game," he says.

"It's real, Jago. It's as real as anything in the world."

And as she says that, a part of Sarah hopes it isn't true. She hopes this is just a wild teenage whim and that she's not actually falling for Jago. Falling in love with a rival would be about the worst thing that could happen. But then they kiss.

And kiss.

And kiss.

And Sarah forgets.

27.338936, 88.606504[lxiii]

CHRISTOPHER VANDERKAMP, KALA MOZAMI

Bardi Turkish Tour Bus, Seats 15 and 16, on the D400 7 km from Kızıltepe, Turkey

Christopher can't stop thinking of Sarah. Of her hair. Her bare shoulders. Watching her run. Looking into her eyes. Her laugh, lacing their fingers together, playing footsies under the table at the diner down in the Old Market.

He can't stop.

He is with Kala and they are two hours from the site in southern Turkey.

The site of her clue.

Her mysterious clue.

They're on a tour bus surrounded by people their age. People drinking and laughing and cuddling and dancing. Kala did some sleuthing on the internet in Dubai and found that a band of self-styled "Meteor Kids" from Ankara and Istanbul were risking their necks to stage some kind of unsanctioned laser-light rave in honor of the unknown ancestors who constructed Gobekli Tepe—and they were doing it *at* Gobekli Tepe. Tonight.

The post on their Facebook page said, *Come party to the end of days where it all began! Lights and transcendence and dance trance in the desert. Wuck the Forld!*

Christopher is listening to a group of girls giggle and gossip in Turkish. He can't understand a word. Sarah used to giggle. He wonders if she still does. He rolls his head to Kala, who sits next to him in the aisle seat. "You're sure she'll be there?"

"For the thousandth time, yes. I spoke with her at the InterContinental."

"After you knocked me out."

"Yes, after I knocked you out." She turns her green eyes to his. "Why don't you be quiet so I don't have to knock you out again?"

Christopher looks away from her. "Okay." He sounds fearful. He *is* scared of Kala, but he's also playing it up. He wants her to believe he is like a puppy or a lamb. Utterly defenseless.

But he is not.

He hates her too much to be afraid of her. Hates what she did to the mother and the girl on the raft. Hates that Kala is a Player, charged with saving some sliver of humanity. He feels sorry for her people, that they have such a lunatic for a representative.

She can't be allowed to win.

And if he can help her lose, he will.

But she can't know this. Not yet. Not until Christopher has a chance to strike. Not until Christopher finds a way to neutralize her superior speed, training, strength, gear—superior everything.

The road goes on. The kids on the bus are getting excited, rowdier. A boy blunders past them and knocks into Kala's shoulder. He gets a look at her—young, smooth, beautiful—and tries to say something clever. She ignores him.

He speaks again and Kala looks up at him with her green eyes and smiles and reaches out and grabs his hand and twists it. The boy yelps and drops to his knees and he's face-to-face with Kala. She says something in Turkish and the boy whimpers that universal acknowledgment: "Okay, okay." He gets up and scampers away.

Christopher pretends not to have noticed the exchange. Still facing the window he says, "Tell me again what Sarah said."

Kala's annoyed. "No more questions. You'll see her at this party."

"All right." He doesn't say anything else. It is late afternoon. The countryside around them is rolling and dry but not bleak. It looks like western Nebraska after the harvest, only without any trees.

Kala frowns.

Kala knows that she is lying. The Cahokian has not returned her call.

Not yet, anyway. She hopes she will. Maybe Kala has misjudged the situation and the Cahokian is a coldhearted bitch who doesn't care for her precious, pining, nuisance boyfriend. Either way, they are going to Gobekli Tepe to seek Kala's clue. If she hasn't heard from Sarah by the time Kala finds it, she'll kill him.

Christopher smiles to himself. He believes his ruse is working. Kala doesn't know anything about him. He remembers going knife hunting for boar with his uncle Richard in the Texas panhandle. He thinks of the chase and plunging the blade into the wiry hide.

All he needs is a blade and an opportunity.

CHIYOKO TAKEDA, KALA MOZAMI, CHRISTOPHER VANDERKAMP

Bardi Turkish Tour Bus, on the D400 7 km from Kızıltepe, Turkey

Five rows back, in a window seat on the other side of the bus, is a small girl in a red wig. She's been bouncing her head to the beat inside a pair of bright blue oversized headphones for the duration of the trip. She has on heart-shaped sunglasses with gold rims. She has pouty blue-lipsticked lips and perfect skin.

Chiyoko knows Kala is there, and that Kala is with a non-Player boy who looks American. An tipped her off—sent her an email about the plane crash, how a Player was on board, how the two mysterious survivors should be investigated. In the days when Sarah and Jago were stalled in Iraq, Chiyoko kept tabs on the Sumerian.

And now, as luck would have it, the Sumerian is heading in the same direction as Jago and Sarah. According to the tracking chip, the Olmec and the Cahokian have been on the move, but are currently stalled at the Turkey-Iraq border. Eventually, all things will intersect, and Chiyoko will be there.

She pinned a bug on Kala's shoulder and can hear every boring thing she and the American say. They are saying nothing now, so Chiyoko is enjoying her music.

And then, over the guitar, Kala's phone rings.

Chiyoko mutes the music and turns up the transmission.

"Yes, this is she," Kala is saying into her phone.

Kala stands and moves into the aisle. Chiyoko can just make out the boy asking, "Who is it?"

Kala doesn't answer and walks down the aisle. "Yes. Again, I am sorry—"

Kala approaches Chiyoko, looks directly at her, doesn't recognize her. Chiyoko smiles to herself, keeps bouncing.

"He is with me, yes."

Pause.

"We are going to Gobekli Tepe. Have you heard of it?"

Pause.

"You're where? What a coincidence. Though I suppose there aren't really coincidences in Endgame."

Pause.

"We'll be there by evening."

Pause.

"That's right. I only want what the Olmec stole from the Calling."

Pause.

"I swear it to you on my honor, Cahokian."

Chiyoko has never heard more false words. Kala oozes with dishonor. If Sarah could see her, she would know not to trust her.

"There will be a party there tonight. When you arrive, call me. I hate to have to say it, but no surprises. Your friend will not survive a surprise, understand?"

Pause.

"Wonderful. I look forward to seeing you too, Cahokian. Blessings."

She hangs up. Chiyoko is about to turn her music back up when she hears Kala say something in Turkish. Her tone is impatient.

Chiyoko looks toward the window, away from Kala, who is behind her. She eyes a thin sliver of mirror on the inside of her heart-shaped sunglasses, which allows her to see what is happening.

The aisle in front of Kala is barred by two large young men. One of them points at Kala, and Kala holds up her hands in front of her. Chiyoko opens a small bag in her lap and removes a small white straw. She sticks it in her mouth and wraps her tongue around it. She adjusts the angle of the mirror and sees two other men behind Kala. One of them is the boy who offended her, the one whose thumb Kala nearly broke.

Chiyoko pities the four fools.

The offended boy moves on Kala. She raises a leg and kicks hard into the boy's stomach. People begin to look at the commotion. Chiyoko kneels in her seat and pivots. She notices the American boy walking down the aisle.

He's not scared, Chiyoko thinks. *He's faking. Interesting.*

Chiyoko looks back at Kala and sees her kick the man behind her square in the jaw.

Chiyoko doesn't smile but is pleased to see martial arts practiced so expertly. Before anyone can act, Kala kicks into a handstand and away from the two flummoxed men in front of her. There is barely enough room between the floor and the ceiling, but Kala flips and lands on her feet, cracking both men across the shoulders with the sides of her palms. One goes down. The other, who is larger, does not.

He grabs Kala's forearm with both hands and yanks her forward. He tries to head-butt her, but she angles her neck at the last second. The man doesn't lose a beat—he starts dancing with his feet, trying to break a toe or an ankle. She is faster, though, and gets her feet up on the armrests behind her. Kala tries to jerk her arm free, but the large man grips her too tightly.

Behind Kala, the insulted boy is now brandishing a small knife.

As the large man continues to wrestle with Kala, the playacting American boy sidles up behind him. "HEY!" he shouts, and the man turns slightly. Christopher lets him have it hard on the eye with a right cross. Ocular bones shatter and the man cries out.

In the same moment, the insulted boy raises his knife. Kala doesn't see him coming.

Chiyoko parts her lips and blows out her cheeks. Without waiting to see what happens next, she turns to the window and pulls the emergency release.

A dart zips through the air. No one sees it. It strikes the boy in the neck. Chiyoko knows how immediate and how painful it is. She had to endure the same kind of dart in her training many, many times.

The boy screams as he seizes in pain, grabbing his neck. Kala wrestles herself free from the man with the broken face. The commotion is big enough now that the bus is slowing down. Hot air from the desert wafts into the cabin as a window is jettisoned onto the road. Kala looks behind her. The boy writhes on the ground. The other attackers are holding up their hands like they don't want any more trouble.

Kala spits and looks at Christopher. "Did you do that?" she demands, pointing at the spasming boy.

Christopher is glowering at the man with the broken face. "He deserved it!"

Kala shakes her head and points at the writhing boy. "No. That."

Christopher sees him. "No."

"Who did?"

"It wasn't you?"

Kala steps past her assailants and grabs Christopher by the arm—*he is strong; I have underestimated him*—and leads him toward their seats.

She looks left and sees the open window.

The girl with the red hair is gone.

HILAL IBN ISA AL-SALT

Church of the Covenant, Kingdom of Aksum, Northern Ethiopia

Hilal kneels on the church's roof. He has been kneeling there for 9,466 seconds. He has contemplated his clue, the simple circle.

Everything.

Nothing.

A circle of stone.

A planet.

An orbit.

A beginning.

An end.

Pi.

3.141592653589793238462643383279502884197169399375105820974944592307816406286208998628034825342117067982148086513282306647093844609550582231725359408128481117450284102701938521105596446229489549303819644288109756659334461284756482337867831652712019091456485669234603486104543266482133936072602491 . . .

No.

Not pi.

Something simpler.

He contemplates the being's words. *The first move is essential.*

Nothing decides everything. The future is unwritten. What will be will be.

The first move is essential.

The first move.

The key.

Earth Key.

The first object of Endgame.

Here.

On Earth.

Placed eons ago by one like kepler 22b. Placed at one of their ancient meeting points. A place of significance.

Earth Key.

What does a key do?

It unlocks.

Opens.

Starts.

Nothing decides everything.

The future is unwritten.

A circle.

A circle of stone.

A disk like the one the Olmec carried from the Calling.

Zero.

A simple circle.

Outside, nothing.

Inside, nothing.

Hilal places his hands on his knees. The world turns around him.

He feels centered, at peace. His heart brims with hope. He hears the atoms of the stone hard beneath his knees urging themselves together. Feels the breath of the cosmos. Tastes the ash of the end. Senses the neutrinos and the dark matter binding, rides the continuum. Hears the low, barely perceptible hiss of the Uroboros, the consuming hum of creation.

He hears those like kepler 22b discussing, watching, judging this game of games.

They made us human.

Looked into the eyes of an animal and gave us perception.

Plucked us from Eden and taught us love and lust and hate and trust and betrayal. All of it. Showed us how to manipulate and form. How to bow down, and pray, and plead, and listen.

They made us.

Everything and nothing.

The first move is essential.

A circle.

A stone circle.

Too many on Earth to choose from.

They made us.

They control something. Not everything. Not nothing.

Hilal's eyes shoot open.

The first move is essential.

The future is unwritten.

The Event is coming.

It is part of Endgame.

The reason for it, the beginning, middle, and end.

Hilal sees, smiles, stands.

Hilal knows.

Hilal understands.

CHIYOKO TAKEDA

Bardi Turkish Tour Bus, Rooftop, on the D400 3.1349 km from Kızıltepe, Turkey

Chiyoko lies flat on top of the bus and waits for it to stop. When it does, she grabs the side and slips to the ground. She lies on her chest on the shoulder of the road and waits. She can hear the bus driver shouting.

She sees Kala's and the American's feet as they scramble off the bus and flag a car. A sympathetic driver slows for them. Seconds later, the driver is on his back in the dirt.

"Get in!" Kala shouts at Christopher.

The American does as he's told. The man whose car is getting jacked stands up and yells as Kala puts the car in gear and tears off. Other people start to get off the bus too. They want to see everything so they can tell their friends later. Film it, tweet it, post it, share it.

Chiyoko cannot let them get away, but she will not risk stealing a car like the brash Sumerian. She stands and eases into the crowd around the door of the bus and makes her way back inside. No one pays her any mind, even with the red wig and the sunglasses. No one knows she played a part in the wild brawl. As she moves through the throng she pulls another straw from her small bag and places it on her tongue. When she sees the boy, his continued spasms drawing a small crowd, she exhales, and the next dart—the antidote—sails through the air, breezing by heads and shoulders. The dart looks like a small bug—no one notices. It hits the boy's neck, and in a minute or two he'll be fine. Chiyoko sits in a nearby seat and waits for things to die down. After 10 minutes and much discussion the bus closes its door and the driver shakes his head and they take off down the road. No one wants to talk to the police, especially the men bloodied by Kala and the American. Not in this part of the country. There is partying to do. And dancing. And playing.

Chiyoko turns her music back on. She bounces her head.

She wants to keep Playing too.

SARAH ALOPAY, JAGO TLALOC

Turkey-Iraq Border, Covert Peshmerga Checkpoint 4

Renzo drives Sarah and Jago through a secret one-lane earthen tunnel big enough for a truck convoy. It's controlled by Kurdish fighters who don't care for official borders. They reach a checkpoint at the end manned by a half dozen men in black fatigues carrying M4s, Kalashnikovs, and Colt service pistols. Renzo stops the car and gets out to speak with the man in charge. Jago sits in the front passenger seat. He has not spoken since Sarah called the Sumerian, since they learned that she is holding Christopher for ransom.

Sarah leans forward and puts her hand on Jago's shoulder. He doesn't move. Christopher is not with them yet, but his presence clouds the car, poisons the air around them. Sarah and Jago spent last night in each other's arms, kissing, whispering, laughing, touching, playing. Two teenagers in the first stage, the delirious first stage, of falling in love. And for the first time since the meteors struck, for the first time since Endgame began, they forgot how they met, why they met, forgot the game they were Playing, which would determine the future of humanity, forgot everything and just loved each other.

Sarah heard the messages from Christopher and Kala this morning, and immediately called Kala back. Jago heard the call and knew what was going on. He didn't ask any questions, didn't say anything. Now, in the car, Sarah reaches for his hand.

"I'm sorry."

Jago casually pulls his hand away. "Sorry for what?"

"I don't know what happened. I guess he tried to find me, and somehow found her."

Jago snorts and stares straight ahead.

"We have to help him and send him home," Sarah continues. "You know we're not going to let her get the disk. It'll be fine."

He shakes his head. "Easier just not to go at all, hm?"

"I have to go. You know I do," Sarah insists. "I would do the same for you."

"You wouldn't have to."

"Jago," Sarah says, and a chill goes through him at the way she says his name. "I'm asking for your help. Please."

Jago looks over his shoulder at her. "You should let him die. There, I've helped."

"No."

"This boy is going to get himself killed. Must have some serious death wish to try following you around. Best to just let the fool have his way."

"I love him, Jago. Don't you understand that?"

Jago smiles in a way that Sarah has never seen before. It's the alpha male smile that he would flash on the streets of Juliaca. It's an angry, painful-looking thing. It causes her to sit back.

"If you love him, then why were you with me last night?" he asks.

"Because I never thought I'd see him again," she explains. "Because I thought that part of my life was over."

"It is. Let him die."

"I'm going to get him, and then send him home. If you don't want to come, fine. Go your own way. But if you do, you're one of them, the heartless killers, and I swear on everything and everyone I love that the next time I see you, I will end your life, and I won't think twice while I do it."

Jago laughs.

"You think it's funny? You won't be laughing as you take your last breath."

He turns toward her.

"I was laughing because I want to hate you, but when you act all hard, and I know you can actually back it up, it makes me like you more."

She smiles. "You just don't want me gunning for you."

Jago knows his pride should be hurt, like it was beneath the Terracotta Army when Sarah clearly outran him. She's challenging him, pushing him. He shouldn't be taking that from another Player. But, much to his chagrin, what Jago feels most is jealousy. Jealousy that this dumb non-Player has gotten Sarah's attention.

"You don't have to swear on your loved ones or whatever," Jago says coolly. "I'm not heartless. I understand love is a strange, strange thing."

"So you'll go with me."

"I'm going for the Sumerian," he says. "She called me out before. I should've dealt with her then."

"Uh-huh," Sarah says, knowing that's not the real reason Jago is going but glad that he is.

"When it's done, you *will* send this silly boy home, right? And we get back to what we're doing, yes?"

"Yes. It's what's best for everyone."

Renzo approaches the car with a smile on his face. Five steel columns descend into the ground at the end of the tunnel, and two men work to raise a mesh wall of camouflage so that the car can pass into the Kurdish region of Turkey.

"You're clear. Come, get out." Renzo is smiling and holding a brown glass bottle and three small tea glasses. He passes out the glasses and pours a cloudy liquid into each one. He raises his glass high. They follow his lead.

"To friendship and death. To life and oblivion. To Endgame."

"To Endgame," Sarah and Jago say. They tap glasses and drink. The liquid tastes like spiked licorice. Sarah scowls, asks, "Ugh, what is this?"

"Arak. It is good, no?"

"No," Sarah says, "it's awful."

Jago laughs. "I like it."

Renzo nods at Jago and pours himself another, drinks, and throws his glass to the ground. Sarah and Jago do the same. Each glass explodes.

Renzo hugs them, kisses them on their cheeks, grabs their shoulders, hugs them again. Before letting Sarah go he says, "Best of luck at the end of ends, but not too much luck."

"If I can't win, I'll make sure Jago does."

"What will be will be."

She smiles, climbs into the passenger seat of the Peugeot. Renzo hugs Jago one last time and whispers in his ear, "Don't be stupid and fall in love. Not until the end is past."

"Too late for that," Jago says.

Renzo smiles. "Then I'll see you in hell, brother."

"I don't believe in hell."

Renzo's face darkens, and he takes a long pull straight from the bottle. "You will, Jago Tlaloc, Olmec Player of the 21st. You will."

Gobekli Tepe.

Man's first known temple, surrounded by barren fields as far as the eye can see. Discovered in 1993 by local shepherds, the complex had lain dormant, intentionally buried by some unknown culture for some unknown reason, for at least 15,000 years. Since its discovery, a mere 5 percent of it has been unearthed, and radiocarbon dating places its provenance in the 12th millennium BCE. This is before pottery, metallurgy, animal husbandry, agriculture, known writing systems, and the wheel. It predates by thousands of years the next comparable stonework structures concentrated in the Fertile Crescent to the south and east. Yet there it is, arriving out of the darkness of the last ice age as a complete mystery. It is a fully formed temple, a fully formed city, a vast array of sophisticated structures dozens of feet across consisting of multiple limestone monoliths, each cut to exact proportions, and each weighing between 10 and 20 tons. Some believe that the monoliths themselves, each one a single rectangular column capped by a 2nd rectangle balanced on top, are the representations of men or priests or gods.

Or perhaps they represent something—or someone—else.

No one knows who made it.

How it was made.

Why it was made.

No one knows what knowledge passed through the minds of its makers.

No one knows the extent of their enlightenment.

No one knows.

BAITSAKHAN, MACCABEE ADLAI

Açgözlü Akbaba Tapınağı, Temple of the Consuming Vulture, Turkey

Baitsakhan puts his hands on the dashboard of Maccabee's Audi A8 and leans forward. "What the hell is this?"

"No idea."

Jalair stops the car. It is nine p.m. and the sun is down. A cloudless purple sky stretches in every direction. They have seen nothing for miles. Only a few cars on the road going in the opposite direction. And now they have finally reached the ancient monument buried in the sand of southern Turkey, the ancient monument of Maccabee Adlai's clue that they decided to investigate. Each of them—Maccabee, Baitsakhan, Jalair—expected to find a dark archeological site. At most, they expected a few security guards and maybe some students or professors camping out.

Instead, dozens of cars and five charter buses are parked in the lot. People their age mill around drinking and smoking. Some of the women are in head scarves, but for the most part everyone looks urban, modern, and free. Most people are wearing colorful glow-stick necklaces. Some are dressed up like club kids—spiked hair, baggy pants, elevator shoes, piercings, jewelry, lots of skin. Music booms from over the rolling hills. Blue, green, and purple lasers dance in the sky, strobing, streaking, sweeping.

"A party?" Baitsakhan asks humorlessly.

"Yes, I believe that's what this is," Maccabee says drily. *I bet he's never been to a party in his entire life.*

"We came here because of your clue," Baitsakhan hisses at Maccabee. "It better not be a waste of time."

"You didn't have any better ideas," Maccabee snaps back.

They get out of the car. Maccabee unbuttons his shirt to the middle of his chest, revealing a long golden chain with a smooth silver sphere the size of a roulette ball weighing it down. He's going to fit in perfectly. Baitsakhan and Jalair, who look like gypsies, couldn't care less about their appearance. Maccabee approaches the closest group of partiers and, in perfect Turkish, asks where they can get some glow necklaces. The kids point over the rise of the hill. He asks how long the party's been going, who's DJing right now, if there have been any police or army guys, if everything is going well. He nods and slaps shoulders and breaks out a quick dance move. He high-fives the guys and turns back to Jalair and Baitsakhan. His smile melts once the revelers can't see him.

"These morons call themselves Meteor Kids," he says. "They're here to, quote, 'Celebrate the end where it all began.'"

"That's funny," Jalair says.

"What's funny?" Baitsakhan asks.

"That they're right," Maccabee says. "It's ironic."

"I don't get it," Baitsakhan says.

Maccabee and Jalair share a look. It is their first look of camaraderie. *He's so young, knows so little, believes he can simply kill his way through Endgame,* Maccabee thinks. *He will only be useful for as long as a closed fist can be useful.*

Jalair opens the trunk and pushes aside a heavy piece of black canvas, and they tool up. Each conceals a pistol in his pants and extra clips, a knife. The blades are ancient and ornate and very sharp. Jalair snaps a leather whip to his belt. Baitsakhan slings a gun belt over his shoulder and across his chest. It has gas canisters and four grenades on it.

Maccabee looks at Baitsakhan. "Really? You look like you're going to war."

"These people all look like lunatics; they're not gonna notice."

Maccabee keeps his expression neutral. *You're the lunatic,* he thinks.

He wonders just how far he should take this alliance with the bloodthirsty brat.

Perhaps, just maybe, when he emerges from the Temple of the Consuming Vulture, he will do so alone.

KALA MOZAMI,
CHRISTOPHER VANDERKAMP

Açgözlü Akbaba Tapınağı, Temple of the Consuming Vulture, Turkey

Christopher and Kala stand in a stone circle 12 feet across. The circle is in a depression. Six monoliths, arranged at even intervals around the circle, tower over them like sentinels from the ancient world. Carved into the stones are clear, concise reliefs of snakes, birds, cats, lizards, scorpions. Part of the circle is still buried in red earth. A 7th monolith is toppled over and half covered by a mound of untouched sand.

Kala, toting a small flashlight, closely inspects this last giant hunk of stone.

Christopher is awestruck. "Are we really supposed to be in here?" They cleared a low wire fence and removed a laughable wooden barrier at the edge of the hole before jumping in.

"There are no rules."

"What is this place?"

"A temple."

Christopher's brow furrows. "What kind of temple?"

"A temple to life and power," Kala answers, distracted. She scratches at the ground with her hands, starts digging.

Christopher runs his hand over the large claws of a carved scorpion. "Who made it?"

Kala works a thin brick from the wall and uses it like a spade. "It doesn't matter."

Christopher shoots her a sidelong look. She has reached a small pile of bricks and is working them free. "It seems like it matters to you."

She glances over her shoulder. "The Great Parents made it, the beings standing guard here, now, for all time. The Prime Annunaki of Du-Ku, my forebears. Yours. Everyone's."

"Oh, right, them," he says with a snicker, remembering the term Sarah used. "The Sky People."

Kala stands bolt upright. Her face is flushed. "Don't mock me, boy. The Annunaki made us, and they were present here, in this spot, thousands and thousands of years before history began. Living gods, beings powerful enough to shape humanity, to create life, and now end it. And you, you child, you laugh at them?" Kala sneers, pointing at him. "You've lived in a little bubble your entire life. All of the world has lived in a bubble. That bubble is about to burst, and all that you believed was real is going to end."

"So serious!" Christopher says, wiggling his fingers. He can tell he's pushing her buttons, so he'll push harder.

Kala takes a step forward. "You want to know what I'm looking for, is that it?"

"I want to know what's going to happen, and I want to see Sarah."

"You'll see her soon enough. And I'll tell you what's going to happen. You are going to die. All of those people"—she points in the direction of the pounding music two hills away—"are going to die. Everyone, except for a very select few, is going to die. Very soon. We—the Players—will decide who lives."

Christopher thinks back to his conversation with Sarah at the airport. He's never paused to think about the context of this Endgame business, what it could mean for the rest of the world. He shakes his head.

"So, you're telling me that the Earth is going to be wiped out?" He keeps his tone mocking, even though his voice shakes a bit.

"Yes. And the winner—me—will decide who survives." Kala smiles at him. "You won't be on the list, Christopher Vanderkamp."

She turns away from him and resumes her work at the bricks, throwing them over her shoulder. Christopher crouches down a few feet away, watching her. He doesn't want to admit it, but she's shaken him up.

"Crazy," he mutters.

She doesn't stop working, ignores him.

"Anyway, there's no way you're winning," he continues. "Know why? Because you're a nut job. The nut jobs never win."

One of the bricks sails over Kala's shoulder and lands right in front of him. He starts to reach out for it. *I could kill her now. . . .*

"Don't get any funny ideas." She says it without looking at him, and Christopher moves his hand away. The bass thumps through the air overhead. The stars stretch out to infinity. He thinks about what he's learned of Endgame, what these Players believe. That humanity came from something out there, in space. There are billions and billions of stars. The idea that there is life out there makes sense, but he's never seen anything that proves it, and he isn't sure a pile of old stones is enough to change his mind. Christopher doesn't believe the world is ending, but these Players do. Kala believes it enough to murder a mother and her child in cold blood. He takes another look at that nearby brick, longing to exact some revenge, some justice.

Kala stands, something in her hands. "I found it."

She turns around, and she's holding a dark, thick metal ring the size of a bangle.

"What is it?"

"A piece."

"A piece of what?"

She runs her fingers over the outside of the ring. Her lips move ever so slightly, as if she is reading to herself. "A piece of—"

"The puzzle," a voice says from above them. A pebble falls into the pit. Christopher and Kala look up at the same time. Standing there, at the rim of the hole, is a man in shadow. He puts a hand on the ground and drops halfway into the pit, landing on a thick block of stone.

"Who are you?" Kala asks. She shines her small light on him. He is squatting. He is short. His eyes are thin and dark, his face sun-beaten, his cheeks round. His hair is black.

"My name is Jalair."

"Who *are* you?" Kala repeats with slow, measured syllables.

Christopher stands. He has a bad feeling.

Jalair scratches his head. "I said my name is Jalair. What's that you found?"

Christopher backs toward Kala. *The devil you know,* he thinks.

Kala pushes her hand into her pocket, hides the dark ring. "You're with the boy. You have the same eyes."

Jalair stands silently and pulls out a gun. He levels it at Kala.

"Tell me about the puzzle piece you've uncovered, Kala Mozami."

She is motionless, says nothing. Christopher is two feet away from her and he can feel the energy coursing through her body.

"Better yet, why don't you let me have a look?" Jalair says.

Kala asks, "Where is Baitsakhan?"

Jalair shrugs. "Around."

Kala takes this literally and looks behind her, but no one is there. Christopher does not take his eyes from the gun. Kala says, "You can shoot me, Donghu, but what I've found will be useless to you if I die. It's inscribed in Old Sumerian, a language so dead as to be unrecognizable."

"But you can read it?"

"Of course."

"Then what does it say?"

Kala shakes her head. "It doesn't work that way."

"How does it work, then?"

"Shoot me and find out."

Jalair considers this. Instead, he swings the gun onto Christopher.

"How about I shoot him instead?"

Kala makes a snapping sound with her tongue. "You're an ex-Player, yes, brother?"

"Yes, sister."

"Then you should know better than to aim for the decoy."

Before Jalair can swing the gun back toward Kala, she is moving.

She's like bottled lightning, running up and along the curve of the wall. Jalair fires at her, once, twice, three times, but she's too fast. Christopher thinks he sees one of the shots brush through Kala's hair, but that's as close as any get.

Kala springs across the pit, grabs the edge of a huge stone, and flips over it, and she sails through the air like a gymnast. Jalair fires one more time, missing again as Kala lands behind him. When he turns around, she hits the muzzle of the gun so that it flips around. It's pointing at him now, and Kala slaps the grip. The back of Jalair's finger depresses the trigger and the gun fires. The bullet passes through his skin, his sternum, his aorta, and the edge of his right lung, and shatters his T6 vertebra before blowing a hole out of his back. Christopher sucks in a breath.

Kala pushes Jalair's lifeless body into the hole with her feet. It tumbles toward Christopher with a series of sickening, muted cracks and thumps, comes to an awkward, twisted stop hanging over a waist-high stone.

Kala has the gun now. She looks at Christopher and says, "Pick up the flashlight and get out of there. We're going."

Christopher forces himself to move. He snags the light from the ground. He is going to be sick. As he climbs out of the ground, he throws up a little.

Kala gives him a disgusted look. "Pathetic."

He stands and wipes his mouth with the back of his hand. He hands her the flashlight. She turns it off.

"Where are we going?" he asks.

Kala keeps the gun low, and points it at him. "We're going to get the key."

"What key?"

"No more questions, no more talking." With her free hand she pulls the ring from her pocket. Looks at it. She points to the north. "Go that way. Now."

Christopher walks past her and heads into the night.

"Stay low," Kala advises. "Someone else is here."

He follows her instructions. He is scared now. No one should be able to do what he just saw her do. Navy SEALs couldn't do what she just did. His right hand begins to shake uncontrollably.

These people are murderers.

He pictures Sarah, her auburn hair, her sunny smile, her laugh. He thinks of her having to fight someone like Kala. He knows if anyone could do it, she could, but the thought terrifies him. And he knows that Kala could kill him immediately and without remorse.

These people are murderers.

Why didn't I listen to Sarah?

Why didn't I listen and stay away?

The sun rises in the west.[lxiv]

CHIYOKO TAKEDA

Açgözlü Akbaba Tapınağı, Temple of the Consuming Vulture, Turkey

Chiyoko has changed into a simple black cotton jumpsuit with a built-in backpack. A tight hood keeps her hair in check. A mask covers the lower part of her face. A thin eyepiece hovers over her left eye. It's a night-vision lens and allows her to see in the dark.

She lies in the dirt above the pit. She watches Kala kill Jalair, hears what happens thanks to the mic that still clings to Kala's clothing. She knows about the puzzle piece. She knows that Kala thinks she is close to Earth Key.

She also knows that Kala is a fool.

She watches Kala and Christopher walk north. As soon as they dip below the rise of the next hill, two others appear from the east. They move quickly, chasing the sound of gunfire. Chiyoko adjusts her monocle, depressing a button over her temple that activates a zoom lens. She focuses on the new figures.

Baitsakhan.

Maccabee.

Interesting, she thinks. *A strange pairing. A dangerous one.*

Chiyoko trains a small telescopic mic on the pair as they make their way to the pit. When they reach it, Baitsakhan drops to one knee and shines a flashlight onto the ground. He utters a string of desperate-sounding words in a language she has never heard before. He disappears into the hole. Maccabee surveys the area around them. His eyes pass directly over Chiyoko, but he doesn't see her. She is invisible. Maccabee waits as Baitsakhan grieves. Chiyoko pulls in a full breath and slips a dart tube onto her tongue. She blows, and the chipped dart sails through the air. It hits the Nabataean on the neck and he doesn't even notice. He just stands and waits until Baitsakhan emerges from the pit, Jalair's whip in his hand.

Baitsakhan scans the ground. He picks up the trail of Kala and Christopher, toes the small puddle of vomit Christopher left behind, grimaces. He looks up at Maccabee and says, "There are two of them. They went this way. We need to find them and kill them."

Maccabee points his flashlight back into the pit. He says, "But this *is* the Temple of the Consuming Vulture. This is where my clue led."

"I don't care. Others are here. They killed my brother. Blood for blood."

"Fine," Maccabee says, not wanting to argue. "But then we come back. There is something here. Something for me. For us."

Whatever Maccabee is looking for, Chiyoko is sure that the Sumerian has already found it. Baitsakhan looks at the tracks and trots away without saying another word. Maccabee shakes his head, turns, and follows him. Chiyoko breathes. She consults the screen on her watch. Sarah and Jago are 48 miles away, traveling 50 mph. She has some time. *I can't risk fighting all three of them, plus the strong American boy. I will follow. As always, follow.*

She rises out of the dirt.

Follows.

Silent.

Invisible.

KALA MOZAMI,
CHRISTOPHER VANDERKAMP

Altın Odası, Ground Level, Turkey

Christopher jogs, Kala right on his heels. He knows the gun is still pointed at him. She's been telling him where to go, left, right, left again, toward that hill, around that stone. He's tried to ask questions, but each has been greeted with an order of "Silence!" They've traveled over half a mile in 11 minutes and the rave, behind them in the night, is an afterthought.

Finally Kala says, "Stop!"

They are in front of an unexceptional mound of earth crisscrossed by long dry grass. It's the only vegetation Christopher has noticed on this barren plain. Kala scans the countryside and drops to a knee. Christopher watches her.

"Are we staying out here all night? Digging stuff up and killing people?"

Kala ignores him and rests the gun in the dirt. "Don't get any ideas," she reminds him.

"I won't. I saw what you can do."

"Good." She clicks on the light and keeps one hand cupped over its beam. It shines on the ring. Christopher leans in, getting his first good look.

It appears to be a simple iron ring, though for something that's been buried for 10,000 years it is in remarkable shape. It shows no rust or calcification. The band of the ring is about an inch thick. Etched into its surface are strange markings and glyphs. Kala extinguishes the light, looks at the small hill.

"It's here," she says and smiles, barely able to contain her giddiness.

"What's here?"

"One of their chambers."

"The Sky People?"

"The Annunaki."

"Let's go say hello," Christopher says, trying to mask his terror with humor. Kala ignores him, grabs the pistol, stands, starts moving around the mound. She doesn't bother pointing the gun at him. Christopher follows, his curiosity piqued. "What's the chamber for?" Kala digs in the dirt again. It falls away in clumps. She digs until she hits stone. A perfectly flat stone with a crescent depression, one in which the ring will fit perfectly. She smiles, inserts the ring, turns. There's a grating sound as a large stone door, at least two feet thick, swings downward, the earth on top of it collapsing. There's a black stone spiral staircase leading down. Christopher takes a step back, shocked. Kala looks at him, elated, shaking with excitement.

"Gold. It's a chamber for the Annunaki's gold."

MgO, Fe2O3(T), & MgO / Fe2O3(T) vs. Fe2O3(T) + MgO[lxv]

BAITSAKHAN, MACCABEE ADLAI

Altın Odası, Ground Level, Turkey

Baitsakhan and Maccabee follow the tracks.

"Do you think they're both Players?" Maccabee asks.

"No. Only one acted. The other was in the pit when brother Jalair was killed. Vomiting."

Maccabee nods. "But the other was a Player."

"No non-Player could kill Jalair," Baitsakhan barks.

Baitsakhan takes off at a jog, eager to catch the murderer. Maccabee follows, less enthused, hoping something worthwhile will come of this. They leave the orbit of the party, passing a ridiculously attired couple making out on a blanket under the stars. The boy wears a feather boa and the girl has a huge rainbow Afro wig that has fallen to the ground. Both wear oversized sunglasses. Maccabee smirks.

The Players move on, unnoticed. It takes them nine minutes to reach the small hill. Baitsakhan stops, kneels, picks up some dirt, smells it. Maccabee moves around the mound, preferring not to play in the dirt with his partner.

Maccabee stumbles, surprised as he almost falls down a shadowed staircase that leads underground. He snaps his fingers. Baitsakhan stands and joins him. They peer into the shadows. Maccabee checks his gun. Baitsakhan takes the whip off his belt, cracks it, the tip snapping violently.

Baitsakhan smiles.

"Blood for Blood."

They start to descend.

CHIYOKO TAKEDA

11 m South of Altın Odası, Turkey

Chiyoko stops short of the hill and takes a knee. Maccabee and
Baitsakhan disappear around the hill and don't come back.

A doorway?

She counts to 60.

Breathes.

She watches the stars imperceptibly twirl across the sky.

Breathes.

Counts to 60 again.

None of the others reappear.

Yes. A doorway.

She consults the tracker. Sarah and Jago have an ETA of 22 minutes.
Maccabee and Baitsakhan are under the mound, going down, down,
down. Presumably, Kala and Christopher are down there ahead of
them.

She checks her weapons. The poisoned wakizashi inside its sheath.
Her shuriken. Her darts. The metal-tipped hojo. Three smoke bombs. A
pepper bomb. No gun. Too much noise, those things, and not elegant
enough. She stands, clicks her watch: the timer rolls from zero; the
digits of the tenths and hundredths fly. She wants to know when Sarah
and Jago are close.

*Follow and watch, Chiyoko. Just follow and watch. Only confront if
completely necessary. Only kill if easy.*

She moves toward the hill, as quiet as a ghost.

KALA MOZAMI, CHRISTOPHER VANDERKAMP, BAITSAKHAN, MACCABEE ADLAI, CHIYOKO TAKEDA

Altın Odası, 25 m Underground, Turkey

Kala has a hard time keeping her heart rate down. It's at 88, 90, 93. She hasn't let it get above 70 in six years.

She and Christopher are standing in a massive chamber as big as an airplane hangar. The walls are rounded and easily 50 feet tall. The ceiling is angled like the inside of a pyramid. Large markings similar to those on Kala's twisted ring are carved on every inch of the walls, telling some ancient story. A golden statue of a creature with the head of a man and the body of an eagle stands guard before an altar at one end of the room. The altar is surrounded by clay burial urns of varying sizes. And everywhere, piled to the ceiling in some places, are massive, glimmering stacks of gold blocks.

"Holy shit," whispers Christopher.

Kala puts her pistol in the back of her pants, trains the flashlight on an ancient torch, and removes it from the wall. She pulls a lighter from her pocket, flips it; the torch erupts. Light bounces off the gold and the walls and rises toward the roof. They're bathed in dense yellow light. Christopher feels faint and sits on the floor. "Wh-what is this place?"

Kala turns a tight circle. "There are underground cities strewn across Turkey. They were dug by Hittites, Luwians, a smattering of Armenians. The most famous is called Derinkuyu. But none I've heard of are as old as this. This is something else. This . . ."

"Sky People," Christopher guesses, still stunned. "Sarah was right. It's for real."

"Yes," Kala says, filling with pride. The people of Gobekli Tepe, the people who once worked the floor of this amazing room, are directly related to her. The ancestors of her ancestors. The original members of her line. "The Annunaki used gold for energy. And they used men to mine it for them. We were their slaves, and they were our gods."

"So this is some sort of power plant?"

"More like a fueling station. One that hasn't been seen in at least fifteen thousand years."

They are silent. Christopher can't fathom the value of the gold that surrounds them. Kala raises the torch as high as she can and peers into the recesses of the ceiling.

Christopher follows the light. "Are those . . . letters?"

Kala frowns. She sticks the torch back on the wall and gets out her smartphone. She makes sure the flash is on, holds it over her head, takes a picture. A blinding white light fills the room. She lowers the screen and looks at the photograph.

"By the gods," she says breathlessly.

"What is it?"

She holds out the phone. Christopher takes it. He can't understand what he's looking at. Dashes and periods and numbers and letters. A jumbled mass of them. He pinches to zoom in. Uses his finger to move around the field. Squints. A massive array of Roman letters and Arabic numerals, as if printed by a huge computer. The signs of modern humans, buried here for 15,000 years. He doesn't understand how it's possible.

But Kala does. She knows that it's a sign.

Earth Key is here. It has to be, she thinks.

"We need to get the key and leave. The boy, Baitsakhan, is up there looking for us," she says, pointing straight up.

Kala grabs the torch and runs toward the altar.

"What about Sarah? Isn't she meeting us up there too?" Christopher calls after her.

Kala ignores him. He watches her go and stays on the ground. He's still recovering from what surrounds them. He breathes. The air is stale and thin. He looks again at the photo of the grid on the ceiling. He stares, stares, stares at the phone, like so many other people in the world are doing at the same moment, playing games, checking email, texting. None of them are looking at anything like this.

Christopher lets the phone fall into his lap. His face is lit from below by the pale light of the screen. He hears Kala moving at the other end of the room. The phone's screen shuts off, going to sleep.

Darkness.

Christopher's mind reels.

He thinks of what he learned in world history, in math, in an AP History of Philosophy class he took in the fall. If this room has been untouched for 15,000 years, then those letters and numbers and signs were put there before writing was even invented. Before *any* kind of writing was invented. Before cuneiform and pictograms and hieroglyphs, to say nothing of Roman letters or Arabic numerals. They were there before Euclidean geometry, before math as we know it, before the concept of knowledge.

Kala's words ring in his mind. *There is so much you don't know.*

Christopher is completely silent. It *is* real. Endgame, the Sky People, the Players. *This picture is proof,* he thinks. Proof of some unknown human history. Proof of extraterrestrial life.

Proof.

Chiyoko passes through the door and starts to descend the stairs. She hears Baitsakhan and Maccabee shuffling below her, trying to remain quiet, unseen. They are rank amateurs compared to her.

Her footfalls on the cut stone are nonexistent. Her breath is a whisper. Her clothing does not rustle. She carries no light, as each of the fools below her does.

The staircase is a tight spiral not wide enough for two people to pass. The wall is smooth to the touch. There are no markings, just depth and more depth.

The sounds below her change. Baitsakhan and Maccabee have reached the bottom. She quickens her pace. She must see what's there, decide how to proceed.

She must see what these boys will do.

Because she knows it will happen soon.

It will happen soon.

Blood will flow.

Baitsakhan and Maccabee stop just short of the vast storeroom.

Maccabee has his hand over his flashlight. His flesh is red and he can see the blurred outlines of phalanges and metacarpals.

The Donghu holds up a fist, jabs himself in the chest. He mouths, *Surprise* and *Neither lives.*

Maccabee nods. *I will guard the exit,* he mouths with a wide grin.

Death is coming, and he likes it.

He turns off the flashlight. They move through the darkness like wraiths, step over the threshold of the underground chamber. There is a lit torch at the far end, near what appears to be some kind of altar.

For a brief moment, Baitsakhan and Maccabee are struck by the size of the room they have entered. The far-off flame doesn't do it justice, but they can't risk any light.

Not until it is done.

Baitsakhan walks in. Maccabee waits in the doorway, his knife drawn, his other hand resting on the butt of the pistol stuffed down the front of his pants. *Let the little monster have his revenge,* he thinks.

Baitsakhan hugs the blocks of metallic stone as he moves toward the torchlight. He knows this place is ancient and untouched.

Sacred.

Something snaps underneath Baitsakhan's foot. He stops, waits to see if Kala notices. She doesn't. He kneels, runs his fingers over what broke underfoot, and discovers a frail leg bone.

A good omen for death, he thinks.

Christopher still sits on the floor when the ghostly form of a small boy passes right in front of him, not more than 10 feet away. This has to be the boy Kala warned him of. Christopher holds his breath and tries to stay calm.

A snapping noise. The figure crouches, stands again. Christopher catches the glint of a wavy blade. The figure moves on, and Christopher's lungs start to burn. He doesn't dare breathe. His hands shake. He grips the smartphone with all his strength, hoping that it doesn't fall to the ground or ring, though there is probably no signal at this depth, in this remote corner of the world. The boy heads for Kala. This is the opportunity he's been waiting for. *I won't warn her.* He has her phone, and a picture of the thing on the celling. That should be enough.

Once they start to fight, I will leave.

Kala opens urn after urn around the man-headed eagle.

All empty.

Yet she knows Earth Key is near.

She feels it.

Here and here and here.

But where?

She walks around the statue. She opens a small stone coffin, sized for a dog or a cat. Nothing inside but dust and tattered cloth.

She stops. She is behind the bird statue. Is the key the eagle? If it is, that's a problem, because it's too big to carry. She holds up the torch again. Turns on her flashlight and sweeps it over the outstretched wings, the elongated neck, the braided hair of the man's head. She keeps the light trained there and moves around to the front. The man's face is flat with deep-set eyes and a broad nose and huge nostrils. His eyes are perfect circles. His forehead is squat. The whole thing is made of gold.

She shines the light up and down the figure.

Nothing.

But then something catches her eye.

Chiyoko walks to within five feet of Maccabee and throws a pebble into the room. The Nabataean's eyes, struggling against the dark, follow the noise, and she walks right past him, unnoticed. She stays close to the wall and works her way behind several large, cube-shaped stones. The night vision in her monocle does not suggest they are precious in any way. They just look big and gray.

She emerges from behind one of them and finds herself staring at Christopher's back. He is crouching, struggling to look toward the rear of the room to see what Kala is doing. From her position, Chiyoko cannot see what's happening, but she can hear that the Sumerian is looking for something. Something that she evidently believes is Earth Key.

Fool.

Chiyoko needs a better vantage point. She scampers up one of the massive metallic stacks littering the chamber. Ten feet above the floor, she sees Kala standing on an altar, working a knife into the head of a statue. Baitsakhan is nearly upon her. She sees Maccabee still standing calmly at the exit, waiting. She sees Christopher where she left him.

He sees Baitsakhan too, and he is not going to warn her. He is Playing. Interesting.

Chiyoko looks up, notices the ceiling, and loses her breath. Words, numbers, signs. She activates a recording device in her eyepiece and zooms in. She takes a careful hi-res picture, takes another and another and another. Earth Key may not be here, but this *is* important. She recognizes the word for gold in at least four languages.

Curious, Chiyoko runs her fingers over the stone beneath her. She draws the wakizashi and cuts carefully into the surface.

And then she realizes what this room contains.

Kala jumps onto the altar and stands face-to-face with the statue. She runs a finger along its jawline. There is a break in it. Up the cheek. She feels under the ear and finds a pin. The other side as well. It is hinged.

She unsheathes her knife and pries the mouth open. Inside is a black orb of glass the size of a baseball that has a perfect triangular hole bored through it. She shines the light on it. Stares at the smooth surface. She sees images: the faint outlines of the continents, the deepening oceans, the towering mountains.

Of Earth.

"I found it," she whispers.

Earth Key.

"I found it."

AN LIU

Liu Residence, Unregistered Belowground Property, Tongyuanzhen, Gaoling County, Xi'an, China

SHIVER.
Blinkblink.
SHIVERblink.
SHIVERblinkSHIVERSHIVER.
SHIVERblinkSHIVERblink.
SHIVERblinkSHIVERblink.
SHIVERSHIVERblink.
BlinkSHIVERblinkblink.
BlinkSHIVERSHIVER.
BlinkblinkblinkSHIVER.
SHIVERblinkSHIVERblink.
SHIVERblinkblinkSHIVER.

An's body seizes. He was sleeping, but no more. It seizes over and over again.

He struggles to keep his tongue in his mouth, away from his teeth.

He fights to keep his fists at his side, his feet in place, his head from flailing. A sound blares from another room, and his convulsing, sleep-addled brain can't figure out what is happening.

The blaring is just like his alarm. It is just like the air horn his father used to blow to wake little An up every day for his training.

His *blink* his *blink* his father.

His goddamned father.

He seizes, again and again, again and again.

This is not a tic, not an episode.

It is something else.

His father.

He was here!

An forces his shaking body to turn over so that he's on his side. And there he sees Chiyoko's talismans, sitting on a soft, red velvet cloth. His body begins to calm.

My father was here! But how? I killed him.

An realizes it was a dream.

The first dream he can ever remember having. His body stops shaking. He stares at Chiyoko's pieces. The tics are still at bay.

But the alarm still sounds.

He sits. Pushes a button. A screen unfolds from the wall. It is full of images of his compound. A Kinect is hooked up to the system and he points at one image. It zooms up. Nothing. He points at another. It enlarges. Nothing. He points at another. It enlarges. Something.

Not a man.

A small, hovering drone, shaped like a dragonfly.

A Player?

He draws a window around it. The camera tracks the drone. It zooms way in. And then—

No. Not a Player. The government. The Chinese government. An is as skilled a hacker as exists, but the Chinese employ hackers of their own. Messing with no-fly lists, running tracking programs, buying supplies—An must have drawn their attention. They have no idea what he's truly up to, no idea about Endgame. To them, he is just a potential terrorist, a dissident.

The government. Not for long. Not a government on Earth is going to survive what's coming.

SHIVER.

He gathers what he has of Chiyoko. Folds the cloth over her. Stands, grabs his go-bag. He opens his closet and gets inside, closes the door, and steps on a lever disguised in the floor. A metal capsule rises around him, and he falls 40 feet, down an escape hatch that he built himself. At the bottom he opens the capsule and walks 678 feet through another tunnel, which leads to an underground garage. He walks through the garage until he finds his vehicle, a black Mercedes SUV with a trailer hitched to it. An gets in, carefully lays Chiyoko out in a silver tray mounted on the center console. Once he's settled, he takes one of her fingernails and places it on his tongue. He turns on the car and puts it in gear. As soon as it moves, a pressure plate in the floor rises, and the world shakes.

The explosion will rattle the damn government a little. Give them some pause. The bomb was big, and dirty, full of radioactive waste. No one will want to come near its crater for a dozen years, even though they only have a few more at best.

I am not a terrorist. This is Endgame. There can be no winner.

He pulls out, drives up the parking ramp; the Beijing safe house is an 11-hour drive away.

He rolls Chiyoko's nail around on his tongue.

No winner but you, my love.

I

II

III

KALA MOZAMI, CHRISTOPHER VANDERKAMP, BAITSAKHAN, MACCABEE ADLAI, CHIYOKO TAKEDA

Altın Odası, 25 m Underground, Turkey

Kala doesn't see him, doesn't hear him, doesn't smell him. Baitsakhan could kill her right now, this very second, with his gun. But that would be too easy. Jalair deserves better. Kala deserves worse. Much, much worse.

He clocks her in the back of the head with the handle of his dagger. She falls hard to her knees, taken completely by surprise. Her head swims, spots briefly flash before her eyes, but the shock of ambush fades quickly. Her training takes over.

She slides to the floor, pretending to be unconscious. As soon as Baitsakhan reaches for her, she elbows him in the gut and jumps to her feet. He barely registers the hit to the stomach, starts toward her, gritting his teeth, scowling. She steps back, reaches for her gun.

"Sumerian."

"Donghu."

"Blood for blood."

Weak, she thinks. She brandishes Jalair's gun and squeezes the trigger. Baitsakhan lashes out with the whip. Its tasseled end snags the muzzle as the slug blasts out. The whip changes the trajectory just enough, and the bullet zings by Baitsakhan's neck, grazing his flesh.

The gunshot reverberates throughout the chamber, bouncing off the hard surfaces, making its way up to meet the mystery on the ceiling. Baitsakhan yanks the whip and Kala's gun clatters to the ground. It slides under the altar, out of reach. He draws out his knife; he has the whip in one hand, the blade in the other. She pulls her own blade and smiles.

"You're faster than Jalair was," Kala says, pouring salt on the wound.

"Do not speak his name, bitch."

She smiles wider. "You'll say hello to Jalair for me after I send you to hell, won't you?"

Baitsakhan doesn't answer. He lunges. He *is* fast. Kala sidesteps, and their knives meet and spark. She hits him hard across the temple with the glass orb and he flicks his whip at her legs, catching an ankle. She strikes at his jugular, but he jumps backward and pulls the whip with both hands. She thumps onto her back, dropping her blade and getting the wind knocked from her lungs.

He pulls the whip again, drawing them together. He steps over her, straddling her midsection. He drops the whip and flips the knife and brings it down with both hands for her head, full of fury and vengeance. Kala reaches up and grabs his thighs and pulls herself between his legs. Baitsakhan's knife impales the ground where her head used to be, just as she punches his groin with the orb. She can feel that he is wearing protection under his clothes, but she knows it still hurts. She springs to her feet and spins.

Baitsakhan is on her. He is not armed. The knife is still stuck in the ground. They are face-to-face. He hisses and grabs her by the ears and pulls. She hits him in the groin again, this time with her knee. She hits so hard she can feel the plastic cup crack. But he shows no sign of succumbing to pain.

He is a Player.

Trained in the ways of combat and pain.

Baitsakhan pulls her ears so hard that the skin behind the right one begins to tear.

She leans forward, into Baitsakhan's pull, and they're so close they could kiss. But instead, she opens her mouth and bites his cheek, her teeth sinking into his flesh.

He cries out and releases her. They separate, and Baitsakhan spits red on the floor.

"Blood for blood," Kala reminds him, her teeth stained red.

"Yes," he confirms, and pulls his pistol from behind his back.

Kala's head tilts. "You wait until now? You could have done it first, and taken the key."

"So that's what that is?" Baitsakhan's eyes just barely drift from Kala's onto the ball.

And that is all she needs. Misdirection. Just like with Jalair. These Donghu are all the same.

Baitsakhan fires, but Kala is on top of him, smashing his wrist with the ball.

This is too easy.

All too easy.

Christopher runs as soon as Baitsakhan pulls the gun.

To see better he flicks on the smartphone just as he reaches the exit, and nearly runs full bore into a smirking young man wagging his finger.

Christopher gasps.

"You lost, kiddo?" Maccabee asks. "No matter. I found you. Pretty soon, you'll wish I hadn't."

Kala jabs an elbow into Baitsakhan's shoulder. The gun goes off again, but Kala has his arm like a vise and the shot hits the dirt. She backs him to the golden altar and rakes her left thumb across the gun's magazine release. The clip falls to the ground. She lets go of his wrist, knowing he will raise the weapon to fire the sole round left in the chamber.

Predictable fool.

She clamps her arm over his and the gun goes off. And that's it. No more bullets in this fight.

She lets him have it with her fists, one of which still contains the glass

Earth Key, pummeling his stomach and ribs. He balls up defensively, tears falling from his eyes. Muscles bruise; bones snap. When he stops moving, she stops too. She steps back. She is disgusted. He's pitiful. "Blood for blood," she says slowly, mockingly.

Christopher has seen kids Maccabee's size before, usually on the football field. He recognizes that cocky smirk from any number of opponents at sectionals. The best way to deal with these types is hard and fast. Christopher loads up and lets fly with a haymaker. But Maccabee catches his fist and holds it. Maccabee's smirk widens into a full-fledged grin. Christopher drops the phone and swings with his other hand. Without releasing his fist, Maccabee blocks the punch and simultaneously hits Christopher hard across his left shoulder. Before Christopher can react, Maccabee raises a foot and brings it down on his knee. The pain is excruciating and the *pop* stomach-churning. The phone lies screen up on the floor, illuminating the pair from below. In accented English, Maccabee says, "What else you got?"
But Christopher has nothing.
"In that case . . ."
The last thing Christopher remembers is the guy's head coming hard for his. Maccabee lowers the boy to the floor, unsheathes his knife, and takes off at a jog toward the altar.
His bloodthirsty partner needs help.

Kala pulls back her hand. It will land squarely on Baitsakhan's throat and collapse his windpipe and his trachea, crush his Adam's apple and break his neck. He stares up at her, his eyes already dead, waiting for the blow.
"Good-bye, silly child," she says. "Blessings."
As she raises her arm, her back lights with a sharp pain, followed by a chill. She cannot move. A hand grips her shoulder and keeps her from collapsing to the floor. She knows immediately that her spinal column has been severed. Her arms and legs are paralyzed.

Her eyes widen. *I am the fool.*

Baitsakhan manages to stand, his face wet with sweat and blood and tears. His eyes red and swollen. His cheek oozing.

"You look like shit," observes Maccabee, his knife still in Kala's back.

"Shut up," growls Baitsakhan. "Let me finish this one."

"Whatever you say," Maccabee says with a snicker.

Baitsakhan spins to Kala and spits on the ground. "Blood for blood, Sumerian," he hisses. "Blood for blood."

ALICE ULAPALA

Knuckey Lagoon, Northern Territory, Australia

Alice pokes the remnants of a campfire with a stick. It is night. The
sounds of the outback surround her. The clicking, the cooing, the
yelping, the hissing. The serenade of a limitless army of crickets.
Home.

The thick Milky Way turns like a wheel overhead. She moves the coals
around, drawing a spiral in them. But not just any spiral. A special one.
A Fibonacci spiral.

Hydrogen, helium, lithium, oxygen, aluminum, scandium, selenium,
cesium, actinium.

The cesium was tricky because originally she thought it was calcium,
but that didn't fit. Also, the clue passed over boron for a reason that
Alice cannot fathom.

But undoubtedly this is what her clue referred to. And it was seconded
with the numbers of the Players' lines.

1, 2, 3, 8, 13, 21, 34, 55, 89 . . . the atomic numbers of the elements of
her clue. Add 5 for boron between 3 and 8, and a 0 and a 1 at the very
beginning, and that's it.

The Fibonacci sequence.

It can go on forever.

Yet starts in nothing.

It is found throughout nature. In shells, in flowers, in plants, in
fruit, in the inner ear. In galaxies. In our very hands: not counting
thumbs eight fingers total, five digits on each hand, three bones
in each finger, two bones in one thumb, and one thumb on each
hand. The ratio of one instance to its predecessor approximates,

sometimes with eerie accuracy, the golden mean: 1.618. For example, $89/55=1.6181818181818\ldots$

Alice rubs her face. Her head hurts. All these numbers and formulas. She's done a lot of studying since leaving the bar in Darwin. Too much for her tastes, but she has to figure this out.

Where do the numbers fit into Endgame? The line numbers, she realized, are also Fibonacci numbers. The Players are like a list of otherworldly isotopes: Mu-2, Celt-3, Minoan-5, Nabataean-8, Donghu-13, Olmec-21, Koori-34, Harrapan-55, Sumerian-89, Aksumite-144, Cahokian-233, Shang-377. But what does *that* mean, if anything?

Where do they fit?

She does not know.

She stares at the fire for 18 minutes. The only sounds are the slight breeze and the crackle-pop of the burning scrub.

Then the yellow, glowing eyes of a dingo appear on the far side of camp.

"C'mere, mate."

The eyes don't move.

Alice holds out her hand. Makes a low, submissive sound.

The dog pads toward her, enters the light of the faltering campfire. A black nose. Mottled fur. Dark eyes.

"That's it. There you are." Alice throws the dog a scrap of charred snake meat. The dog sniffs and gobbles it up.

"Was just wondering what I should do, mate."

The dog looks up from its snack. Cocks an ear. Hell, she got answers talking to some American tourist; might as well try a dingo.

"Should I stay and wait for round two, or leave Oz and go out for this first key?"

The dog looks at her seriously. Points his nose to the heavens. Sniffs.

Alice looks up too. Sees a massive green-and-orange-tailed shooting star streak through the sky.

The Player and the wild animal, each looking as feral as the other, lock gazes.

The dog sits on its haunches.

Alice nods deeply.

"Yeah. I think you're right. Round two it is. When it starts, I think I'll go after that little wanker that chopped Shari's finger."

The dog lies down. Puts its head on its forepaws.

"Yeah."

The Milky Way.

The dark.

The little fire.

"I'll wait."

Lord Krishna's home, swallowed and gone.[lxvi]

CHIYOKO TAKEDA, KALA MOZAMI, MACCABEE ADLAI, BAITSAKHAN, CHRISTOPHER VANDERKAMP

Altın Odası, 25 m Underground, Turkey

Chiyoko watches Maccabee carry Kala's frozen body to the exit. She can hear and see everything from her perch. Baitsakhan has the black orb. He paid for it with blood and pain and a huge helping of humility. Christopher is moaning but still unconscious. When they reach the exit Maccabee pushes Christopher aside with his foot. He lowers Kala onto a large waist-high stone.

"You're welcome, by the way," Maccabee says, not quite feeling the gratitude he expected for saving Baitsakhan's ass.

Baitsakhan grunts.

Pompous fool, Chiyoko thinks.

She considers killing them. She would do Maccabee first, then the boy. But it's too risky. She can kill only one at a time, after all, and that split second, even with his wounds, might be all that the Donghu would need.

No. There has been enough underestimation here for one night. Patience.

"This is it, Maccabee." Baitsakhan holds out the ball. "Earth Key. She found it for us!"

"Let me see that," Maccabee says, unconvinced.

Besides, one will eventually kill the other. And before that happens, they will probably eliminate at least one other Player. They are idiots, but for now they remain useful.

Baitsakhan sweeps an arm through the air. "Look at this place! It has to be." He draws his knife and points it at Kala. "Isn't that right, sister?"

"Get screwed!" she says in partially formed words.

"She's got a lot of spunk," Maccabee says, chuckling. He gestures to Baitsakhan. "Bring the light closer."

Baitsakhan does. "My god," Maccabee says, staring into the orb. He sees the contours of the continents and the oceans and the mountains, all right there, alive in his hand, just beneath the orb's surface. "I think you're right."

Christopher struggles to get up and says, "Wha—?"

The Players ignore him.

Baitsakhan leans in to Kala's face and says, "What else do you know? What was your clue?"

Kala is fading. "I said, get screwed."

"Where is Sky Key?" Baitsakhan asks. He lets the point of his ancient blade rest on her chest, between her breasts.

"You'll never find it." She coughs, her mouth full of blood. "Not smart enough."

"I don't intend to find it. I intend to take it. Just as I have taken this."

"Just as *we* have taken this," Maccabee interjects.

Baitsakhan says, "Yes. We."

"Won't happen," Kala mumbles.

"It will."

"He'll kill you first." She points her eyes at Maccabee. "He'll kill you soon, child."

"Mind your business, dead one," Maccabee snarls.

Baitsakhan kneels in front of her. He lets his blade rest on her thigh. "If you won't tell me, I'll kill you."

She coughs again. "I'm already dead."

Maccabee looks at his fingernails. "You're right about that," he says absently.

Kala ignores Maccabee. She locks eyes with Baitsakhan. His gaze is like stone. Hers is something older, and harder. "I am home, Annunaki," she whispers in Sumerian, a language only she can understand. "I am sorry that I come empty-handed. Peace and blessings."

Baitsakhan nods. "This is for my brother, Jalair. The gods take him."
And he drives the knife into her chest.

Christopher has propped himself up and sees it all. He is mortified, riveted. Baitsakhan twists the blade as blood covers its handle. Kala whimpers, a hole carved right through her heart. He pulls the knife free and stands. He is finished.

And so is Kala.

I should have listened, Christopher thinks, overflowing with fear.

"Hey." Maccabee snaps his fingers in Christopher's face. "Who are you? Why are you here?"

Christopher is too broken to lie. "I'm Christopher," he says, unable to peel his eyes from Kala's still bleeding body. "I know Sarah Alopay. Kala was going to ransom me."

"Can you contact Alopay?" Maccabee asks.

"Yes."

His newest captors share a look.

"This just gets better and better," Maccabee says.

Maccabee hauls Christopher to his feet and drags him to the doorway. Christopher is wasted, pale, gone. Chiyoko has never seen a more frightened look in all her life.

Poor boy, she thinks.

Maccabee drags Christopher into the stairwell and disappears. Only Baitsakhan and Kala remain. Life clings to her like late-morning dew to a spider's web. Baitsakhan sneers, "Blood for blood," and throws the torch onto her lap. Kala whimpers, smoke billowing, her flesh searing, clothing melting, and Baitsakhan walks away.

As soon as Chiyoko is sure he's gone, she drops silently from the stone and pulls the wakizashi from her belt. Kala sees her through the flickering tongues of flame and manages a small smile. Chiyoko draws the blade swiftly across the Sumerian's throat.

Kala's eyes go dark, her arm falls outstretched, index finger extended at 166°30'32".

Rest, sister.

With the tip of her weapon Chiyoko prods Kala's still-burning body until she finds what she's looking for. Using the blade, she cuts the cloth and picks up the ring. It rattles down the length of the steel and stops at the hand guard. Chiyoko stares at it for a moment, feels, senses, knows she got what she came for.

Kala did too.

Chiyoko secures the ancient ring and looks at her tracker display. Jago and Sarah are less than 15 km away. They'll be in the parking lot soon.

It's time to go and meet them.

Time to get the disk.

Time to Play Endgame.

It's full of stars.^{lxvii}

CHRISTOPHER VANDERKAMP

Audi A8 Leaving Gobekli Tepe

Christopher is dragged up the stairs, into the night, toward the party. They skirt around the rave until they reach the parking lot, where he is thrown in the back of a black sedan. He slides to the far door. His leg is killing him. He puts his face in his hands and begins to cry.

Maccabee gets behind the wheel, and Baitsakhan is in the passenger seat. Baitsakhan turns around and studies Christopher, his swollen lips curled in distaste.

"If you try to escape, I will gut you," Baitsakhan warns. "And if you keep crying, I will gut you."

Christopher tries to get himself under control. He can't bear to meet Baitsakhan's eyes. He hated Kala with all his heart, but no one deserved that. These two are monsters.

They pull out of the parking lot, Christopher staring out the window. He sees the glow of the lasers and the smiling people and a girl running giddily across the parking lot. They have so much to live for, these happy kids. They're just like he was before the meteors fell, just like Sarah was. He's glad they don't know what he knows, that they're able to live freely and in the moment. At least for now. Christopher remembers Sarah's words: *Endgame is a puzzle. The solution is life.* But he realizes that she didn't tell him everything. Endgame might hold the key to life, but Endgame itself is death, just as Kala promised. *But the game is death,* he thinks, as if he is speaking to Sarah.

And then, as he stares blankly out the window, wondering what Baitsakhan and Maccabee are going to do to him, and if he's about to die, and how it's going to happen, and how terrible it's going to be, he sees Sarah, behind the wheel of another car, passing them.

Just like that.

Was she real? He doesn't know. Can't be sure. She comes and goes, and fades into the distance. She is gone.

The game is death.

He plants his hands on the glass and he knows. He's going to die. He's going to die and he will never see Sarah Alopay again.

SARAH ALOPAY, JAGO TLALOC, CHIYOKO TAKEDA

Peugeot 307 on the Şanlıurfa Mardin Yolu, Route D400, Heading East

A black Audi screams past the 307 as Sarah and Jago pull into the parking lot at Gobekli Tepe. They were expecting Kala and Christopher, not all these cars and buses and revelers.

"How're we supposed to find her in this?" Sarah asks, waving her hand in front of her.

"Look for someone like us," Jago answers, the M4 resting in his lap. "Someone with guns."

And that's when Sarah sees her. A girl in a black bodysuit, a hood, a mask. Yeah, that definitely fits the description of a Player. Sarah points her out.

"Told you," Jago says. He clicks the safety off. "Easy."

When the girl sees them, she tears off her hood and spreads her arms out wide. It isn't Kala.

"Is that . . . ?"

"The mute," Sarah says.

Chiyoko works her way to the driver window, signing frantically. She makes a show of demonstrating that her hands are empty.

"What the hell is this?" Jago says, his voice low. "Why is she here?"

Sarah rolls down the window. "Are you with Kala?" she asks.

Chiyoko reaches for her phone and the notepad program she can use to communicate. She hears a gun cock within the car and stops, glancing up.

"Hands where we can see them," growls Jago.

Chiyoko sighs.

"Where's Kala?" Sarah asks again.

Chiyoko shakes her head at Sarah and draws her thumb slowly across her throat.

"Dead?"

Chiyoko nods.

"You killed her?" Jago asks, leaning across Sarah to get a better look at Chiyoko.

Chiyoko ignores Jago's question, the answer too complicated to communicate right now. Instead, she points to Sarah, then clasps both her hands over her heart in a loving gesture, then points at Sarah again.

"My . . . my friend?" Sarah asks hesitantly. "My *boy*friend?"

Chiyoko nods. She points down the road at the pair of taillights that are quickly melting into the night. Then, she holds up two fingers.

"Two of them?" Sarah asks. "Took Christopher?"

Chiyoko nods.

Jago claps sarcastically from the passenger seat. "Shit—next time bring something to write with."

Chiyoko frowns, gestures at her pockets, then at his gun.

"Don't blame me," he says. "This is Endgame, sister. You know the drill."

"Hell with this," says Sarah, putting the car in gear. "We've got to catch them. Whoever they are." With Christopher in trouble, Chiyoko is an afterthought. "Thanks," Sarah shouts out of the window as she steps on the gas.

"Whoa!" shouts Jago as Chiyoko leaps in front of the car, blocking their path.

Sarah barely has a chance to hit the brakes. She grips the wheel with both hands. "What the hell, Mu?"

Chiyoko holds out her sheathed short sword and slams it flat on the hood. She makes a grand bow, as if she's presenting the blade to Sarah and Jago.

"I think she wants to come with us," Jago says.

They don't have time to negotiate. Sarah leans her head out the window. "All right, come on, but don't try anything!" From the corner of her mouth, to Jago, she whispers, "If things get weird, kill her."

"Gladly."

Chiyoko opens the back door. As she gets in, she hands her sword to Jago. And then Sarah guns the car in reverse.

"I guess I should thank you," Sarah yells as she cranes to look out the rear window. "If we save my friend, it will be because of you."

Chiyoko bows again. When she straightens, she sees some of the lights on the HUD creeping along the bottom of the windshield. She points at them as if to ask what they are.

"Oh, you're in for a treat," Sarah says, piloting the car backward at 50 mph.

"Yeah," says Jago. "We're full of surprises."

Sarah yanks the parking brake and they spin around. She throws the car directly into 2nd gear and drops the pedal and they're off. She extinguishes the headlights as they hit the pavement. As soon as she does, the inside of the windshield transforms. They can see everything in front of them. The road, the sky, all of the stars above. The brake lights of the unsuspecting Audi. As Chiyoko looks around, she sees that all of the windows are night-vision equipped. She blows out a long ascending whistle that conveys her amazement.

"I thought you were a mute," Jago quips.

Chiyoko reaches into her pocket, producing her cell phone. She begins typing frantically. When she's finished, she hands the phone to Jago, who reads the message.

"Listen to this," he says to Sarah. "It's Maccabee and Baitsakhan we're chasing. They've got your . . . friend. He's got an injured leg. Chiyoko here promises, on her honor, to help us and not kill us—so long as we let her examine the disk afterward." Jago narrows his eyes at Chiyoko. "I don't know."

Chiyoko snatches back her phone and types another message.

"Well?" Sarah asks.

"She says her line used to care for the disks. Says she knows stuff about them." Jago eyeballs Chiyoko. "You going to share some of that knowledge, shy girl?"

Chiyoko nods grudgingly.

"Then I guess we've got a deal." Jago reaches under his seat. "You want a gun?"

Chiyoko claps once.

Jago asks, "Twice for no?"

She claps once again.

"Good enough," Jago says. He passes her a two-tone sterling-and-black Browning Pro-40. She grabs the stock.

"On your sword and honor, right?" Jago asks before releasing the barrel. "You aren't gonna betray us."

Chiyoko gives him a curt nod.

He lets go. "All right. In case you forget, I've got this." He pats the M4, the one with the grenade launcher mounted under the barrel.

Sarah drops the 307 into 4th gear and they go from 94 to 114 in two seconds. The Audi is fast, but the crappy-looking 307 is faster. They snake along the road; all the turns are tight, fast, and low, the wheels screeching, the engine roaring. Sarah's an expert driver, and within a minute they're 50 m behind the A8. And judging by the casual driving of their targets, still undetected.

Chiyoko rolls down her window and takes aim. Jago rolls down his window and braces the M4 on the side mirror.

"Ready?" he asks.

Chiyoko nods.

"Fire!"

Chiyoko fires three rounds and Jago a short burst. The slugs hit the Audi and glance off it in sparks and flares.

"Bulletproof!" Sarah exclaims.

The Audi swerves and accelerates. Chiyoko fires two shots at the tires, but they appear to be solid rubber. Sarah takes a hand from the wheel and draws a square on the windshield with her finger; the image zooms in. She can see Christopher whipping around and gazing with fear out the back window.

353

"Be careful!" she shouts.

"What? It's bulletproof, right?" Jago says, squeezing off another round.

"Jago . . ." Sarah says quietly. "Please."

Jago pulls his gun inside and rolls up the window. "Eh, it was worth a try."

The Audi swerves as its occupants try to figure out who's attacking them. Sarah clicks the 307 into 6th gear and pulls alongside the sedan. Shifting across the backseat, Chiyoko finds herself right alongside Maccabee. He cracks his window and Baitsakhan reaches across, sticks out a pistol, and fires five rounds at the 307. Chiyoko doesn't even flinch as the bullets explode on the window in front of her.

Jago jabs his finger at his window and says, "Yeah, bitches, we're bulletproof too!" Sarah lets up on the gas and they drop a half car length behind the Audi.

"Well, what now?" Jago asks, spinning to Chiyoko.

She motions for her sword. He frowns but hands it over. Before he can even ask what Chiyoko wants the blade for, she has rolled her window back down and is climbing out of the car, onto the roof.

Jago looks at Sarah, wide-eyed. "Wasn't expecting that."

Sarah rolls the window back up and concentrates on keeping the car straight. As Chiyoko steadies herself on top of the 307, Baitsakhan lobs a grenade toward her. She casually slaps it out of the air, redirecting it to the shoulder, where it explodes on the side of the road, doing no harm. "¡Dios mío!" Jago exclaims in awe.

Chiyoko's face appears in the windshield and she motions at the Audi.

"Get closer," Jago says.

"Trying."

A turn is coming as Sarah edges to within a couple of feet of the Audi. They are going 85 mph.

And then Chiyoko jumps.

She lands flat on the roof and reaches for the edges to steady herself. Sarah drops the 307 behind the Audi.

Baitsakhan opens the passenger window and sticks out a pistol, but Chiyoko kicks it out of his hand. The gun sails into the air and Baitsakhan's hand disappears back into the car. Chiyoko draws the wakizashi and drives it straight down into the rubber seal between the rear window and the roof of the car. It goes to the hilt and she slides it along the window and the rubber pops out. She pries the glass outward and, in a single piece, it comes free, sliding across the highway behind them.

"You gotta be kidding me," Sarah says.

Christopher—confused, scared, shocked—gapes out the rear window. And sees Sarah.

Chiyoko reaches into the car and grabs Christopher by the arm and hauls him onto the trunk, where he is out of Baitsakhan's reach. Then she motions for Sarah to come closer.

Sarah urges the 307 right behind the Audi's bumper. Maccabee passes Baitsakhan a new pistol just before Chiyoko picks up Christopher and vaults onto the hood of the 307. Christopher, clinging to the edge of the hood, is white as a sheet.

Sarah yells "Hold on!" and slams the brake. As they start to slow down, Baitsakhan shoots. A bullet grazes the back of Chiyoko's head; another hits Christopher in the leg.

Jago arms the grenade launcher of the M4, leans out the back window, and pulls the trigger.

"Adios, amigos."

The grenade streaks through the air. Before it reaches the sedan, the car's brake lights flare and front doors fly open. The grenade sails through the back window and explodes. Sarah eases the 307 to a stop. Chiyoko helps Christopher off the hood. Jago opens one of the rear doors. Christopher and Chiyoko fall into the backseat, and Chiyoko closes the door. Sarah puts the car back in gear and takes off.

"Everyone all right?" Sarah asks.

Chiyoko touches the back of her head. Her fingers come back bloody, but the cut isn't deep. She flashes Jago a thumbs-up. Christopher, who's had too much for one night, is passed out. But the wound on his calf doesn't look like it's bad.

"His leg's grazed," Jago says. "They look fine to me."

Sarah lets out a relieved sigh. "Chiyoko, that was—"

"Unreal, I've never seen anything like that," Jago interrupts.

Chiyoko shakes her head as if to dismiss them, makes a drinking motion. Sarah takes a bottle of water from the center console and hands it to her. Chiyoko opens it up and dumps it over Christopher's head. He wakes with a start, pushing away from Chiyoko, gazing dazedly around the car.

"Sarah—it's you—holy shit—who are these people?"

"Players, Christopher. This is Jago." Jago looks at him, nods slightly. "The crazy-ass ninja is Chiyoko. This is Endgame, and you shouldn't be here. I want you home, where it's safe."

She wants it to sound like a lecture, but Sarah can barely keep a straight face. Her boyfriend just chased her halfway around the world and, without any formal training, took on Players. Sure, he needed rescuing, but it's still pretty awesome. Christopher smiles at her eyes in the mirror. She smiles back. Their love is still alive, still strong, still there.

I found her, Christopher thinks. *It will be better now. I can deal. I found her.*

"Rest up, amigo," Jago says. Sarah hears the tension in that last word and doesn't like it. "We need to put some miles behind us and then we'll have a look at that leg."

"All right," Christopher says, still staring at Sarah in the mirror.

Jago shakes a bottle of pills. "Take one of these."

"What is it?" Christopher asks.

"Oxy," Jago says.

Christopher takes the pill and within minutes is asleep. Sarah watches him in the mirror as she drives. She makes no effort to calm her heart, or slow it down. It's beating fast because of Christopher and she likes it. She watches him and doesn't think of Jago, or of Endgame.

I love you, Christopher, but you should have listened to me, she thinks.

Fear creeps into her. He could get hurt again. Only next time it could be worse.

She looks back to the road.

You should have listened.

Hadean,[lxviii] Archean, Proterozoic, Paleozoic, Mesozoic, Cenozoic, Anthropozoic.

BAITSAKHAN, MACCABEE ADLAI

The Şanlıurfa Mardin Yolu, Route D400

Maccabee and Baitsakhan lie in the dirt on the side of the road. Jumping from a car going 53 mph hurt. A lot. Maccabee has broken his nose for the 6th time in his life, as well as dislocated a finger, bruised several ribs, and suffered dozens of scrapes and cuts. He sits, takes the bridge of his nose between the heels of his hands, and pops it into place. He clears his throat and spits a wad of blood on the ground. "Baitsakhan?"

"Yes." Baitsakhan is 30 feet to Maccabee's left, also just sitting up. He has a cracked right patella, a gash on his left forearm, a sprained wrist. "I'm here."

"You in one piece?"

"More or less." He pulls a canister from his belt of explosives and unscrews it. He takes out four iodine swabs and a suture kit. "Still have your gun?"

Maccabee touches the grip. "Yes."

"Can you get us a ride? I have to stitch a cut."

Maccabee rolls his eyes. "Sure. And I'm in one piece too. Thanks for asking."

"You're welcome."

"You have the orb—Earth Key?"

"Of course. I'll never let it go."

"Good." Maccabee stands. His body creaks. He straightens his back. Vertebra click. "That was not fun."

Baitsakhan has a flashlight between his teeth. "No." The cut on his arm is deep and filthy, four inches long. He takes another canister from his belt and unscrews it and pours the liquid over the cut.

Alcohol.

Burns.

He doesn't cringe or whine. He tears the swab package open and runs the iodine along the cut, under the flesh, working it in and around. Fresh blood dribbles into the dirt.

Maccabee turns to the road and starts walking. "Sorry about Jalair," he says over his shoulder.

Baitsakhan doesn't respond.

Maccabee walks up the embankment. The Audi is 100 feet up the road, completely ablaze. Nothing is salvageable from it. He pulls out his gun, flips the safety off.

Baitsakhan runs the curved needle through his flesh, working quickly. He still doesn't make a sound. He ties off the suture, rips off a piece of his shirt, wraps it around the wound. He stands, walks toward Maccabee. "Anything?"

"Not yet."

They wait for several minutes. Baitsakhan raises his wounded arm and points. "There."

"Get down," Maccabee says.

Baitsakhan eases his battered body to the ground. Maccabee steps into the middle of the road. A pair of motorcycles approaches. Fast motorcycles. The headlights hit Maccabee, and he waves his hands, feigns a look of fear. Neither of the bikes slows down. They are 200 feet away and closing.

"Not the Good Samaritan types," grumbles Maccabee.

So he raises his gun.

One head shot and the bike on the left goes down and skids over the road. The other bike slams the brakes and swerves, but Maccabee sights the driver and pulls the trigger and it goes down as well.

Baitsakhan stands. "Well done."

Maccabee blows over the muzzle and smiles. They each walk toward a bike. Baitsakhan reaches his first. The driver is dead, but the passenger, a young woman, is not. Baitsakhan thinks he saw them at the party but doesn't care. He leans over her. She's scared.

"Devil!" she hisses in Turkish.

Baitsakhan reaches down and takes her quavering head in both of his hands and snaps her neck. He pulls her and her boyfriend off the bike and lifts it up. He looks over at Maccabee as he's finishing off his driver with a final shot. They bring the bikes to the middle of the road, rev the engines. Maccabee shouts, "Let me see the key!"

Baitsakhan removes it from the inside of his jacket and holds it up.

"What do you say we go celebrate a little?"

"Celebrate?" Baitsakhan asks, as if it's some kind of alien concept. He thinks about his brother and his cousins, the blood that's been spilled. They would want Baitsakhan to enjoy this victory. He nods and works the orb back into his clothing. "Yes. Celebrate. I think we deserve it."

SHARI CHOPRA

Chopra Residence, Gangtok, Sikkim, India

Shari tries not to think about Baitsakhan. She is home, and it is peaceful, just the way she left it before the Calling. She thinks she'll stay here for a while and rest. But then she feels the ghostly numbness where her finger should be, and she thinks about hunting down the Donghu and killing him.

She has not made up her mind.

Shari is on one knee. Little Alice is sitting on the other. Her dark hair is in pigtails. Her eyes are big and wet, like smoothed river stones. Shari is hugging her daughter's shoulders. Jamal is standing over them, beaming. Little Alice is holding one of Shari's hands. "Where's your finger?" Little Alice asks.

Shari shrugs. "I lost it."

"How?"

"An accident."

Little Alice is not a prospective Player. Jamal knows of Endgame— knows everything—but Little Alice knows nothing. Shari would like to keep it that way, but she knows she can't. Not once the Event happens. Not once the world begins to end.

"Did it hurt?"

"Yes, my little *pakora*, it did."

"How much?"

Shari releases her daughter's body and stretches out her arms. She pulls her hands close together, so that only a few inches separate them. "Only this much," Shari says.

"Oh."

Jamal kneels. Shari puts her hands back out as far as they will go and says, "But being away from you hurt this much, *meri jaan*, this much."

"Okay," Little Alice says, smiling, and she bounces off Shari's knee and runs away, down the grass lawn, toward a loitering peacock at the end of the garden. The southern face of Kanchenjunga looms over the hardy shrubs, its jagged peak white in the sun and blue in shadow. Jamal watches their daughter. He is two years older than Shari. "Where is your ring?" he asks quietly. For Shari, his voice is like a blanket and a warm fire and sweet milk all together.

"I lost it too," Shari says matter-of-factly. "But I will get it back, my sweet. Even if I have to fight the god himself, I will get it back."

Jamal puts a hand on his wife's thigh. "I hope it doesn't come to that."

"It won't. A little monster masquerading as a boy has it. He will return it."

"You're going to chase him?"

Shari looks at Jamal. There is a darkness in her eyes that wasn't there before the Calling. Gently, he puts a hand on her shoulder. "I don't know yet," she answers.

"Take some time," Jamal says. "Stay with us for a while."

Shari nods, watches her beautiful daughter running through the grass. Endgame is in motion. The Event will come soon. Perhaps before it does the other Players will come first, to hunt her, to hunt her family. She flexes her remaining fingers, thinking about how quickly everything can fall apart.

Later that night, after they've gone to bed, Shari wraps her fine hands around Little Alice's slumbering neck and squeezes. Squeezes. Squeezes.

The girl's eyes snap open. She smiles. Mouths, *Mama*. Cries tears of joy. Even as her body writhes and spasms and dies.

Shari holds on to the warm neck until the pulse stops. She lets go. Brushes the hair from her daughter's face. Leans in and gives her a kiss.

She turns to her own bed. Jamal still sleeps. Shari looks to her hands and there it is. A knife from the kitchen. Shining steel. Bone handle. The one she uses to dice garlic and *dhania*. She puts the point over his heart. Waits. Waits. Waits.

Plunges.

The rich blood sprouts along the blade and Jamal looks at her and says, "Thank you, sweet." As he dies, he reaches out his hand and takes hers and holds it until he can't anymore. When she pulls the knife out of his chest, the ring that the Donghu stole comes with it.

Shari lifts it up. Looks at it. Licks off the blood. Swallows.

And then she is an elephant on a green expanse of grass and the stone circle is there before her, iconic and permanent. She bellows her grief, the sound reverberating off the stones.

A dream.

She sits bolt upright. Covered in sweat. Little Alice is crying in the bed next to theirs; Jamal is there, soothing her. The moonlight filters through the cool mountain air and into their cozy house.

This peace cannot last.

I must always keep a gun. A gun with three rounds in it.

She sees the old standing stones of her dream, placed by druids, and knows.

Earth Key is there.

I will not tell.

Another can have it.

18.095, -94.043889[lxix]

SARAH ALOPAY, JAGO TLALOC, CHIYOKO TAKEDA, CHRISTOPHER VANDERKAMP

Fatih Sultan Mehmet Bridge, Istanbul, Turkey

Chiyoko takes her hands off the wheel and claps. Claps again. Sarah and Jago each wake with a start, their reflexes buzzing. Christopher still sleeps.

They are in Istanbul.

It's evening. Chiyoko guides the 307 across the Mehmet Bridge. The black strait is 210 feet below. Boats of all sizes move through the water in the same lanes once used by Minoans, Greeks, Romans, Cypriots, Caucasians, Moors, Israelites, Egyptians, Hittites, Byzantines, and every kind of person from every walk of life that the world has ever seen.

Jago flips a computer terminal out of the back of the passenger seat and searches for hotels. He finds a nice one and punches it into the car's navigation system. Chiyoko claps once in thanks.

"I'm going to book us into a really nice hotel. Might as well play Endgame in style, right?"

Sarah smiles at Jago. Chiyoko nods in agreement.

Christopher stirs. Rubs his eyes. "How long have I been out?"

"Not long enough, *pendejo.*"

"Jago," Sarah scolds.

Jago folds his arms and mumbles something vulgar in Spanish. Sarah, in the passenger seat, turns to face Christopher. "How's your leg?"

"Numb, but okay. Toes move and everything. We going to a hospital?"

Jago snorts.

"We'd rather not. Let's have a look at it first." Sarah runs her hand over the knee, which is still slightly hyperextended. She pushes down. "How's that feel?"

"Not great, not terrible." She wiggles the knee from side to side. "And that?"

"She set my shoulder the night we met," Jago muses, gazing out of his window. "A night I'll never forget . . ."

"Yeah, why's that?"

"It was explosive," Jago says, flashing his studded teeth at Christopher. "She is good with her hands, yes?"

"Shut up," Sarah says, "or I'll cut yours off."

Christopher looks from Jago to Sarah, his eyes widening, confused.

Sarah shakes her head. "It was nothing like that. We had to jump off a moving train before it blew up."

"Things blow up around you guys a lot, don't they?"

"That's what Endgame is," Jago says.

"And look at me," Christopher replies. "Little old rookie right in the middle of it."

"Right where you shouldn't be," Jago says.

Christopher turns to face Jago. The backseat suddenly feels too small. "You got a problem?"

"Yes," Jago says simply, "you're a sack of meat, and I don't want to carry you."

"Meat? I'd knock your fu—"

"STOP IT!" Sarah shouts.

"I'd kill you before you touched me," Jago sneers.

If Christopher was thinking straight, he'd remember what happened when he tried to punch Maccabee in the underground chamber.

Around Sarah, though, his old high school instincts kick in. He's not backing down. Christopher starts to move, but Sarah sticks a hand between the two boys in the backseat. "Chiyoko, pull over. Feo, you're riding up front."

Chiyoko stops the car, a slight smile on her face. *Boys. All the same.*

Sarah gets out and opens the rear door. Jago eases onto the sidewalk.

"He doesn't belong here," Jago whispers as he moves around her. Sarah gets in back; Jago sits up front. Chiyoko pulls the car into the flow of traffic.

Sarah puts her hand on Christopher's knee. "I'm sorry. None of this is easy."

"I heard what he just said," Christopher complains.

Sarah sighs and says, "And you know what? He's right. I'll get you back on your feet, but when I do, you have to go home. Nothing's changed since the airport in Omaha. You shouldn't have followed me. You *shouldn't* be here."

Christopher recoils. "I'm not going anywhere, Sarah. I've seen this much. I know about these Annunaki, these maker beings, our screwed-up history—I'm going to see the rest. For Christ's sake, I was on that damn plane crash, did you know that? The one all over the news?"

Jago gives Christopher a mildly impressed look. "You were?"

"Yeah, me and that psycho Kala chick." Christopher thinks of the murdered mother and daughter. Knows that they will haunt him for the rest of his life. "We were . . . we were the only survivors," he lies.

Sarah puts her arm around Christopher's shoulders. Jago faces front, not wanting to see this. "God. I'm so sorry."

"Yeah, don't sweat it," Christopher says unconvincingly.

She squeezes his broad frame. Remembers what it was like to hug him, to be held by him. No one speaks for a while. Sarah asks Chiyoko to stop the car again. They pull in front of a pharmacy.

"I'm going to get some things for that leg, including a pair of crutches," Sarah says, looking Christopher in the eye. *"That you are going to use to take your ass home."*

"Whatever," Christopher says as Sarah climbs out and closes the door behind her.

An awkward silence descends in the car.

"Do you talk?" Christopher finally asks Chiyoko.

She shakes her head.

"Oh, that's cool. I never thanked you for rescuing me from those two kids, so, thank you. They were bad news."

Chiyoko bows slightly.

"Speaking of that—since you were in that big gold room spying on us, why didn't you help? You know, before the little one stabbed Kala, before they kidnapped me?"

Chiyoko's eyes shift but she is otherwise motionless.

"Fine, don't answer," Christopher mutters. "You Players are all the same. Out of your minds."

Jago turns to the backseat, looks at Christopher, smiles, the diamonds in his teeth throwing off a sinister light. "This is Endgame, bitch. Best get used to it."

AISLING KOPP

Lago Beluiso, Lombardy, Italy

Aisling's eyes are closed, as they have been for the last five hours, 23 minutes, and 29.797 seconds. Her back is straight. Her legs in half lotus. Her fingers laced in her lap. She sits before the cave painting of the beautiful woman she's started referring to as the Mu, adrift on an open sea, the disk in her hands, death all around her.

Aisling waits for the painting to whisper its secrets. For her clue to unfold some new and immense knowledge within her brain. For something—anything—to happen. She sighs and opens her eyes. Nothing is happening.

"This is bullshit," she says, her voice echoing through the cave. It's strange to hear the sound of her voice, dry and scratchy. Isn't talking to yourself one of the first signs of dementia? She flops down on her back and grabs her satellite phone out of her pack, calls her grandfather. It was on his advice she climbed all the way up here, his fault she's doing nothing when she should be out there Playing. He answers on the 3rd ring, his voice riddled with static.

"Now what?" she says, by way of greeting.

"Hello, Aisling," he replies, a smile in his voice. "How's it going?"

"How long am I supposed to stay here, Pop?" she complains. "It's been days and I'm no closer to figuring this thing out. *If* there's even anything *to* figure out. Maybe you misinterpreted my clue."

"I doubt it," her grandfather replies grimly. "Tell me what you see."

"Paintings. Old-ass paintings. One is a weird-looking lady on a boat, floating around after—well—it looks like the world has ended, ya know?"

"And what else?"

Aisling glances to the other painting. "Twelve people gathered at—"

Aisling slaps her forehead. For the first time, she recognizes the stone monoliths that surround the 12. She feels like an idiot, should've recognized it sooner. It's blurry, and rotated, and missing some pieces, but it's the same place she's studied and visited. It is a place sacred to her line.

"—gathered at Stonehenge," she finishes, glad Pop isn't there to see her slip up.

"Hmm," he says. "One of our places."

Most consider Stonehenge to be a burial ground, a healing station, a temple.

It was these things.

But more.

Much more.

Aisling has had the astronomical significance of Stonehenge drilled into her since she was a child. The Heel Stone—a rough-hewn 35-ton monolith that lies 256 feet northeast of the ruin's center—marks the exact point on the horizon where the sun rises on the summer solstice. Other parts mark the winter solstice, sunrises and sunsets, moonrises and moonsets; parts that have been destroyed predicted solar eclipses. Which means, to those who want to understand, who want to believe, that whoever built the turn of massive rocks understood not only that Earth was spherical but also that it had a place in the known universe.

All of this circa 3000 BCE.

A simple circle of stone, but it symbolizes so much.

Aisling stifles a yawn.

"What are they doing at Stonehenge?" Pop asks.

"Screaming, mostly," Aisling replies. "There's a Dia coming down from space ahead of a fireball. Most of the twelve look freaked out. Except for one—the same lady from the boat—she's fitting a stone into some altar."

Her grandfather is quiet, mulling this over. Aisling stands up and goes to the pictograph, runs her fingers across the rough wall, touching the fireball that careens down from space.

"It's pretty morbid," she says.

"Aisling," her grandfather begins hesitantly, "what if you have the order wrong?"

"What order?" she asks, stepping back from the painting, taking it all in.

"You said that the Dia comes with its fire, and then the woman uses the altar."

"Uh-huh," Aisling says, patting her pockets for a stick of gum. "So?"

"What if the woman uses the altar, *and then* the fire comes?"

Aisling freezes, a stick of spearmint halfway to her lips. She looks at the chaos of the first pictograph, then turns her head, looking at the desolation of the second. The lone woman with her disk.

"She won," whispers Aisling. "And she's alone."

She whips her head back to the first painting. Stonehenge. The altar. The stone disk. The Mu.

"Aisling? Are you still there?"

"It's a cycle," Aisling replies, thinking of the words her long-dead father used before he went mad. "We're all part of an endless cycle."

HILAL IBN ISA AL-SALT

Church of the Covenant, Kingdom of Aksum, Northern Ethiopia

"I know I am right," Hilal says. Hilal takes Eben's hands. The old master looks wary, but his protégé is enthused.

"But why? Why do we have our traditions, and our knowledge, and our secrets, if what you say is true?"

"Because it is a *game.*" Hilal takes his hands away, pinching the bridge of his nose. "Or, perhaps, it's a test. A game within a game. A way to prove not just the worthiness of our line, but of all humanity."

"Slow down," Eben cautions. "These are dangerous thoughts."

"True thoughts," Hilal insists. "Certainties."

Eben ibn Mohammed al-Julan asks wearily, "But why would the being give you this clue?"

Hilal has wondered this himself. He meditated long on the circle that kepler 22b forced into his brain. Hilal believes he understands it, but he can only guess at the being's true motivation. So he guesses.

"It was a mistake. It has to be. A circle has so many meanings. Too many. But paired with his words, it comes into focus. He said it. The Event is part of Endgame. The reason for it. The beginning, middle, and end!"

Eben strokes his chin. "I don't know."

"Or it *wasn't* a mistake!" Hilal shouts, his mind on overdrive. He knows he is right, feels it in his gut, like faith, and he must convince Eben. "Perhaps he *wanted* one of us to figure it out."

There's a spark in Eben's eyes: long-held ideas being reconsidered. He says, "Or perhaps they are testing your worthiness. This is a parable of sorts—we kill, therefore we must *be* killed."

"If that is so, Master Eben, I must tell the others."

Eben cocks his head. His dark skin is weathered. His brilliant blue eyes are troubled. "This is unexpected."

"Of course it is. The future is unwritten. The being meant something else—that anything is possible. Our very history—that we have been visited, altered, taught by the beings for millennia—would suggest that anything is possible. Master, I must warn the others!"

"If you are wrong, you will be playing from behind. They will have advantages that you don't, ideas, alliances, ancient objects, Earth Key."

"But if I am right, it won't matter. The future is unwritten."

"Perhaps."

Hilal shakes his master's arms. Peers deeply into his eyes. Hilal is full of love and life. The Coptic cross that is tattooed over his chest and stomach hums with electricity. "Fathers Christ and Mohammed would agree. Uncle Moses. Grandfather Buddha. All of them would say it is worth a try. For love, Master Eben ibn Mohammed al-Julan, for love."

The wizened ex-Player takes one of his hands and places it lightly on Hilal's eyes. They close.

"Why do we believe in these figures—the Christ, Mohammed, Buddha—when we have seen the true forces that shape life and knowledge?" Eben asks his young Player this question not for the first time. It is a familiar refrain amongst their line. A powerful one.

"Because," Hilal answers, "we believe that one person *can* make a difference."

The sun wobbles 11.187 cm and peels off a flare of historic magnitude. It explodes into the void with the power of 200,000,000,000 megatons of TNT. The CME is so massive and intense and fast that it will reach Earth in only nine hours and 34 minutes.

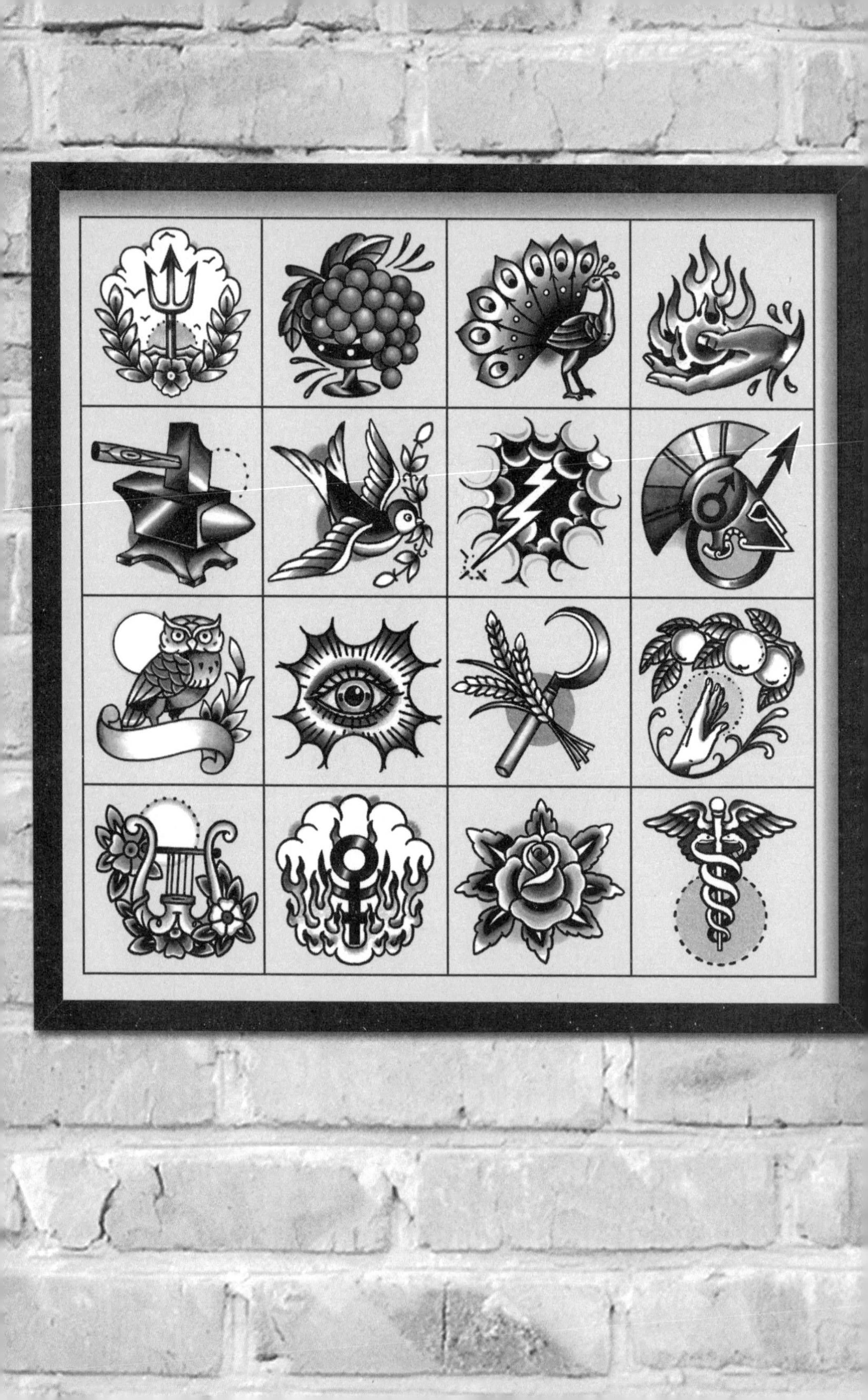

MACCABEE ADLAI, BAITSAKHAN

Sürmeli Hotel, Suite 101, Ankara, Turkey

Maccabee can't sleep. He's spread out on a couch just big enough for his body. He rolls onto his side and looks over to the bed where young, brash, murderous, vengeful Baitsakhan is curled up.

Asleep.

With a smile on his face.

They're sharing a hotel suite in Ankara. They disagreed about the best way to celebrate their acquisition of Earth Key. Maccabee wanted women; Baitsakhan would only agree if he could kill them when they were done. Maccabee wanted a drink; Baitsakhan insisted he would never touch the stuff. Maccabee wanted to see the city; Baitsakhan hates any city but Ulaanbaatar.

So they bought an XboxOne and played *Call of Duty: Ghosts* until their eyes fell out. Maccabee got killed more than Baitsakhan, which is why he's stuck on the couch. He looks at the scar on his hand, the scar caused when he made a blood bond with the boy. He knew it was a lie. He knew Baitsakhan was lying, too. He runs his fingers along the grip of his pistol. He could take the pillow and hold it up and shoot the boy and that would be it. He could take Earth Key and Play on.

He could.

The sleeping boy snorts.

Grins.

His brother just died. He should be mourning. What is wrong with him?

Maccabee picks up the gun with one hand, the pillow with the other. Puts the barrel into the face of the pillow. He flips the safety, puts some pressure on the trigger. The pillow will muffle the sound. Allow him to work in silence.

Baitsakhan screams. Maccabee jumps. The gun does not go off. He lets the pillow fall on top of it as Baitsakhan scrambles with the sheets, as if they are suddenly infested with snakes and rats and scorpions.

"You all right, Baitsakhan?"

The boy yells and works his hands into his clothing, pulls out the orb, which is white-hot and glowing. He juggles it as if it is 1,000 degrees, throws it across the room. Maccabee reaches out, catches it, and the light inside dims. It is not hot at all. If anything, it is slightly cool. Baitsakhan looks around as if there are more creepy-crawly things coming for him. Finally his eyes settle on Maccabee. "How are you holding that?"

"Why couldn't you?"

"It was burning me." The young Player holds out his hands. They're red, blisters already forming.

"It's not burning me." Maccabee gives the orb a good look, turns it in his hand. "I think there's a message here."

Baitsakhan stands. "Where?"

"Here."

The Donghu crosses the room. "I told you it was Earth Key."

"I don't dispute it, brother," Maccabee says.

"It is only a matter of time until kepler 22b confirms it."

"Maybe it's doing that right now. Look."

Baitsakhan peers into the orb. Reaches out a finger and touches it. His skin sizzles and he recoils. "Ack!"

"I'll hold it, brother. Don't worry."

Baitsakhan leans forward tentatively, looks. First there is a symbol.

Then a face.

"The Aksumite!" the two say together.

The map of the world swirls into view, and zooms in, and in, and in. They are looking at rural Ethiopia. For a brief second, a point of light is illuminated, as if there's a star inside the orb. It vanishes; Maccabee looks at Baitsakhan; Baitsakhan looks at Maccabee. They both smile. At the same time, they smile. "Time to Play."

SARAH ALOPAY, JAGO TLALOC, CHIYOKO TAKEDA, CHRISTOPHER VANDERKAMP

Millennial Residence Hotel, Istanbul, Turkey

Sarah realigns Christopher's dislocated knee back in the car before checking into a four-star hotel on the European side of Istanbul. They each get their own room. She needs some space, if only for a night. Christopher is sturdy on the crutches, and a cortisone shot would probably do him wonders, but Sarah doesn't want to give him any more reasons to stay, so she doesn't bring it up.

As they make their way to the elevators, crossing the hotel's bustling lobby and looking like rock stars who have been partying too hard, Christopher quietly asks, "Sarah, can I talk to you?"

"Not now, Christopher. I'm exhausted."

"It's important."

"A bath, food, sleep—they're more important."

"Fine." Christopher shakes his head.

"I'm sorry."

"Forget it," he says over his shoulder.

They pile into the elevator. Christopher and Jago stand on opposite sides, Sarah in the middle, Chiyoko close to the doors. None of them speak. Their rooms are on the top floor. *Ding ding ding ding ding ding ding ding.* The doors open. They exit the elevator and go their separate ways.

Christopher orders a burger.

Chiyoko sits on the floor and meditates.

Sarah draws a bath.

Jago knocks on her door.

She opens it.

"Can I come in?"

She moves aside.

Jago takes five steps into the room and turns. "We should leave them. Tonight."

The door closes and Sarah leans against it. She's spent. "I know."

"So let's."

"I can't."

Jago frowns. "Why not?"

Pause. "Chiyoko should see the disk before we cut her loose. We made a deal with her. And she might be able to tell us something useful."

"She can't tell us anything."

Sarah rolls her eyes. "She could help us find Earth Key."

Jago waves this away. "Fine. We'll grab her on the way out. We should leave *him*. It's not right to bring him along."

"Don't be so jealous."

"I'm not."

She shoots him a look.

"Okay, maybe a little," he admits.

She sighs.

"You're going to have to leave him eventually. Unless you plan to spend the rest of Endgame rescuing him."

"He can hold his own," Sarah replies, but the words are hollow.

"Because he was captain of the football team?" Jago chuckles. "He'll die if he stays. You know I'm right."

"Maybe. Probably."

"Let's leave. Consider it an act of mercy."

Sarah slides down the door to the floor. Jago steps forward, crouches in front of her, and runs his hand down her jawline. She nuzzles his fingers. "If I thought he would go home, we would leave, but he won't. He'll follow me again. He'll continue to put himself and me—and you, as long as we're Playing together—in danger. No, for now he has to stay."

Jago lets his hand drop away. He doesn't know how else to reason with her. He doesn't know why he even cares about what happens to her or Christopher. He shouldn't. Sarah looks up at him, as if she's reading his mind. "You won't leave me, will you, Feo?"

He thinks for a moment, remembers Renzo's warning not to fall in love. But he also knows he's going to Play Endgame the way he decides to Play it. And though Christopher is a nuisance, Sarah has proved her worth, and saved him more than once. With Christopher, what will be will be. With her, what will be will be, whatever happens between them. And he wants to make it happen between them.

Finally, he says, "No. I won't. On my line and honor, I swear it. Not until . . ."

"Right. Not until the end," she says sadly.

"Not until the end."

A moment. "Thank you, Jago. Now that this has started, I know I can't do it alone. It's too . . . bleak."

"Yes," Jago says quietly. "It's not as glorious as we were raised to believe, is it?"

Sarah shakes her head. They're quiet for a while, both of them thinking about the future, and each other.

"If we get Earth Key, maybe we'll be able to figure out when and where the Event will strike. More than winning, I want to save the people I love. I haven't spoken to my parents since I left home. It would hurt too much if I did." Sarah pauses, looking at Jago. "This is why I chose you, Jago. You're honest. You like me. Maybe you love me. I . . . I love life, Feo, not this. Not Endgame. I hate it. Christopher, in spite of the fact that he's annoying as hell right now, is my friend. And I want my family, my friends, to live." Pause. "I want yours to live also. What can I say? I'm weak that way."

Very slowly Jago shakes his head. "No, Sarah, that doesn't make you weak. It makes you human. That is why *I* chose *you*."

She holds out her hand. He takes it. "What are we going to do?"

"Win," Jago says. "Somehow we are going to win . . . together."

MACCABEE ADLAI, BAITSAKHAN

Bole International Airport Runways, Addis Ababa, Ethiopia

Maccabee and Baitsakhan descend the narrow gangplank of the jet they chartered from Ankara to Addis Ababa. The sun is bright. The air is hotter than hot, thick with the odors of gasoline and tar. Baitsakhan's neck is wrapped in a black-and-white kaffiyeh that he bought in Turkey. He wears blue jeans. A new white T-shirt. Dusty riding boots. Maccabee has on one of his expensive linen suits. No tie. White Adidas shell-tops. He smells like a nightclubber. They load into a waiting Land Rover with their small but heavy bags. Maccabee drives. Baitsakhan sharpens his knife in the passenger seat.

"This is how you do it," Maccabee says, glancing over at his young partner.

"Do what?"

"How you Play," Maccabee answers, wishing he could see the two of them through a camera. "In fucking style."

Baitsakhan scrunches up his eyebrows, shrugs. "I prefer knives."

Maccabee shakes his head. "There's no talking to you."

SARAH ALOPAY, JAGO TLALOC, CHIYOKO TAKEDA, CHRISTOPHER VANDERKAMP

Piccolo Gato Ristorante, Trieste, Italy

Before leaving Istanbul, Chiyoko shows Sarah and Jago the image of the grid of letters and numbers and signs from the golden chamber near Gobekli Tepe. Christopher says he saw it too. "It was the most amazing thing I've ever seen."

They have no idea what, if anything, the grid means.

But they know it means something.

They check out of their hotel. They drive west and leave Turkey. Cruise through Bulgaria. Pass through Serbia. Visit Croatia. Glide through Slovenia. They barely speak. Christopher is stewing in the backseat, and Sarah pretends not to notice. Jago and Chiyoko take turns driving while Sarah puzzles and puzzles and puzzles some more over the grid and her clue, wondering if they fit together in some way. She makes little progress. Breakthroughs are not forthcoming. She finds it all very frustrating.

After many hours and miles of silence they reach Italy, stop for the night in Trieste. 1600 km. 994.19 miles. Including breaks, 20 hours, 43 minutes, 29 seconds.

They check into another hotel. See the Adriatic. Go to dinner. A heaping family-style bowl of creamy, spicy penne rigate at a plastic table on the sidewalk. They watch Italians stroll. *This wouldn't be so bad if it were just a vacation,* they think. All except Chiyoko. She does not have any illusions about normal life; she simply bides her time. Jago has a glass of red wine. Chiyoko drinks tea. Christopher stretches out his leg and has a beer. He has another. And another.

Sarah abstains, sticking with *acqua con gas* and slivers of lemon. The awkward silence continues. Sarah works all through dinner, scribbling into a notebook. Christopher cranes his neck, hoping he can help. Jago stares icily at him. Chiyoko doesn't mind the drama, actually. She's glad her three companions are at odds. It keeps them quiet.

Over dessert Jago asks, "Do you want to see it, Chiyoko?"

Chiyoko claps once. She gingerly sips her tea and tries not to look too excited. Jago picks up his backpack. He unzips it. He reaches in and removes the stone disk.

Sarah looks up from her work.

At last, Chiyoko shows some measure of wonder as she cradles the disk in her hands. She runs her fingers over the grooves. Stares at its markings.

Home, she thinks to herself. *Soon you are going home.*

She lets it rest in her lap, bows her head to Jago in thanks. "You're welcome," he says, glancing at Sarah. "We did have a deal, right?"

Sarah knows what that look means: they've satisfied their debt to Chiyoko. Now, they can move on. Leave her and Christopher behind. Sarah pretends not to notice, looks away.

"Cool rock," Christopher says, who sounds as though he's had too much to drink.

Chiyoko takes out her phone and taps a quick message. She hands the phone to Jago. *Thank you for showing me this. I would like some time to study it.*

Jago frowns at the message, hands the phone to Sarah. After she's read it, Sarah and Jago lock eyes. *It's like they're communicating without speaking,* Christopher thinks. *Just like Sarah and I used to back at home.* Christopher is suddenly jealous of this Player, his stupid accent, his ugly scar, his ridiculous teeth. He grabs the phone out of Sarah's hand. "Study what?" he asks. "It's a rock."

They ignore him. Sarah looks at Chiyoko. "Do you think it will lead us to Earth Key?"

Chiyoko nods vehemently.

"We've got a lead on a guy who specializes in these disks. It's why we're in Italy," Jago says. "We'll be visiting him tomorrow; you can study it on the way."

Chiyoko cocks her head, asking, *Who?* Jago smirks at her.

"Can't tell you that, obviously. You'll see soon enough."

Chiyoko nods as if she understands. She already knows the identity of their so-called expert, overheard during their conversation with the little troll man at the Terracotta Army. Musterion Tsoukalos.

Yes, someone needs to show him this, Chiyoko thinks.

Jago takes the disk back from Chiyoko, her hands lingering on it for perhaps a moment too long. He eases it back into his bag. "Maybe you know something this specialist doesn't," Jago says to her. "For now, we can continue to help each other, yes?"

Chiyoko takes her phone back from Christopher. She taps out another message. *Whatever information I find, I will share with you.*

Jago nods. "Good."

"Thank you, Chiyoko," Sarah says, smiling.

Sarah returns to the puzzle, flips through her notes, thinks.

Christopher puts his arm across the back of Sarah's chair. She doesn't seem to notice, or chooses to ignore it, focusing on her work. However, Jago notices. He stands up abruptly.

"Long day. I'm turning in."

He turns and walks toward the hotel, the bag bouncing innocuously on his back.

After a few more minutes, Chiyoko puts down a wad of euros and stands. She claps once. Sarah looks up from her work, rubs her temples. "You too?"

Chiyoko nods, eyes Sarah's notepad.

"Yeah, you're right. I should give it a rest." Sarah looks to Christopher. "What do you say?"

"Sure, I'll go back. But I want to talk."

Chiyoko is not interested in these . . . feelings. She claps once, spins on her heel, and goes. Sarah closes the pad and lets her hand rest on it.

"Fine, Christopher. Let's talk. But let's do it here."

He rubs his face, which is still bruised from where Maccabee struck him. "Sarah, I'm not going home."

"I know."

"I wo—wait. What?"

"I know you're not going home. You're too stubborn to do anything that makes sense."

Christopher is dumbstruck. He expected more of an argument. A young couple walks by on the sidewalk. They are very attractive. Her high heels click the pavement. His loose shirt flaps open at the chest. Christopher can't help but watch them. "God, that could have been us," he says longingly.

Sarah shakes her head. "Maybe once, but not anymore. Our time—our chance—it's gone." Her voice shakes slightly as she says the words.

"It doesn't have to be."

"It does. You may think you understand what's happening, but you don't. Yes, you've heard us talk, but you don't really know what's coming. You don't understand what's at stake."

Christopher thinks back to what Kala told him about the destruction of civilization, how each line is fighting for its survival. "I know more than you think, Sarah."

Sarah curls her lip, figuring this for more bluster. "You don't know shit. Not about me, not about Jago, not about Chiyoko or Kala or Maccabee or Baitsakhan. You don't know shit about Endgame, and that will never change."

"I saw Kala killed," he says, holding Sarah's gaze. "And before that, on the life raft, Kala killed a child and her mother for no reason. You think I don't get what you guys are all about?"

"I'm sorry you had to experience that," Sarah says, touching his arm. "But it's nothing compared to what's going to happen. It's called the Event—"

Christopher interrupts. "Yeah, everyone on Earth dies except for the winner and the people in his or her line, right?"

"Yes," Sarah says, taken aback. "You know about that?"

"Kala liked to talk," Christopher replies. "I don't actually believe it, and neither should you, Sarah. Aliens with gold-powered ships or whatever? Come on. Nothing has the power to just wipe out a planet."

"You haven't seen what I've seen," Sarah says matter-of-factly but with a hint of sadness. She wishes she didn't believe too. "I want you to go, Christopher, because I love you. I want you to go because I don't want to watch you die. I want you to go so I can have a better chance of winning. And of saving you. Of saving you and Mom and Dad and everyone we know back home. But having you here, it's not making it any easier."

"Assuming I even believe all this crap about the Event—why the hell would I just go home and wait around while you fight for the fate of everyone we know?" Christopher shakes his head, bewildered. "If it's like you say it is, we should call the army or something."

"That's not how it works."

"How it works sucks, then."

Sarah can't argue with that. For a while they don't speak. The distinctive sound of a European police siren wails from some nearby street, bouncing off the stone and concrete of the old Italian city. A boat in the harbor sounds its low horn. A dog barks. Someone passes, saying *"Ciao, ciao, ciao,"* into his mobile.

"You have to go. Please."

"No."

"Yes."

"It's not going to happen. If you don't want me looking for you all the time, you have two options: kill me or let me come with you. I pledge myself to you, Sarah. You got that? I pledge myself to you."

"Endgame is not for you."

"Bullshit. If what you say is true, then it is *precisely* for me, for people like me. So I'm staying. I can help you."

"No. You can't. Not like this."

"I can."

"Jago won't like it."

"Screw Jago. He's a punk."

"He's not."

A long pause. Christopher eyes her. She quickly changes the subject. "If you do stay, what are we going to do with that leg?"

He smiles. "Get me a cortisone shot. I've played entire football games with worse."

She rises. She is tired and feels defeated. There's just no convincing him.

"All right. We can do that. But right now, I have to go to bed."

She starts past him but he grabs her arm. If it were anyone else she would react, dislocate his shoulder, gouge his eyes out, break his leg. But it isn't anyone else. She spins and he pulls her close and gives her a huge, heartfelt kiss. And in spite of everything, she kisses back.

Christopher says, "I'm telling you, Alopay. That *can* be us."

She shakes her head, whispers, "No, Christopher. It can't."

32.398516, 93.622742[lxx]

HILAL IBN ISA AL-SALT

Aksumite Communications Outpost, Kingdom of Aksum, Ethiopia

Next to the ancient church carved from stone, among the tall cedars, is an unremarkable wood-and-mud hut with a thatched roof. It has no windows and only one low door, which Hilal must duck to walk through. But inside the hut, the walls are metal. The floor is concrete. The furniture is spare and utilitarian. A string of generators, buried deep underground so no one can hear, provide electricity. A series of high-speed satellite uplinks is hidden in some of the taller cedar trees, disguised as branches. The data they send and receive is encrypted. Every bit. Every byte.

Hilal tries to locate as many Players as he can electronically. Only once he has done this will he enter the field and contact the remaining Players. One by one. He hopes there is enough time.

He knows it is a small hope.

For the others must be closing in on Earth Key.

They must.

Still, he has located active Gmail accounts for Shari Chopra, Aisling Kopp, Sarah Alopay, and Maccabee Adlai. He has hacked each and will open a new draft and write his message into each account. He won't risk sending it. He would like to avoid the prying eyes of the online police in all their forms. He prays that these four check their email, that they will see.

He prays.

He writes his message. He selects the text. Copies it. Opens a browser window. Accesses Aisling's drafts pane. Opens a new document.

And is about to hit paste when the power—the quintuple-backed-up generated power—goes out.

The inside of the hut is dark. Dark as pitch.

Hilal raises his head from the dead computer screen.

The message wasn't transmitted. He is still the only one who knows.

How could they lose power?

He listens.

And he knows.

The keplers did it.

They *want* the game.

They want to see what happens.

The keplers want it.

As he stares at the black screen, a knock at the little door.

A hole rends the magnetic field. It acts like a funnel. All the radiation of the sun from that moment of the flare.

All.[lxxi]

It snuffs out all power, spins all electrons, jiggles all quarks.

It affects everything. Yet it is invisible.

As if it is nothing.

SARAH ALOPAY

Grand Hotel Duchi d'Aosta, Room 100, Trieste, Italy

Sarah says good night to Christopher, wanders through the hotel. Goes back outside. Sits at the bar and orders a glass of white wine and doesn't drink more than a sip. The kiss has left her wanting and confused.

She leaves the barmaid a €100 note and walks through the halls. Everything—the wood, the wallpaper, the carpet, the paint, the metal, the memories—is as good as gone. The Event, the aftermath, the death, the madness, will see to that.

When her legs stop moving, she is staring at a door that is not hers. Room 21. She can sense him behind that door. She knows he isn't asleep. She thinks about that time in Iraq, on the couch in Renzo's garage. In the airplane lavatory. She rests her forehead against Jago's door. She almost knocks, but stops herself. She will stay with Jago. Play with him. Maybe fall in love with him, maybe die with him. But she will be with him until the end. They still have time.

She thinks about the girl from Omaha. The one everyone loved and admired. The girl who could've had a normal life. Who wanted a normal life—but in reality, never had one. Not even close. With a sigh, Sarah turns away and walks down the hall. She stops in front of a different door. She is going to leave the boy behind this door. She may never see him again when she says good-bye. And though she loves him, and has loved him, she knows their time is coming to an end. With Christopher, she doesn't have any more time. This is it.

She knocks.

She hears movement on the other side, and it takes a moment or two for the door to swing open.

"What's up?" Christopher asks, surprised. "You want to argue more?"

"No." She steps into the room and presses a finger over his lips and she pushes the door shut with her foot and she says, "Just shut up."

CHIYOKO TAKEDA

Grand Hotel Duchi d'Aosta, Room 101, Trieste, Italy

An runs.

Through a field of flowers.

They're thick around his ankles.

He falls.

Gets up.

Runs.

Falls. Gets up. Runs.

The soles of his bare feet are brown and slick.

The sky is heavy with billowing clouds.

Raining down numbers and letters and signs.

They strike his head and neck and arms.

A large stone *O* slams into his back.

He falls.

Doesn't get up.

Rolls over.

Dies.

Chiyoko's eyes snap open at 2:12 a.m.

She inhales a stab of air.

She lies on top of the sheet, naked, alone; her fists are balled, her toes curled. The windows are open. The cool sea air drifts across her skin. The small hairs on her stomach rise. She gets goose bumps on her arms. She brings her hands up, reaching for the ceiling. She relaxes. The dream of An fades.

She sits up, swings her legs over the bed. It's just like the night the meteor fell over Naha. Just like the night the first round of death came to Endgame.

Time to Play.

She stands. Goes to the chair and pulls on her black jumpsuit.

Everything is in its place, as always. She tucks her hair into her collar and pulls on the hood. She draws the cowl over her face. Only her eyes. Her dark, empty eyes.

She slips into her soft shoes, puts the Browning that Jago gave her in her belt, double-checks the safety. She walks to the door, places her ear on the wood. Waits. Turns the handle. Pushes the door open. Steps out.

She pads silently down the hall, hears the night clerk's television behind the check-in counter, hears the hum of the HVAC, hears the springs of a bed rhythmically bouncing somewhere close by.

No one can hear her.

She crouches in front of Room 21, slides a lock pick from her sleeve, opens the door, steps in, takes her time letting the door close slowly without a sound. She turns around. Light from the street sifts through a curtain. Jago sleeps alone, shirtless, on his stomach. Chiyoko is surprised. She thought the Olmec would have won out over the dopey American boy. But no matter. It's better that he is alone. She sees the knapsack on a chair by the window.

Careless.

She picks it up, opens it, reaches into it; the disk is cool beneath her fingers. She pulls on the straps of the pack to tighten them, kneels and goes through the pockets of Jago's pants, finds and removes the keys to the 307.

Very careless.

She walks to the bed, stands over Jago. She takes out her wakizashi. Its steel is 1,089 years old. There is no telling how many people it has slain. She runs her fingers over the sheath, thinks how easy it would be to kill him now. He will be coming after her, Chiyoko knows. He will be angry, righteous, vengeful. But he was honest with her, and so was Sarah, and she will not kill a Player while he sleeps.

She turns and without a sound jumps through the window. Her left hand grabs a drainpipe and she slides down to the street, black as night, quieter than death.

She leaves the wakizashi behind, penance for breaking her word. On it is a small square of paper.

She walks to the 307, opens the door, sits, starts the engine, drives away.

HILAL IBN ISA AL-SALT

Aksumite Communications Outpost, Kingdom of Aksum, Ethiopia

There is another knock at the door of the little hut.

The beings must be trying to cut him off. To stop him, now that he's figured out the secret of Endgame.

But he can still fight. If that's what is knocking, he can still fight.

The darkness inside his hut is his friend.

He grabs his favorite weapons, slides to the wall next to the door, and waits.

Knock knock.

Knock knock.

No more knocking.

The door is kicked in. Two figures enter the hut—one short, one tall—and when they're all the way inside, Hilal slams the door shut behind them.

The darkness.

He twirls his arms and moves into the space he knows so well. In each hand is a machete.

Black polished steel.

Ebony grips.

HATE engraved on one, *LOVE* on the other.

He has a gentle soul, but do not test it.

He hits something and hears a wail and a *thump* on the floor. Flesh and bone, he knows the feeling well.

Very well.

A desperate gunshot follows. The slug ricochets around the metal walls and misses Hilal, but by the pained grunt across the room, he thinks it might have grazed one of the others. He splits them, moves through the room, and jumps onto a metal table that none can see but that he knows is there. He slams a machete down, cleaving a computer monitor in two. Sparks fly and the room lights up for a millisecond. Long enough for Hilal to know what he's up against.

The Nabataean.

And the Donghu on the floor, injured.

Hilal thrusts out his right arm, turns the blade flat, crouches, and spins like a dancer. The machete arcs toward the Nabataean's head. But Maccabee luckily drops to the floor, and Hilal's razor-sharp blade only severs half an inch of hair from his head.

"The door!" Baitsakhan yells. "Open the door!"

All right, injured one, Hilal thinks.

He backflips off the table and over the Nabataean.

Another shot. Muzzle flash. The bullet flies between Hilal's legs. A close call.

Yes. I will give you some light.

His feet hit the concrete floor silently. He slides to the door. He presses his mouth close to the metal wall, knowing the acoustics will transport his voice to the other side of the small room.

"Here!"

Another shot, aimed at the reverberations of Hilal's voice. Not even close.

Another ricochet. Hilal waits to hear if it strikes one of them.

It doesn't.

No matter.

He throws the door open.

Maccabee turns to shoot, but Hilal steps forward and smacks the end of the gun with both machetes at the same moment. The weapon clatters to the floor. Hilal brings the blades up hard and fast, uncrossing them, searching for more to slice and maim. Maccabee raises his arms too, but when the blades impact his wrists they strike metal cuffs concealed under the Nabataean's fine linen suit. Maccabee flashes a sinister smile. Hilal grimaces as he retreats into the light of day. These killers smile when they come for him. It sickens him, and he will pray for their souls after he's disposed of their bodies.

Baitsakhan rises to his feet. His eyes are full of hate. He exits the hut and throws something. Hilal smacks it to the ground with a backhand swipe.

The thing clunks to the soft ground under the cedar trees.

It is a hand.

Baitsakhan's own hand.

"You lost something," Hilal says. He knows never to speak during a fight, but he also knows that words can hurt more than any weapon.

Baitsakhan's wrist spurts blood. "Gun!" he says as he tosses his pistol to Maccabee, who snags it from the air.

Hilal throws the machete and it *whomp-whomp-whomp*s through the air and strikes the pistol as it goes off. A wedge of dirt rises at Hilal's feet where the slug hits. The pistol flies to pieces. The machete takes a small piece of one of Maccabee's fingers before flying past him and embedding in the trunk of a tree. Baitsakhan throws a small black object at Hilal. Hilal backpedals and with his remaining machete smacks it like it's a baseball. It sails into the deep green cedars and explodes.

A grenade.

Hilal hears something only he understands. A stone door sliding open. It is but a whisper.

Baitsakhan stalks toward him, his eyes empty and vacant. He's losing blood, delirious, and kill-crazy. He throws another grenade. And another and another. Hilal hits them all away with his machete.

They each explode in the distance, sending shrapnel whizzing past. Maccabee, suddenly less enthused about this operation, takes cover. After the last explosion, Hilal runs backward at alarming speed, never taking his eyes from his attackers. He heads for the clearing, for the secret church carved from stone. The place where the stone door has just been opened.

Where Master al-Julan will be waiting.

"You're dead!" Baitsakhan barks, full of hatred, now cradling his wounded arm. The color is fading from his face.

Hate makes you weak, brother, Hilal thinks.

Maccabee pops out of cover. He has a grenade of his own, but he takes more care than his young partner did. He pulls the pin slowly, holding onto the lever so it won't explode, waiting for his moment.

"How did you find me?" Hilal shouts at his assailants as he continues to backpedal. He is only 24 feet from the church, but he must know how they found him, why they come now of all times.

"Earth Key showed us," Baitsakhan says.

"You don't have Earth Key."

"We do."

"Impossible." *I would know. We all would.*

"Show him."

Maccabee doesn't show him the dark glass orb. Instead, he throws the last grenade and at its apex shouts, "Now!"

Maccabee hits the deck, and the Donghu too. This grenade is different. Hilal knows he cannot bat it away like he did the concussion grenades. This one is incendiary.

It is fire.

Mere inches from the church's trapdoor entrance, the air above Hilal is engulfed in flame. The fiery tongues lick, devour, swallow. They burn his clothing and his shoulders and his head. They consume him as he goes down down down into the impenetrable room beneath the ancient church.

The fire subsides; the burns remain.

More darkness, but he is safe now.

And he is not alone.

The last thing he remembers is the smell of burning hair and the pain.

The searing pain of fire, the searing pain of hell.

This is Endgame.

SARAH ALOPAY, JAGO TLALOC, CHRISTOPHER VANDERKAMP

Grand Hotel Duchi d'Aosta, Trieste, Italy

Sarah wakes at 5:24 a.m.

Her dreams were geometric. 9,466 shapes. Rectangles. Tetrahedrons. Spirals. Crumpled polygons. Circles. Parabolic lines stretching to infinity.

She is close, so close to figuring out this grid from the golden chamber in Turkey, and figuring out her clue.

She stares at the ceiling.

Shapes.

Numbers.

Letters.

Signs.

Christopher snores next to her. She'd forgotten all about him. The puzzle has dominated her thoughts. Fooling around with him last night—it helped her forget about Endgame. For one night she was normal, just like that couple they'd watched strolling by the restaurant.

They didn't sleep together. Just lay in each other's arms and kissed and felt and touched. It was fun, but now, just before the sun rises, Sarah bites her lip and tries not to scream. It was cruel, what she did. Spending the night with him not only because it was her last chance to kiss him but also because it would be easier to sneak away in the morning. If she had stayed in her own room last night, or in Jago's, Christopher would be up before any of them. Up and waiting.

She might still be able to sneak off, but what she did won't push Christopher away; it'll only keep him closer. Jago was right. Sooner or later, Endgame will kill Christopher. And Sarah doesn't want to watch him die.

Jago was right. She isn't normal. Time to embrace that fact.

But this confusion is fleeting, because right now, as she's lying in bed, the puzzle sizzles at the forefront of her mind. She almost has it. If only the incessant pounding from down the hall would stop.

Wait—pounding?

Sarah slips out of bed without Christopher so much as stirring. She is still wearing the clothes from the day before. She steps into the hall and sees Jago at her door, looking like he's about to kick it down. He's wide-eyed, furious, panicked. He has Chiyoko's sword in one hand, a crumpled piece of paper in the other.

"Jago," she whispers, rushing over to him.

He sees her. They meet in the center of the hallway.

"The disk! She took it! The mute!"

"What?"

Jago thrusts the note at her. Sarah reads it, her stomach bubbling with dread. *I am no longer tracking you. On my blade and honor, it is true.*

"Goddamn it, Feo! How did you let her take it?"

"I don't know . . ." Jago answers, trailing off as his eyes drift over Sarah's shoulder, toward Christopher's room, just starting to realize where she came from.

"Let's go get her."

Jago slaps the front of his jeans, feeling his pockets. "No!"

He takes off at a run down the hall. Sarah yells after him, "Where are you going?"

"The keys!" Jago shouts over his shoulder as he crashes into the stairwell door. "Bitch took the keys!"

Sarah glances at Christopher's closed door before sprinting after Jago. She arrives on the street only five seconds behind him, but that's long enough for an enraged Jago to punch through the window of the nearest car. Sarah stands on the hotel steps as Jago paces wildly back and forth, clutching his bruised fist. It's still dark. The air is cool and damp. The bell of a buoy can be heard in the distance.

"It's gone," Jago barks. "The car. The disk. She took everything except her fucking sword." Realizing he's still clutching the weapon in his damaged hand, Jago tosses it disgustedly onto the ground.

Sarah comes down the steps. "It's okay, we can fix this." She picks up the wakizashi and gently touches his shoulder. "Let me see that hand."

Jago twists away from her. "What is this 'we'? You've been playing me too, just like the Mu. But worse."

"I'm not playing you. Calm down."

"I screwed up, let her get the drop on me, it's true," Jago says, nodding wildly. "But you're sleeping with that dumb little boy? This whole team thing is over; we're done."

"You need to calm down," she says, trying to keep her cool.

"What the hell is going on?" Christopher asks as he emerges from the hotel. He looks tired and bleary, but also has a little swagger going as he comes down the steps. Jago's teeth grit; the veins along his neck stand out. Sarah's worried he'll punch out another car window, or worse.

"Chiyoko took the disk and our car," Sarah says curtly, wishing Christopher would just go back inside.

"How the—?" Christopher asks incredulously, but cuts himself off when he notices the look on Jago's face. "Damn, dude. Fall asleep on the job?"

Christopher doesn't see it coming. Jago's hand lances out, flat and sharp, right for Christopher's throat. Luckily, Sarah does see it coming, and she steps in and deflects the blow. Christopher, caught off guard, stumbles on his bad leg and falls to the curb.

"What the—!"

Sarah cuts him off before he can make this situation any worse. "Go back inside, Christopher. Get our things. We need to get moving."

Christopher stands slowly. Jago is still staring at him, fire in his eyes, and Christopher can tell the only reason he's not attacking is that Sarah stands between them. "You sure?" he asks Sarah.

"Go."

Christopher hobbles back into the hotel, Sarah and Jago face off on the sidewalk. There's only about six feet separating them. They look like two tentative prizefighters, neither eager to make the first move.

"Don't you ever try to hurt him again," Sarah tells Jago warningly.

"You keep him around, that tells me that you want him dead. I figured I could speed up the process."

Fed up, Sarah flicks a jab at Jago's face. He deflects it and grabs her wrist. She spins, drives an elbow into his ribs. She can hear the wind go out of him, but his grip doesn't loosen. He yanks her arm, hard, pinning it behind her back. As pain shoots up into her shoulder, Jago snakes his other arm around her neck. With her free arm, Sarah fires an elbow into his face, but he lowers his head, letting it bounce off his crown.

All of that takes 2.7 seconds. They're close together now. Almost a hug, but more like a choke hold. She can feel him breathing. He can feel her heartbeat.

He says into her ear, "Do you really want to do this?"

"Promise me you won't hurt him."

"Why would I do that?"

"For me."

"For you? You just betrayed me. I should kill you."

"You ever been in love, Jago?"

"Yes."

"Ever been in love with more than one person?"

"No."

"It's not easy."

"What are you saying, Cahokian?"

"You know what I'm saying."

He loosens his grip.

"If you're playing me, I'll kill you."

"I'm not, Jago. But if you think I am, kill me now. I don't want to go on with someone who'd think that of me."

Loosens a little more.

"I'm not going to be his friend or help him."

"We'll leave him eventually. I swear. I was going to do it today—that's why I spent the night with him. So we could sneak away."

Jago can tell she isn't lying. "All right."

"I didn't sleep with him, Jago. We just . . ."

Jago can tell she isn't lying about this either. "It's all right."

"Just promise you won't hurt him until we can leave him."

"I promise," Jago sighs, letting her go. They step apart, look each other over, both of them breathing fast, starting to sweat a little. There's energy between them, but they need to focus on the task at hand.

"We'll need a new car," Sarah says.

Jago points across the road at a late-model Porsche Carrera convertible. "There."

He pulls a knife from his back pocket. Sarah follows him across the street. Christopher emerges from the hotel, carrying their bags, hobbling fast to keep up with them. They disturb a flock of 56 pigeons, which jump into the sky and start to turn in a wide circle. Jago holds the knife over the soft top of the car. He is going to cut it open and steal it.

"Wait!" Sarah says.

Jago pushes in the knife.

She reaches him, stays his arm before he can cut any more.

She watches the pigeons turn. They are fast. She can hear their wings sluicing the air. "I think I've got it."

Jago gives her a wild, simmering look. "Got what?"

"The puzzle, Feo. The puzzle!"

"What good is that without the disk?"

"I don't know. But if I've solved it and she hasn't gotten too far, maybe we can head her off."

He pulls the knife from the car's roof. "I'm going to kill her."

Sarah walks around the car to a low wall near the edge of the water. "She didn't kill you," she points out.

Jago doesn't answer. He paces. Sarah sits. Gets out her notes, the folded copies of the grid from the golden chamber of the gods.

Christopher watches. He keeps his distance from Jago.

Sarah writes. She starts slowly, starts going quicker. She marks up a printout of the grid, crumples it, throws it on the ground, marks up another, pushes it away, another, another, another.

Stops.

She holds it up. "Here."

Jago takes it. He doesn't understand what she's drawn over the random assortment of letters and numbers. "What is it?"

"Look. Here and here and here." She points. Continues to point. The first is a dash, then eight letters, then a dash.

-EARTHKEY-

"Now. Here, here, here." Repeats, indicating a different pattern.

DIRECTIVES.

He looks at her in shock.

"You did it?"

She nods. They are rapt. "There's more. Here."

He says the numbers as she points. "Five-one-point-one-eight, negative one-point-eight-three, and four-six-point-zero-nine, one-zero-point-one-two."

"Yeah."

"What about the rest?" Jago asks, pointing at the numbers that clutter Sarah's papers.

"The rest is junk."

"They're coordinates, aren't they?"

She looks at him eagerly. "Yes!"

"To where?"

She beams. "Not sure exactly, but somewhere relatively close."

Jago gets out his smartphone. "I'll look it up."

"The first one, I remember that from when we were in Mosul and I was mapping all those points from my clue." Sarah pauses. "It's Stonehenge."

Jago looks up from his phone, matching Sarah's excited look. "A stone circle."

"Yes."

"Like the disk. A circle of stone."

"Yes!" She grabs him by the arm and squeezes excitedly.

He looks back to the phone. Punches the other numbers into a tool server called ~geohack. Holds it up for Sarah to see the map. Christopher watches with his arms crossed over his chest. They haven't even looked in his direction in minutes. He watches Sarah's easy rapport with Jago, the way they bounce ideas off each other, their energy. Last night feels hollow to him. He edges closer, but doesn't know what to say, doesn't know how to make himself useful. Doesn't know how to make Sarah see him as her partner, instead of Jago. Sarah pinches the screen to zoom in. "The Alps."

"No roads."

"But there's a lake. Lago Beluiso."

"We need a plane, not a car," Jago says wistfully. "One that can land on water."

Christopher grandiosely holds out his arms. "I've got a floatplane," he interrupts. "But it's parked on Lake Michigan."

Sarah rolls her eyes. "That's not funny, Christopher."

He ignores her. Reaches out and points toward the water. "Seriously, though. I've got one just like that." They follow his finger to a bright orange Bush Hawk four-seater, floating on the water right in the middle of the marina. "Same color and everything. I don't know how you missed it. You know, being *Players* and all."

They ignore his attitude. Sarah looks at Jago. "I guess we're not stealing a car after all."

"No," he replies, smirking, "we're stealing a plane."

34.341568, 108.940175[lxxii]

CHIYOKO TAKEDA

Tsoukalos Residence, 20 Via Cereto, Capo di Ponte, Italy

Chiyoko pulls the 307 onto a round gravel driveway and parks next to a black vintage Ferrari. The "house" before her is a sprawling Italianate mansion surrounded by stands of cypress and birch. It is completely isolated.

She sits in the car for a while, mapping out exactly how this encounter will go. She does this by writing phrases on a series of index cards. It's not the first time she's interrogated a person with just index cards. Chiyoko knows some people find her silence intimidating. The cards, she thinks, make it even worse. When she's ready, she gets out of the car, grabbing Jago's backpack from the passenger seat.

She has changed clothes. A short pleated skirt and leather Mary Janes and a yellow polo shirt. Her hair is pulled into pigtails. She has on a thin coat of makeup and is wearing her Lolita-esque heart-shaped sunglasses. She approaches the huge oaken double doors. She checks the time. 7:36 a.m. She pushes the doorbell. The barking of some large-sounding dogs comes from within. Seventy-eight seconds later she hears the clicking of the dogs' nails on the floor inside. An eye slit slides open and a man says, *"Chi è?"*

Chiyoko holds up the first card. It's written in English. *I am mute.*

"Ah . . ." he says hesitantly.

The 2nd card reads: *Do you speak English, please?*

"Yes," he answers.

Chiyoko flashes a bright smile. She shifts her backpack, making sure that the man notices she's brought a gift. Another card. *I am here on behalf of Cheng Cheng Dhou.*

"Dio," the man says worriedly, and slides the slit shut.

Chiyoko removes the disk from the bag. She searches above her. Sees a camera in a corner of the porch's overhang. She holds the disk out. She knows Musterion is afraid, so she turns one knee in toward the other, like a little girl might.

"Dio," she hears the man say again. One of the dogs barks. She lowers the disk and holds another card up to the camera. *I am his niece. He wanted you to have this.*

Twenty-seven seconds pass.

A lock is thrown.

Another.

Another.

Chiyoko puts the disk in the bag, slings the bag over her shoulder. She pulls down the hem of her skirt. The dogs bark; the door opens.

A short man with a high, perfect pompadour reins in two massive cane corsos. He's still in his pajamas. He has on fine leather loafers. Chiyoko curtsies. The man offers a tentative smile. "Please, come in. I apologize for the dogs. You were . . . unexpected."

The dogs growl. Musterion pulls them back. Chiyoko concentrates her chi. She looks each dog in the eyes. As she does, they sit back on their haunches. The one on the left whimpers. She kneels and scratches it under the chin. Its dim black eyes go soft.

She looks at Musterion with a disarming smile. She hands him a card. *Are you alone here?*

Musterion's hand trembles as he reads the message. "Just me and the dogs. Why?"

The dogs gurgle with pleasure, their tails beating happily on the floor. They don't notice their master's sudden apprehension. He's having second thoughts about this girl who he's let into his house. She hands him another card.

The disk belongs to Stonehenge, correct?

"I think . . . I'd like you to leave," Musterion says. He snaps his fingers at the dogs, but they pay him no mind. Another card.

How do I use it?

"You're one of them," Musterion exclaims, apprehension and terror filling his voice. He starts to back away, tugging on the leashes. Chiyoko stands up. The dogs watch her expectantly, as if she's going to give them a treat. Instead, she produces a coil of rope. Her hojo. Musterion drops the leashes, turns, and runs. Chiyoko unfurls the hojo and it slings around his neck. She pulls, and he comes crashing to the floor. The dogs bark merrily, like it's all a game. Musterion tries to get up, but Chiyoko stands over him. She puts her heel on a pressure point in his chest and his right lung collapses. As he gasps for air, she holds a card in his face.

How do I use it?

When he answers, she shows him his final card.

AISLING KOPP, SARAH ALOPAY, JAGO TLALOC, CHRISTOPHER VANDERKAMP

Lago Beluiso, Lombardy, Italy

Aisling hasn't decided what she should do. Go to Stonehenge? Or stay and wait, knowing she's safe, knowing more Players are going to die? Now that she's settled in, and may have figured out the cave paintings, she's kind of enjoying the sideline gig. Camping suits her.

Aisling is hunting. She's sick of that cave, with its morbid prophecies. The cool air clears her head as she tries to decide how long to procrastinate and what exactly she believes.

As a baby, her dad spirited her away to this very place. Aisling thinks she could've been happy growing up here.

An engine echoes off the sides of the mountains. Aisling thinks nothing of it. Milan is relatively close to the west; there have been many small planes since she began her vigil. She returns to the task at hand. Pulls the white rabbit from the snare and slices its stomach, pulls out the guts. She takes a flap of skin and begins to tear. She pauses.

Something is different.

This plane is low.

Getting lower.

The engine growls and sputters and she knows.

Someone is coming.

Coming to see what she's seen.

She wipes her bloody hands on her jeans and grabs her rifle.

No more waiting.

Much like her father's peace was shattered, so is Aisling's.

Lago Beluiso is a long lake with steep mountains on all sides. Christopher is at the controls. He's logged more hours than Sarah or Jago. He took flying lessons while the assassin kids were learning krav maga.

"Finally good for something," mutters Jago, but Christopher ignores him. He feels good. He even rests a hand on Sarah's leg and she doesn't brush it off. They pass over Beluiso from north to south and turn. He noses down and decelerates, and the plane bumps along the lake. He steers it to the western shore and cuts the engine. Jago jumps into the water and wades to land, consulting a GPS. He wanders into the woods. Sarah jumps into the water, follows him. Christopher leans out the door. "I'll wait here. That grade's too steep for my knee."

"We'll be back as soon as possible," Sarah replies. "Good flying."

Christopher nods and tries to suppress a smile. Watching Sarah and Jago puzzle out that number crap—which Christopher still doesn't understand, and probably never will—he'd felt hopeless. But now, maybe there is a use for him after all. Jago has already moved into the woods. Sarah smiles and follows, jogging up the steep hillside.

Aisling moves into position. The rifle is heavy; the carabiners on her harness clank. The Pirana descender is pulled tight over two loops. She has to get to a place where she can have a good look at these visitors.

These Players.

Pop taught her to shoot first and ask questions later. That's how she planned to Play Endgame. But after staring at those paintings, Aisling is reconsidering that course of action. She flies through the woods, leaping logs and rocks and depressions.

What if they're friendly? What if all this can be avoided?

She tightens her grip on the barrel.

What if they're not and what if it can't?

* * *

Up up up.

Fast and faster. Sarah moves to the front, leaping like a fawn. Jago keeps up, but not easily. Sarah stops. Jago does too. She crouches. Points. Jago sees it. A dark green cord in a small loop lying across a deer track. A game snare. Jago sneers. "A Player is here."

Sarah nods, draws her pistol. "Not Chiyoko, though. She'd have no reason to set that trap, not since this morning."

"Agreed." He inspects the positioning device. "We're close. About a hundred meters."

Besides the pistol, the only weapons they have are their bodies and Chiyoko's wakizashi. The rest of the hardware was all in the 307.

Sarah cracks her neck. "Let's go."

Aisling skids to a stop on a cliff high above the cave's entrance. She grabs the rope, checks the anchors, pulls a small set of very high-powered binoculars from a case on her side. She peers down the mountainside: nothing. She lets the binoculars hang around her neck and works the rope through the descender, moves the rifle's strap across her body. She turns her back to the lake and sets her brake hand and plants her feet wide and jumps, scaring a nearby hawk and sending it into the sky.

Sarah and Jago reach the edge of a small clearing as a hawk suddenly takes wing overhead. Something, or someone, startled that bird. They each wonder, *Who?*

There are footprints everywhere.

Not one of the larger Players. Not Alice, Maccabee, or Hilal.

But a girl.

There is a small pile of sticks near a gash in the rock. A cave. Without speaking they agree that whatever's in there must be what the clue is leading them to. Sarah holds up three fingers.

Two.

One.

Fist.

They dash across the clearing. The hawk cries out, its screech echoing over the vast alpine bowl.

The hawk wails. Aisling brakes and twists 180 degrees. She scans with the binoculars. The camp is still empty, but she hasn't been watching it for the last 46 seconds. She hangs there for another minute, waiting for a sign, but none comes.

She turns, resumes lowering herself.

Sarah flicks on a flashlight and checks the chamber. A bedroll. A pack against the wall. A fire circle. A stack of wood. A pile of animal bones. Drawings and notes in charcoal on an otherwise blank section of wall.

"Empty," says Jago.

"No Chiyoko, at least."

"Lucky her." Jago walks across the room, shining his own light. "Look at this," he says slowly.

They stand before the ancient picture Aisling has been contemplating for nearly a week. "That's us," Sarah says with wonder. "All twelve of us."

"Or something like us," Jago agrees.

"The monoliths . . . Stonehenge."

"And there is one of kepler 22b's ancient cousins."

Jago stuffs the GPS in his pants and takes out a smartphone. He snaps a picture of the painting.

Sarah runs her hands over it. "This figure has a disk. It looks . . . it looks like she's putting it on this rock." She places her finger on a stone with a dagger drawn in it.

Jago lowers his phone. "Or putting it *in* it."

They stare in silence.

Here is their story, their future, their past.

Everything and nothing.

All the time.

Here and here and here.

"You think . . ." Sarah trails off.

"This is how we're supposed to use the disk to get Earth Key. . . ."

"It has to be," Sarah whispers in awe.

Jago snaps close-ups of the painting.

Sarah points at the red ball above the scene. "What's that?"

"The sun? A moon? kepler 22b's home?"

Sarah shakes her head. "It's one of the meteorites. Has to be. This is our story, or part of it anyway."

"I suppose so."

Sarah takes one of Jago's hands. "I've seen enough, Feo. We need to leave."

Jago nods, his face grim. "We need to get that disk back."

They miss the 2nd painting entirely. The one of the woman on the ocean, floating alone, after Endgame.

They don't have the revelation.

Not like Aisling.

Aisling stops on a narrow ledge above camp and checks again. And there they are.

Two of them.

Unexpected.

She swings the rifle off her shoulder. She flips the lids on the scope, throws the bolt, lets the air out of her lungs, steadies herself. These motions come naturally to her; she's done this many times before, feels comfortable killing from a distance. But she's not going to kill this time. Not yet. She eases her finger off the trigger. She wants to get a better look at them before she decides what to do.

Life or death?

She can't get a bead on the girl from this angle, but she can see the boy. One of the skinnier ones. Jago Tlaloc? Or the Shang? It's hard to tell. If it's the Olmec boy, he didn't seem too bad. Unlike the Shang, Jago didn't blow anyone up during the Calling. The Shang, on the other hand, he deserves to die. She touches the trigger, feeling the coil taut beneath her finger. Aisling squints. "Come on," she mutters. "Turn around. Let me see your beautiful face. . . ."

Sarah emerges from the cave behind Jago. She glances over her shoulder at the cliff rising behind the trees. A glint on the lower half of the rock—a scope.
"Run!" Sarah shouts. "Run for the trees!"
Jago doesn't need to ask why; he trusts her, and he moves immediately. Sarah runs too, aiming over her shoulder with her pistol, firing toward the cliff.

A chunk of rock explodes next to Aisling's shoulder. She flinches. Cover fire so they can get to the safety of the woods. Aisling should've taken the two of them out when she had a chance. Unless . . .
How would I react if I saw a sniper rifle aimed at me? Aisling wonders. *It's all a cycle,* she hears her father say. Which means that maybe it can be broken.
Aisling fires a shot into the air. She wants to get their attention. She lets the gun down from her cheek.
"I am Aisling Kopp, La Tène of the 3rd line. Whoever you are, listen!"

Sarah and Jago hunker down behind a thick tree. They crane their necks, trying to get a look at their assailant, but they can't see the cliff face anymore.
"She can't see us," Jago says.
"Do you have the disk?" Aisling shouts, her voice desperate.
Sarah frowns at Jago. "How does she know about that? She couldn't have seen you take it at the Calling."
"Listen, if you have it, and you know what to do with it, do not use it!"
"She's bullshitting," Jago says. "Just trying to prevent us from getting Earth Key."
"I repeat, DO NOT USE THE DISK!"
Sarah whispers, "Screw her. Let's get out of here."

Jago dips his chin in agreement.

"If you have it, don't go to England. It wi—"

But Aisling's voice is drowned out by the guttural echo of the Bush Hawk's engine jumping to life.

"Chris heard the shots," Sarah says.

Jago stands and turns his back on the clearing. "We need to get out of here and intercept Chiyoko." He moves furtively down the steep slope.

Sarah follows, glancing only once over her shoulder. She can still hear the Player on the cliff yelling, but she can't make out the words. Something bothers her about what just happened, but she can't quite put her finger on it.

Aisling continues to shout, but the unseen plane's engine is too loud, and Aisling's voice is out of range. She angrily slaps the side of the cliff and flails in her harness. They wouldn't hear her out and she didn't shoot them. Not her most productive day.

The heavy rifle languishes in front of her. Aisling looks at it as if she just noticed it. "Well," she says, "there's still time."

She pulls it to her shoulder. Raises it, slides the bolt, chambering a round. The lake stretches out below her. The sound of the engine roars. They'll have to rise in order to escape. Easy pickings.

"I tried talking," she says to herself. "Now let's try this other thing."

Christopher is relieved to see Sarah, and disappointed to see Jago, emerge from the woods. They splash into the water and clamber onto the plane.

"What happened out there?"

"We got shot at," Jago says.

"Sounded like a big gun."

"Get us out of here," Sarah says. "We got what we came for."

"Cool," says Christopher, not bothering to ask what new piece of alien mythology they dug up this time. They put on the headphones and mics and Christopher grabs the control stick and moves the plane around, lets out the throttle.

"Stay low and behind the trees for as long as possible!" Sarah says into her mouthpiece.

Christopher punches the throttle and the plane lifts into the air. He holds the craft close to the water's surface until they reach the edge of the lake.

"Here we go!" He pulls back hard and they move up, up, up.

Aisling pushes her eye to the scope.

There you are.

Breathe.

Fire.

Bolt.

Repeat.

A port-side windows blows out as a round tears through the fuselage.

Christopher jogs the wheel, and the plane waves back and forth.

Sparks fly off the prop as another round grazes it.

"You got this?" Sarah asks, turning pale, grasping Christopher's arm.

"I got this," he says, teeth gritted. He's not going to be in another plane crash. He banks hard left.

"What the fuck are you doing?" Jago screams. The mountain is right in front of them like a wall.

"Closing the damn gap."

Jago scans the cliff face and sees a muzzle flash. A round tears through the port wing.

Christopher pushes the throttle harder.

"Pull up, pull up, pull up!" Sarah yells.

Aisling abandons the scope and fires at will.

She fires her 5th shot.

Wing again.

One hundred meters and closing.

6th.

Pontoon.

7th.

Blade.

8th.

Fuselage.

It's overhead and screaming up the mountain as she fires her 9th shot.

The plane growls and strains. Droplets of gas spray.

The plane disappears over the mountains to the west.

Aisling smiles.

You won't get far.

CHIYOKO TAKEDA

Malpensa International Airport, Milan, Italy

At the Milan airport, on her way to Heathrow, Chiyoko composes an email.

Dearest An,
I am en route to Stonehenge. I will soon have Earth Key. I will have won the first round. Before I Play on I will come to you, dearest. I will give you more of me. I will.
Yours until the End,
C.

She hits send.
She'll soon be winning.
She'll soon be there.
She'll soon be with him.
Soon.

HILAL IBN ISA AL-SALT

Church of the Covenant, Kingdom of Aksum, Northern Ethiopia

"They can't, they can't, they can't." Hilal ibn Isa al-Salt's voice is weak and muffled, delirious.

"Hush now. Be calm, Hilal." Eben is by his side, on a stool, working over a surgeon's stainless-steel table. A small pewter Christ watches them from the wall.

"We would know." Hilal is covered in burns. His arms, face, chest, and head are loosely wrapped in gauze.

"They can't have it. We would know."

"Yes, Hilal. Hush now."

"I could be . . . I could be . . . I could be wrong. . . ." He fades out. Eben ibn Mohammed al-Julan ties off Hilal's good arm. Grabs his wrist and turns it, taps the inside of his elbow. Hilal jolts back to consciousness.

"I could be wrong!"

"Peace, Player." Eben takes a needle from the table, primes it, pushes a finger against a plump vein, lays the cold steel on the skin, pulls the plunger, pushes it slowly in.

"I could be wrong," Hilal says. "The Event could be inevitable; it could be . . ." He trails off, fades again. Eben pulls the needle free and applies pressure. The pulse is still good. His respiration normalizes; there is no pain. Eben looks at the Christ. The lamplight flickers. The power is still gone. The generators still dormant. But he has spoken with someone on a hand-crank radio, learned that a solar flare knocked everything out, but only in northern Ethiopia.

He prays.

Because what out there can direct a solar flare? And how would it know what Hilal was attempting to do?

He prays more.

Grits his teeth.

The beings are not supposed to meddle.

AN LIU

Liu Residence, 6 Jinbao Street, Apartment 66, Beijing, China

An Liu reads Chiyoko's email 134 times.

His body can't stop

SHIVERblinkblink-SHIVERSHIVERSHIVER

SHIVERblink-SHIVERSHIVERSHIVER-SHIVER

BlinkSHIVERblinkblink-blink-blinkSHIVER-blinkblinkblinkSHIVER-blink

SHIVERSHIVER-blink

can't stop shaking.

He crawls across his Beijing safe house to her remnants on the soft red cloth. It takes him 22 minutes to travel 78 feet. It has never been this bad. Never.

BlinkSHIVERSHIVERblink-blinkSHIVERblinkblink-blink-blinkSHIVER-blinkblinkblink-blink.

He touches her lock of hair, and his body still trembles but not as badly.

He won't *blinkblink* won't wait.

After he set off the dirty bomb in *SHIVERblink* in Xi'an, his homeland is too hot anyway.

He *blink* will go.

Blinkblink he will take his toys *SHIVER* and go to his love.

He will change the way he Plays.

And when he finds her, stands in her presence, stillness.

427

SARAH ALOPAY, JAGO TLALOC, CHRISTOPHER VANDERKAMP

Malpensa International Airport, Milan, Italy

One of Aisling's shots nicked the Bush Hawk's gas line and they had to make an emergency landing in another lake, 17 km to the west. They abandoned the Bush Hawk and hiked into the tiny town of Bondione and stole an old Fiat. Since touching down on the lake it has taken them five hours and 17 minutes to reach the airport.

Too long.

Sarah navigates the Fiat into the covered lot north of the terminal and winds up the ramp. The trio is silent. They are frayed, exhausted, filthy. They pass car after car. The vehicles belong to people. People on trips. People working. People vacationing. People living their lives.

Not thinking that it's all going to end.

Sarah slams the brakes.

"Damn it!"

"What?" snaps Jago, peering around for snipers.

She points.

"The Peugeot!"

She pulls into an empty spot next to their old car. The big flower on the hood seems to mock them. Sarah says, "At least we know Chiyoko was here."

"*And* we know she's got a big head start," Jago adds.

Thinking of the plane crash he and Kala had to endure, plus the emergency landing of the Bush Hawk, Christopher says, "Maybe this is a sign that we should drive."

Sarah kills the engine. "No. This means we *have* to fly. We've gotta catch up."

"She'll get Earth Key as soon as she can," Jago adds. "We have to be there when she does."

Christopher folds his arms. "All right," he says, disappointed.

Jago turns in his seat. "*You* could drive. We'll meet you there."

Sarah snickers, in spite of herself. Christopher frowns, but tries not to take it personally. He's decided to endure Jago until Sarah gets tired of him. He's sure that, eventually, she'll get tired of him.

"Screw you, Tlaloc," Christopher says. "I haven't left yet, and I'm not going to now."

Jago opens his door. "Too bad."

They get out and check the 307, digging the spare key out of a secret compartment behind the rear bumper. They open it up; everything is still in place. The guns, the computers, their clothing, personal items. Their various passports and visas, their extra credit cards. The med kit, including five preprepped shots of cortisone. Sarah injects two into Chris's lame knee. He winces but feels better immediately. He leaves a crutch in the car, opting for only one. They clean up, pack their carry-on bags.

"What should we do about guns?" Sarah asks.

"You can't bring them on a plane," Christopher says.

"You figure that out all by yourself?" Jago asks.

"Screw you."

"Kidding, amigo." Jago opens a case and produces a small semiautomatic pistol unlike any Christopher has ever seen. It is white with a matte finish. "We *can* bring these on a plane," Jago says proudly.

"Ah, I forgot about those," Sarah says reverently.

"What the hell are they?" Christopher asks.

"Ceramic and graphene-polymer plastic pistols," Jago says, turning one in his hand. "Everything down to the ammo is nonmetallic. Completely invisible to imaging equipment."

"What—you're just going to carry them on board?" Christopher asks.

"Nah, we'll check a bag."

"Okay," Sarah says slowly. She picks up the 2nd pistol and slides in a clip and grabs an extra one. Jago does the same.

Jago looks at Christopher. "You want one?"

Christopher shakes his head. "I'm good, dude."

Jago snorts. "Good. We only have two."

Sarah puts a hand on his arm. "Ready?"

"Hell yes."

They're not happy to do it, but they leave the rest of the guns and black-market electronics behind. Jago tosses Chiyoko's sword into the trunk as well. They close the trunk and lock the car.

"I'll be back for you, baby," Jago says, patting the hood affectionately. They leave and walk along the sidewalk and into the terminal. From force of habit Sarah counts the number of armed people. Fifteen black-clad officers with Beretta ARX 160s. Two K-9 units with large Alsatian dogs. Two undercovers smoking cigarettes with the obvious bulk of shoulder holsters under their sport jackets. All minding their business and watching the throng.

Christopher watches Sarah's eyes, noticing the cops too. "Maybe we should ask one of these guys if they've seen a little Japanese cat burglar?"

"Don't even joke," Sarah says, focusing her eyes straight ahead. "No delays."

Christopher limps a few steps behind her and Jago. He is, Christopher realizes, a pretty big delay on his own. He tries to keep up. They queue at the British Airways desk. They wait patiently. No trouble. They move up when the line does. They don't talk. They stare at their smartphones, just like everybody else. They don't look at all like they're Playing a game for the fate of the world. They don't look like the types who would carry high-tech guns through an airport.

"Avanti!" the desk agent calls.

Sarah and Jago pocket their phones and approach the agent, looking no more suspect than a pair of dusty, travel-sick kids on a gap year. Christopher leans on the counter next to them. He hands over his real passport. Sarah and Jago use fakes that Renzo made them. New identities. They buy tickets for Heathrow. The earliest flight leaves in two hours. No one asks any questions, and the bag with the guns disappears down a conveyor belt. Jago chuckles as they walk away from the desk. "By the way, friend," he says to Christopher, "our luggage is in your name."

Christopher's eyes widen. "You fuck."

"It's fine," Sarah says, placating Christopher but giving Jago a stern look. She actually doesn't think it's a bad move. On the off chance that the guns do raise red flags, it'll be Christopher who's questioned. She and Jago can slip away and move on. They'd come back for him after confronting Chiyoko.

As they walk through the tunnel toward the gate, Sarah and Jago once again outpace Christopher. It was just yesterday that Sarah spent the night with him, but now all that is forgotten. Aside from when she let him put his hand on her thigh in the Bush Hawk, they've hardly touched, and now it's Jago who she feels more connected to. The two Players are focused but also excited, crackling with an energy that Christopher can't understand.

He's not excited about the trip to Stonehenge. He doesn't care about Earth Key, or the Event, or the Sky People. Now he only cares about Sarah.

Christopher is afraid.

Afraid for her, and afraid for himself.

Afraid because he can't stop thinking that one of these two Players is going to die.

MACCABEE ADLAI, BAITSAKHAN

Saint Gabriel General Hospital, Addis Ababa, Ethiopia

Baitsakhan is down two cousins, one brother, and now one hand. But he still has Maccabee Adlai. They are at a private hospital in Addis Ababa, paid for by Maccabee. Baitsakhan sits in bed, slurping ice water through a straw. During the rushed surgery to save him, he received 12 pints of blood, two of them donated by Maccabee himself, a universal donor.

"First the Aksumite, then the Harrapan," Baitsakhan says, already thinking about the scores he has to settle.

Maccabee sits in a wooden chair next to him, intently studying the orb in his hands. "I don't know."

"Blood for blood, brother. Blood for blood."

Maccabee shakes his head. "No. We have to change tactics. This can't be about revenge."

Baitsakhan rubs the gauze on his stump. "Why not? If we kill them all, then one of us will win. Not counting us, only eight remain. Maybe fewer."

A dull light grows in the orb. "No, Baitsakhan. You weren't listening to kepler 22b. One of us *can* win if all the others are dead, but we are guaranteed nothing. We still need the keys. We still need to satisfy the Makers."

Baitsakhan spits on the floor. "We have one of the keys already. Trust, brother. My way will work."

Maccabee is silent. The orb begins to glow, but the light is not overpowering. Baitsakhan is so consumed with murderous fantasies that he doesn't notice. Images flicker within the dark globe. A jagged white peak. A dead tree. A vast fire. A little girl playing in a yard, a peacock, a person screaming. A rough circle of stones. A labyrinth cut in a field of wheat. A distinctive three-stone arrangement.

Stonehenge.

The image of Stonehenge stays, grows, changes to show a figure, a person, walking through it. It's the Mu, Chiyoko Takeda.

Maccabee clicks his tongue. A revelation. "This isn't Earth Key, Baitsakhan."

"What?"

"It isn't a key at all." Maccabee stares at his partner with searing eyes. "It's a transmitter."

"A *transmitter*?"

"Yes."

"Transmitting what?"

Maccabee looks at the orb again. His lips curl into a sneer as the Mu picks her way through Stonehenge. "Showing Endgame. It's not meant for us. It's meant for . . . *Them*, the keplers."

Baitsakhan's eyes flicker. It dawns on him too. "Then this is . . ."

Maccabee leans forward eagerly. "Yes. It's better than a key. Much, much better." He stands. Holds the orb over Baitsakhan's lap. They watch together.

Watch the beginning of the end.

OK, look through here, and see the swan and what lives beyond beyond.[lxxiii]

SARAH ALOPAY, JAGO TLALOC, CHRISTOPHER VANDERKAMP

River Avon, West Amesbury, Wiltshire, England

It is 4:53 a.m. when they arrive. Sarah is at the wheel of their rental car. The headlights are off. The monoliths rise before them, looming shadows, dark and empty.

Stonehenge.

Ancient sentinels of rock.

Keepers of secrets.

Watchers of time.

Christopher leans between the front seats. "So that was made by the Sky People?"

Sarah shakes her head. "Humans made it. The Makers showed them how, and why."

Christopher still doesn't get it. "Well—how, and why?"

Sarah stares. "We're about to find out."

Jago peers through a pair of binoculars they bought at an airport gift store. They are not very good, but they'll have to do.

He squints. Scans. "Nothing." He lowers the binoculars. The three of them watch a low bank of clouds roll in from the west, its edge blotting out the stars. "Maybe no one's here," Jago says.

"At least not that you can see with those bird-watchers," Sarah replies.

"Isn't that weird?" Christopher asks.

"What?"

"Well, this is a pretty big tourist site, right? Shouldn't there be security or something?"

"He's right," Jago says.

"Endgame," Sarah breathes, and they know it's true. Somehow, this place has been cleared for their arrival, just like the Big Wild Goose Pagoda was. What transpires here will be outside the gaze of the uninitiated. More—They will be watching. The keplers. Somehow, They will be keeping score.

Jago lifts the binoculars back to his face. "Maybe we beat her—"

Christopher points. "There!"

The shadowy outline of a figure steps into full view from behind one of the monoliths. The person spins. The person is holding something circular and heavy.

"Bingo," Sarah says.

"Let's go get our key," Jago says.

From the outside moving in:

1 Heel Stone.

56 holes.

4 station stones.

29 holes.

30 holes.

30 sarsen stones.

60 bluestones.

5 sarsen trilithons.

19 bluestones.

1 sarsen Altar Stone.

Stonehenge.

AN LIU

Route A344, Amesbury, Wiltshire, England

The motorcycle screams between An Liu's legs, eating up the asphalt and the crisp night air of the southern English countryside. He piloted his own jet from China, stopping once for fuel at a small strip in Romania. He couldn't wait. And since he decided not to wait, his tics subsided. Chiyoko.

So near.

Almost there, my love. Almost.

When he is two kilometers from the old monument, he stops. He parks his bike on a side road and gets some things he might need from the saddlebags—some toys he smuggled in his jet. He walks to the top of a small hill. He surveys the land with a high-powered night-vision scope. Sees the stones. Can't see Chiyoko. Not yet. But he knows she is there. He can feel her. She is like a sun made just for him, throwing light and heat, giving him life. He looks more. More. Here and here and here.

And there.

A small car. Parked in a little depression on the side of the road about one kilometer from the site. Three people. Two with guns.

He zooms in.

He recognizes two. ·

Players.

Cahokian.

Olmec.

He watches them talk and prepare; he watches.

He lowers the scope.

He is glad he brought some toys.

SARAH ALOPAY, JAGO TLALOC, CHRISTOPHER VANDERKAMP

River Avon, West Amesbury, Wiltshire, England

Jago slaps a cartridge into his ceramic-and-polymer gun. Clips the holster to his belt. Sarah straps her pistol around her thigh, pulls her hair into a ponytail, sticks an extra clip, her only extra clip, into her back pocket. Christopher paces. He's been given the job of getaway driver. He is not happy about it, but he understands.

Sarah turns to him. "Bang bang . . . bang. Two shots, and a third one a second later. That's the signal. If you hear it, come and get us."

"Got it."

Jago looks to Sarah. "Ready?"

"Yeah."

Jago walks to the top of the depression and surveys the area around Stonehenge. Sarah takes Christopher by the arm. Squeezes. "Wait in the car."

"All right."

"Keep your ears open."

"If you don't signal, how long should I wait before coming in after you?"

Sarah shakes her head. "If there's no signal, we're dead and you can go. You *have* to go, understand? It won't be safe here. Don't come and look for us. My Endgame will be over."

He nods solemnly. "You're not going to ditch me now, are you? You could just get what you want and leave and I'd never know."

Her eyes are stern, honest. "I won't. I promise." She pauses, looking down. "Listen. What happened at the hotel . . ."

"We can talk about it later," Christopher says, feeling a fresh surge of dread. *Later,* he thinks. *If there is a later.*

Jago whistles. They turn. He spins his finger through the air. Sarah leans forward and gives Christopher a peck. "I have to go. I'm sorry it's like this. It's not what I ever wanted or expected."

Before she can get away, Christopher wraps his arms around her. "I'm sorry too, Sarah. Go kick some ass, and I'll see you soon."

"I'll be right back."

They both smile, Sarah spins away, and without looking back jogs up to join Jago.

"I love you," Christopher says to himself. "I love you."

CHIYOKO TAKEDA

Stonehenge

This is Endgame.

Chiyoko sets the disk down. Looks to the heavens. Gray clouds hang low over England and the world. Mist drifts over the rolling green landscape. The stars, the clear sky, they're gone. Clouds blanket the world.

She stares at the disk, which is resting in a barely perceptible cutout on top of the Altar Stone. No one, until Chiyoko arrived a short while ago, ever knew why the cutout was there. The disk fits into it, but not perfectly. She reaches out and lets her fingers grace it, smiles, knows this is the last step to acquiring Earth Key. She puts both hands on the disk and presses.

Presses.

Presses.

She lifts her hands and lets them hover over its grooved surface, gathers her chi in her fingertips; the Altar Stone shudders slightly.

The ground rumbles.

Her legs begin to tremble.

A partridge calls out in the distance.

She thinks of An.

Tortured An.

Absent An.

You should be with me. Life is not the same as death. You should see.

This is Endgame.

CHRISTOPHER VANDERKAMP, AN LIU

River Avon, West Amesbury, Wiltshire, England

Christopher sits in the driver's seat, tapping the wheel nervously. His leg bounces. He pushes the clutch in and out, in and out. He runs the shifter through the gears. He looks at the sky expectantly.

He can barely take it.

It has been 23 minutes since Sarah left.

With him.

Christopher's imagination runs wild. He doesn't know what to do. He wants to go find them. He gets out of the car. Walks around it. Gets back in. Puts on the seat belt. Holds the key in the ignition and starts to turn. Doesn't turn.

If he smoked, he'd be smoking.

He rolls down the window. The sky is incrementally brighter but still dark. It will be a drab dawn. Fitting for the occasion.

He is gray inside.

He waits, wraps his hands around the top of the wheel, squeezes it, turns his hands over it.

"Screw this."

He puts his hand on the key, and as he begins to turn it, he feels a cold, round piece of metal pushing into his temple.

"Don't," a young man's accented voice says.

Christopher's eyes shift to the side mirror. There, in a black jumpsuit covered with straps and trinkets and grenades and canisters, is the torso of a skinny kid with a concave chest. A kid Christopher could pummel in seconds flat.

Only the skinny kid has a gun.

"Hands on wheel," says An Liu in stilted English.

How did he sneak up on me? Oh right, another fucking Player.

Christopher does what he's told. An steps away from the car.

"Open door. Show hands. Get out. Too fast I shoot. No show hands I shoot. Silencer. Understand? Say yes."

"Yes."

"Good. Now do it."

Christopher does. He stands and faces An, keeping his hands visible. Christopher is surprised he isn't more nervous. This is the 4th Endgame kid he's run up against—not counting Jago and Sarah—and the 4th to kidnap him. He also looks the weakest.

"Catch." An tosses something at Christopher and he catches it reflexively.

It is a grenade.

"It armed. You let go, it blow."

Carefully, Christopher turns the grenade over in his hands. "It'll kill you too."

"No. I make it special. Small explosion. Take your arms, stomach, maybe heart and lungs. I stay safe. Just get splattered. Gross, yes. But I not die. You understand, say yes."

"Yes."

"Good. Turn away. No look."

Christopher's heart races faster now. He wonders if these Endgame kids have any advice on controlling heart rates. He should ask Sarah. He turns back to the car, and without making a sound, An approaches him and slips a rope around his neck, pulls it tight. An steps away from his quarry and lets out the leash. There is nine feet of slack.

"I make bombs. Special bombs. This rope special. Part around your neck is bomb. I have trigger. I trip it, you lose head. I have other trigger. Biometric. I die, you lose head. It is active now. Understand, say yes."

"Yes," Christopher manages to say. The leash is tight; his hands are sweating, his heart hammering.

I should've listened to Sarah, he thinks once again. *I shouldn't be here.*

"You can drop grenade now."

"It won't blow up?"

"No. I lie. But I not lie about rope. You test me, you lose head. Understand, say—"

"Yes."

An smiles. Christopher drops the fake grenade.

I should have listened.

"Good. Now, walk. Walk to Stonehenge. We go. We go and see our friends."

SARAH ALOPAY, JAGO TLALOC, CHIYOKO TAKEDA, AN LIU, CHRISTOPHER VANDERKAMP

Stonehenge

The Altar Stone shudders.

Chiyoko's charged fingertips tingle.

Her knees shake.

But it stops.

She steps away and gives it a puzzled look.

The disk isn't working.

What? Why?

A voice interrupts her thoughts.

"You're doing it wrong."

Chiyoko spins. Two shuriken, hidden in her sleeves, fly from her hands. Sarah sways and catches the zinging metal blades between the thumb and middle finger of each hand. Sarah smiles. "You're not the only one with skills, Mu."

Chiyoko holds up her palms in a sign of peace. Sarah steps forward. "Surprised to see me?" Chiyoko's eyes look rueful. She claps once for yes, and makes an apologetic bow. She points at Sarah, holds up two fingers, cocks her head. She's asking where the others are.

"Here," Jago says, stepping from behind the upright of the southernmost trilithon, the one with the dagger carved in it. His pistol is aimed at Chiyoko's head.

Chiyoko's body is still, but her eyes dart from Jago to the disk to Sarah. Sarah looks at her. "Here's the deal. We're going to take the disk back and win Earth Key. You have a choice. You can let us get the key peacefully and leave. Or you can make one wrong move and Jago will blow your head off."

"With great pleasure," Jago adds. "I'm awake this time, *puta*."

It doesn't seem like much of a decision to Chiyoko. She can't give these two the disk, can't let them have Earth Key. The disk belongs to her line, to her people. This is how it has been and how it always will be. Chiyoko keeps her hands visible and still, her breath even. Her chi is now in the pit of her stomach, balled up and ready. She hears the spring on Jago's gun depress.

Jago says, "You're taking too long."

Chiyoko makes a confused gesture at the stone disk and the altar. She makes an open-handed shrug, clasps her hands together in a beseeching motion.

"Stop moving," Jago warns.

"You want to know how it works?" Sarah asks. "Is that it?"

Chiyoko glances hesitantly in Jago's direction before nodding.

"I solved my puzzle. It led me to answers. If you'd stuck around, maybe we'd have shared it with you."

"But now you can go to hell," says Jago.

Chiyoko fumes silently.

I was rash. Stupid. I was not patient.

She takes a step backward. Jago squeezes the trigger; it is 0.7 mm from firing. Chiyoko bows her head in defeat, gestures toward the disk.

Sarah steps forward. "Good decision."

Jago gestures with his gun. "Stand over there, Mu. Slow and steady."

Chiyoko looks at his gun, gauging the distance, trying to figure out if she could disarm him. Jago mistakes her look for apprehension. "Don't worry. I won't shoot. Unlike you, when I make a deal, I honor it."

Chiyoko does as she's told as Sarah slips the shuriken under her belt and steps to the Altar Stone. She cups her hands around the disk. She can feel its power but knows it's misplaced.

She begins to lift it and whispers, "This is it."

But before she can turn the disk, a cocksure voice with a Chinese accent says, "No, Cahokian. Not yet."

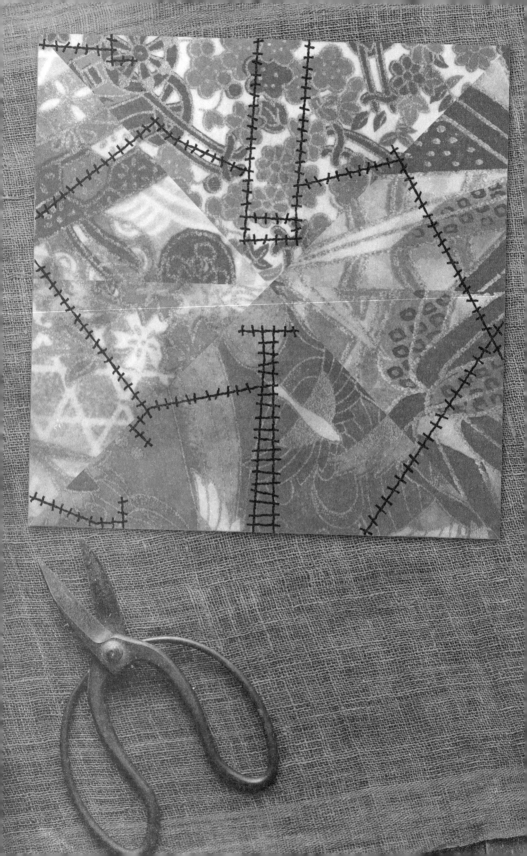

ALL PLAYERS

England. India. Italy. China. Turkey. Ethiopia. Australia.

Sarah spins, draws her gun, aims. Jago keeps the pistol steady on Chiyoko. Chiyoko only moves her eyes, but Jago can see the emotion in them. She is sad and she is relieved. She is curious.

Christopher appears from behind the northernmost group of stones in the outer circle. His expression is steady and defiant. A black cord is looped around his neck. Sarah's gun follows and waits. After 2.3 seconds An Liu steps into view. His forehead is in her gun's sight. She begins to pull.

"Don't," An says. "Rope has bomb. It kill boy if I die. Biometric switch. I also have trigger. You do what I say or boy die. Lose head. It goes boom. You understand?"

Jago asks, "What the hell are you doing here? He with you, Chiyoko?"

"Chiyoko help me in China," An explains. "I help her now. You give her what she need to have Earth Key. You do it now or boy die."

"Shoot this chump, Sarah," Christopher says, his voice hard and searing. "He's bluffing."

An pulls on the leash. "Quiet. Not bluffing. Don't be stupid."

Sarah puts more pressure on the trigger. She knows Christopher better than any person on Earth. She knows that he's lying—that he doesn't really believe An is bluffing. Christopher wants Sarah to shoot An because he is afraid of what will happen if she doesn't. He's afraid she won't win. Christopher's eyes plead with her. Sarah swallows hard.

Chiyoko claps her hands insistently. An glances in her direction. She makes a calming gesture, shaking her head. *Life is not the same as death,* she says in her mind, willing An to hear. An understands that she does not want this to happen. Not this way.

But An doesn't see it that way.

Chiyoko has never wanted to speak so badly in her life.

Jago fires a single round over Chiyoko's head. She feels it graze a stray hair. "I said don't move."

Chiyoko freezes.

Christopher's voice cracks as he says, "Shoot him. He's bluffing."

"No bluff."

"Shoot him."

Sarah stares down An Liu. The disk is behind her. The dagger stone is just to her right. All she needs is a moment.

"Shoot him. Do it."

An slides farther behind Christopher. Sarah doesn't have a clean shot.

"Don't. He die."

"Don't move!" Sarah insists.

An stops. She only has a bead on the side of his face, his ear.

"He's full of shit, Sarah. Shoot him. Do it now."

"I don't have a shot."

"Sure you do," Christopher says. "You're Sarah Alopay. You always have a shot. Do it."

Sarah suddenly feels sick to her stomach. She watches An. Jago watches Chiyoko. Chiyoko watches An. An watches everyone, his gaze twitching between them.

Christopher's eyes are locked on Sarah Alopay. She looks at her high school boyfriend. Her beautiful, reckless, pigheaded high school boyfriend who has no business being here. She remembers Jago telling her that her love does not make her weak. That it makes her strong. That it makes her human.

But this is Endgame.

She cannot afford to be human anymore. She cannot be normal ever again. She has to be something different. Something more. Something less.

She is a Player, the Cahokian, fighting for her line.

Fighting for her family.

Fighting for her future.

Fighting for *the* future.

"I love you, Christopher," she says quietly.

He nods. "I love you too, Sarah."

"Give Chiyoko disk or he die!" An screams.

"I have since the moment I saw you, and I always will."

"Same with me. Always have, always will. Now waste this scrub."

"Give Chiyoko disk or he die!" An screams again.

She smiles a sad and tender smile. "You should have listened to me, Christopher. This is not how this should be ending."

A look of fear and resignation washes over Christopher. "I know. I'm sorry."

Sarah's smile fades; her face changes. Christopher watches as the girl he loves melts away and becomes something else. Something he doesn't recognize. Something hard, efficient, and ruthless. Something he fears. He doesn't want to live in a world where the Sarah Alopay he knew and loved is replaced by this one. She stares at him, gun steady, eyes locked, smile gone. They could always tell what the other was thinking, even without words. It was one of the things they loved most about each other. They always knew what the other would do before they did it. And what Christopher knows now is that she *is* going to do it. She is going to take the shot. The only shot she has, the only shot that can take An out.

"You always talked about choice, Sarah. About how we all choose who we are and what we're gonna do. But you were wrong. You don't have a choice. You never did. This is what you were born to do, what you were destined to do, what you have to do."

She stares at him.

"So do it. I forgive you, and I'm sorry for putting you in this position," he says, his voice just above a whisper. "Do it and win. Win for me."

Sarah nods, and very quietly says, "I will."

Christopher closes his eyes. Sarah pulls the trigger. The bullet spins out of the chamber, sails through the air, and strikes Christopher James Vanderkamp in the middle of his head, boring through his skin, skull, and brain, killing him instantly.

The bullet continues through the back of Christopher's head, through the air between Christopher and An, and strikes An Liu square in the forehead. His skin peels away, his neck snaps back, and he is thrown to the ground.

And as An falls, Christopher Vanderkamp, dead but still standing, explodes from the chest up. Poof, he is gone. Blasted into red mist. His lower half collapses and falls to the ground in a heap.

An wasn't bluffing.

Time slows.

Everyone but Sarah freezes.

She spins to the Altar Stone, grabs the disk, and dives toward the stone with the small dagger carved into it. She slides the center of the disk over this carving. It's just like in the cave painting in Italy, except it isn't the Mu claiming the key; it's the Cahokian.

She holds the disk in place, but realizes after a moment that she doesn't have to. The giant blue sarsen rock envelops the disk, as if each is made of mercury. The disk starts spinning very rapidly, and the center of it, a small globe covered with hieroglyphs, the size of a marble, falls out and into Sarah's hand. The giant blue sarsen rock swallows the rest of the disk, and there's a massive boom, which explodes across the English countryside.

Chiyoko runs toward An. Jago struggles to keep his gun on Chiyoko. The ground rumbles, and everything is vibrating. The air fills with electricity, and though it is dawn, the sky darkens. The ground sways so violently that they have trouble standing.

Chiyoko reaches An and drops to her knees next to him. She places a hand on the nearest rock for support.

But it is not steady.

It is moving.

Up, out of the ground.

Fissures open underfoot, but not in straight lines, as they would during an earthquake. They open in circles. Circles moving against one another, like the wheels of a gigantic machine. Everything shifts as something long hidden rises from the earth, tearing Stonehenge apart. Sarah is on the innermost ring. She's on her knees crying, sobbing, her chest heaving, tears running down her face. She has the key. Earth Key. One of three. And she just won the first stage of Endgame. The first stage of the game that will determine the future of everyone she knows and everyone she loves, her friends, her family. She has a chance to save them all. All of them but one. The one she loved the most. Christopher. Crazy, stubborn, beautiful Christopher. She knows she warned him not to follow her, asked him to stop and go home, told him Endgame was dangerous and could get him killed. And she knows An was going to kill him regardless of what she did. But still. Still. Crazy, stubborn, beautiful Christopher. Dead. A bullet in his head. A bullet she fired. He was going to die, so she decided she would take him. An act of love. And though it breaks her heart, she knows he understood. She saw it in his face, and in his final words, "Do it and win. Win for me." So she will. She clutches Earth Key in her hand and she sobs and she swears to herself that she will honor him, and honor their love, and honor his final words. She will win. And she will do it for him. As the stone takes her higher, she swears on her heart, her family, and her line, she will win, and she will win for him.

Jago, Chiyoko, and An are on the second ring, also going up, but not as high. Chiyoko is trying to stay upright, caressing An's face, looking for vital signs. She thinks she can feel a fading pulse. The last pangs of life leaving his tortured soul. She is happy that he came for her, but why? Why did this have to happen? Why couldn't he understand? Why couldn't he Play for life?

Chiyoko hates Endgame in this moment. In a life filled with training and death, filled with hatred for her burden and her destiny, she hates it more than she's hated anything.

Chiyoko smiles, leans over, and kisses An's cheeks. The ground is moving crazily now. An looks peaceful. Not tortured. And at least they are together. At least they are together.

Life is not the same as death, she thinks.

Chiyoko moves her mouth. She tries to speak. Tears spring to her eyes. "I have to go now," she wants to say. "I have to go, my love."

She stands and turns. The ground is rioting. The monument growing below them is a monstrosity. She is about to raise her hands in surrender and move toward Jago, but the sky darkens behind her.

"Look out!" Jago shouts, a jittery blur not 20 feet away.

Chiyoko spins. A cool blast of air strikes her face just before a 21-ton piece of stone falls on top of her, crushing her below the stomach. She collapses next to An, his motionless body unharmed by the ancient rock. Chiyoko reaches out and takes his hand.

Takes his hand and dies.

Jago watches Chiyoko die. In spite of himself, in spite of Endgame, in spite of his training and her betrayal, he feels sorry for her. But there isn't time for feelings. Not now.

Jago tries to find Sarah amongst the spinning, turning wheels of the moving Stonehenge, and glimpses her standing in the center ring, the blue sarsen stones of the horseshoe rising above her like the bars of a cage.

She steps to the loose edge of her section, her heart racing, tears in her eyes, thinking of Christopher, thinking of the key and the others to come. She watches the ground as the stones spin, sees what was hidden underground. It's a massive version of a new, pristine Stonehenge. An otherworldly structure that was buried for ages. One that man mimicked aboveground. But this structure wasn't made by man; it was made by gods, by Annunaki, by Sky People, whatever they are, whatever you want to call them. It was made by those who made us. And it's not stone, but metal, glass and gold, materials unknown, by processes unknown. As it continues to rise on the telescoping circles, the stones at ground level fall like megaton dominoes, a giant boom as each plows into the ground. Amid the chaos Sarah notices that they are falling in a pattern, pointing to the undisturbed Heel Stone 256 feet away.

Lying beyond this is the gray ribbon of road, the parking lot, the countryside, England, Europe, the rest of the world. A world that will never be the same, that will soon descend into irrevocable chaos, that will never understand why this madness just shot up from the earth, will never believe who is responsible for it.

"Sarah!" Jago screams, but he is drowned out by a massive sonic boom. They're both thrown to the ground as the sky lights up. Sarah's ears ring and her head swims, and she manages to stand. The Heel Stone is gone. In its place is a perfect hole 15 feet across. The Heel Stone moves up and out of the ground, traveling like a missile on a beam of white light, moving through an opening in the cloud cover, roaring toward the heavens. Within seconds, it is gone.

The light, though, the light remains. A beacon surging into space. Sarah is reminded of the beam shooting from the top of the Great White Pyramid in China. She is drawn to the light, can't turn away. Something there is calling her. As she moves, the ringing in her ears strengthens, becomes deafening. She stops at the edge of the beam, reaches for it.

Yes.

Yes.

Yes.

A voice in her head.

Yes.

Jago screams her name, but she can't hear him. All she can hear is the ringing, the voice in her head saying, *Yes yes yes*. She drops to the ground, drawn toward the light. She reaches for it, her arm moving into it. The light is bitter and cold and bites at her skin and calls to her *Yes Yes Yes*. She steps into it *Yes Yes Yes* and she's immediately lifted 30 feet into the air. Her eyes go white—a blinding, terrifying, crushing white—and in her mind she sees:

Marcus, festering, buzzards and worms devouring his flesh.

Kala, rotting, half burned in a room of gold.

Alice, sleeping, a mottled dog curled at her feet.

Hilal, weeping, covered in bandages, watched over by an elderly man.

Aisling, moving through the forest, stalking a deer, rifle in her hands.

Baitsakhan, seething, fixing a steel hook to his wrist.

Maccabee, staring, transfixed by a white-hot orb of light in his hands.

Jago, kneeling next to Christopher's body, staring in awe.

Chiyoko, dead, one hand clutching An's, the other outstretched, finger pointing 175°21'37".

Shari, cooking, a small girl tugging at her pants.

She sees kepler 22b, surrounded by others like him, her, it, smiling, applauding.

And she sees the light, infinite and unending, moving through space, millions of miles, billions of miles, of space.

The key is in her hand.

She's ahead of them all.

If they want to win, they will have to take her.

And she will be ready for them.

Sarah Alopay, daughter of the Bird King and the Sky Queen, the 4,240th Player of the 233rd line, will be ready for them.

She can feel the key in her hand.

She can feel Christopher in her heart.

She will be ready.

For him.

For him.

She opens her eyes.

The light disappears.

She falls back to Earth.

Sarah Alopay.

Daughter of the Bird King and the Sky Queen.

Bearer of Earth Key.

Falls.

This is Endgame.

So many years ago, love,
That soon our time must come
To leave our girl without a home;—
She's like her Mother, love, you've said:
At her age I had long been wed,—
How many years ago, love,
How many years ago?

SHARI CHOPRA

Chopra Residence, Gangtok, Sikkim, India

It has only been 11 days since Shari Chopra unraveled the clue that the Sky Gods put into her head. Now she's mashing chickpeas with the flat side of a cleaver on a plastic cutting board, and she has not thought of Endgame for 58 hours, an extraordinary stretch.

A small black-and-white television with a coat hanger for an antenna is tuned to the only station it can get. A Bollywood dance routine fights its way through a pattern of snow. The song is about love and how wonderful it is. A plump brown chicken prances across the floor tiles, and Little Alice chases after it, calling, "Here, dinner, dinner! Here, dinner, dinner!" And they disappear into the yard.

Shari laughs to herself—her daughter is so much like she once was—and doesn't notice that the music on the television has stopped. But then she hears the voice. . . .

Esteemed Players of the lines, hear me now.

Him.

Her.

It.

kepler 22b.

She turns to the screen. The image there is of an odd but good-looking man, vaguely Asiatic, with round eyes and high cheeks, a thin nose and full lips. His hair is dark and parted down the middle. He wears a collared shirt open at the neck.

A strange disguise.

Earth Key is found, the Beacon sent, the Event is triggered.
Congratulations to the Cahokian of the 233rd for finding it,

possessing it, and bringing the Event to the Unwitting Billions, most of whom are going to die. It will occur in 94.893 days. Now you must find Sky Key. Live, die, steal, kill, love, betray, avenge. Whatever you please. Endgame is the puzzle of life, the reason for death. Play on. What will be will be.

He disappears, and the movie comes back. The music is ridiculous, flippant, inconsequential. Shari takes a deep breath.

Triggered?

Little Alice stands on the kitchen's threshold.

Triggered?

She points at the cutting board.

Triggered!

"Mama, you got a boo-boo."

Shari looks down, sees she's pressing the knife deeply into the side of her finger.

"So I have, *meri jaan*," she says, moving the knife and wrapping her hand in a dishtowel.

"Mama, who was that man on the TV?"

Shari looks at her daughter with sad eyes.

"Don't worry about him, cupcake. Nothing he said concerns you."

Shari scoops up Little Alice, wraps her in her arms, carries her outside to the patio. Jamal is there, drinking a glass of iced tea. He immediately recognizes the ashen look on his beloved's face.

"What happened?"

"Ninety-four days," she repeats.

"The first key is found?"

"Yes," she says, bouncing Little Alice on her knee.

"Will you be leaving us?"

"No, love. I'll stay here with you. My Endgame is different. They will pursue, search, hunt, and kill. I will wait here, with you. And our beautiful girl. And they will come to me. Eventually, they will have to come to me."

Jamal knows she's not telling him something. He waits. Little Alice laughs, swatting at a butterfly as it floats by.

"They will have to because of what the Sky God told me."

"What was that?"

"It told me where the next key is found. And it told me that I was the only one of the twelve who knew."

"But you won't go get it?"

"No. I won't have to. You see, Sky Key is here." Little Alice bounds off her lap, her feet pounding the soft grass. She chases after the butterfly.

"What?" Jamal asks.

"Love—I am the Gatekeeper."

Little Alice chants, "Sky Key! Sky Key! Sky Key!"

Jamal reaches out and takes Shari's hand. They look at each other and smile, lean in, and share a long, sweet kiss.

94 days remain.

94 days.

94.

(Endnotes)

[i] http://goo.gl/fSY56u

[ii] http://goo.gl/zHrfYj

[iii] http://goo.gl/rUy2K8

[iv] http://goo.gl/mW1Ujm

[v] http://goo.gl/7CmnxY

[vi] http://goo.gl/eO75bR

[vii] http://goo.gl/WFFBxL

[viii] http://goo.gl/yKvD7S

[ix] http://goo.gl/0Jd79r

[x] http://goo.gl/qRHKVS

[xi] http://goo.gl/g08vg8

[xii] http://goo.gl/ZclYxr

[xiii] http://goo.gl/03wyVH

[xiv] http://goo.gl/nsDpUd

[xv] http://goo.gl/9UfHnE

[xvi] http://goo.gl/4eH8qy

[xvii] http://goo.gl/4Zvyyr

[xviii] http://goo.gl/iSxWzy

[xix] http://goo.gl/7fbd8f

[xx] http://goo.gl/dN5zT1

[xxi] http://goo.gl/Bxppok

[xxii] http://goo.gl/rCML6Q

[xxiii] http://goo.gl/KAqMtJ

[xxiv] http://goo.gl/NZrR9A

[xxv] http://goo.gl/JMbynN

[xxvi] http://goo.gl/trcuKd

[xxvii] http://goo.gl/AnsqvN

[xxviii] http://goo.gl/jldbxB

[xxix] http://goo.gl/W7ttrv

[xxx] http://goo.gl/IXA4gL

[xxxi] http://goo.gl/y7Ot8b

[xxxii] http://goo.gl/gRnH32

[xxxiii] http://goo.gl/nFDOKP

[xxxiv] http://goo.gl/jkCeh9

[xxxv] http://goo.gl/5LnY9E

[xxxvi] http://goo.gl/Xq7IZt

[xxxvii] http://goo.gl/2lXkal

[xxxviii] http://goo.gl/mWfUFX

[xxxix] http://goo.gl/0DeKBX

[xl] http://goo.gl/gQ1BHx

[xli] http://goo.gl/AX0Nyc

[xlii] http://goo.gl/BxGSS7

[xliii] http://goo.gl/9VM4Nc

[xliv] http://goo.gl/aw0DDa

[xlv] http://goo.gl/JxJJVK

[xlvi] http://goo.gl/lWBDOz

[xlvii] http://goo.gl/H4PqPk

[xlviii] http://goo.gl/n0XNKF

[xlix] http://goo.gl/fSY56u

[l] http://goo.gl/PWDfdL

[li] http://goo.gl/15ik6L

[lii] http://goo.gl/h4SMgp

[liii] http://goo.gl/hHq0QD

[liv] http://goo.gl/41d8TJ

[lv] http://goo.gl/QrM06C

[lvi] http://goo.gl/TXRDMF

[lvii] http://goo.gl/49dau2

[lviii] http://goo.gl/L2NUlv

[lix] http://goo.gl/STSyJS

[lx] http://goo.gl/VnC1ks

[lxi] http://goo.gl/7Dc2KZ

[lxii] http://goo.gl/qia5sb

[lxiii] http://goo.gl/jTAVgz

[lxiv] http://goo.gl/xwGqwd

[lxv] http://goo.gl/X8rmEY

[lxvi] http://goo.gl/UOh3zZ

[lxvii] http://goo.gl/mMurZ8

[lxviii] http://goo.gl/VJLCtT

[lxix] http://goo.gl/qa02uc

[lxx] http://goo.gl/x65wnj

[lxxi] http://goo.gl/RS3t9u

[lxxii] http://goo.gl/Sv75sw

[lxxiii] http://goo.gl/bsbWUU

The Endgame Gold is on display at:

Caesars Palace

3570 S Las Vegas Blvd, Las Vegas, NV 89109

www.endgamegold.com

For complete rules and regulations go to:

www.Endgamerules.com

Decipher, decode, and interpret.

Search and seek.

Search and seek.

Search and seek.